LUCKY

ELITE DOMS OF WASHINGTON

ELIZABETH SAFLEUR

Copyright ©2017 by Elizabeth SaFleur. All rights reserved, including the right to reproduce, distribute, or transmit in any form or by any means. For information regarding subsidiary rights, please contact the Publisher.

Elizabeth SaFleur LLC
PO Box 6395
Charlottesville, VA 22906
Elizabeth@ElizabethSaFleur.com
www.ElizabethSaFleur.com

Edited by Patricia A. Knight

ISBN: 978-1-949076-07-3

ELIZABETH
SaFLEUR

Dedicated to Erica, who has brought much joy to my life – "just like that."

Big love to Laci-Rose, Samantha Sparks, Gemini, Destiny Ray, Dr. Candy, Cherry Noire, Velvet, Sunny Champagne, Divine Springs and Aurora for their dance inspiration, support and friendship over the years. I love you, ladies.

Special hugs to Gemini, the real-world inspiration behind the fictional Cindy inside these pages, and who I'd never expect to give up swearing. Also, XOXO to Samantha, who is always eager to read my stories and tell it to me straight.

Becky and Ally, you truly are the bestest betas ever! And, a huge thank you to AJ Renard, my constant go-to source for BDSM accuracy and overall great friend to the entire BDSM community.

To Virginie, thank you for sharing your genoise cake recipe. It's delicious!

One final note! This book is a work of fiction, not reality. My characters operate in a compressed time frame. A real-world scenario involves getting to know one another more extensively than my characters do before engaging in BDSM activities. Please learn as much as you can before trying any activity you read about in erotic fiction. Talk to people in your local BDSM group. Nearly every community has one. Get to know people slowly, and always be careful. Share your hopes, dreams and fears with anyone before playing with them, have a safeword and share it with your Dom or Domme (they can't read your mind), use protection, and have a safe-call or other backup in place. Remember: Safe, Sane and Consensual. Or, no play. May you find that special person to honor and love you the way you wish. You deserve that. XO, Elizabeth

1

"Derek, oh good, you're here. I meant to tell you earlier," his assistant said. "Cirque canceled at the last minute and Sam from Aerobesque Studios is filling in. I promise—"

Jesus. That woman is going to splat to her death on my club's hardwood floor before the doors even open tonight. That was Derek Damon Wright's first thought as he threw up his hand to silence his assistant. Twenty feet above his elevated dance floor a lithe female figure dangled precariously upside down in a graceful arch from a silver hoop, her arms stretched for the ground. Nothing like killing all the nerve endings on the back of your knees ...

As she spun, a spill of hair swung in a chestnut aura around her head and shoulders while a flutter of skirting revealed tiny booty shorts that outlined the most perfect ass he'd seen in a while—and that was his second thought.

In a balletic motion, the dancer swung herself upright to sitting, while her curtain of hair cascaded down her back to frame that perfect ass.

She craned her head upward. "The lyra is still a little loose."

ied on the catwalk above the rigging
tion point of that hoop thing she'd called
something new every day.
ched nervously as Stan spider-crawled along the
it girders fifty feet in the air. *Fuck ... get it right, Stan.*
nile the dancer seemed nonchalant about the rigging, he couldn't afford to be. *Jesus, don't let her kill herself.* The last thing he needed was a near-death on opening night.

Stan finished his fiddling and gave her a thumbs-up. The dancer stretched into a split with one foot on the lyra and the other pointed toward the floor. *Nice stretch.* Great legs, too, he thought, which should have turned him back to his office. He hadn't expected to find this woman spinning and disregarding gravity when he popped downstairs to check on a liquor shipment.

She tucked her body backward and slammed her too-good-to-be-real ass onto the metal tubing. At the rate she was going, she'd have bruises all over tomorrow.

His imagination erupted into visions of securing her to the hoop in a four-point bond. His hands began to itch like they did when they hadn't held rope in a while. His all-work-and-no-play the last few months had officially caught up with him.

He should go. He didn't need distractions on opening night, especially those of the female variety, but he couldn't tear his eyes away. Whether it was his club owner reaction in the face of an impending death or a purely male admiration for a beautiful female, he couldn't have said.

Her bare feet made a delicate thump on to the floor as she disengaged herself from the lyra. She squinted up at Stan. "Good to go. Silks?"

A long swath of purple fabric snaked to the ground in a hiss. Enough parachute material to wrap around his Ferrari —twice—swayed from the girders and pooled on the floor.

Lucky

After grasping the twin pieces and tugging as if checking their security, she hoisted herself upward in an effortless hand-over-hand. She captured the silks between her two feet and pushed herself higher. Her tight ass didn't show an ounce of jiggle. He would have known given the amount of female flesh he'd had the privilege of enjoying over the years.

Great, she was climbing higher. He couldn't leave now.

When she slipped on the fabric and cried out, he rushed forward, shucking his Tom Ford suit jacket as if it were made of day-old newspapers. He grasped the swaying fabric. "You okay?"

"I'm fine." She grinned down at him. Dancers all came from the same beautiful gene pool. However, this one? Her smile alone would open a thousand doors.

"I see you're not afraid of heights," he said.

"Not anymore." She tilted backward and her legs spread into an upside-down V. His hold tightened on the fabric. She was at least twenty-five feet in the air. After securing one leg in a manner he couldn't decipher, she wrapped more material around her waist, then pulled it over her knee and ankle.

"Step back or take your chances." Even upside down, her smile held something unique, as if she meant what she said.

"Well?"

He left little to chance so he stepped backward a tad. Before he could calculate descent of drop, and whether he'd break one arm or both when trying to save her, she launched into a full-body barrel roll toward the floor. He bolted backward. His heart had to be on the outside of his chest by the time she halted her spin and bounced mere inches above the hard surface.

He masked his shock. What he'd just witnessed was dangerous as hell. God, what it would be like to take a woman with such body confidence and rig her up…

Her long, glossy hair brushed the surface of the floor as

she floated in a flat spin a mere four inches off it, more mesmerizing than the many feet of lilac silk shimmering in the light.

His assistant's clapping gave his heart another jolt. He'd completely forgotten Jills was standing behind him—yet another clue his head wasn't completely in the game for tonight's opening.

"The press is going to love that. Can I get a quick pic? Send it off to Channel Nine?" Jills raised her cell phone and the telltale click of the phone camera going off in rapid succession broke through his oh-so-fun vision of the dancer bound and spinning—fully nude. Did she have tan lines?

The dancer righted herself and hopped two steps to remove a piece of silk wound around one ankle. "No photography flashes. If one goes off..." She shrugged apologetically.

Derek placed his hand over Jills' furiously working fingers. "Keep photographers outside, Jills. Red carpet them, but only let them in after the show, private seating in booth three."

Jills let out a disappointed sigh. "Consider it done."

He cocked his head toward the dancer. "You've been doing this for a while. If something is important for your safety, consider it handled."

"Thank you." She stepped forward and offered her hand. "I'm Sam Rose." He returned her handshake, noting the calluses on her palm that contrasted sharply with the smooth skin on the back of her hand.

"Derek Wright. Sam is short for Samantha, I presume?"

"Oh, just Sam." Her tiny skirt swished when she stepped down the three steps to the main floor. Her spill of long honey-brown hair swung in time with her movements, a lovely affirmation of her femininity. Too many Washington DC women wore bobs to deny their gender and sexuality. He joined Samantha, who was staring at the mural on the wall behind the dance floor.

"This is big. Is that a depiction of the Arctic?"

"Greenland."

"But those are glaciers."

"Yes, Greenland is iced over. Iceland is green."

"Oh, yeah, I remember that now." She beamed.

She gazed around the club lit with colored lights that washed it in a blue cast. His designers used lights to create an atmosphere of a high-end ice cave. The ambiance fit his mood of late.

One of his lighting people—a new guy—whistled from the rafters, and a swell of white light cascaded over them both.

"You need a spotlight, baby." The guy winked down at her.

Derek shot his gaze upward. "Her name is Miss Rose. Make sure she gets good lighting, and without the commentary. You know better than that."

The man gave him a salute. "Sure thing, boss man."

Her eyes widened. "Oh, God, you're the club owner? Mr. Wright? I'm sorry. I didn't recognize you." Color tinged high on her cheeks. "I thought you were in PR or modeling for the Viking atmosphere."

Public relations? Kill him now. "You haven't been to one of my clubs? Strikers, Torrid?" Normally, his clubs were restricted to elite clientele, but on looks alone, any of his doormen would usher in this woman without hesitation.

She shook her head.

"How many club performances have you done, Samantha?" He'd never call her Sam. No woman who looked like her and who could spin and fall so adeptly and gracefully should have a man's name.

"Oh, plenty." Jills had sidled up to them.

Samantha sent her a warm smile. "Some. You're our first

5

high-end club. But we've done charity performances at the New Theatre on U Street and in our studio."

He dipped his chin toward her. "I'm flattered to be your professional debut."

"Thank you, and don't worry—"

"I'm not worried, Samantha."

"Just Sam."

Okay, her smile was a lethal weapon. Was she single?

His number-one rule smacked him upside the head in answer. After one negative experience ending in exorbitant legal fees to defend his good name, he never again became involved with someone who worked for him. Now he had a penchant for recording his business dealings in his office as evidence of his business-only behavior.

Of course, that didn't mean he couldn't admire the beauty before him and let his imagination have a little fun.

"Holy shit." A female voice harpooned across the room. "It's fucking huge."

"That's what she said," Jills chirped. She and Samantha glanced at one another and burst out laughing.

"Uh, that's Cindy. She's dancing with me," Samantha said.

"I guess it's good we play loud music." Given the pair of lungs he'd just encountered, he'd be fined for profanity if not. The woman had a mouth the FCC down the street could hear.

"That wouldn't matter." Sam laughed. "But she's the best. Really. Don't worry—"

"Not worried, Samantha." No matter what she preferred, this lady was a three-syllable woman.

"You're not worried a lot, are you?"

Was he? He reluctantly turned away from her contagious smile to face Cindy.

"It's about effing time we danced somewhere good." She righted a rolling suitcase in front of him. "Hi. This club is uh-

Lucky

mazing. Club Frost, huh? Yeah, I can see it. You're not worried those white leather couches are going to get dirty?"

"No, not worried, and thank you. I'm Derek. Club owner."

"Cindy. Dancer. Aerial artist. *Single*."

Her grip, as well as her language, rivaled a sailor on shore leave. Yet she also was a looker. His patrons would appreciate that perfect dark skin and bright hazel eyes, not to mention biceps that promised great capability.

"It's a pleasure to meet you, Cindy."

"Cin, don't you want to practice?" Samantha pulled her toward the silks. He could overhear her hushed whispers. *Are you crazy* and *I can't believe you said that* reached his ears.

He let out a low chuckle.

"You have no idea the effect you have on women, do you?" Jills waved her hand at him. "That blond Greek god thing plus the good breeding and manners. You're like—"

"No one." He sent his gaze back to the two women now tittering around the silks. "Like no one. But they're… " He nodded his head to the two women. " …something." The "something" bothered him, but the feeling would wear off. It always did where women were concerned.

"I knew you'd like her. Sam empowers women through dance. When you think you can't, she shows you that you can. That's why I thought she'd be perfect for you."

"I'm a woman who requires empowerment?"

"No, a perfect gentleman. Too perfect." She grinned over at him. "I'll show them the dressing room."

"No, I'll do it." He was an unwilling partner in Jills' never-ending endeavors to fix him up. Courtesy was courtesy, however. He'd show the dance team where they could prepare for their performance. As most women usually did, they'd brought a lot of stuff. Letting someone weaker than him lug half their body weight when he could help would be poor manners.

Hoping his dance floor wouldn't be the scene of grisly near-death later on, he strode to where the two women stood. He should insist on gymnastic mats for these ladies despite Samantha's stellar demonstration. Danger wasn't on his to-do list.

"Ladies, let me show you where you can get ready."

Samantha responded with one of her killer smiles. Perhaps he should reassess his rule about mixing business and pleasure. He could do endless things with thirty feet of parachute silk.

2

"This dressing room *rocks.*" That pretentious, overly-designed club space on the other side of the door just redeemed itself. Samantha ran her gaze over the individual makeup tables that ran the length of the wall. Lighted mirrors hung over ten stations with individual garment racks assigned to each one. How did she get one of these? She'd kill to have this area in her dance studio.

Derek threw her a curious look. "I'm glad you approve."

"I'll make a note not to drop any makeup." Cindy pointed down at the impractical tufted white chairs before each countertop.

Derek hung her bag on the nearest rack. He jutted his chin toward a small bar in the corner. "Help yourself. You'll find snacks and bottled water along with sodas. No alcohol but—"

"Oh, we don't drink before a performance," Sam said.

"Good. Do you want dinner now or later?"

"Dinner?"

"From what I saw earlier today you'll need to keep up

your strength. Do you eat red meat? We also have vegetarian and vegan fare."

"I can't eat. I'll throw up," Cindy said. "But you go ahead, Sam. I'm good with these." She attacked a bag of chips.

"Maybe after?" Sam asked.

"I'll tell the chef. Doors open at ten. Break a leg, ladies." He paused in the doorway and winked. "But not literally."

Sam's stomach stupidly flipped and her lips would not stay professional. They kept stretching into a flirty smile.

After Derek had fully closed the door behind him, Cindy lurched toward her. "Oh. My. God. He's not only hot, he wants to feed us. And, not that white bread sandwich crap in vendor boxes. We so owe Jills a fruit basket for recommending us. I totally expected a sleazy old guy, not a Norwegian god straight out of the movies. I mean his pictures don't do him justice."

"Don't tell me. You stalked him online."

"Of course I did. As soon as Jills called today."

"I had no idea he was the owner."

"You've never heard of Derek Damon Wright? You really do need to get out more, Sam."

No, and good thing, too. If she'd known about him in advance, her nerves would have demanded weeks of practice, new costumes, and a bikini wax. During his earlier regard, her red flags flew up, out, and on fire—even standing in the middle of a fake ice cave. Men always gawked at dancers, but Derek's eyes drove deep under her skin, assessing and questioning. And she'd thought he'd been hired as an Alexander Skarsgård look-alike to make the place look "Viking."

"Don't you think this place is a little over the top?"

"With a name like 'Frost' of course it's ridiculous. But, hey, so long as his checks don't bounce. But then I can think of a few ways he could pay us." Cindy rolled her hips.

"Don't you think of anything else?"

Lucky

"With that guy walking around?"

Cindy was right. Derek's good looks likely unnerved every woman who found herself in his presence. He had stood in his club like a conqueror. Heck, he'd likely conquered many over the years—especially of the female variety.

She couldn't nail down the color of his eyes even in the dressing room's brighter light. Not green, not blue, not gray, they were something all mixed together. The colors shifted as if they couldn't make up their mind.

He'd focused so intently on her as she tested the rigging, and like a rookie she'd nearly missed a pivotal wrap on the swan dive. You didn't make those kinds of mistakes and live.

She peered into the mirror. Dark circles were emerging from under her concealer. Not the best way to make a first impression on The Viking. Her makeup bag made a ringing *thunk* when it met the counter.

"Okay, real marble." She traced a finger over the rich gold veins running through the surface.

"That guy has more money than God," Cindy said into her bag as she pulled out their opening number costumes. "Inheritance. Some big-time New York family. This new club is only one of *thirty* that he owns all over the world."

"Let's hope he marketed this place well, then, and it's packed with potential dance students. We need to double registrations before the end of the year. Without more students, my expansion plans will be dead in the water."

The pop star Pink had made silks popular. However, once someone tried to pull their entire body weight up and over their head and failed, they often never returned.

Sam's stomach churned. Could they keep everyone's interest tonight? Her grandmother said wealthy people were different, and you had to present something they hadn't seen before. Ordinary wouldn't cut the mustard or get you invited back.

Thank God she brought The Alien Killer, her favorite white bodysuit that glowed in black lights. What else did she bring? She rummaged in the clothes bin Cindy brought.

"Cin, did you remember the Man-Eater?" Oh, please, let it be here, she silently prayed. She'd scored the fire engine–red bandage dress at a consignment store last year. The dress appeared impossible to dance in but had hidden slits and vents that stretched, showing just the right amount of skin at the right time.

"You and your costumes! You could be in a grocery bag and you're still going to cause a stir." Cindy swiveled on the white stool. "It won't matter."

Oh, yes, it will. Her grandmother, also a dancer back in the day, had told her: *If you're ever caught with nothing but a bed sheet, turn it into a Greek Goddess toga. Anything less is pure laziness.* Not that her grandmother would ever be caught dead in a sheet. But Sam understood the sentiment.

"Clothes make the man," she said.

"Which would make Derek a well-dressed Viking. Did you get a load of that suit?"

She had. *Tom Ford.* She'd had a brief, holiday-working stint at Nieman Marcus last year and watched a man nearly have a heart attack at seeing the $3,858 price tag on a Ford charcoal gray jacket that looked curiously like the one Derek wore.

She pulled out three other dresses, not at all what she wanted. There had to be something in here she could use, something that fit the high-class, modern atmosphere of the club.

Derek's club was dead opposite of those sleazy strip clubs from West Virginia and Virginia Beach that called weekly seeking "eye candy" to "dress up the place." Just because she

Lucky

offered pole dancing, burlesque, and aerial art dance classes didn't mean she or any of her students stripped for money. She considered what she did and what she taught her students to be art—empowering and transformational art.

Cindy drew a long swatch of lipstick over her generous lips. "I can't believe Wright looks better than his pictures."

"Obsessed much? How do you feel about switching *Writings on the Wall* to the ending number?"

"Whatevs." She swiveled to face Sam. "Derek couldn't take his eyes off of you."

"Okay, we're switching the two songs."

"Your refusal to admit it means you saw it, too." She dropped her voice to a husky growl. "*Ooo, let me hold the silks for you*. Yes, I was watching in the doorway."

"Stalker." Her cell phone vibrated in her bag. Speaking of which…

"Don't answer it." Cindy put her hand on Sam's arm. "Or I am marching you to the courthouse for a restraining order."

"I don't have time for an RO." Sam hit "decline" on her phone. She hoped never to see Craig again.

"You have the worst luck with men," Cindy said. "Except for me. I haven't had a date in an eon. Hey, I have an idea. Sleep with Viking Derek."

"Cindy. Dance, remember? That's all we're here for."

"Hey, I saw him slap down that lighting guy, and he schlepped our crap ton of stuff to the dressing room for us. And, hello? Dinner? Hard to beat courtesy like that. Remember what your grandmother and I have told you. When a man shows you who he is, believe him. Motto stolen liberally from Maya Angelou."

"Doesn't matter. He's got *playboy* written all over him."

"Even better. He'll know what he's doing. If he knew what *we* could really do… " Cindy stood and rolled her hips in a figure eight. "We'd be dancing here every night. Ooo, I have an even better idea. Make Derek your baby daddy. Then you could own half of Frost. And your kids would be gorgeous."

"I hope you show this much enthusiasm during our performance."

"Oh, I will. Just think. When you're pregnant with Derek's *baby*, I'll get all the solos." Her smirk wasn't helping Sam's concentration.

"Not going there. The next guy I date will be one step up from a priest."

"You won't be getting close to the altar with one of those. Still, I should have warned you about Craig. The minute I saw his manicure, I knew he wasn't right for you."

"Or David or Keith." She'd run out of fingers to count the number of players she'd encountered in DC All the male population cared about was getting ahead in their careers and servicing their overabundance of testosterone, and she wasn't into females.

Cindy's sympathetic face didn't help. "You okay? You don't look so well."

"The usual nerves."

"You never get nervous. Unless … you *like* him!"

"Like you said. He's nice. Normal." *Sort of.*

"Let's hope he's not. Did you get a load of his feet? You know what they say." She winked and widened her hands as if measuring a trophy fish.

3

Derek stared through the two-way glass that lined one wall of his office at the club floor below. "T-minus ten," he said to no one. He didn't want to think of the imminent onslaught of humanity. After dozens of these openings he should have had enthusiasm in spades. Why did anyone think *fake it 'til you make it* worked?

Jills' telltale heel clicks signaled that she'd entered his office. "A line down the block."

"Good. Security?"

"In place."

"Bartenders?"

"Ready." The clicks moved closer.

"What's wrong?" She crossed her arms. "This is the fourth opening I've done with you, and you're all"—she waved a hand over his chest—"Zen-like. Did your mother cancel her trip in?" Her hand flew to her lips. "Oh, I shouldn't have asked that. Sorry. Go back to Zen."

Laughter, unexpected given the circumstances, bubbled up. No, his mother hadn't canceled her parachute into Washington. In fact, her timing moved up to coincide with his grand opening. After all, maximum disruption was her style.

As if on cue, his cell phone vibrated in his jacket with likely yet another of her voicemail messages. He let out a long breath to counter the reminder's effects—annoyance with a healthy dose of resignation.

"Jills, you worry too much." He turned to her. "Everything's fine."

Fine, he repeated in his head. In three days, however, life would be great. He'd be lying prone on a lounger in St. Thomas for fourteen days straight and forget all about this new club he'd lived and breathed for the last six months. His penthouse renovations had stalled, and it was the perfect time to leave. He couldn't wait to get the hell out of his nation's capital. Hell, he might even stay in the Caribbean longer now that he'd decided to promote Jills to manager of all his DC clubs.

"You should ask her for a drink after her performance."

"Who?" He knew damn well *who*.

"Sam."

"Samantha. You know I never get involved with people I hire." Jills never knew when to leave well enough alone, but it was her tenacity and attention to detail that made her so valuable. Nevertheless, her job description did not include relationship advice.

"I know. And it's a shame. I've taken her classes, and *Samantha* could use a decent man in her life. She's had a hard time."

He turned sharply to face her. "I'm sure she has the boys lined up around the block."

"That's been the problem, actually."

The mirrored wall shook, cutting off their conversation. Loud thumping music had erupted from below, Lights had dimmed. Ten p.m. had arrived, and instead of elation, an all-too-familiar numbness blocked out the blitzkrieg. He needed a vacation, that's all.

Jills extended her arm in invitation. "May I escort you to your patrons?"

"I'm watching from here." He turned to her. "You're Wright Investment's DC Club manager. Starting right now."

"W-what?" She flushed. "But we agreed to wait for another week and—"

"Still uncomfortable being promoted?"

She threw her arms around him. "Oh, thank you, Derek."

He eased her off him. "Thank yourself. You earned it."

"But who's going to take care of you when I'm so busy taking care of everyone else?"

"No need." He pitched his jaw toward the elevator. "Go. Manage."

"Thank you. Again." She scooted out with a visible spring in her step. He should have promoted her a year ago. It was time for him to move on from micromanaging his assets.

For thirty minutes he watched the club fill to capacity and ignored that ever-present, niggling discomfort that had grown beneath his skin in recent months. Ah, such discontent was par for the course. An early-thirties, what's-next-with-my-life kind of feeling. Nothing more. After all, he had more than most men could dream of.

Washingtonian magazine called him the luckiest man in DC, as if he shit gold bricks. He was many things, but lucky wasn't one of them. Yet who was he to complain?

His work had rewarded him, handsomely. His life had surpassed all the men's magazine's promises. *Travel + Leisure* showcased places he'd visited years before they became the "it" vacation spots. Suits hung in his closet before *Esquire* magazine made them popular. *Architectural Digest* had been on him for five years about photographing his penthouse overlooking the Potomac.

Jills considered him a decent man. That was even funnier than the lucky comments. He wasn't that respectable in life's grand scheme. He owned entertainment facilities. He wasn't curing cancer.

Two familiar couples had entered the main floor of the club through the dry-ice smoke of the entranceway curtains. Jonathan, his fiancée Christiana, and Mark and his wife Isabella were intercepted by an enthusiastic Jills, who led them to their reserved half-moon booth facing the dance floor.

Jonathan had Christiana glued to his side, and Mark left even less room between him and his better half.

"Overprotective men." He had to admit, however, his friends had found love—or love found them.

He'd dabbled in the whole boyfriend-girlfriend thing a time or two. Yet he never quite understood the appeal to lock oneself to one person—and he certainly didn't have the best role models in his family for how to conduct a relationship. Military boarding school starting at age ten was the perfect antidote to understanding the family dynamic. Forcing a square peg into a round hole only resulted in frustration—and splinters. He had the scars to prove that fact.

Jills beckoned a waitress to the table. She would be magnificent as Frost's new manager. Now he could move on to … whatever he wanted.

As if he knew what that was.

He should go downstairs and greet his friends. His feet didn't move. His feet understood nothing was sadder than a fifth wheel between two couples. He told himself to man up and head downstairs anyway when Christiana and Isabella began bouncing in their seats, clapping. Samantha's form appeared at the steps on the far side of the dance floor.

Her shadowed, regal carriage was more pronounced among the people swaying and undulating to the synthesized music. A moving spotlight ran over her like a lighthouse beacon, illuminating the glow-in-the-dark stripes swirling around the torso of her bodysuit.

Derek absorbed the enchanting curves of her outstretched leg and her bare shoulders peeking from cutouts in the fabric. Her chest expanded in a long inhale as if she was taking in the crowd's energy for a minute. He found himself taking in a long breath with her.

Remarkably, people noticed she was about to take over the floor and stepped backward, giving her room. With that neon suit, how could they not see?

For reasons unknown to him, he hit the speaker button on the window panel and let in the tidal wave of sound.

He'd planned to let the DJ make the welcome announcement. He wasn't sure why he'd changed his mind in that second, but he had. He tapped into the DJ booth with his headset and alerted him of the new plan. He then picked up the microphone that connected into the DJ's sound system.

"Ladies and gentlemen, this is Derek Wright. I would like to welcome you to Club Frost." Cheers cut through the music's thumping backbeat. "Tonight, we offer you a special performance by Aerobesque Dance Studios. A few rules. No photography please. Put your cell phone away. Yes, I mean it. Instagram can wait."

The crowd laughed.

"What you are about to see is beautiful, but we don't want anyone running to the stage to get a selfie."

"You'll lose an eye to a pointed foot!" Cindy, who now stood behind Samantha, had screamed into the crowd, which earned more cackling.

"What she said. Please make room on the dance floor for the Femme Fatales."

A swath of dark purple fabric fell from the ceiling in a sharp flap. He was impressed that Stan, who stood on the catwalk above, knew exactly where to let it fall and at what rate, given a few people still milled around the dance floor.

Two bouncers immediately escorted the remaining patrons off the floor. He didn't need to be here at all. Now that Frost was open, perhaps he'd leave for the Caribbean in the morning.

Samantha took the final step up to the dance floor and walked so confidently to the silks his own spine straightened. Smooth skin and delicate sinews showed through the keyhole cutout in her bodysuit.

Men crowded the edges of the dance floor. Of course, they did—the lechers.

She turned and fell in a dramatic crouch near the dark purple fabric. A muted spotlight clicked on, dousing her in cool light. The music dropped out leaving nothing but a cacophony of annoying voices.

A bright horn chord hit and her arm shot to the sky. Her fingers curled around the fabric and she rose in an undulating body wave. "Writing's on the Wall" by Sam Smith—the James Bond theme song. The music fit. She had *Bond girl* written over every confident move. He wouldn't be surprised if she had hidden knives in that bodysuit that taunted him with its slits and cutouts.

With an inspiring bicep curl, Samantha twirled in a pencil-straight hold on the fabric. How did she make it spin so easily, and hold that position for so long? Her feet grasped a bunch of fabric, and once more he got to watch her very fine ass pivot back and forth as she climbed the silks. On a solid chime, her legs vaulted backwards, sending her into an inverted V. The crowd clapped.

"Wait for it," he whispered. They hadn't seen anything yet.

As she hung upside down, she swirled the fabric in the pool of light, which sent her twirling once more.

Upside down, her hands wrapped fabric around her waist

and then around her knees several times. She released into a cascade of cartwheels that left her bouncing ten feet above the hard floor. As it had earlier that day, his heart dropped with her.

Sam Smith crooned about risking it all and breaking his fall. *Apropos.*

She pulled herself up once more only to cascade her body forward into a drop. Her whole body jerked hard into a pose, leg bent like a gazelle frozen in the air. She righted herself only to climb again.

God, don't let her hurt herself. A part of him was still concerned for her safety, even though she'd obviously been doing this for years. Tension crawled up his spine. Without realizing, he'd been taking in gulps of air. He'd seen every Cirque de Soleil show, usually entertaining clients, without a single heartbeat skip. But this dancer was here on his dime and with her came instant liability.

Derek momentarily ripped his eyes from Sam's form and gazed at the crowd sitting at the tables littering the club. What do you know? They were paying attention. Some more than others, like the men. He felt one side of his face lift in a smirk. They probably were imagining what he'd been earlier. Samantha Rose was sex-on-silks.

For long minutes, she worked the fat ribbons as her body blended with the music—or was the music dancing to *her*?

Wrap.

Climb.

Wrap.

Climb.

Two men edged closer to where she danced. He fingered his headset in his hand. If necessary, like if they moved another inch, he'd have his guys move in. They didn't.

Samantha spun faster. She straddled, kicked, and spun more. Pitching her whole body forward, she twirled in space as the two split pieces of fabric caught her on Sam Smith's last croon. Like this afternoon, he grew tired but oddly energized watching her.

She eased down and took a little bow toward the crowd that clapped appreciatively.

"Good choice, Jills," he said to the glass. "You were right. She is better." Better than anything he'd seen in a while. It made him feel good for some reason—as if he hadn't seen everything in life yet.

He huffed. He must be tired. Plus, his overly dramatic mother had left yet another overly dramatic message that he continued to ignore.

Cindy stalked up the steps toward Samantha. The lyra dropped from the ceiling. The two women clasped a side of the large hoop. A duet? He had to give them credit. Their energy rivaled the Olympic gymnastics team.

They each snaked a leg onto the lyra and flipped backward. The kills-the-back-of-the-knees thought he had earlier came back to him, which made his own knees ache. Then they climbed upward, only to twist lithely into a pose as the lyra spun.

The crowd's reaction puzzled him.

The women held martini glasses, pointed, and smiled. Men leaned down to listen to their dates whisper in their ear, their eyes never leaving the two dancers. He'd never seen such attention to the entertainment in his clubs before. Whomever they brought in was usually given as much thought as the music—only noticed if it was awful.

Cindy left the stage, leaving Samantha who once more climbed the silks. The crowd erupted into applause. Except one or two buffoons who continued to sling back tumblers of liquid courage and engage in conversation. What was wrong with those people?

A light cold sensation seeped through his palm. Without

thought he'd placed a hand on the glass. Samantha twisted and moved into various poses that left him dizzy. He pushed off the window with every intention of going back to his desk.

After another few minutes defying gravity, Samantha did a quick bow and skipped off the floor, while Cindy prowled through the crowd and grasped the lyra.

His eyesight tracked Samantha, whose form moved back into silhouette as she left the spotlit area. Did that guy reach out to her? He should go down there and make sure no one got any bright ideas to hit on his dancers. He turned toward the door and the spell broke.

Damn, he was interested in this woman. He hadn't been caught off guard by mere attraction in years.

He glanced back to see a young man intercept Samantha at the edge of the dance floor. She jerked her head toward the green room and he followed.

She had a boyfriend. Naturally she did. "Men around the block, like I thought."

He strode to his desk. It was time to clean it out for Jills' takeover and head down South.

In fact, he'd order his jet fueled and leave tonight.

4

As soon as the dressing room door clicked shut behind them, Samantha turned to Craig. "What are you doing here?"

"A few of us from the office are checking out the new club. What are *you* doing here? This place is so not you."

She felt her chin rise. "How would you know?"

"Jesus, you're still upset. We weren't exclusive, ya know." He glared down at her with narrowed eyes.

"Get over yourself. Why have you been calling me, anyway?" She'd waited five dates before having sex with the guy and then he asked out one of her students—one of her *younger* students. Really, who cared?

"Look, I need your help. Senator Keeley's gonna make a run for president in the next election. He's going to take me with him."

He wanted a letter of recommendation? She'd never wanted to smack the smugness off a person so badly.

"Good for you. Now I've got to change." She turned away.

"I'm glad I ran into you." His body hovered over as she pulled out her next outfit. "I need just a second. Uh, some people might come around asking about me. You know, security clearance stuff."

She straightened. He couldn't be serious. He wanted her endorsement?

"I couldn't leave my request in an unsecured message."

"Unsecured. You that important now, huh?"

"Look." He scrubbed his perfectly manicured hand through his brush of hair. "You were the last woman I was with and we did some things together, stuff that doesn't need to get out. The Senator is rather conservative."

"You're worried I'd talk about your porn collection? Or how you needed it so you could get it up?" She shouldn't have said that. "I shouldn't have—"

"You mess this up for me, Sam, and I swear to God." His teeth clenched so hard a muscle twitched in his jaw. "You wouldn't want your dance moms to find out how you like it, either."

"Excuse me?"

"People will believe anything, especially if it comes from a senator's aide. I spin for a living, remember that. Tell them I'm as vanilla as it gets and everything will be fine. I won't be forced to make you look worse."

She crossed her arms over her chest. "You saved me the trouble of breaking up with you. We're not compatible. I date *in my species*."

He had the nerve to laugh. "You mean I'm not a nice guy from Maryland with a dog and yard waiting for you to spit out a couple of kids. You got that right."

She bit her tongue on the insults she wanted to hurl at him, as loud clapping from the other side of the door signaled she wouldn't have time.

The DJ's voice thundered on the other side of the door. She had to get out there *now*. The same outfit would have to do.

"Send them my way. I'm happy to tell them *all* about you," she said at the doorway.

He grasped her arm once more. "Tit for tat, Samantha. Remember that."

∽

Derek rose and stretched his back. His life had been reduced to signing his name on checks, this last batch taking nearly fifteen minutes. He found himself staring down at the club floor once more. He couldn't make himself go down there despite the fact that his friends must be wondering where the hell he was.

A lithe figure draped herself backward in a silver hoop shimmering with tiny white lights. Graceful. Beautiful. Not Samantha.

A quick scan and he found her standing near the dressing room door. Two guys were trying to chat her up.

"Just look at her. Trouble for sure." It was not lost on him that he'd spoken out loud to himself many times tonight. He was losing his mind.

Where was her boyfriend? Ah, there he was, ordering the $300/glass whiskey by the look of the bottle in the bartender's hand. The guy glowered at where Samantha stood caged between those two guys. Boyfriend pounded his fist on the bar and the two girls nearby jumped. A lover's quarrel? Jealous tirade?

Derek picked up his headset and hit number two. Chaz, the security lead, answered immediately.

"Sir?"

"Those two guys with Samantha Rose, the dancer. Move them away from her." They were likely harmless but they stood too close to her and he'd be damned if they'd continue to imprison her against the wall. "And that guy that bought

Lucky

the Macallan. Down at the end there? One more fist pound and he's out."

"You got it, boss."

Chaz never questioned his actions, which was why he was at every opening Derek had. He glanced over at the two security men at the end of the bar, both in suits in an attempt to blend in with the patrons. They nodded at the orders that had been delivered into their earpieces.

He also had the enormous satisfaction of watching Chaz divest Samantha of the two womanizers himself. Samantha flipped her long braid over her shoulder, as if shaking off whatever the hell those guys had been saying. Perhaps he would go downstairs, make sure Poseur Boyfriend didn't spew any of his jealous anger over her. The guy stayed at the bar. *Okay, boyfriend, man up and go get your woman*. He didn't budge.

Derek studied him. Pressed khakis, button-down, closely cropped hair with just enough gel. Nothing about him offered an ounce of originality. How did she end up with that guy?

Easy. DC was filled with *that guy*.

He half-hoped boyfriend would do something foolish. He could ban him from this night forward. Being turned away once usually bruised the ego of his sort enough to turn them off the place forever. Derek could withstand the negative PR of one guy telling all his equally poseur friends that Frost was a dead zone.

His eyes drifted to the empty silver hoop gleaming in the low blue light. Samantha and Cindy both had disappeared. The show was over.

∽

Sam's hands cramped worse than when she'd taught three

pole dance classes in a row. Rolling her wrists in the air, she hustled through the dressing room door. She could only hope Craig had left. He'd want to get back to the action, the total opposite of where she hoped to be soon—her bed.

Feet propped up, Cindy swiveled back and forth in the impractical white chair before her makeup stand. Just as they did on Sam, dark circles ringed her eyes. Today had been long for them both.

"Cin, why don't you go home? I can get help loading the car. I'll leave the silks and lyra until the morning. Swing by on my way to the studio to pick them up."

"I'll take you up on that." A loud pop sounded when Cindy swung her legs down and stood. "My hip is killing me. Damned inverted split. Hey, did we get paid?"

"Oh, no." Sam dropped her bag. "In the rush, I forgot to ask Jills."

Cindy stood and waved her hand. "Go. Retrieve money. I'll guard our stuff."

"No, go home. You look exhausted."

"You sure? I mean leaving you here—"

"I'm fine." She led a limp Cindy to the door. "See you tomorrow. Uber home, and text me when you get there, okay?"

"Yes, *mother*."

She peeked through the dressing room door at the main floor as Cindy hobbled toward the exit. Strobe lights streaked across writhing dancers undulating to the heavy bass beat. At the end of the bar, two girls in skirts with their butt cheeks hanging out leaned against one another and giggled about something a bunch of guys had said. Yeah, so not her scene.

After shaking her hair loose from its braid and changing back into her skirt and her favorite Aerobesque T-shirt studded with real Swarovski crystals, a gift from her grandmother, she loaded her costumes and her grip back into the large rolling suitcase. Getting through that crowd with it and her bag would be a challenge. She'd make it work. She was strong. Then she'd find Jills.

As she inched her way toward the exit, she bumped clueless patrons all along the way who ignored her *excuse me*'s and *pardon*'s, which she voiced every foot. Who could hear her? The music hadn't seemed that loud when she'd danced.

It took her twice as long as she'd anticipated to finally slip through the curtains hiding the exit door. With a sigh of relief, she reached toward the bar to open the heavy steel door and startled as a beefy arm appeared and slammed it down for her.

"Hey, great performance. Let us help you with that."

"Thanks…"

"Let me take that." The taller of the two men pulled her bag from her shoulder.

"Uh, okay." Honestly, her arms welcomed the lighter load. She followed them out through the exit door.

As soon as her foot hit one of the concrete steps down, the military-looking guy grabbed her bicep. His grip was a little harsh, but then perhaps she wobbled on the outside as much as she felt inside. Fatigue draped her from head to foot.

Mr. Tall and Dark put her bag on the hood of her car, sandwiched between a black SUV and a Jeep. How did they know the Corolla was hers? Maybe they worked for Derek.

"You're pretty," he said.

She swallowed. "Thanks. My boyfriend thinks so."

"You don't have a boyfriend." Mr. Military moved too close. Her radar pinged. *Both* of these guys stood too close.

"Sorry, I do. He's inside." She forced a wry smile. "Don't you work here?"

Mr. Tall and Dark huffed. "In this dump? No way."

A slice of anger lit her up inside. Derek's club was excessively over-the-top but not a *dump*.

"Don't you have girlfriends waiting for you inside?" She fumbled in her purse. Where were her keys? Her Swiss army knife was somewhere in here, too. Did she have mace?

Finally, her fingers touched metal. She pulled out her keys and they immediately slipped from her nervous grasp to the ground.

Mr. Military bent down and scooped them up. He didn't hand them over. "What's your hurry? Let us buy you a drink."

"Thanks, guys. I appreciate it. But it's been a long night."

"Yeah. Bet you have lotsa long nights." His sneering tone carried unwelcome implications.

Oh, no. Not good. Not good at all. A sense of vulnerability slithered down her spine. What had she been thinking? She let two strangers follow her into an empty alley. *Stupid. Stupid.* She glanced over his shoulder at the too-far-away street. Cars rushed by—or as fast as a car could in downtown Washington, DC on a Saturday night.

He continued to toss her keys in his hand and peer down at her with hard eyes.

Should she scream? Her breath came more quickly and her heartbeat pounded in her temples. Her eyes darted around the vacant alley and then to the steel exit doors. Short of a miracle, she had to handle this situation herself. What did self-defense teachers say to do? Run or go kicking and screaming, she recalled. *Or something like that.* The guy smirked down at her and she latched onto a sliver of anger that punched through her fear. She straightened and held out her hand, though it trembled a bit. "My keys, please."

"Sure sweetheart." He put one arm on the hood of her car and leaned down. His breath stank of liquor; his attitude reeked of danger.

Lucky

She winced as his beefy hand ground her keys into the tender flesh of her palm, bruised and aching from dancing.

"But, first, how about a private performance?"

"No." She pushed both hands against his chest to get away. He never moved. He grabbed her arm and slammed her face-first over the hood of her car. When his crotch met her backside, her heart slammed into her throat. *Oh, shit.* His hand trapped her wrists and stretched her forward until her toes barely touched the asphalt. A small whimper escaped her. This was not going to end well.

Her whole body shuddered as a loud bang reverberated against the walls of the alley. Through the curtain of her hair, she caught sight of a figure in the doorway. The iron grip on her wrist released, and she stumbled away from her car. Her knees slammed into the hard blacktop and her palms met gritty crumbles of black pavement.

She looked up and recognized the figure as one of the club bouncers. He was at the base of the stairs now.

"Gentlemen." He pointed at a camera in the corner trained down on them. "I suggest you run like hell." He cracked his knuckles and chuckled. "Or stay around to see how much leeway the boss has given us to deal with losers like you."

Tall guy huffed. "Fuck, man. She's a dancer. What do you think that display in there was all about?" He angled his chin toward the club. "She's looking for a hook-up."

Her stomach lurched in anger at his voicing what most men thought. If you were a dancer, you must be begging to be mauled. She swallowed a rising *fuck you.*

"Miss Rose, will you accompany me over here?" The mountainous bouncer's tone had softened but she appreciated its lethal edge.

Before she could get two steps, Military Thug dug his

fingers into her upper arm and whispered, "DC Pole Studio says hello. Watch yourself, slut."

What? DC Pole? A few years ago she'd taken two classes there. She'd wanted to know what generated all the fuss about these new aerial dance classes. The classes hooked her—two measly classes she regretted taking to this day.

"What's it going to be, gentlemen?"

Two more men dressed in black from head to toe exited the steel doors and descended the steps with military precision. After one glance, her two attackers choose option one. Instead of running, with one final sneer in her direction, her assailants swaggered down the alley. They *swaggered!* She swayed with the need to hurt them, to terrorize them as they'd terrorized her. Her reality expanded and contracted until it was all she could do to remain upright.

The two guys in black from Frost each supported one of her arms and helped her back up the steps.

"You okay?" The Mountain asked when they got her to the landing. He frowned at the clots of blood on her knee. A wet sensation trickled down her leg.

"I'm fine. I'm used to it." The harassment didn't usually morph into anything quite so physically threatening.

"That's a shame. But shit like that doesn't happen here. Derek makes sure of it."

"Derek." His name sounded strange in her head. The platform tilted a little, and she grasped the iron railing. Her vision grayed. *No, no.* She wouldn't go down.

"Hey, you need to sit down. You might be going into shock."

"I refuse to."

He laughed, the first time she saw that serious face crack into something resembling a smile.

"Good for you. I'm Chaz, by the way. Come inside. We'll

get you fixed up, and you look like you could use a drink." He held out his hand.

No, not a drink. *Payment.* She needed to be paid. Then she could go home. "Is Jills still here?" Her need for payment trumped her reluctance to return to the club.

"Let's go see."

One of the men in black took a handkerchief from inside his suit jacket and handed it to her. She pressed it on her knee. Damn, she had classes to teach tomorrow. Hopefully, she only scraped some skin.

Chaz-the-Mountain led her back through the exit door and ushered her through the curtains with a gentle hand at the small of her back. As they traversed the club toward the bar, the crowd parted at the sight of the men. The thumping music drilled into her brain.

She felt herself helped into a half-moon bar stool, polished metal so sleek she was sure her butt cheeks would reflect off the surface. Her feet dangled in the air, her legs too shaky to rest on the footrest of the stool. They sure liked impractical furniture.

"Greg, get her a drink, will ya? I'm finding Derek." Chaz slapped the bar and stepped back.

"Oh, no, please don't bother him." So she still had a voice. "I need Jills."

"Miss Rose, Derek will have my head if I don't tell him what happened."

"No, please. Just Jills."

The bartender leaned closer so he didn't have to shout over music. "Hey, what can I get you? On the house." He gave her a wide smile, which oddly comforted her, a surreal contrast to the terror she'd felt only moments ago. It was hard to focus. Why was she still here?

"I forgot to ask about our check." Not that the bartender could do anything about it.

"Oh, my God, what happened?" Jills appeared in front of her and clasped her arm.

She must have winced as Jills immediately dropped her hold. "Oh, sorry, did that hurt? Greg, we've got to get her back to the dressing room. I have a first-aid kit there. Chaz. Where is he? And the others?"

Greg's face shot up. "Mr. Wright."

"Samantha." Derek pushed Jills aside.

Her eyes slanted toward his.

"Now they're green," she said without thinking. His face began to fade as pinpricks colored her sight, and the last remnants of any fear drained from her body. She gripped the bar's cool edge. Nausea hit her hard as the masculine smell of a man's expensive suit mixed with the dry ice smoke wafting from the dance floor. She felt herself lifted as if she weighed no more than a bird. She fought the urge to faint. She'd been through worse than this. She would not faint, damn it.

5

"What the hell?" Derek's anger had rocketed from zero to 70. "Why was she allowed to go to the alley *by herself?*"

Chaz had shifted on his feet. "Sir, we got to her before … those two guys didn't—"

"Where is she?"

"At the bar. Shaken up. But—"

Derek had been out of his office chair and down the emergency exit stairs before Chaz had finished his sentence.

He pushed himself through the throng of clueless people and cursed under his breath. How dare anyone try an attack at his establishment. He arrived just as Samantha tumbled off the stool and into his arms.

He hadn't carried a woman in years. Her skin and muscles working against his, her breath warming his neck, felt both awkward and nice. The circumstances that placed her in his arms, however, chilled his appreciation.

Where was her boyfriend? No time to find out. Blood ran down her leg onto his hand.

Chaz and Jills stepped into his private elevator with them

and hit button three on the console. "Thought you might need help with the doors," Chaz said.

"I'll call the police." Jills' head bent to her cell phone.

Samantha lifted her head from his shoulder. "No, please." As if she'd been slapped, panic filled her face.

"I've got this, Jills." He'd assess Samantha's adamant plea for no police later.

The elevator stopped and the doors opened automatically. After stepping into the small alcove, Chaz threw open the wide double doors to Derek's office but wisely didn't step through. "Mr. Wright, they'll never get in here again."

"Security footage. Find out who they are. Mark them immediately. City wide."

"Done."

After tonight, the two thugs, provided they could be identified, would be ostracized from nearly every venue in Washington. When Derek designated someone "persona non-grata," those patrons became undesirable to restaurants and clubs across the sixty-eight square miles of DC

"Jills, the club is yours. Send my apologies to Jonathan and Mark that I didn't stop by. Tell them … work. No details."

"Yes, sir." She and Chaz stepped backwards into the elevator, both wearing masks of reluctance.

He'd met Samantha hours ago, but he understood their sentiment. From the first moment she stepped into his club today, he'd recognized her universal appeal.

He'd bet money authenticity ran through her veins with not an ounce of contrivance—the rarest of the rare in Washington. He'd been on the receiving end of manufactured charm and Samantha didn't give off that vibe. Jills' words about her were starting to make sense. She displayed an indisputable vulnerability that lured unscrupulous men to do barbaric things and everyone else to rise to the occasion to protect her from them.

He set Samantha down on the longest of his leather couches, and she immediately pushed herself to sit upright. "I should go."

"Whoa, there. Let's talk a bit first."

Her eyes rose to his face. "I'm not going to sue you."

Sue him? Well, they were in DC. You couldn't throw a rock without hitting an attorney.

"On the contrary," he said. "I take such affronts to my employees and guests personally. It will never happen again here. You have my word. Where's your boyfriend? He should get you home."

"Who?"

"That gentleman you were speaking with before?"

"Craig?" She huffed a little. "Not my boyfriend. A WMD."

"Weapon of mass destruction?"

"Washington Mistake Date. That's what Cindy calls them."

He laughed. "Sounds appropriate. Where is she?"

"She Ubered."

"By herself? It's one a.m. I'd have sent her home in one of my cars."

"You have more than one?"

"A few."

He strode to the credenza behind his desk and pulled out a small first-aid kit. After wiping blood off his hands with a tissue, he returned to Samantha. She swayed a little on his couch.

"Let's take care of that knee. Then I'll take you home."

"I have a car." She sat forward when he handed her an alcohol wipe. She dabbed her scraped knee and winced.

"I insist." He ripped open a bandage wrapper.

She grimaced once more as he stretched the bandage over

the cut. "No, really." She tried to stand and ended up hopping on one foot. He steadied her as she tested her scraped leg. "See? Minor battle wound."

He huffed out an amused breath. How interesting. She was trying to make him feel better, when it should have been the other way around.

She kept opening and closing her fists as if they cramped, and her pupils appeared dilated. She was not all right—at all.

"Sit." He eased her back down and then strode to the bar on the other side of his office. "Your preference?" He could use some tequila.

"Water would be nice."

The cold air from the mini fridge soothed the heat that had risen in his face. He pulled out two small bottles of water. Forget the alcohol. Keeping a clear head would be the wiser choice.

She flushed anew and her gaze darted from his when their fingers touched briefly in the hand-off. She wasted no time chugging half the contents. When her lips released the empty bottle with a soft sucking sound, his mind flew to other times he'd heard something similar and his cock twitched in his pants.

"I didn't realize I was so thirsty."

Jesus, that smile.

"More?" he asked.

"No thanks. Uh, I hate to ask you this, but we're hoping to get paid tonight?"

"Jills didn't pay you in advance? Most performers wouldn't even show up without payment." Samantha's lack of business acumen caused a prick of concern. He went back to his desk and drew out a large checkbook from his drawer. He lifted a pen and then set it back down.

"Frankly, I don't know your going rate."

"Three hundred dollars. Is that okay?"

Lucky

"Three hundred?" Surely she kidded. She deserved ten times that after the performance he'd enjoyed.

"If that's too much—"

"Not at all." Hell, after tonight, she should demand a Brinks truck back up to his alley and unload his safe.

He reopened the drawer and drew out a fountain pen. Something about drawing live ink across the check felt appropriate for the beauty sitting before him. After signing his name, he rounded his desk and handed over her payment.

"Oh, no, Mr. Wright. This is too much." She fiddled with the edge of the paper. "I told you it's not your fault about those two guys, and I won't—"

"Derek. And I'm not paying you off if that's what concerns you." He nodded to the paper in her hand. "One thousand dollars is your new going rate. Consider this a business lesson. You should never ask for less than that, and now you can, because you've already earned it."

She cocked her head. "You're … kind. Not arrogant at all."

He didn't know why, but he'd had never had a greater compliment, especially when she blushed a delicate peach.

"Oh, that sounded better in my head. I mean, most people who've made it in this town are not like you. You're actually great."

"You've been hanging out with the wrong people."

"Probably. Thank you for having us dance. And for the business advice." She lifted the check.

"Believe me, the pleasure was all mine."

She took his outstretched hand. He disliked the thought that after tonight he might not see her again.

"I promised you dinner," he said. She shouldn't drive yet, and what was the harm? Fulfilling one's promises was merely being polite—despite the impolite stirrings below his belt at the thought he'd get to spend another hour with her.

6

Dinner? With Derek Damon Wright, the Viking?

Oh, why not? Perhaps Cindy was right. This was the kind of man who would make a girl feel good and lucky and…

"Sit." His eyes turned blue, like a storm had blown in.

She put her butt back on the leather cushion. Was he angry? No, his tone was more do-what-I-say than anything else. Men did that when they were worried. She had caused a problem for him tonight.

He picked up the phone from its cradle. "Georges, send up my favorite and a bottle of Chardonnay. Nothing too oaky." He dipped the receiver under his chin. "By the looks of what I saw tonight, you need it."

"May I have sparkling water and a Diet Coke?"

"Cancel the wine. Sparkling water and Diet Coke." He replaced the phone in its cradle. "Diet soda is terrible for you."

"So is being attacked."

"Touché. Dinner is the least I can do."

"I-I'm sorry." Once more she said something that her head

Lucky

and mouth couldn't agree on. "I shouldn't take any more of your time."

"I'd welcome the company." His eyes scanned her leg. "You need to elevate that."

The bandage had turned a deep purple from blood. Guess her scrape was deeper than she thought. *Great*. She had four classes to teach tomorrow including an advanced pole dance private lesson. It was hard to stick to a pole when bleeding, and nothing got blood out of parachute silks. She should know.

Maybe she could take the day off. That bonus he'd handed her? It would go a long way in helping pay the rent. Given the expensive material of his suit, the extra seven hundred dollars over her usual rate was likely his pocket change.

"Lift." He pointed to the armrest on the couch.

She placed her leg so it hung over the end toward him. She also pulled down her skirt, which turned out to be inadequate coverage under the circumstances. "It'll stop bleeding soon."

"You have experience with this?" With deft fingers, Derek removed the soaked bandage and placed another.

"Sure. Dancers fall."

"We should get this attended to."

She grimaced when he retrieved an ice pack from a mini fridge and laid it over her throbbing knee.

"I can have a doctor here within an hour," he said gently.

"Seriously?"

"Of course."

"It's one a.m."

"So?"

She shook her head and tried to push herself up. "You know what? I teach tomorrow—"

"The knee"—he dipped his chin downward—"is saying to take the day off."

"We dance through the pain."

"Glad I didn't know that while I watched you."

"What did you think, by the way?" Her nerves waited with anticipation. She wanted to dance here again. A thousand dollars made up for random alley encounters, especially since she'd seen his bouncers in action.

"You're one of the best dancers I've ever seen."

She snickered. "I doubt that. But thanks."

"I can't imagine anyone doubting your ability. Been dancing long?" He sat down next to her and ran his hands through his hair. The blond strands glinted with copper in the light thrown from the glass lamps placed around his office.

"Since I was twelve."

"Have you ever done anything else?"

His comments didn't feel like small talk. He seemed genuinely interested. Or he was delaying her. He probably wanted to make sure she wasn't going to faint. *Whatever.* Either reason felt good, as if he cared.

"No, even though twelve is actually considered quite late for someone who wants to dance professionally. I finally convinced my parents to put me in ballet under the guise of it changing my tomboy ways."

"My mother put my brother and me into cotillion when I was eight. But unlike you, we tried bribing her to get out of it. It didn't work. Now if they'd taught us aerial work..."

"I can teach you. Men take my classes. I mean..." What exactly? Like Derek Damon Wright would waltz into her studio and join the men's pole class? *Ha.*

"What days?"

He couldn't be serious. "At their request, Fridays at five

Lucky

p.m. I think it's so the guys can go out with their arms all pumped."

His laughter doused her in pride that she'd amused him.

"Sadly, Fridays are a work night for me, and my patrons couldn't care less about my arms."

"That's a shame," she said. "I mean, being in the business of making sure others have fun, but not having time for it yourself."

"You're right. Any ideas on that front?"

Okay, he was definitely flirting with her.

Another sting ran through her leg, and she flinched. Concern replaced the amusement in his eyes. Dumb knee, interrupting everything.

Was he inching closer? She could smell his delicious aftershave, and up close, his blond, scruffy, five o'clock shadow revealed more red. She wanted to touch the shock of hair that ran across his forehead. Of course, she didn't. She didn't do such things. It's just he was being so casual and fun with her.

His large hand descended on the ice packet as if to hold it in place. "You know you should press charges against those two guys."

She barely heard his words as his intimate gesture sent all her blood reserved for brainpower straight between her legs.

"It doesn't help," she finally said.

His eyebrows arched. "This has happened before?"

"Sort of. It doesn't matter."

"Okay, spill it, Samantha Rose. You're holding out on me."

"I can't imagine anyone holding out on you." *Gah.* How inappropriate could she be?

"Don't be so sure."

"Maybe if you worked on your arms?"

"Is that all?"

A trickle of icy condensation dripped down the side of

her leg. "Sorry for the trouble." She dipped her chin toward where his hand still lay. No manicure, thank the gods.

"You aren't trouble." He released her knee, and she caught the plastic before the pack slipped off completely. "A woman like you must attract all sorts of unwanted attention."

"What do you mean, a woman like me?" She hadn't meant to snap, but she was *so over* being accused of something she was innocent of. She knew she attracted male attention. Was that her fault? Was she supposed to join a convent?

"My apologies. Entertainers are often harassed. Unfairly, I might add."

"I've been unlucky, that's all."

Derek seemed as if he wanted to say something else but a loud clunk from behind the double doors sounded. He rose to greet a man in a black T-shirt and jeans pushing a cart into the room.

"Sir, where would you like it?"

"By the window, please."

Samantha caught a heavenly smell. She rose even though her leg protested the movement.

The waiter uncovered the plates and arranged the food in an artful display.

"Chicken Parmesan?" She hadn't meant to breathe the words. Thick, glorious cheese laced a red sauce poured over a hefty-sized portion of chicken. She'd have to do three spin classes to justify one bite. Her stomach rumbled as usual not understanding the concept of calorie restriction or even calorie appropriateness.

"You like?" Derek asked.

"Love."

The man disappeared through the door, and Derek pulled out her chair for her. She hobbled over and realized the large glass overlooked the dance floor.

"Spying on your patrons?" she teased.

Lucky

"Always."

She grasped her lip between her teeth. The thought he'd been watching her stirred up her insides, and rather than make her nervous, his admission intrigued her.

He took the ice packet from her and pushed her chair in so her knees tucked under the little cart. After settling into a chair opposite her, he held up a glass of water in a toast. "To a very successful performance, and hopefully, a longstanding partnership between Aerobesque and Wright Entertainment."

Oh, score. She hadn't dared to hope she had a future here based on what had happened tonight. She lifted her glass to meet his. Then, she went ahead and did what she told herself never to do. She let herself pretend she belonged here, with this man, having dinner in a private office of an entertainment executive because he liked her—or at least her dancing despite the fact she'd attracted loser men left and right tonight.

God, she hoped she didn't prove unlucky for *him*. Because she was having more fun at that moment than she'd had in months, and he seemed so honest about his attention. Not at all as if he wanted to hustle her into bed, though she wouldn't mind if this guy had been trying to seduce her.

He lifted his fork. "Please. Dig in."

She tried to eat delicately even though he continued to stare at her. She felt like a vagabond in her short skirt and T-shirt. Her floaty white dress would have been perfect for this setting. Or her tango dress. Oh, yeah, she should have changed into *that*. Halfway through her chicken Parmesan she forced herself to lay her fork down. She could at least meet his manners halfway and not gorge herself like a pig.

"Is anything wrong?" he asked.

"Not at all. Everything's better with cheese."

He smiled. "I tend to agree."

"Unless it's on cake."

"True." He ran his finger over his bottom lip. "You're an unusual woman, Samantha Rose."

"Because I don't like cheese on cake?"

He grinned and shook his head before his face grew serious. "Jills tells me your studio's motto is empowerment."

"Yes. A lot of women who come to me are looking to feel better about themselves. They haven't always had it easy."

"She said the same about you."

Why would Jills say that? Did he feel sorry for her? She shrugged. "That makes me ordinary. Everyone has rough times." Except by the look of him and this palatial office, he hadn't had many of those.

"Speaking of rough times…" He abruptly stood. "You've had quite a night. Time to get you home."

It was her time to stand, but she didn't want to. Her leg didn't hurt very much, but she liked being here with him—despite the fact his interest in her likely fell in the please-don't-sue me realm.

He pulled out her chair. "Thank you for making my grand opening a success." He stood close enough that his breath whispered through her hair.

"Thank you for … well, everything." She ignored the impulse to kiss him and instead, held out her hand like a professional.

He took it but not in a handshake, more like a gentle cradling of her fingers.

"So you'll dance for us again."

"We'd love to." More like a *hell yes.*

"Good." His lips parted and his eyes dropped to her mouth but quickly raised to eye level once more. "Before we go, remember something for me."

"Okay." Her fingers warmed in his hand.

"Remember you get to choose the men in your life. Just

because a man shows interest doesn't mean you have to return it."

First business and now romantic advice? He was beyond sweet. He was honest-to-God chivalrous ... and hot. He was most definitely hot.

"That guy I saw you with earlier," he continued. "Not the two thugs, but the WMD. Forget him if you don't want him. You deserve better."

She'd like better. She'd like a gentleman, like the man who now held her hand.

"I should hold out for a white knight?"

"Or at least a real man." He still didn't release her fingers. He stayed in place—not moving forward but not retreating, either. He stared down at her as if waiting for her to make a move. Intelligence shone from his eyes, something she hadn't noticed before, adding to his all-American good looks.

Oh, what the hell. She leaned up and kissed him on the cheek.

A thrill crept up her spine at the scratch of his rough five o'clock shadow against her skin. Derek was a *man*. The contrast between Derek and her last three years of immature dates rose sharply in her mind. So, this is what a real-world, noble man looked and acted like—and she understood she'd never been with one before.

"I'll try to remember all your advice."

He smiled down at her and made no move to step backward despite her inappropriately close stance. She needed to seal the moment so she wouldn't forget tonight. She leaned her whole body into him, and this time she didn't reach for his cheek. She went straight for his mouth.

That rough beard touched her skin once more. But his lips—oh, his lips—were soft and warm and pliable and within seconds took over her whole mouth. As their lips clung together, his hands moved in as if seeking more. One hand pressed gently on her back and the other clasped the back of her neck, his thumb digging into the crease behind her ear.

Oh, my.

When he broke the kiss, he kept his lips close to hers.

"Hmmm," he growled. He peered down at her as if he couldn't make sense of what just happened. Truth be told, she wasn't quite sure, either, despite her epiphany a minute ago.

"Um, I'm not sure why I did that." Actually, she did know, but she cared about his assessment of her.

"You're trying to seduce me."

"Maybe."

"I'd hoped so."

"Really?"

Breaking contact completely, he stepped back and sat against his desk, his arms folding over his chest. "But what if you're just using me?" One side of his mouth arched up.

"What if I am?"

"I've always been a man of service."

"Ah, a knight *and* a gentleman."

"Gentle may not be in my repertoire."

At visions of him manhandling her, she dug up new courage. Oh, yes, definitely a real man.

"What *is* in your repertoire?" she asked.

He grasped her waist and pulled her between his spread thighs. Her mind stopped when his mouth softly descended on hers, this time politely and hesitantly, as if asking her a question. She dipped her tongue into his mouth as an answer. "Gentle" exited the building.

He pushed himself to standing, which pitched her backward. He surged past plunder and *conquered* her mouth. She had liked making the first move, but his kiss rewrote the script. She liked him taking over even better.

Lucky

An hour ago, two men manhandled her as if she was an object to use. Derek's rough treatment, however, came from pure appreciation and desire.

He broke his kiss and regarded her with hesitant eyes as if weighing his options. His indecision hung in the air like stale smoke. Oh, no. He couldn't stop now. In the last five minutes she'd crossed some invisible line and she wasn't going back. She was a young woman, who until that moment, let other men decide everything for her—including whether or not she was worthy of their attention. She had *waited* for them. Tonight she no longer waited, and what do you know? This man in front of her responded. She'd never see men—or herself—the same way again, and that understanding fueled her courage.

She ran her fingers over his abdomen, circled her palms around his waist and let them leisurely explore the muscled ridge in the small of his back. She had to remind herself to breathe.

"I like your smiles." He stared at her lips.

"They like you back."

He brought out her inner seductress and she liked her.

His lips firmed themselves over hers once more. A curious sensation took over that morphed into a single, pointed, no-hesitation decision. She was going to have sex with this man. Oh, yes, she was going to break her loser streak with a man who had *winner* written all over him. She was going to do something, be something, different. *The chooser.*

The minute she had that thought, he spun her and lifted her until she sat on his desk. Jesus, he knew how to move a woman around. But strangely, she hadn't been overpowered. She had been complicit.

He lifted her leg so it rested against his hip. "Does your leg hurt?"

"What leg?"

His eyes, now more gray-green, sparked with intention. "Good. We should keep it elevated."

"Whatever you want, doctor."

His full smile eased something inside her, and his list of titles grew. Viking. Gentleman. White Knight. Doctor. If he cooked, she'd swear someone had built him to order —for her.

The way his fingers slowly caressed the inside of her knee as he held it parallel to the floor sent a crack of lightning to land between her legs. Like she needed any more incentive to keep going. *Not*.

Her ballerina slipper dropped to the oriental carpet with a soft plunk. Neither of them moved to retrieve the wayward shoe.

"Keep your leg here. No matter what." His hands molded themselves around her calves as if measuring her size. She sucked in her breath as his hand moved up and down in a slow massage.

Okay, so much for *her* seducing *him*. Sweet baby Jesus, she did not want him to stop.

His phone rang and his private elevator hummed with movement all at once, followed by an urgent knock on the door. Chaz's voice boomed, "Those guys are back. Alley."

She startled at the emphatic voice. "Those guys, as in—"

"Don't worry." Derek eased her leg down.

"You say that a lot."

He turned his face to the door. "Do what's necessary. I'll be down in five."

He helped her stand. "I'll be back. Don't leave."

Her knee stung as her circulation reallocated and blood rushed down her legs. Her bravado shifted, too. What was she thinking? Having sex with a man she didn't know, no

Lucky

matter how great he seemed, was a bizarre end to this even stranger evening.

Now alone, leaning against his desk, her body itched to run. Manners, she reminded herself. She'd leave a note before jetting out.

She moved papers around looking for a pen. But what would she say? Thanks for the bonus and almost seduction and let me know when you want us to dance?

Her grandmother had told her lonely people did desperate things. She'd proven that point. Only she was the lonely heart and he was … what?

She shouldn't leave. He was *amazing*.

No, she should go. Everyone thought a dancer was easy. Yet, he hadn't acted as if she was being slutty.

"Decide," she gritted out.

She circled his desk, knocking her knee against his ungodly throne of a chair. "Shit." The sharp pain radiated up her leg and dissolved all remnants of her earlier euphoria.

She opened the top drawer of his desk. If she was going to leave she had to leave a note. He had to have a pen somewhere in this palatial office. Instead, she found a small keyboard and a screen inside. Her own image shone back at her. She darted her eyes around looking for cameras. Nothing was obvious, but the screen clearly was trained on where they'd nearly *done the deed*. He'd taped them? She'd come so close to giving the man an exclusive porn video.

She picked up a pen that lay next to the screen—*her face on a screen!*—stuck her tongue out at her own image—*so mature, Sam*—and scribbled across the old-fashioned blotter on his desk.

Thanks for everything, but I don't do porn.

She took a deep breath. "What a buzzkill."

7

Derek hit *end call* on his cell phone. Until today, he'd never called a woman more than once in his life. After the third unanswered call, he'd left a message on Samantha Rose's cell phone, a number his ex–special ops friend, Mark, had easily obtained.

As soon as Derek said his name into the message, he realized he'd crossed the crazy line. Getting involved with anyone with whom he'd exchanged money was akin to putting a gun to his head. He'd been the focus of attempted seduction by hundreds of women, and yeah, he realized how arrogant that sounded.

Yet he'd enjoyed hearing Samantha's friendly voice in her greeting, a sharp contrast to the "note" she'd left. He recognized angry handwriting, though he couldn't understand where her irritation came from. What had she meant? *"I don't do porn."*

As soon as he was able to get away from Frost the night she'd bolted, he'd driven by her house, her address also easily found. Her beat-up car sat in the driveway. Her house was

Lucky

pitch black, as if abandoned. Her two returning attackers had eluded capture and he'd been disturbed about them being on the loose, especially since he hadn't known where Samantha had disappeared to. He didn't go to her front door. Jills intimated she'd had bad luck with men. Nothing like a man you'd almost seduced banging on your door at four a.m. to seal that bad luck.

Jesus, he'd turned into a stalker. He only wanted to make sure she was okay. It didn't help every time he imagined her face and those luscious legs his dick made like one of the flagpoles in front of the Capitol Building. Hell, he pretty much sported an erection 24/7 since he'd met her.

If he had any sense left, he'd drive to Dulles Airport, get on his plane, and head to St. Thomas as he'd decided last night. Jills had things under control with Frost. Besides, what could go wrong in a nightclub?

Plenty. Opening night proved exactly how much, which only reminded him of those idiots who assaulted the woman he was curiously, inanely, irrationally obsessed with after spending, oh, two hours with her?

Nothing about her computed. She'd acted as if she wanted him and then she bolted. *Typical female.* They get what they need and bail. When he returned to his office that night, he'd experienced a crushing disappointment. Disappointment wasn't a state Derek entertained.

Okay, no more "firsts." She wasn't paying attention to his calls—or the one, unwise message he'd left four hours ago.

"So, go to work, man," he said to himself in the mirror. He exited his private office bathroom and dropped into his desk chair.

His mood brightened once he actually got something important done. Receipts for the opening proved high. His liquor distributor found a tequila he'd been after for a while.

The *Post*'s review of Frost was as expected: stellar. Yes, overall, today had turned out to be a better day than it had begun.

Then his phone rang and it was *not* Samantha returning his call.

"Yes, Mother."

"He finally picks up."

"I had a club opening."

"You couldn't spare one minute to call your mother back?"

"I couldn't have spared a minute to talk to God." *But you could spare an hour for Samantha.*

"Hmmm, no matter. I came to town."

"Mother, tell me where you're staying, I'll swing by—"

"Later. Always later. But I need your help."

He threw himself backward until his chair groaned. "How much?"

"You think I'm calling for … for money? No, this is worse. Much, much worse."

She lobbed that mystery to put him on edge. Little did she know, she couldn't say a thing to him that would impact his emotions. Not after years of listening to her emergencies, which usually meant something akin to missing a Neiman's sale.

"Fine," she huffed. "I'm at the Oak."

"Lunch tomorrow. Does that suit?"

"I suppose it must."

Jills softly knocked on his office door. "Got to go, Mother. Work calls."

"That's what killed your father, you know. Too much work." She hung up.

If only his father had worked himself to death. Instead, a random mugging in Rockefeller Center ended the man. Oh, the ironies of life. Franklin Wright had more money than the

Rockefellers did in their heyday, but a two-dollar bullet ended it all. He supposed he shouldn't blame his mother for moving him and his brother from penthouse to penthouse while she auditioned potential second husbands. He'd grown up with some of the best views New York City had to offer, at least until he was shipped away to school.

"What do you need, Jills?"

"The police called."

On top of Samantha bolting from his office without so much as a good-bye, the thugs who'd assaulted her had returned for God-knew-what but disappeared before Chaz and his boys could nail them.

"Video footage give the police any leads?" He should have encouraged Samantha to press charges against those goons. Now they'd likely never be caught.

"Too grainy. I still can't believe that happened to her. I talked to Cindy—"

"And?"

"Sam's taken the last two days off. I didn't want to bother her at home. I mean, after the incident here. I'll try later."

"When you talk to her ask her…" What? Why she bolted? He should shut up. Women talked amongst themselves and were stellar at filling in blanks that shouldn't exist, like how he *might* want to see her again. Even basic questions could be interpreted as one step from a forthcoming marriage proposal.

"I'll find out how she is. She's not the type to sue in case you're wondering."

"I know."

Jill cocked her head at him. "I knew you'd like her."

Like her? How about she irritated the hell out of him.

Over the years, he'd mastered interpreting smiles, gestures, and flinches. Yet everything about Samantha was a delicious, nearly magical contradiction—from her calloused hands to the soft skin on her neck. Guileless but sassy in all the right places, she proved no pushover yet no brat. Most of all, he couldn't figure out why she'd intrigued him.

And when she'd kissed him? A move so innocent it had the power of a Mata Hari seduction. Nevertheless, he wouldn't be undone by a woman. He undid *them*. He loved turning on a woman, turning her inside out with pleasure, dominating and leading her through the maze of her desires.

He wanted to be dead opposite of the White Knight she'd named him. He wanted to fuck her into oblivion.

Jills dropped her voice to a whisper. "Georges mentioned you had a private dinner with her after her performance."

"The least I could do. Don't read too much into it."

"Then you don't care if I tell you where she'll be tonight."

His face lifted to stare at her despite his ego refusing to admit his interest.

"It's none of my business."

"Yes, that new Argentine restaurant on Fourteenth Street? Malbec? Where she'll be giving a tango demonstration for atmosphere around seven thirty p.m.? Wouldn't interest you at all. Or the fact that she'll be dancing with a hot Latin guy who has been trying to go out with her ever since—"

"It matters not to me."

"Uh-huh. Shall I make a reservation for you?"

"I don't need reservations."

"True. Then I guess my work here is done." She turned on her heel, but not before sending him a knowing look that plainly stated he'd be having Argentinian asado tonight, right at seven thirty p.m.

The minute Samantha wrapped herself in parachute silk to courageously barrel roll toward the floor, he knew. She was exactly the type of woman a man could get lost in. Only he didn't get lost, and it was time to end the enigma of Samantha Rose—starting with why she tried to seduce him and then fled. Women didn't run from him.

He needed to find out what happened.

~

Samantha's phone vibrated in her back jeans pocket. The screen showed a missed call. At least it wasn't from the paranoid Derek Wright. At first she didn't recognize his number as the one that had been ringing her phone for the last forty-eight hours. Mystery solved when Derek left a short message earlier that day. He'd had the gall to sound a little annoyed. She swiped and deleted the message. Why had she been keeping it anyway?

"Maya, no!" Samantha scooped up the wiggling little girl before she fell face-first into the humidifier. She loved Tuesdays when she could babysit her friend's two-year-old.

Balancing the squirming cutie on her hip, she pressed her foot on the protruding floorboard.

"Humidity is too low. Cindy, before you lock up tonight, can you be sure to refill the tank?"

"Sure thing. Hey, when does Erica pick up her kid? This place is starting to look like a fucking daycare."

"Cindy!"

"Sorry, sorry. This no-swearing thing is hard."

"She'll be here soon." She tickled the little girl's belly and was rewarded with a baby chortle.

"I hope she gets here before the pole party. We've got six girls coming tonight, compliments of our gig with smokin' hot Derek—"

"You mean because we gave a stellar performance at Frost and caught the eye of one maid of honor desperate for something unique for a bridal shower."

"Sure thing. Whatever you say." Cindy handed her Maya's little pink sweater.

"Maya, not the hair, not the hair." She unclenched the baby's fist, releasing a clump of her ponytail.

"Sanasanasana." The little girl arched her back and kicked.

"Samantha," she repeated, as if an almost-two-year-old could say that many syllables.

The little girl's curls shook in all directions in a defiant no. "Nononononono."

"Okay, okay." She plopped the little girl on her feet. Maya took off running into the center room, leaving a tiny pink sock behind. Sam scooped it up.

"So when are we going to dance at Frost again?" Cindy asked.

"I don't know." *Never.* She'd purposely left out her near-miss seduction and then finding out he had hidden cameras everywhere.

"I still can't believe Craig showed up and had the nerve to ask you for help."

Yet another half truth to Cindy about what he really said. Cindy would insist they confront him when she'd rather forget the other night had happened. She still debated cashing Derek's check. She'd been in Washington long enough to know once a check was cashed, it meant something, like an agreement everything was fine. Things were not fine, though she had only herself to blame.

"There's something else I need to tell you before you bolt," Cindy said. "Joanne left a scathing message on the studio voicemail. I deleted it. I know. I know. I shouldn't have since you should report this harassment to the police. The same with those two guys from Wright's club, by the way. Maya, no!"

The little girl had slapped the mirrors hard, leaving

Lucky

smudgy handprints behind. She let out a wail at Cindy's bark.

Samantha lifted the little girl into her arms once more. "The mirrors will survive, won't they, Maya Princess. Cindy, no police. Joanne will grow tired soon enough. My little studio can't be affecting DC Pole's business that much." She hoped. She was getting tired of the threats. Things happened in threes, right? Craig, the guys in the alley, and Joanne made the triad of doom. Statistically, the end was near.

"Sananananana." Maya demanded to be put down.

"Up, down, up, down. I don't know how her mother does this." Cindy backed up a few steps. "It's why they're born cute. To lure us into *ooh*ing and *aah*ing until they unleash their devil side. You sure you want one of these?"

"Children are easier than some adults." The last few days had proven that theory.

Maya clung to Sam's legs and peered up at her. "Gooooose."

"Your mom is bringing the juice boxes." She fought the urge to squish the little girl until she burst. All that irresistible baby chub softness begged for hugs. How did her mother survive being away from her? She ran her hands through Maya's soft dark curls.

"You are cute and you know it, don't you, princess?"

"Your kid with Derek will be cuter." Cindy waved her hand.

"Ha." Her light response did nothing to quell the pang that hit her in the chest.

She was born with her biological clock ticking. In recent years, it'd grown to the decibel level of a Japanese wadaiko drummer. There was just one problem around starting a family—no baby daddy.

"Okay, but you finally have to spill it. How big is he?"

Cindy had been asking her that same question for the last two days.

"Like I said yesterday and the day before, nothing happened." Rather, something *almost* happened. Then, the cameras-in-the-office happened. Too many happenings for her. At least, like Craig, he'd proven the truth of her grandmother's often-given advice: *pay attention to what they do, not what they say*.

"Upy, upy, upy!" Maya's little chubby hands grasped the air. She lifted the little girl once more.

"Ooh, you're getting to be such a big girl." She smoothed down Maya's hair, now damp against her forehead. Sam had to choose more wisely in the future. She only had six years left until her ovaries would put up an out-of-order sign. Age thirty-five, the year her gynecologist said was the last easy year to get pregnant for most women, waved at her in the distance like a red flag before a charging bull.

"If what you say is true, I can't believe you'd bolt before testing the man's assets," Cindy said.

"I should have never told you about our dinner."

"It goes against the sisterhood to keep almost-sex with a guy that hot from me. So tell me, did you at least get close enough to, ya know, guess?"

The bells rang on the door downstairs.

"I'm leaving." She put Maya down. "I hear your mother coming up the steps, little princess. Cindy, you're off the hook for babysitting."

"Thank the Lord." She glanced down at the little girl. "Even if you are cute."

Maya was more than adorable. The little girl was everything Samantha wanted all rolled up into bouncy energy and pink cheeks.

"Aren't you supposed to be at the restaurant by now?"

Oh, crap, she was going to be late.

She blew Cindy a kiss, grabbed her bag holding her tango shoes and her favorite red dress from the hook on the back of the door, and turned to leave. She nearly crashed into Erica.

"Hey, Sam." She shot her gaze around her. "Maya baby."

The little girl squealed and pounded toward them. "Mamamamamamama."

Each syllable from the little girl's rosebud mouth pounded into her heart.

8

Derek led Sarah to the curved booth for two near the dance floor at Malbec. They had a great view of the space.

"This place is quaint. How did you hear of it?" Sarah asked.

"Jills."

"She always did have her finger on the pulse. Speaking of which, how is *your* new place?"

"It's just another club."

"There's the guy I know and love. Bored and nonchalant." She laughed lightly. "So, when did your mother get in town? You have that look on your face."

"That obvious?"

"You had a club opening the other night—which I'm sorry I missed, by the way. But I know what that means. A fly-in from the maternal unit. That's also why you wanted to have dinner, right? Have legitimate plans to keep you occupied?"

"Sarah, I would never use you like that."

"It's okay. You'd do the same for me."

True. Whenever Sarah's stepmother was in one of her fix-Sarah-up moods, Derek was Sarah's convenient "date" to

Lucky

keep Claire Marillioux-Brond off her back. They were like brothers-in-arms committed to repelling annoying mothers who would never leave this Earth with unattached children. He considered Sarah and the other members of their closely-knit group his best friends and real family. They showed up when needed, not with an eye to cause disruption.

"Thanks, Sarah. I have an unavoidable lunch with her tomorrow."

"You sure you're fine with me ditching you in about two hours?" she asked. "M is up to no good again. It's time for his final lesson."

"Going to release him?"

"Not on your life. I'm just going to let him think I am."

Sarah's Femme Domme status was legendary at Club Accendos. Hell, probably nationally. He wouldn't want to be the one displeasing her—and he didn't have a submissive molecule in his body.

By the time they placed their orders, they were well into their second cocktails.

"Jonathan tells me you moved back into Accendos during your penthouse renovations. I haven't seen you in any of the playrooms," she said into her gin martini. "A few of the subs have been asking after you."

"Haven't been feeling very sociable."

"Having a Dominant crisis, are we?"

"I don't believe in crises."

She laughed. "Neither do I. It's not the first time one of us has gone missing for a bit. Jonathan went dark when he fell for Christiana. So…" She turned to him. "Are you going to tell me why we're really here?"

"I hear the food is amazing."

She gave him a knowing smile, which only reminded him how another woman's smile had blown him wide open.

Samantha peered between the two red curtains separating the kitchen from the main floor. What in the hell was Derek doing here? She recognized the stalker pattern; coincidentally showing up where she performed was the first play. Yet he'd brought a date. That didn't add up.

She studied the woman dressed in rich burgundy velvet, her dark mahogany hair shining in the candlelight. In a word, gorgeous. She sat so confidently next to him, she had to be his significant other. She wasn't flirting, but there was no mistaking she believed she belonged there.

Samantha had googled him when she was home resting her knee. By what she could find, he was single. *But clearly taken.*

So, in addition to him taping his exploits, he was involved with someone. *Great.*

She'd had run-ins with taken men before. One notable episode came to mind. Out of nowhere, a seething woman threw her date's martini in her face. Her face! Turned out the thrower was her date's *wife*. With any luck, martini woman served divorce papers on him the next day. She never saw either from that moment forward.

What were Derek and his girlfriend talking about? The clang of dishes in the background, sizzling oil in pans, and shouts from the chef drowned out the packed dinner crowd's banter.

This place was definitely not like Frost. She'd changed into her dress in a broom closet while Edwin stretched and warmed up against the doorway to ensure no one would enter while she changed. She'd felt like the hired help—at least until she changed.

As her dress's ruffles cascaded down her torso, she trans-

Lucky

formed into a femme fatale clothed in heavy, rich, crimson fabric—a woman desired by every man who saw her. She held on to that sensation with every breath in her body as she watched Derek's date laugh at something he said.

Thank God she hadn't slept with him. Purpose stiffened her spine. In one or two minutes on the dance floor she'd bring him to his knees—without ever having to say a word. She wanted him to know what he'd missed out on Saturday night.

The first chord rang out, beckoning them onto the stage. Edwin led her through the curtain. Tango music had always pulled forth her inner siren, and it worked its magic now. At the first plucking notes of the violins and the cadenced low boom of the bass, every muscle screamed to stretch out and move.

As soon as her foot hit the cheap parquet floor, she turned to Edwin, who stood tall and regal on the other side of the floor. She grasped the red cloth of her dress and swung it behind her. A jolt of energy swirled up her body.

The average length of a tango is three minutes—one hundred and eighty seconds to showcase the power and vulnerability between two people. The full story of love played out between two bodies, instantly intimate, instantly at war, set to the rippling notes of violins, a bass and an accordion.

She reached into the musical notes and let go. Hands up and flourishing, she circled her rib cage, feeling a pleasant stretch across her belly. She curled her finger at Edwin and then pulled an *amague*. As he rushed to her, she flipped him away. He grabbed her anyway and snapped her against his body.

They moved together across the floor to the accordion's notes. Quiet words from the small tables around the dance floor swirled around them. They soon posed in front of Derek's booth along the back wall.

His green-blue eyes hooked on hers immediately. The woman next to him cocked her head at him as if she understood immediately some connection had been made between Samantha and him. Funny, his date didn't look pissed. She appeared entertained. So she was used to his playboy status. The thought made her angrier.

"Mantenha o seu abraço," Edwin said. *Hold your embrace.*

She had nearly faltered but regained her footing quickly. She had moved to this song before. She knew exactly where he might lead her.

Her feet moved quickly and then slowly, following Edwin wherever he led her. She circled his foot with a pointed toe. Edwin spun her and she collapsed her legs so he could throw her into a dip. One last chord and the dance would be over. Edwin collected her and spun her out until she held on to his fingertips. She curtsied while he bowed to the tables, her back to Derek's booth.

Just before Edwin could pull her back for the second dance, Derek's voice drifted over the opening chords inches away from her.

"May I cut in?"

"The dance demonstration isn't over," Edwin said. He tried to pull her closer, but her body resisted. She'd grown stiff as a board seeing Derek stand there in his elegant suit, his face relaxed and confident like he hadn't just asked another woman to dance in front of his date.

She was vaguely aware a couple rose from their small cocktail table nearest them and joined the threesome on the dance floor. The ice had been broken—by Derek—the signal obvious to all patrons they could take the floor. Demonstration over.

Edwin dropped her hand and turned toward the stiletto-

Lucky

heeled woman now standing on the edge of the floor. The woman smiled when he bowed toward her. Had Sam entered the Twilight Zone?

The music changed to a slower beat. Derek extended his hand.

"That's not how you ask for a tango."

"I know. But old habits die hard. I was taught to ask first." He raised his eyebrow and nodded.

She placed her hand in his and let herself be pulled into an *abrazo*. The embrace might as well have been a sexual claiming. Their bodies crashed into one another.

He quickly dropped his handhold, sending both arms to circle her. Okay, what the hell. Let's see if he could dance. Most men had no idea how to move on a dance floor, let alone Argentine tango. Derek exuded confidence but that didn't necessarily translate into capability—especially in her world. And, the dance floor was *hers*.

His hand moved across her lower back. Three steps later he proved he could lead, which irritated her more than a bit.

"You ignored my calls," he said.

"Of course I did." The floor swam under her vision. *Look. Away.* Peering into those blue-green-gray-whatever eyes of his wasn't wise, though she'd delight in seeing him squirm.

She bent one leg outward and tossed the edges of her skirt behind, revealing more skin than what would be considered appropriate for a demonstration in a public place. She didn't care. Let him see what he wouldn't have. She'd blame it later on the dress, whose ruffled layers demanded to be put to good use—like driving a man to distraction.

He drew an arm around her waist and pulled her tightly to him. "If I recall, you weren't ignoring me in my office."

She gasped. The *nerve*. "That's before I knew you like taping the women you seduce."

"If I recall, you were the one coming on to me." His annoyed tone was beyond belief.

"That doesn't explain the cameras." She wanted him to know she *knew*. "I don't appreciate being videotaped without my knowledge or permission. In fact, I believe that's illegal."

The rhythm caught her heart. More quick steps backward relieved a fraction of the tension between them. He twirled her and her body unwound toward the edge of the dance floor. She let her leg extend so far she touched someone's foot. A gasp sounded behind her followed by light clapping.

Derek didn't let their bodies remain separated for long. He drew her up and quick steps brought them back to center.

"I wasn't taping anything. It was a live feed. How long have you been in Washington? You do know you're on camera every time you enter any building, walk down any street."

"But not while we were…"

He twisted her so she faced outward, essentially ending all conversation. His breath ran hot in her ear. "I wasn't taping us. I wouldn't do that to you."

"How would I know that?"

He pushed her forward with his body. "Believe me or don't believe me. But I find your accusation repugnant and unbecoming of you."

He admonished her? Well, didn't that take the cake? Okay, perhaps he told the truth—at least about his videotaping habits. Except he was here with another woman and that kept her anger intact. Plus, he could dance, which maddened her further. He probably danced all the time with that woman who appeared to be giving Edwin a run for his money. Edwin's gaze remained riveted to the woman's confident face. Derek's date might be playing him, too, right?

"You and your girlfriend dance often?" *Change partners?*

He turned her to face him once more. His forehead wrinkled and then softened as if he finally understood the question. "No. It's hard to do *anything* often with a girlfriend when you don't have one."

"Lover then."

"Sarah"—he glanced over at her and Edwin, dancing quite well together—"is one of my best friends from another club. I'm not romantically involved with anyone."

"Most men lie about that stuff."

"I never lie."

Her irritation deflated like a balloon by the sincerity in his voice, and she swallowed a small lump that refused to go down her throat.

"I assumed…"

"Never assume." He nearly growled the words.

He turned to encircle her once more and lead her backwards. She looked away and he twirled her in response, her leg hooking around his. His solid body fed her confidence, or yearning, to lean in more. *Great*. Now that her hormones realized he was single and not a closet pornographer, they started a celebration.

It's just the dress. And the music. It drove through her heart. She felt it in her pelvis. The *bandoneón* striking, hot and precise.

"Won't Sarah be annoyed if I'm monopolizing you?" she asked. "Friends or not, she's still your date."

"Would you be jealous, if you were in her shoes?"

The teasing tone annoyed her. "Arrogant much?"

He dipped her backward. "You have no idea."

He pulled her up so suddenly, she took a sudden intake of breath and a familiar pang hit her between her thighs. A tendril of hair escaped and fell across her face.

The music stopped.

She stepped backward and nodded, as was customary at ending a tango. She was nothing if not a professional when it came to her chosen field. "Thank you for the dance."

"Are you sure that's all you want?" he challenged.

9

As soon as Derek's foot stepped outside the restaurant's front door, thunder rumbled overhead. A surprise rainstorm was all they needed to add to tonight's turmoil.

Derek signaled his driver with his free hand, his other clutching Samantha's fingers. After he opened the door of the black sedan, her hand pulled free from his clasp. She balked at slipping into the back seat. Still unsure? *Join the club*.

Derek wasn't impulsive, which made the entire night, and what he now planned to do, inexplicable. However, Samantha's man filter was out of whack. Their conversation on the dance floor had revealed her fear of being taken advantage of. Her vulnerability demanded his attention. On one hand, he wouldn't allow himself to be pussy-whipped, despite his recent abnormal behavior. On the other hand, allowing this magnetic woman to be in the world, unprotected and open game, was akin to throwing a Christian into a gladiator ring. His hand found its way to her face. "When we get to your house, you'll tell me if you wish to finish what you started."

"What I—"

"Yes, in my office, remember?"

"Y-yes," she repeated like a tongue-tied schoolgirl. "But Sarah…"

"She let me know in no uncertain terms she has plans later with someone else. A man friend. Do you want to ask her?"

"No!" She looked stricken. "I have a car."

"Leave it."

"I'll get towed."

Jesus, this woman argued with him constantly. His palm itched once more. Tying her up would be incredibly satisfying. His mind's eye flashed a vision so real, he almost lost sight of Samantha's face a few inches from his.

He'd rig her up. Settle into a comfortable chair. Watch her writhe a little. He'd take some time to figure out why the hell this woman compelled him so.

"It's right over there." She pointed to a beat-up red Corolla. "Follow me?"

His body seized at the thought of trailing behind her, letting her lead. If only his penthouse renovations were complete. He had planned several rigging spots where he could work.

"Just this once?" she asked.

He nodded an affirmation. *At least she asked.*

As his driver wound his way through the streets of northeast DC, he kept a close eye on her taillights—or one of them anyway. The right one was burned out.

Damn, he almost wished he'd never met her. He'd already gotten too invested. Yet he couldn't walk away now.

Her old arts and crafts home off Porter Street surprised him. The dichotomy of her beat-up car and the large home added to the complexity of Samantha Rose. While old, the house would sell for $2 million in the overinflated world of DC real estate.

"If you don't hear from me in ten, go home, Rich," he said to his driver. He shouldn't assume anything, right?

"Yes, sir."

Exiting the sedan, he approached Samantha cautiously but with growing interest. She trembled under an inadequate pent roof over the side door. He took keys from her shaking hand and inserted the one he guessed would work into the lock. Two hard shoves and they were inside a mudroom.

"I could leave you here." He placed her keys in her hand. Her expression said "stay," but he needed to hear her speak the words.

"No, come in."

"Roommates?"

"I live with my grandmother. This is her house."

Oh, great. If an older woman met them with her hair in curlers, he'd have to move to plan B, as in, *Samantha, see you later*. After stepping inside, he found grave silence.

Linoleum from the 1950's and 1970's-style appliances in avocado green dated the kitchen. A basket of fresh fruit sat in the center of an old farmhouse table. The small space was spotless, smelling of apples and ammonia.

"Something to drink?" Her keys clattered to the table.

"I'm fine. Your grandmother—"

"Can't hear a thing. She's deaf." Samantha flipped off the side alley light. "There. Now she knows I'm home. It's our signal. Don't worry. Nothing wakes her once she sees the light go off."

"I'm not worried."

"Is that why you're backed up against the refrigerator as if a woman in curlers will appear with a rolling pin to beat you?"

"Get out of my head." He threw her what he'd hoped was a casual smile as he eased off the cold metal of the refrigerator door. He was usually good with women. Just not their parents, or in this case, grandparents. Chalk it up to another childhood scar from being trotted out by his mother in a little man suit at age five to stand before his grandfather's massive desk to be assessed.

He sucked in a long slow breath and regained his mental footing. It wasn't difficult. He was no longer that little kid.

When he moved forward, a photo hung by a magnet on the refrigerator released and drifted to the floor. He picked it up.

"You and Cindy at the beach?" The two of them sat in sand squinting into the camera lens. "Hmmm, dangerous. Being friends with your co-workers."

"What a strange thing to say. I count all my students and instructors as friends. Isn't Jills your friend? You seemed…"

"Friendly?" He scratched his chin. "While at work, yes. Her life is her own after hours. Keeps it uncomplicated."

"Must be lonely."

Lonely? Hundreds of people surrounded him most nights. "How's the knee?"

She lifted her dress and revealed a large bandage under her fishnet pantyhose. "Better."

"Take off your stockings."

Her lips parted at his command, but she lifted her dress and eased the stockings down her legs. The fabric had left tiny harlequin square indents in her skin. Hmm, the patterns a rope dress would leave taunted his imagination. "Where are your bandages?"

"There's a first aid kit over the fridge."

"No, stay there. I'll get it."

"Grandma says most accidents happen in the kitchen, so why have the bandages in the bathroom?"

The first-aid kit was exactly where she'd indicated. "Smart woman."

Lucky

He pulled out a chair and rested his foot in the center of the seat. He patted his knee. "Up."

She fanned her leg upward and rested her calf on his thigh. A glimpse of a black lace thong lit up his cock like a firecracker.

"You heal quickly." He gently pulled off the bandage.

"Where did you learn to dance?" she asked. "Not many men know how."

"Cotillion, remember?"

"And they taught you Argentine tango?"

"I learned a lot of things there. Like how easily women get the upper hand. Tango leveled the playing field." *Among other things.* He eased her leg down, losing sight of that lace he wanted to rip to shreds to bare her sex.

"Is always having the upper hand important?"

"Always." That familiar click of the tables turning hung in the air between them. "Control matters to me—in all areas of my life." Tonight she needed to see him as he really was—not the club owner, or the man who questioned her date choices, or even the man she was attracted to. And, yes, she was definitely interested in him. One mystery had been solved this evening. He could tell there were many more secrets to crack where Samantha Rose was concerned.

She clung to his hands as he helped her up. She pressed her whole body forward into him. All these signs urged him forward despite his earlier misgivings. He was used to being on the receiving end of flirtations, but Samantha brought a completely new level to the man-woman dynamic. She *lured* him. He was sure she didn't know her power. She'd have wielded it more frequently by now.

"Can I tell you something?" she asked. "About Saturday night."

"I wish you would."

"I realized something important. I have terrible taste in men."

Her intelligence about her situation eased the knot of concern he'd been carrying around. Perhaps he needn't worry about her, but then he'd have to agree her attempt to seduce him in her office meant *he* was a bad choice. He likely was.

He moved a curl of hair over her shoulder. "You alluded to that."

"The way you were with me. It was so different it made me see what was possible. So, that's why I…"

"Tried to seduce me."

She flushed. "Yes."

"So you *were* using me." He laughed. Her words didn't upset him at all. On the contrary, relief coursed through his veins. He understood seduction. It was the morning after that perplexed him, that female desire to continue, to *cling*.

"So, as someone who's been used in the past, when I saw the screen in your desk—"

"It gave you a good excuse to leave. You were thrown back into the cycle of men not being honest with you."

She nodded.

"Well, Samantha Rose." He hoisted her onto the table. "What do you want tonight?"

"I'm not sure."

"Uncharted territory?"

She nodded.

"Me, too. I guess we're stuck."

Her eyes widened. She eased off the edge of the table and turned her back to him. "Can you help me with my zipper? It gets stuck sometimes, too."

∽

With deft fingers, he lowered her zipper. The faint *zlip* was the only sound to accompany the tick-tock of the clock on the sideboard credenza.

Straps fell over her shoulders followed by her dress falling to the floor. The scratch over her belly awoke something inside her. She turned so she could see his eyes, more gray now. Before they'd been blue-green.

Freed from the armor of her dress, she found everything about him to seem larger than she recalled. His height was greater, his shoulders broader. The pronounced angles in his face drew more elegant lines than she'd appreciated earlier. Even that gentlemanly vibe he threw off was grander.

On the drive home, she had tried to talk herself out of going any further with him. She'd listed what little she knew about Derek Wright: kind but direct, confident but with unsettled eyes, normal yet breathing the rarefied air of a privileged world. In the car, she came down to one reason to be here with him, right now, like this, with her dress puddled at her feet. She wanted to be.

His hands reached around her ribcage. His eyes never left her face as he unsnapped her bra with one hand.

"Wow." She hadn't meant to say it aloud. But his bra removal skill, and resulting smirk from her remark, said he probably could do many other things with those hands. She was going to find out. Her bra made a soft slap as it hit the vinyl floor.

When his gaze locked on the sight of her bare breasts, a deluge of feminine power solidified her earlier decision. He would honestly *appreciate* her. Respect wasn't anything she'd thought of before, not really. What a mistake, because now as she stood before a man who honored her thoughts and feelings, respect was all she could think of.

"Wow, indeed." He reseated her on the table. He leaned

his hands on either side of her legs and gazed down at her intently for one endless minute.

"You like?" she asked.

He grasped her ass and yanked her to the edge so her crotch connected with his. "I like."

So did she, because now she knew his size. Cindy would have been impressed.

His hands cradled her face. As his fingers massaged the back of her skull, his eyes roamed over every inch of her heated cheeks.

"Do you like surprises?" he asked. "Cameras notwithstanding."

"Love them."

"Good. This one time I'm going to tell you what I'm going to do. Next time, I won't."

There was going to be a next time? "Okay."

"First, I'm going to kiss you so hard you'll lose your ability to stand. You'll be short of breath. Your world will become my mouth."

Good start.

"Then I'm going to rip that thong off you. I'll send something tomorrow to replace it. But only so I can rip it off again because I know one thing, Samantha Rose."

"What?" she breathed.

"Once I'm inside you, I'm going to want to be there all the time. Deep inside." On his last words, he ground his pelvis against her now soaked panties.

Yes, please.

His mouth came down on hers. He did rude things with his lips and tongue. True to his word, she was breathless by the time he stopped.

His fingers wound their way through her hair and pulled her head back gently but with intention. The fingers of his other hand slipped into her thong, and he yanked hard. A thrill ran through her whole body at a telltale ripping sound —until the tear stopped. *Stupid lycra material*. She wanted the fabric to be shredded so he could ravage her like he'd promised.

He chuckled slightly. "Best laid plans… "

She returned his laughter but then stopped when he whisked her panties down her legs in a nanosecond. Being stripped of her dress and exposed to him fully touched a vulnerable place inside her, as if her earlier courage lay in a heap at her feet along with her dress.

"Hey, no fair. I'm naked and you're not."

He fisted her hair a little tighter. "We'll get there."

"When?" The lights were bright in the kitchen.

"You would be fun to tie up."

Her mind's eye wrapped her in a series of rope patterns. She could almost feel the itch. She licked her lips. "Okay."

His eyes narrowed a bit. "Into bondage, are we?"

"Maybe." She'd be into anything this man was into because her insides were ready to explode.

"Too bad we don't have some of that parachute silk here. I could wrap them around these"—he regarded one leg—"incredibly luscious legs and keep them still. Though I'd rather like seeing you come undone." The vision of all the positions he could put them into tumbled into her mind. *Oh, yes.*

He brought his lips and hot breath close to her ear. "And once I have you bound and helpless, how should I take you? Missionary? From behind? Against the wall?" He pulled back to face her. "Or all ways?"

She inched her legs further apart and nodded.

∽

Derek dropped his hold on her hair and stepped backward. This woman was too good to be true.

Was she fishing for his sexual proclivities? Nothing about her spoke of seeking gossip or blackmail material, and she appeared quite sensitive to that possibility for herself. He dismissed his suspicions.

Was he being careless? Probably. He didn't care. His cock overruled any over-thinking on that front. He had to be inside this woman. *Now.*

He supposed he should have stopped to further assess her scene play experience, but where would she have encountered kink? In some kid's shared apartment with play toy handcuffs and a tickler?

That conversation would come later—and there would be a later. He was certain of that fact thanks to the saucy curiosity he read on her face. Her inexperience demanding to be overturned intrigued him. She'd called him a gentleman. He was. When shown a door, he'd been taught to open it.

For him, she was a place he hadn't yet visited or a fantastic book he hadn't yet read. So much to discover, and not only because she was uncharted territory for *him*. He got to be new to *her*.

He unbuckled his belt. After zipping it through the loops, he doubled it in his hand and waited. He assessed her breathing, where her eyes landed, what she did with her hands—all signs of whether she was turned on or scared.

The hungry look in her eyes and her pink tongue reaching out to touch her lip strengthened his resolve to keep going. He wasn't yet sure if she fueled his dominance on purpose or by accident.

He laid the belt next to her. She didn't flinch when the leather touched her thigh.

After peeling off his jacket and casually draping it over one of the chairs, he rolled up his shirtsleeves. He stopped her hands from reaching out to touch him.

Lucky

"No helping, ballerina. Hands back by your sides. Palms on the table." He purposefully increased the volume of his voice for effect. Her delicious pout made his mouth water. *Such beautiful lips.*

"You're going to help me in other ways. In fact," he said, lowering his zipper, "in many other ways."

Her teeth nibbled on that pink, plush lower lip. "Mine," he said without thinking and grasped that tender lip between his. Yes, this mouth would be his in many, many ways.

Hands clutched at his still-clothed ass and pulled him harder in toward her. *Bad little ballerina*. Without letting go of her mouth, he clasped her wrists and pulled them up. Lowering her back to the table surface, he pressed her arms over her head.

"Keep them there." He worked her mouth over for long minutes until she ground her crotch into him with unmasked desperation.

Something hit the floor. A saltshaker rolled under his feet.

With one hand, he got his pants and briefs down to his ankles. His cock popped free and slapped the inside of her leg. She raised her legs high until her ankles rested on his shoulders. Fuck that she didn't wait for him and positioned herself. He was ready to fuck her.

He'd been hoping the night would end like this. He retrieved a condom from his wallet and rolled it on in one long glide.

When he pushed his cock into her slowly, she moaned as every inch penetrated her. He waited for her to squirm, the signal she'd adjusted. Instead, his bad little dancer grasped the edges of table and pulled herself closer to him so no space existed between them.

"Stop."

She stilled at his bark. *Good girl.*

In his mind, he level-set his own expectations. This was sex, pure and simple, with the most basic introduction to being topped. If she listened to him at all, he'd take that as a sign to demand more and then demand more still until he hit a wall.

"Don't move," he said.

"But I want to—"

"Samantha. Let me take you."

Her chin dipped in recognition of his words. "Yes, please."

Oh, she fueled his dominance all right. But, Jesus, he wouldn't last if she kept making those noises. His mouth swallowed her little mewls that were driving him insane. Now that her hot breath mixed with his and their connection was complete, he prayed he wouldn't come before she did. She didn't wait.

She keened in his mouth as he ground into her, hitting her clit repeatedly. Sweet relief came to him next. He hadn't had sex in a while. Now he had an inkling about the tantric bullshit that Alexander had always preached. As they said, rewards come to those who wait.

He reached out and touched her face. "You okay?"

"Oh, yes." She cracked a new smile—one he hoped to earn again after their second round. That first time was far too short, and he'd allowed much leniency despite his inclination earlier to bind and tease her until she submitted. He'd verbally address that with her later.

"Samantha, about surprises."

Her eyes cleared with excitement. "Yes?"

He pulled his trousers up and hastily secured his belt. After easing her up to sitting, he grasped under her ass and lifted her. "Your room."

"Upstairs."

With some guidance, and many prayers he didn't run into her grandmother despite Samantha saying she couldn't hear, he carried her up the stairs. One glance at her old-fashioned brass headboard and his cock thickened to a painful degree. With six feet of rope and a few hours, he could spend all day testing those metal scrolls.

His gaze caught several feather boas hanging on a hook on the back of her bedroom door.

What do you know? The universe provided.

~

Samantha pulled on her arms. Derek had slipped a scarf Samantha had thrown in a corner over her eyes and tied her arms with feather boas, cheap dime store ropes of itchy feathers in red and black that had been hanging on the back of her door for years.

She hoped this "surprise" he talked of would come soon. The light tickling around her wrists would eventually drive her mad.

A rustling in her nightstand drawer was just another long string of unexpected sounds and sensations produced by Derek in the last five minutes. She liked it. She spent so much of her days choreographing, trying to remember steps and directing others to do the same, that not knowing what happened next brought a strange, sweet peacefulness. She so rarely stood—or in this case lay—on the other side of entertainment.

Derek let out a laugh. "Do you always have chocolate in your nightstand table?"

Ah, he'd found her hidden stash of Ferrero treats. "You never know when a sugar craving will hit."

"Spoken like a true woman." The scrape and crinkle of the plastic tray made her mouth water. "Half-empty," he mused. "I suppose it's important to keep up one's strength. Especially in bed."

Was he chewing? "Hey, no fair. Do I get any?"

"Maybe." His voice was muffled. "They're good."

More crackling of wrappers reached her ears. Then a slight cool disk touched her cheek followed by the smell of chocolate. He'd laid one, unwrapped, on her cheek. He placed another on her other cheek. Several more soon dotted her chest. She could smell the chocolatey goodness.

"That wasn't exactly what I had in mind," she said carefully. If they fell, he might eat them.

"I'll let you have any that you can keep on your body."

She almost nodded but then thought better of it. They perched quite precariously on her face.

Derek's chest hairs brushed across her thighs. He'd finally gotten undressed, and, damn, she missed the show.

The bed dipped. Was it bad she was concerned about the chocolate caramels falling? The sandpaper of his rough beard scratched the inside of her calf. Derek crawled in between her legs, his breath growing closer to… He pushed her legs further apart. Thank God she'd shaved that morning.

"Ah," she cried out when his lips met her opening. Her chest expanded as he licked slowly up her crease and sighed.

"You taste better than the chocolate."

"Nothing's better than chocolate." Oh, except for what he did with his tongue. She took slow, shallow breaths. Her mind alternatively focused on that chocolate smell and how slowly and lightly he sucked on her clit. One of the chocolates dropped off her cheek. The other one wasn't far behind in falling to the pillow.

Good God. Without thinking, she let her back bow, and miraculously the caramels clung to her skin, likely half-melted to her chest by now. Her thin comforter bunched up under her clenched fists as he licked, sucked, and licked more.

He stopped suddenly. "Need some chocolate strength?"

Lucky

"No." She eased her thighs closed to capture his large body between her legs. She didn't want him to go anywhere.

"None of that," he tutted and pushed them wide again. "I've just gotten started."

"Good," she breathed.

He climbed her body. A chocolate caramel popped off her. Yep, it had started to melt.

He ran the sweetness over her lip, and she craned her neck hoping to grasp it with her lips. The devil snatched it away. "I didn't say you could have it yet."

"Sadist."

"Not really. But if you need one, the gentleman in me could oblige."

Was he serious? "I'd rather have a Ferrero."

He chuckled, and the sadist put the chocolate back onto her chest. "Then let's make sure they stay on." His mouth latched onto her pussy before she could take a half breath—and this time he ate at her as if *she* was made of chocolate. The gentleman didn't stop for a really long time.

10

Derek stretched his leg and his foot touched air. Samantha's queen-sized bed wasn't big enough for one person, let alone two. His eyes cracked open. Sunshine escaped through the bed curtain and rudely attacked his face.

He sat up at the soft click of a door closing down the hall and creaking floorboards. He was alone.

Her room, which he'd barely registered last night, was surprisingly large. Yet who could notice anything with a nude and bound Samantha?

The 1970s retro alarm clock read nine a.m., a time he rarely saw cross any timepiece.

In addition to the inadequately sized bed, two chairs circled a large round cricket table in front of a double-hung window. A tailor's body form draped in a flesh-colored silk, half of it studded in crystals, stood in the corner. He could envision the costume's purpose. In certain lighting she'd appear nude and lit by stardust. He appreciated the look, though a jolt of jealousy that anyone might stare at her believing she was naked bewildered his usual morning-after stoicism.

Lucky

He swung his legs toward the table and his eye caught rolled-up paper. He'd studied enough architectural plans to recognize what they were.

He stood, and before he could reach them, a picture in an oval frame caught his attention. A woman held a large feather fan like a half clamshell behind her head. She was a looker. She had Samantha's large eyes and cleft chin. Man, they had a lot of personal photographs in this house.

The door gently opened and Samantha peered around.

"Your mother?" He lifted the frame.

"No, my grandmother. I was just saying good-bye to her. She's gone to the deaf school to volunteer."

"I'm sorry I missed her," he lied.

"She wants to meet you."

"You told her I was here?"

"Sure." She pulled on a black Nike sport jacket.

He returned the frame to its dusty spot on the table. "Your grandmother danced."

"She was a burlesque dancer back in the day. Nineteen sixties."

"She must be proud that you followed in her footsteps."

"Sort of. I've never taken the stage in that way … if you know what I mean."

So, her grandmother was a *real* burlesque dancer, likely entertaining men with a show that would have been tame compared to today's standards but scandalous in her day.

"Your parents?"

"Florida. Retired early. I see them twice a year. They wanted my grandmother to live with them, but she refuses to leave this house." She waved her hand. "I'm the grateful recipient of that decision."

"You take care of her."

"We take care of each other."

"What are these?" He picked up the design plans and

unrolled them. "Says Aerobesque expansion on the top." He held down the edges as he unfurled them on the bed.

"Don't you want to get dressed?"

"No. You started construction yet? I know a thing or two about expanding spaces." Being friends with co-workers and living with family were all a mystery to him. But this? *This* he understood— the joy of creating something that didn't exist before.

"It's not a big deal. I mean, it is to us. I'm hoping for more students soon."

"By the look on my patrons' faces the other night, I'd say students will be knocking down your door soon. You should give demonstrations at my club until you've finished with your expansion. I have high ceilings."

"I know. And thanks. That's generous."

"Not really. You'll guarantee a crowd. Why not move to a place more centrally located?"

"I heard people get used to coming to one location, so this is the building next door. Students don't like change."

"You got that right."

"Employees are the hardest part of any business," he said. "Finding them, training them, only to have them leave for something better. Making sure they don't steal."

"You have employees who steal?"

"All the time, in a variety of ways. Free drinks to friends, free drinks to themselves, slipping themselves a handful of bills because they think they were entitled to a greater tip. The list is endless."

"That's terrible."

"Comes with the territory."

"My instructors would never."

"Don't be too sure."

"For someone with a great sense of humor, you're pretty cynical."

Lucky

"You think I have a great sense of humor?"

She laughed. "And selective hearing."

He pulled out the second design and laid it on top of the first, which he already could tell would never work. "The first thing to understand is whatever the construction company quoted you on this renovation, add twenty percent. They all lie to you to get the job."

"I don't have extra money."

"Then you'll need to low ball your contractor." He glanced at an undersized boiler room sketch. Whoever did these plans wasn't completely on the up and up. "You haven't selected anyone yet, have you?"

She shook her head. "I'm going to meet with someone today—"

"Cancel it." He grasped the end of the chintz chair and pulled it to face the table. "Sit. We need to prepare you."

~

We? Was she really talking business with one of the most successful entertainment investors on the East Coast? At least that's what Cindy had called him. To add to the ridiculousness of the situation, he was still nude. Paying attention to anything other than his impressive man parts proved difficult.

Derek's large hands held open the plans and he studied them intently. "You've got some problems here. I'll send you the names of some reputable contractors—and a new designer. I'll also tell you who to avoid."

"That's nice of you, but you don't need to."

"Yes, I do. You need my advice." He winked at her, which made her want to match his naked state.

"You're so humble."

He laughed out loud, flashing white teeth in that flawless

face on top of his flawless body. A body that had her pinned to her kitchen table—which she needed to remember to bleach today before she left—and done unspeakable, carnal things to her body even later in her bed. He'd withheld the chocolate for over an hour.

For another thirty minutes he gave her a list of questions to ask a contractor, which she furiously took down in her phone to email to herself. Wow, he knew a lot.

A quick glance at the time showed ten thirty a.m. She'd barely make it to her studio to teach her eleven o'clock class.

"Oh, man, I'm so late. I have to go." She stood.

"When are you free later today? There's more to discuss."

"Um, three? I have to teach a class at six."

"Can you swing by Frost later? I'll make calls this afternoon to some people I know." He rolled up the plans and tucked them into the tube he found under the table.

"That fast?"

One side of his mouth lifted. "I give the building industry a lot of business."

"Wow, you move fast." She wanted to expand her studio, but Derek's pace was a cha-cha when she was thinking more like a waltz.

"They're preliminary talks, ballerina." He tucked a stray strand of hair behind her ear. "Not commitments."

"Okay. Three o'clock. And thank you."

"Believe me, the pleasure is all mine." He reached for his shirt. *Damn*. His tight abs and broad chest made her mouth water. She wanted to melt more chocolate—on him. But she had to go teach if she was going to keep her studio open, let alone afford sweets.

11

Jonathan's rumble resounded in Derek's ear. "There are not enough secure lines in Washington to keep this a secret long." His friend and fellow Accendos member had that right.

"True. Alexander probably already knows we're up to no good. But he's turning sixty next year. It's the big one."

"Something tells me Alexander is going to live forever."

"We can only hope. So, the question is hold his surprise party here or take him down to The Regal? St. Thomas will be great that time of year. You know I'll make whichever one work. I just need the dates."

"April 24."

"Let's do the Caribbean." Carson's rough voice cut in. "Sorry I'm late. Clients. This a secure conference line? You know Alexander will find out otherwise."

Derek and Jonathan laughed together at their attorney friend's usual paranoia.

"We were just discussing that," Jonathan said. "But the gentleman in him will refuse to acknowledge if he did find out. He'll play along like he doesn't know."

The word *gentleman* produced an unexpected happy jolt that traveled up his spine. It conjured up a vision of Samantha and all the non-gentlemanly things he wanted to do to her later. Hell, had already done to her.

"Okay. Regal it is. Shouldn't we check with Sarah, Ryan, Mark?" Derek asked. "As fellow Tribunal Council members, they wouldn't want to be left out."

"I'll talk with Sarah and Mark," Jonathan said.

"I'll see Ryan tomorrow at Accendos. London wants to go."

Derek chuckled. Carson's little masochist wife got antsy if she and Carson didn't "work it out" at Alexander's club, Accendos, at least once a month.

He wondered how Samantha would respond to Club Accendos and its atmosphere. He'd eventually have to broach the Dominant-submissive discussion with her. He'd never had the "introductory talk" before. Samantha seemed to enjoy their time together, though enjoying feather boa bondage was hardly an indication of a submissive bent.

The women he'd gotten involved with in the past few years came from Accendos and were already deep in the lifestyle. He should talk with Jonathan. Lord knows the man liked giving advice and with his fiancé, Christiana, he'd gone through the same scenario Derek now found himself in. Christiana had been new to their world when Jonathan met her. Carson was fortunate, having discovered London's proclivities immediately from the woman herself.

How did others do this? Slog through the endless negotiations not knowing what lay on the other side? How not to have them get too attached?

The door to his office opened without so much as a knock, and his earlier good mood was knocked completely off its axis.

"Gotta go, gentlemen. I'll check dates. Let me know what

the others say." Not waiting for a response from either, he returned the phone to its cradle and turned to the intruder.

"Hello, Mother."

∼

Samantha parked her car in the same spot where she'd been attacked, not because she was trying that whole get-back-on-the-horse thing, but because it was the only free space she could find. Paying twenty-five dollars an hour to park in the garage next door was ridiculous.

As she rounded the corner of the building to go to the front, she wondered if she should have called Derek first. Would the doors even be open? Turns out they were. She waltzed right into Club Frost as if she were expected. Shrouded in dim lighting, the empty dance floor cast a lonely vibe.

Two men stood hunched over boxes behind the bar. Probably readying themselves for tonight's crowd. It was Wednesday after all, the night when people in Washington began their weekend partying.

One of the guys dressed in black head-to-toe straightened. "Greg," she said, stepping up to the shiny metallic bar. "You may not remember me—"

"Samantha Rose, of course I remember you. How are you? Feeling okay?" His dazzling smile put her at ease immediately.

"I'm great. I'm looking for Derek? He asked me to stop by to talk business," she stated in a matter-of-fact tone. She needn't have bothered. No amusement triggered by potential gossip lingered in his eyes.

"He's upstairs. And, hey, we have your lyra and silks from Saturday."

Oh, wow, *how* had she forgotten those?

"Give me your keys. I'll put them in your car for you while you go upstairs."

"Thank you. It's in the alley." She handed him her keys with no hesitation. The courteous vibe she got from Derek ran deep in Greg as well. Besides, who'd steal her car? Or smelly silks and a lyra with two dents in it?

"Go on up." He indicated the small elevator door in the corner she recognized from the other night. "I'll buzz you in."

She took a deep breath and headed to the discreet elevator. She wore her swishiest skirt. The fabric grazed across her legs and made her feel soft and feminine—and now that she had had an effect on Derek, her female side was feeling large. Plus, skirts provided easy access in case business wasn't the only thing on his mind.

She stepped inside, her belly buzzing in anticipation. She was going to see Derek, and she was as giddy as a kindergartner.

~

"Mother." He pecked her on the cheek. "What a nice surprise."

"Is that all I get from my favorite son? Especially since he stood her up for lunch today."

Damn, he'd forgotten he had a lunch date with his mother.

"My apologies."

She presented her other cheek. When he laid a second, chaste peck, the cool bands of her diamond and ruby rings touched his cheek.

"Your cell phone seems to have died, as well." She pulled her handbag up on her elbow, a move mimicking the Queen of England. "Your downtown office said you'd be here."

Lucky

He'd been on his mobile half the afternoon and had ignored all incoming calls. A quick glance and he could tell half a dozen messages had been left, some by Jills and his downtown office assistant, likely warning him about the pending maternal invasion.

"I've been very busy, and this week has been pivotal." *In more ways than one.*

"You're right about that." She turned to him. "Especially given the news I have to deliver."

If she said she was getting divorced for the fourth time, he'd have to consider moving to the Caribbean for good.

"Have a seat." He sat himself on one of the two leather couches.

She pulled out a linen handkerchief from her purse and dusted the seat before perching herself.

So typical. "Worried I'm behind in my cleaning bills?"

"Not at all. This is pure silk." She ran her hands over her ivory skirt before sitting down and setting her handbag on the table that separated them.

"So, shoot. Why are you here, Mother?"

She sighed and crossed her legs. "It's your brother."

"What do you think Bret has done now?"

"It's not what I think. It's what he's *doing*." She dropped her voice to a hush. "It's what he's done. He's gotten involved with an event planner."

"Ava is not an event planner anymore. She's a property manager and from what I hear, a damn good one."

"Language, Derek Damon." She fussed with her pale pink jacket. "So, you knew? Naturally. I'm the last to know anything when it comes to you two. And it doesn't surprise me she's retired, living in the lap of luxury at your resort."

"Our resort. We own it together. And Ava is working, Mother, at her insistence. Or, so Bret tells me. I'm sure he'd love nothing more than to have her pregnant and barefoot." And probably nude 24/7. Unlike him, Bret couldn't wait to correct their childhood by starting a family. He only hoped his brother knew what he was doing.

"Children! Good lord, I hope not. He'll never shake her then. For God's sake, you two are going to be the death of me."

"Oh, don't worry, Mother. You'll never see me procreating. I see no reason to pass on these genes."

"I'm sure there was an insult to me in there somewhere. I refuse to acknowledge it. Contrary to what your brother and you think, I love you both. Deeply. I've loved all my children, and wanted nothing but the best for you all." She clutched her heart with all five diamond-ringed fingers. His own heart squeezed at her words. If she brought up their childhood, he'd be forced to become rude.

She moved on. There appeared to be a God after all. "Now tell me, are you going to help me or not?"

"With?"

"*Bret*. Have you been listening at all?"

"He's a big boy, Mother. Now, I have a date. You're at the Oak, right?"

"A girlfriend? Don't tell me. An event planner."

"No, a dance studio owner."

"A *dancer*? Are you and your brother out of you minds?"

Her words stopped when he held up his hand. "I am not having this conversation with you."

"Look, there are women everywhere trying to ensnare men like you. I thought you of all people would understand. *A dancer* must see you as a meal ticket from God. If she gets pregnant, it won't change a thing about what happened before…"

Later he'd assess whether or not he heard the elevator door open, but he knew for certain he'd never expected

Lucky

Samantha to step in right at that moment. Otherwise, his next words would have never left his mouth so vehemently. He knew how women worked, sort of.

"Mother. I am *not* marrying Samantha. Happy? Now, go to your hotel and I'll see you later." He'd expected to rise, turn and march her to the elevator. Instead, he found Samantha standing behind him, her face a mask of shock.

He walked over to a stiff Samantha. He embraced her in a hug and smoothed back her hair.

"Hi. How are you?"

"Fine." She seemed a little stunned at his sign of affection.

"Hello." His mother stepped forward and offered a diamond-studded hand. "I'm Betsy. Derek's mother."

"Sam."

"What an unusual name for someone so pretty," she drawled in her usual judgmental tone. "Are you the dancer my son is not going to marry?"

Derek grasped his mother by the elbow and led her toward the elevator. "Mother, I'll call you later."

"Later. It's always later with you two." She gave him a peck on the cheek. Before pulling back, she whispered, "You don't have to go there. Not everyone is cut out for family."

He prayed Samantha hadn't heard that last part. Their family's past wasn't anything he'd discuss with anyone.

∽

Samantha kept silent as Derek's eyes followed his mother's perfectly straight back until she disappeared behind the elevator doors. The woman wore vintage Chanel and carried an honest-to-God Kelly bag. With a mother like that, no wonder Derek dressed as if he was about to be called to a state dinner at the White House.

She should have worn something more conservative than

this skirt. In the past, it always had made her feel free. Now? She felt cheap.

Derek scrubbed his hair, turned and flashed her a smile that didn't reach his eyes.

"I'm happy to see you, Samantha."

"Your mother wasn't." Which was the oddest thing, as most mothers loved her. It was their sons that didn't carry that same sentiment.

You had sex with him. You loved it. It was your decision. Take a breath.

She'd known this man for days. Besides, his moratorium on marriage was not unfamiliar. The fact he'd spoken so adamantly had thrown her, that's all. She was also sick to death of being looked at like she was one step up from being a stripper.

He pointed at the tube sticking out of her bag. "Let's take a deeper look at your plans."

She pulled her bag higher on her shoulder. "I've been thinking. You're used to big projects, and this is small potatoes—"

He slipped the tube free. "Samantha, no project interests me more than what I'm holding in my hands right now." He straightened. "One exception. What I held in my hands last night. Now come over here. You're too far away."

One step and she was flush against his chest. His grin warmed the frost his mother had laid with her words. *And his.*

"About what you overheard. My mother doesn't bring out the best in me. She's worried about gold diggers."

"I'm not out for—"

"I know, Samantha. Like I said, forget her. I have."

Had he? The last thing she needed was to be accused of having self-serving designs on him. Yet, did that mean she

Lucky

was once again being seen as "have fun" material and not much of anything else? She had put out desperation vibes before.

Time to play it cool.

"Okay, I'll forget it." She took the plans back from his hands and uncapped the top. "Besides, you were the one who told me never to assume anything. Why should you presume I'd want to marry you?"

He grinned down at her, appearing remarkably relieved but also intrigued. He scratched his chin. "You're right. You just want my high ceilings."

"Now you're getting it." She unfurled the papers in the tube and they leaned over her plans together.

"So, this bathroom size isn't up to code. You need a window here … and here."

Curiously, going back to business felt good, like he didn't see her as a one-night stand or an opportunist. There had to be something in between, right?

"Who did you use as an architect on these?" he asked.

"He's an architectural student, the boyfriend of one of my students." She flushed a bright red. "I told you I don't have money to hire."

"I understand. I'll get my guys to redo your plans. Then we'll get more solid construction bids. Two of the best outfits in town said given the age of the building and the size you want, you can expect something around forty—"

"Thousand?" She straightened and backed up. "I can get other help."

"Boyfriends of students who did construction during the summer?"

"At least I can afford them."

"There are codes to follow, you know."

"But forty!"

"If you need a loan—"

"I'm not taking your money."

"Wasn't offering it. I can set you up with a banker."

"Listen. I appreciate this. I really, really do. But this is too much."

"Dinner then. Tomorrow."

She wasn't sure she heard him right. "What? I have to teach."

"Call in a substitute."

"It's my favorite class."

Derek cocked his head.

"I'm not missing it." She hoped her tone wiped that stunned look off his face.

"Then leave the plans here with me. I'll get the fixes handled and bring them to you. Then you can decide what to do."

"That fast?"

"Like I said, I know people in the business. They'll fix the issues so at least you'll have workable plans to use as you wish. I'll take you to dinner after class. Then we'll discuss how you can get it done without spending forty thousand."

"I teach until nine on Thursdays."

From his annoyance, she surmised people rarely argued with him. She rather liked his stern gaze. The angles in his face sharpened, and his eyes flashed more blue than green.

"Have Cindy take over your later classes."

"Maybe."

"Yes." His hands circled the back of her neck.

"You're bossy." *And hot.* Those little circles he made with his fingers on the back of her skull could melt the polar ice caps.

"You have no idea how bossy I can be," he said.

"Okay, I'll work it out," she said softly. His unyielding

desire to see her filled her with confidence. Plus, he had likely left scorch marks on the nape of her neck with his magical fingers.

So what if his mother didn't like her? She wouldn't be part of their dinner date.

12

Derek eased himself out of the driver's seat into the fall sunshine and stretched. The dance studio's Florida Avenue address wasn't as bad as he'd supposed. As he rounded the corner, he slapped the tube in his palm in rhythm with two boys drumming on plastic buckets on the corner.

Nichols & Farnsworth Architects had charged him four times what a cursory mock-up might otherwise cost. They'd also scratched her previous plans immediately once they pulled up the building address where she wanted to expand. He only hoped she didn't pay that architectural student a dime like she'd said given what she got—a worthless idea. Thanks to his contacts, with careful rearranging, her new plans realized an extra fifty square feet of dance space, and Aerobesque would have three rooms versus two.

As for her balking at $40,000? He could spend that in an afternoon. Yesterday, over a cup of coffee, he *had* spent that much on a design for a new adult pool at Regal Resorts, a place he should be right now. The addition of a clothing-optional section of the property had proved to be the best

Lucky

move he and Bret had made yet. They already needed to expand due to the growing waiting list for bookings.

He should take Samantha to Regal. On second thought, he'd be crazy to put her nudity on display.

The metal steps clanged loudly as he jogged up to the door. He headed into a dusty alcove. The 1920s row house had to be one step away from being condemned. A glance at the similarly run down commercial building next door where she wanted to move her studio, and he had to hold himself back from handling the project for her. That place had hidden additional costs written on every brick. He should fund the renovation himself.

Of course, money made things messy.

By the time he reached the top of the stairs, he'd decided. He'd help her obtain a loan and settle for being her business advisor. It'd be easier.

Cindy sat behind a card table that doubled as a desk in a corner of the tiny room. She glanced up from a laptop and grinned. "Hello there, handsome," she said over thumping music.

"Cindy, how is the life of an aerial artist?"

"Still single, damn it." She slapped her hand over her mouth. "Sorry. Trying not to swear so much."

"How's it going?"

"Hard as hell. Sam will be done soon."

He nodded. "I'm in no rush."

He glanced at two women who sat beside one another on a small couch, typing furiously into their phones, while a third woman in yoga gear leaned against the wall, her eyes fixed on him.

Ah, Washington women—they were either Working Women in business suits constantly tapping into a phone or Fitness Moms in gym clothes with French manicures that touched only organic food for kids' lunches. Both types had perfected nonchalant motherhood.

"Sam told me about your advice on the expansion. Thanks for that. We could use the help." Honest warmth radiated from Cindy's face.

"It's what I do best."

"That's not what I heard," she whispered.

His ego flickered with self-satisfaction over the possibility Samantha had been impressed enough to share anything about their time together with Cindy. Another first to add to the accumulating list of inaugural moments thanks to Samantha Rose. Normally he'd cut off anyone who'd shared any detail about him with anyone.

A loud gaggle of giggling erupted from behind the curtain followed by a drum roll of feet. He stepped backward just in time. Seconds later, a herd of diminutive female bodies in pink tights and sparkly T-shirts burst through the curtains in a tangle of tiny humans. He'd have backed up to avoid them, but where would he go in this room that was basically an alcove?

"Girls! Girls!" Cindy called out. "Don't forget the form Miss Rose told you to take home." She handed out bright pink pieces of paper. Their grabby little hands clutched at them.

"Thank you, Miss Cindy," a chorus rang out. *Wow. Loud.* For such little bodies, their lungs rivaled Cindy's.

They jumped up and down and generally bounced in all directions as if they'd mainlined pure sugar. A few of them rushed to the three women who barely registered their space had been invaded.

One of the girls threw herself in between Working Mom's iPhone and her face. "Mooooom."

His stomach turned over at the whine.

Lucky

Samantha emerged from behind the curtain and beamed at him in the doorway. "I see you met my Lyra Ladies."

He inched his way toward Samantha, careful not to step on any of the girls, and placed a kiss on her cheek. "Meet is an overstatement. More like a hit and run." His casual laugh sounded fake even to him.

"You don't look worse for the wear."

"Floor's mine," Cindy said, high-fiving Samantha before scooting through the curtain. He caught the flash of a lyra hanging from the ceiling in the other room before the fabric fell back into place. Perhaps he'd follow her inside. There was bound to be more space.

When three young women jogged loudly up the stairs, he honestly felt his molecules constrict. How would they fit? Was there enough oxygen in this ten-by-ten landing?

"Derek!" Christiana bounded up the stairs and threw her arms around him in a hug. *Thank God, an adult.*

"You two know each other?" Sam asked.

"Derek is one of Jonathan's friends. It's how we met. Your new club was so much fun last weekend."

"I'm only sorry we didn't connect."

"Oh, we knew you were busy. Sam and Cindy were awesome as usual. Sorry we didn't get to say hi, Sam." She hugged her. "We left early. Jonathan got ideas."

I'll bet.

"Anyway, Derek, I'm glad to see you're finally getting some recreation in." Christiana threw Samantha one of those secret looks women give each other. "See you two later." Jonathan's fiancée disappeared behind the curtain.

A little girl pushed past him and launched herself at Samantha. She latched on like a leech around Sam's legs. "Thank you, Miss Rose. I like to spin."

Samantha crouched down and took the little girl by the

shoulders. "You did very well, Amber Lynne. Next time don't forget to keep your knees bent, okay? It's how you stay on." The pink sprite disappeared into Samantha's arms in a hug.

When released she peered up at him. "Is this your boyfriend?"

"This is Mr. Wright. He's helping us make our studio bigger."

The little girl threw her matchstick-sized arms around his legs. His hands automatically rose in the air. She was so thin he might break her. The girl's grip was striking, however—if one liked being clung to by a baby orangutan.

Her large blue eyes flashed up at him. "Make it really, really big. We need a million more hoops so all my friends can come and spin and then when we're bigger we all want to climb the ribbons and then we'll be real dancers and we'll go on stage and men will throw flowers at us."

"You mean they give you a bouquet when you take your curtsy," Sam said.

"Yeah, but like a *million* of them." She stressed *million*, as if it was her favorite word.

"Amber Lynne, why don't you go get your dance bag and meet me out here?" Fitness Mom had sidled up to him. The little girl took off like a shot.

"I thought I recognized you, Mr. Wright. I've been to Striker's many times."

He gave her a courteous, single nod. "I appreciate that."

"You should go to his new club, Frost. It's beautiful." Samantha grinned at him.

"I'll be sure to do that." She turned to Samantha. "Sam, thanks so much for letting her come to class." She turned back to him with a wave of her hand. "Amber Lynne doesn't turn seven, Sam's minimum age, for another four months. But talent can't be denied, can it?" She threw him a sure

Lucky

smile as if to say her daughter was headed straight for Broadway if she had anything to do with it.

"I'm delighted to have her in my class. She's a natural."

Fitness Mom positively beamed under Samantha's diplomacy.

Amber Lynne jogged back to her mother, a too-large bag slung over her tiny shoulder. "I want ice cream."

"You don't need the calories," she whispered down to her little girl.

Ah, get the food dysfunction in early, he thought.

"But *Mooom*." She let her bag drop and her pouty gaze dropped toward the floor.

"Next time I'll bring some," he told Amber Lynne. "What's your favorite flavor?" The room had grown so hot, ice cream sounded perfect.

"Pink!" Amber Lynn announced. Obviously she liked strawberry. It'd match her outfit.

Through gritted teeth, the girl's mother smiled. "How sweet." A Samurai sword couldn't have cut him deeper than the sharp look she threw his way. *Whatever.* Kids annoyed him. Moms who ensured future problems annoyed him more.

Fitness Mom turned on her heel, pulling the little girl toward the stairs.

Samantha's wistful gaze followed her smallest students and their cooing mothers until their high-pitched voices faded down the stairway. He turned Samantha's face toward him. "So, this is your favorite class."

"Yep. Those little girls are so cute. I love them."

The look on her face told him everything he needed to know. He'd seen that look before. *She wants kids. Like yesterday.*

The tube he'd been carrying squeaked under his death grip. His palms had grown sweaty in the stifling room.

"Derek, are you okay?"

"I'm fine."

"You look a little freaked out."

"Just warm." He pointed to the folding table that held a laptop and little else. "Let's look at your plans."

A loud banging up the stairs had them both turning. A woman with a death grip on a little girl's hand stepped up into the tiny office space. *Another one?*

"Hi!" She held out her hand toward Samantha. "I'm Jocelyn Davies. Perhaps you got my message?"

Samantha took her hand. "Oh, yes, thanks for coming by."

He'd be sure a hand sanitizer was installed in her bathroom. Where was her bathroom in here anyway? Perhaps he could scoot out and avoid the little girl's dark eyes and those looks she kept darting at him every few seconds.

Samantha crouched down to the little girl. "And who are you?"

He'd never heard that airy, pulled-back voice from Samantha before. It was as if she approached a scared animal.

The girl's mother answered, "Jessica, say hello to Miss Rose."

Her thin, soft "hi" made his body feel too big for the space. His suit was too tight around him. The very air wasn't meant for him. Overall, Samantha's world of kids and dilapidated townhomes and more kids wasn't even on his planet. And, yeah, he knew how shitty that sounded.

Samantha chatted up the woman and her daughter for a few minutes. He would have left, but the woman stood at the top of the stairs and blocked his exit. There was nothing for him to do but let his mental calculation spin into overdrive over recent developments and his newfound, inescapable situation.

Her business was in trouble. *Easy fix.* She wanted kids. *Deal breaker.* She was hot as hell and in the most unusual,

Lucky

authentic way. *Fascinating.* She argued with him constantly. *Another deal breaker.* He didn't share power. Everything about her led to one outcome. *Dissonance.*

So much for having "the talk." He steadied his breath. Inhale through the nose, exhale from the mouth.

"Just let me know if that sounds like something you'd be interested in," Samantha said to the woman.

"Wonderful. I'll be in touch."

What had they talked about? He'd barely heard a word while engaged in a breathing meditation he used often to calm full-on panic.

After the woman led her daughter down the stairs, one slow step at a time, he inched toward the stairway.

"Derek?" Her soft tone stopped him. The utter lack of demand in her voice made him pause before bolting.

He stopped and turned. In a moment of self-preservation, because he was a selfish bastard and this may be the last time he saw her, he drank in every detail of her glossy hair and her large eyes. Yet even with all the deafening sirens inside his head, he couldn't make himself leave. Something was wrong, so very wrong. He should be halfway down Florida Avenue by now.

"I know why you're worried," she said after a few seconds ticked by. "Remember I overheard what you said to your mother this morning."

He had no idea what to say. Children were irreversible. After the death of his own brother, the pain still haunted him. He'd never willingly leave himself vulnerable to experiencing such a thing again. Hence, no children.

"Remember my mother doesn't bring out the best in me."

"It's not the first time I've heard a man panic at the C word. It's okay."

No, it wasn't. It was *never* just "okay" when it came to women wanting a family. Somehow he always ended up back in the same place—at this point where the woman wanted *more*, and less suited him fine. At the same time, a slice of anger cut through his own sense of self-preservation at the thought that anyone would reject Samantha.

She blinked up at him as if waiting for his next move. Strangely, the urge to bend her over that inadequate card-table-turned-desk grew. He'd bind a calf to each table leg, bare her pussy, redden her ass cheeks.

"You're perfect for … that." Jesus, he couldn't even say the word "children." He needed some air. He swallowed hard. "Anyone who says you aren't isn't worth your time."

"So you're not worth my time?"

He walked into that one. He shook his head in answer. *Let's stop this…* What was this? He sounded like a girl even in his own head.

"Then what's the problem?" she asked. "It's not like I've proposed to you."

"You want kids."

"Most people do."

"I won't."

"Won't." She said the word slowly.

"Right."

Her eyes moistened. "Who says I'd want to have kids with you? Why does every guy believe I'm after his gene pool?"

Because it's written all over your face, sweetheart.

He should leave. Yet if he bolted, he'd be like every other guy in her long line up of WMDs. He wasn't interested in family, but hurting her wasn't what he'd intended, either. He hadn't expected to reach this place with Samantha so soon.

"I'm going to tell you something. It's going to sound bad. I don't mean it like that. But I don't know how to say it any other way and not be honest. You were unexpected. And I don't get surprised."

"I thought you liked surprises."

Lucky

"I give them. I don't receive." He rubbed his chin with the frustration of not doing exactly what he wished—abandoning this conversation, dragging her into the side studio and binding her with those silks like he'd imagined. God, he was a bastard. On top of everything else, he'd done a terrible job of shaving this morning.

"Duly noted," she said.

He leaned against the wall and pulled her into him. "I'll strike you a deal. Let's start over. I don't know what's going on here with you and me, but I'm willing to see you more—"

"Willing." Her word hit him as hard as a thrown stone.

Jesus, any modicum of charm he'd ever possessed had fled the building. "I'd like to spend time with you. The trouble is, your version of *spending time* might not be mine." Hell, probably not even close.

She chewed her lip. A few seconds ticked by, and then she raised her gaze. "So what's your version?"

It wasn't lost on him that she provided a much-needed opening.

He let go of her. "I'll show you."

He might regret what he was about to do, but his skin had perfected the thick hide needed to live the life he'd been forced to lead. If she never wanted to see him again after tonight, it wouldn't be the first time a woman had made that decision about him.

"You got Cindy to take over your classes?"

"Yes."

"Good. I'm taking you somewhere."

"Where?"

"You'll see."

After she disappeared behind the curtain to retrieve her things, he put his idea into action. Either she'd be scared off for forever tonight, or her dreams of rugrats and a house in the suburbs would be put on hold for a while. His plan was a hell of a risk, but he didn't get rich from playing it safe.

By the grace of God, Alexander answered his phone.

"Alexander, is the rooftop pool free? If not, can you make it so? I'm bringing a guest. First timer. Important. Very, very important."

13

Samantha had often wondered what lay behind the long line of boxwood and azalea bushes on Q Street. She was about to find out. She often took the street as a shortcut to Wisconsin Avenue and always slowed down near this section of road to admire the flowering bushes on either side of the sidewalks.

Derek pulled her hand onto his thigh and smiled as they waited for an iron scroll gate, flanked by two large lion statues, to crack open.

"Ready?" he asked.

She nodded. He hadn't said much on the drive over, only that they'd be visiting a friend.

Derek's wheels crunched on the limestone driveway as they pulled up to a bona fide, right-out-of-the-movies mansion. Her grandmother had been right about the rich being different. She imagined the outdoor lighting bills alone rivaled her rent payments.

Tonight, however, Derek had shown the opposite of her grandmother's wisdom about the wealthy. He'd proven to be the same as every other man she'd ever met—terrified of being trapped. *Only he's not like every other guy, either.*

Here she was anyway—wherever the hell *here* was.

A tall elegant man in formal wear stepped off the bottom step of a circular staircase and opened her car door. "Welcome."

Derek jumped out immediately and was around his car in seconds. "Alexander, thank you for meeting us."

"My pleasure. This must be the very talented Samantha Rose I've been hearing about. I'm Alexander Rockingham." His hand engulfed her fingers. "Welcome to Accendos, my home."

"It's nice to meet you." Samantha smoothed down her thin sweater, a little embarrassed she hadn't thrown on something more befitting the atmosphere. At least she wore her favorite stiletto boots.

"Derek said you have the best view in Washington. It's kind of you to have us drop in like this."

"Derek is a special friend. Besides, my home is open 24/7." He cocked his head. "You look so much like someone I once knew." The regal man turned to Derek. "I understand only the pool, Derek?"

She glanced up at Derek. "A pool?"

"On the rooftop."

"It's October." *And fifty-five degrees out.*

They didn't react to her stating the obvious, instead gestured for her to follow them.

Her heels crunched on limestone gravel as Derek headed her toward a small circular staircase, and her gaze traveled along the ivy crawling up the side of the building. A man pushing a wheelbarrow caught her attention, then disappeared around the corner. Or, at least she thought it was a wheelbarrow. Who could tell from this distance?

She followed them up the stairs and inside. She'd have pressed the whole too-cold-to-swim issue if she hadn't been

Lucky

muzzled by the beauty of the entryway. Inside the oval portico, dozens of white French tulips spilled from an enormous silver urn atop a large round table. Oil paintings hung on the walls, and thick carpeting over hardwood floors muffled their steps.

A rustling on the other side of the hall snapped her attention forward. Two men in black sporting earpieces stood like sentries on either side of a gabled door. They barely acknowledged the newcomers' presence as Derek's hand pressed against the small of Sam's back, urging her forward.

"They don't bite," he whispered in her ear.

No, she'd thought of something more savage—like kill.

"You sure I don't need a security clearance to visit?"

He smiled down at her. "Actually, you do."

Seriously? She'd been teasing him. They followed Alexander's broad shoulders down a long hallway, and she was once more moved to silent awe when they passed a woman in a long, ivory gown sitting astride a man's lap on a bench. The silky material bunched at the waist showing off her legs all the way to her... *Oh, my, no underwear*. The men walked past without a second look.

Derek paused in front of yet another gabled arched door. "Alexander, we're going to take the long way."

The men passed a knowing look. "Are you sure? Has she—"

"A hunch."

"I don't need to remind you of our protocol."

"No, you don't."

The older man stepped aside. "By all means. It was nice to meet you, Samantha. I hope to see you again soon." He turned on his heel and left them at the enormous wooden door.

"Samantha. About being tied up—"

"Shh, not so loud." She glanced at the couple a mere twenty-feet away. She needn't have bothered to hush him. The couple was kissing and grinding like teenagers.

He let out an amused puff of air. "I probably should have prepared you. But you said you like surprises, and I like to give them."

She sucked in a sharp breath. "You're not going to demand an impromptu performance. People do that to me all the time." This mansion appeared to have high enough ceilings.

"I'll bet. Here, you only dance if you want to." He swung open the door and a cacophony of sounds crashed over her like a tidal wave.

She blinked. Closest to the door, a nude woman lay face down on a black padded bench. A spanking bench? She'd once seen one in a movie.

In fact, her first thought was she'd stepped onto a movie set. The room had a surreal quality that her brain couldn't quite sharpen to reality.

Samantha threw a glance at Derek, who'd stepped deeper into the room.

"Where are we?"

"This room is called the Library."

She grasped his arm and followed one step behind as he inched forward. She blinked, waiting for her brain to click into gear, doing what it always did when faced with something new. She broke down each piece and movement, step by step, until she caught a pattern.

Black ropes in a crisscross design over the back of the woman lying on the bench.

A red strap pulled taught through her lips.

A man's hand on her back.

A long tail of red and gold braids hanging from his tight fist.

She startled and glanced over her shoulder when the door clanged behind them. A huge man in all black had closed the door. After releasing the handle, he stepped back into a military-straight stand and his gaze moved over the room.

Her attention returned to the man lording over the prone woman. He pulled his arm back and struck the woman bound to the black-padded spanking bench. The woman jerked in her bonds, and Samantha jumped. Derek paused and circled her shoulders. "He's not harming her."

"How do you know?"

"Pain, if mutually agreed upon, is fine. Actual harm is against the rules."

"Rules?" She sounded like a zombie.

"Yes."

She took a moment to look from one side of the room to the other. A statuesque redhead leaned against a tall bookshelf filled with ancient-looking books, while a man with jet-black hair ran his hands down her bare breasts. She groaned contentedly.

A flash to her right caught her eye. A woman smacked a stick lit with fire over a man's bare torso glistening in sweat.

Derek's arm encircled her shoulder and led her deeper inside. They passed a nude man with long blond hair lying on his back on a massage table. A military-looking guy in leather pants and bare feet hunched over him, whispering, as he massaged the naked man's enormous erection.

"It's a sex club," she whispered. She'd heard of them, those dark seedy rooms in the backs of nightclubs or suburban, concrete-floored basements outfitted like a dungeon.

"Not exactly," he responded. "But sex definitely happens here."

"Do you…"

"Yes."

Her gaze darted to his face. "Why did you bring me here?"

"To show you my version of spending time." He smiled down at her. "And like I said, Alexander's home has the best view in Washington."

She hadn't thought to ask what kind of view.

He dropped his embrace and held out his hand. "Ready to go upstairs?"

Was she? New hormones she didn't know she possessed rose like floodwater. Excitement, embarrassment, intrigue, wonder, and fear consumed her mind and body. She knew stuff like that went on. In this day and age, who didn't? Curiously, she wanted to run but also stay. She might never get another chance like this again and she wanted to learn more. Why not?

"Is this the view you wanted to show me?"

He chortled. "No, come."

As they traversed the rest of the space, a cacophony of sounds both titillated and unnerved her. Male and female groans competed with one another. The creak of ropes followed the sharp thud of long leather tails against flesh as a bound and suspended woman lurched from the impact.

Once they reached the far end of the room, Derek gestured her to step inside an open elevator. "Is there more … up there?"

"We'll be alone."

When the doors closed and the scene disappeared from view, her lungs demanded more air. She hadn't realized she'd almost stopped breathing when she stepped into—what did he call it?—*the Library.*

"You do that stuff?"

"Some of it. Are you appalled?"

"No. More like it makes sense."

Derek had been different from the get-go. The fact that he was into BDSM shouldn't have shocked her. He had tied her up with boas.

Lucky

"You're not a sadist, are you? I mean, you withheld chocolate from me for over an hour the other night."

He laughed. "Samantha, you're truly not like any woman I've ever met. But, no, not a sadist."

She let in the pride that naturally arose from his words and also a little relief he wasn't into hardcore pain.

The elevator creaked to a stop and he yanked open the old-fashioned cage door. A short hallway filled with potted palms led to an open archway. One step through the arch and the night sky spilled out endlessly over the rooftop terrace.

A redwood plank floor warmed the space, the long lines of the boards framing a large infinity pool that seemed to drop off the side of the building. Large potted trees and raised beds of flowering plants created small alcoves fitted with sleek chaise lounges, chairs, and tall, silver heat lamps that glowed a dark orange.

Her boot heels clicked softly as she followed a trail of small recessed lights around the pool. The pale moon shrouded in wispy clouds decorated the glassy surface—the reflection of the night sky above.

"No one else is here?" The silence oddly both comforted and unnerved her. Given what she walked through downstairs, she half-expected to be met with men in leather vests and executioners' masks and writhing nude women. Instead, she'd stepped into a Better Homes & Gardens magazine spread.

"I requested the rooftop for us."

"You can reserve it?"

"Benefits of being part of this club's governing body."

"I don't get this place." She turned to him. "I mean, downstairs … and then this."

"Accendos is unusual."

She cocked her ear at soft piano chords drifting in the air. "Chopin?"

"Sounds like it," Derek said.

"Huh. One minute it's the Playboy mansion and another minute it's a 'tour of homes' stop."

He smiled. "Alexander would like that. He doesn't like being a foregone conclusion."

"Who does?"

"Come. The view's spectacular." When he extended his hand, she took it.

He led her up a raised deck. A large cream-colored sectional couch circled a fire pit the size of one of her lyras, the gas-lit flames dancing. What was it about rich people and light-colored furniture?

Three steps up and Washington unfurled below in an urban carpet of glowing white, gold and red lights winking up at them. Treetops masked most of the home's roof area except for one wide section allowing a view of Georgetown. Distant traffic sounds floated in the air. She walked to the chest-high glass wall that lined the length of the rooftop.

"It is beautiful up here. How high are we?"

"On top of the fourth floor of the new wing. The house sits on a hill, rather high for DC."

They spent long minutes gazing over the city. She relished the moment of silence as it gave her time to think, or rather let the swirling emotions called up by their walk through the sex arena to settle.

Derek's world was so different. Two hours ago, she held onto an almost-seven-year-old as she tried to balance in a lyra. Now, she'd walked through a sex club and stood gazing over Washington four stories up with a cool breeze ruffling her hair.

A thought occurred. Perhaps this was his way of asking her if *she* fit with *him*.

She turned to him. "You brought me here to shock me."

Lucky

"Perhaps." He studied her face as if waiting for a certain reaction.

"You're trying to scare me off?"

His brow wrinkled. "Did I?"

"No." She was only afraid—truly afraid—of one thing: investing in a romantic dead end again. To date, Derek proved to be nothing like the guys she'd known before. She didn't like being labeled, so it was only fair she not do the same to him.

"If I asked you to bring me here sometime, would you?" So what if she didn't know what the hell he was into? Desire spiked whenever she was near him. She wanted him in ways she didn't even know about yet.

"You mean engage in a scene with you in the Library. Specifics are important."

"Yes."

"You're not ready."

His response knifed through her pride. She'd never been afraid of experimentation. If she had, she never would have learned anything in her life, and her life had been filled with learning new steps.

"How do you know?" she asked.

"I just do."

Oh, hell no. She wouldn't be a foregone conclusion either—like she was marriage material or she wasn't. Or she was a sex goddess or a prude.

A slight steam rose from the pool surface and gave her an idea.

She stripped off her sweater, her skin immediately pebbling in the too-cool air. It took little time to shed herself of her boots and jeans. She made a show of unhooking her bra, and then turned away from him to draw down her panties so he got a full view of her ass. When she glanced back, his eyes remained fixed on her butt. *Good.*

"I imagine it's heated?" she said over her shoulder. She skipped to the edge of the pool and dove into the water that hit her like a warm bath. He wasn't the only one who could play the shock game.

14

Little vixen. Her intrigue was gasoline thrown on this unreasonable fire he had inside for her.

The truth of her words—*to scare me off*—bounced in the space between them. She was right. He had wanted to frighten her, to hear her admit they weren't going to work out. She lured him into considering subjects he'd abandoned long ago, like love, family … children.

He walked to the edge of the pool and surveyed her glorified nudity silhouetted from the lights shining up from the bottom of the pool. She treaded water, her hair slicked back and her white teeth glowing in the dark in one of her lethal smiles.

Her confidence about her effect on men was obvious. Little did she know, she'd presented her tight ass with such impudence and full-on womanly confidence, he wanted nothing more than to redden those cheeks until they glowed. She wasn't the only one assured of their abilities.

"Provoking me?" he growled.

"I could tell it was heated and I was cold."

"Next time you'll ask me first."

"Or?"

"There won't be a next time."

Her face fell. *Tough*. She wanted to know how this worked. He'd show her.

She swam to the wall closest to him. "Come in with me? It is a nice night for a swim."

"Turn around. Face away from me toward the center of the pool. Arms on the edge. Let your body rise up. Show me your breasts."

She hesitated.

"Now."

"Bossy." She did what he asked and let the buoyancy of her body put her into position. Her breasts broke the water's surface.

He sauntered to the end of the pool, away from her. "Very nice. Keep them there." He crossed his arms and watched her body rise and fall in the water in time with her breaths. "Up, Samantha. I want to see those nipples pucker in the cold."

"Will you…"

"What?"

"Come in with me?" She swallowed. "Please?"

She'd asked mildly. It was a start.

After shedding his clothes, he dove in and swam, underwater, until he reached her. His hands found her legs and split them open. He swam up between them.

Her mouth had dropped open at his aggressive taking of control. *Good.*

She needed to stop grasping for the upper hand. As refreshing as her unexpected responses were, relinquishing control to her—to anyone—wasn't on their dance card. At the same time, rushing into dominating her without understanding her desires could shut her down for good. He needed her to ask for it.

He pulled her from the edge until she was forced to cling

Lucky

to him, her crotch settling right above his growing arousal. He spun her in a few slow circles until they stood right where he wanted them. Her hair fanned out in the water like beautiful, dark sea grass.

As he rubbed her pussy up and down his erection, the outside world faded in the fog created from the pool's heat. Pool water was no friend to sex, but she looked delicious and her gasps egged him forward.

"More," she said. "Show me more."

"Maybe." Truth was, she wasn't ready for what he really wanted. "When we are here—if we are ever here again—and after extensive vetting of limits, I'll decide when and how we do things."

"Always?"

"Always."

God, she was wet; her tell-tale slickness moved over his cock. He changed angles until he was flush against her clit, grinding in little pulses, pulling her toward him and then releasing her. Waves rippled on either side of them, her arms fanning out like a snow angel.

"I like how you're doing that," she breathed.

He stopped. "Then agree to follow my lead."

She tried to raise her head but couldn't. Her whisper reached him anyway. "Yes, sir."

He was positive she didn't mean the honorific in the way the submissives two floors below would. Regardless, his cock responded to the word "sir" in its usual way. He thickened and ached to spear her deep. *Fuck*, he could come, hard. He rubbed against her clit once more, despite the danger of going off too soon.

She moaned loudly, and her nipples taunted him as they puckered more despite the ninety-degree pool temperature. He pulled her up and wrapped her legs around his middle, still not penetrating her. She ground herself down, her strong legs squeezing his torso, rising and falling in a remarkably steady rhythm. Her teeth sank into his shoulder when she released. He held off. For men, coming in the pool was grounds for immediate revoking of pool privileges.

She lifted her head and gazed into his eyes. "Man of service. Good thing no one was around."

"Yes, normally there are several people peering up through the glass bottom window."

"What?" She peered over her shoulder. First-time guests often mistook the swirled blue pattern below as part of the pool bottom design. Only later did they realize they peered at an optical illusion, blue carpeting in a hallway through a glass bottom. He was rather disappointed someone hadn't strode by. He'd like to know whether or not she enjoyed exhibitionism.

"Oh, my God." She pushed at his chest and tried to get her legs down. "You knew."

What did you know? Not an exhibitionist, which was strange given her profession.

He chuckled and held her fast to him. "As a dancer, I'm surprised you don't like being watched."

"Hello? Costumes?"

"No one's down there ... yet."

He let her slip through his arms and she was at the edge in two strides.

"Stop." His tone caused her to cling to the side and turn to him.

She blinked.

"Swim back to me."

"What if I don't?"

"I'll march you downstairs, strap you to the spanking bench and tan your ass with my bare hand." He wouldn't, really. At Accendos, whenever a guest was involved, a third party not involved in a scene must witness the guest's consent before any serious play could ensue. He could still threaten a spanking for effect.

"Promise?" She threw him a smile that could only be characterized as daring. She lifted herself from the pool. "Catch me."

Little devil. She openly defied him. Perhaps she didn't know what to ask for. Perhaps she didn't want anything at all and was jerking his chain. It was time to uncover that secret.

He took his time climbing out of the pool via the shallow end steps. He stalked toward her, her shivers growing more pronounced with each of his steps. She didn't run. She either had second thoughts or wanted to be caught—badly.

Samantha's eyes fired. He admired her spunk, her talent, her body. The fact she knew her impact on him was they problem. She believed she had him by the balls, which was yet another state he did not entertain. True, a jagged longing to bury himself inside her started when they walked through the Library. As she'd clung to his arm, he'd detected no fear in her, only curiosity. Nothing could have made him harder.

He did have one, immediate issue, however. How should he start the conversation about his proclivities? Hell, his way of life. He'd have to show her. Come to think of it, a spanking wasn't really a scene, was it?

With no fanfare and no words, he swung her up and carried her back to the raised area where a fire blazed in an artful display. They'd need it. The water had warmed their skin but the heat dissipated quickly in Washington's dry fall air. Her ass would be on fire soon enough with what he had planned.

He had her over his lap in seconds.

"This is not a scene. But I'm going to spank you. Hard."

Her next movement was so subtle he could have missed it, but Derek didn't miss signs. The tiny grind of her ass into his lap confirmed his suspicions. The body doesn't lie when it comes to the most basic emotions. Fear, anger, and desire started in the physical self and invaded the mind as fast as flames could consume a candlewick.

She wanted him to spank her.

Derek shelved his impulse for one more second. He fisted her hair and she moaned. "Do you want me to spank you?"

"Does anyone?"

"Yes. So ask me if you want it."

"Spank me?" Her voice was barely above a whisper, but he heard her anticipation.

"You say Iceland if you want me to stop."

She ground her hips into his lap once more.

He wasted no time giving that glorious, to-die-for ass a hard smack. Holding back would have been disrespectful of her wishes. Three more swats and she squirmed, but he never heard "Iceland."

After settling her on his lap, he pinched her chin so she was forced to look up at him. "This is what you were hoping for?"

Unshed tears glistened in her eyes. "I like flirting with you. Sorry, not sorry."

"I can tell. You like being chased. All women do." He slid a finger over her cheek, capturing a stray strand of hair. "But know this. The fastest way to drive me away is with manipulation. You don't need to work that hard to get my attention."

From her first smile, so blatantly charismatic and direct, he knew he'd have the potential to fall into her so deep he couldn't get out. He'd have to tread carefully.

"I wasn't trying to manipulate you."

"Good. Now about what we saw downstairs."

"You said I wasn't ready."

"You are now." He tucked a strand of hair over her shoulder. "Tell me what else you saw that intrigued you."

15

Samantha didn't know how to answer his question. An idea skirted the edge of her mind, refusing to be nailed down. That his finger made small circles on the side of her breast didn't help her focus.

Break it down, she told herself.

He'd spanked her. She'd *liked it*. She more than liked it. Is that what she wanted?

She shifted on his lap, her ass igniting from rubbing against the soft hair on his legs. Wetness pooled between her thighs and it wasn't from the swim.

"Samantha." His low growl only made her wetter.

"Um, the way the men looked at their partners."

"But you don't like to be watched by others?"

"I'm observed enough when I'm dancing, but I'm not *seen* —if that makes any sense." She knew men gawked at her with avid titillation, a far remove from being valued or esteemed. In fact, the word *leered* came to mind when remembering past attention.

"Those people down there," she said. "They looked at each other like they'd won the lottery. Is that silly?"

"Not at all. Because they have in a way."

"Can you tell me more about who comes here?"

"No. Privacy for everyone here is paramount."

She liked his answer.

"And what goes on downstairs?" Her gut told her he wanted to do more than the slap and tickle of her former lovers. Perhaps his boas and chocolate play had been merely a test.

"We only walked through the largest of the rooms at Club Accendos."

"There are more rooms?"

"The club consists of four main playrooms, twelve bedrooms, sixteen bathrooms, give or take. There's a pool out back, and gardens that you must see in the daylight. There's more."

"Playrooms?"

"Places to indulge."

"And Alexander lives here."

"Yes, and sometimes others when they need to. To many, Accendos is the closest thing to a home they have. Alexander once took me in during a darker time. I was one of his lost boys."

His eyes glowed a smoky gray blue. *Sadness*. That was the unsettled cloud she'd seen in his eyes the first night she'd met him.

She placed her palm on his chest, over his heart in an overwhelming urge to draw herself closer. "Can you tell me more?"

"I'd rather show you, if you're game."

She lifted herself up to stare at him. His lips had arched into a sly smile.

"I love games." She readjusted her crotch on purpose so she ground a little on his erection.

Lucky

He grasped her hips, stilling her with such absoluteness her heart nearly stopped, too.

"Remember when I said I control the pace of our time together." He placed his fingertip against her lips, stopping her words. "You understand the lead-follow technique. If you take my direction, you'll receive many, many good surprises. You said you like surprises."

She nodded.

"We're going to start slow." He set her on her feet. "Walk over to the other side of the fire."

After circling the firepit, she purposefully stepped close to feel the flame's warmth—as if she needed to feel any hotter. He sat with his muscled thighs slightly apart, his cock proudly displayed, half-erect, as if he hadn't a care in the world. *Pure Viking.*

"What do you want me to do?" The question burst forward from the knot in her throat. She knew what she wanted to do—draw that luscious looking cock into her mouth. The harsh spike of desire shocked her. Hell, tonight she'd had an orgasm in a mansion's rooftop pool and been spanked. Why not go for the motherlode?

The corner of his mouth gave a wicked tilt. "I saw on your web site that you give lap dance workshops."

"Dance? I can do that." She started to move back around the fire toward him.

"No, stay there. You need to hear my rules first."

"In a lap dance, the dancer always sets the rules."

"Not here." He ran a finger over his lip as his gaze traveled the length of her body. The sad cloud in his eyes cleared to a fiery dark blue.

∽

"Widen your legs." Derek settled back into the cushions and enjoyed the view. "More. I know you can."

When she inched her ankles wider, her spectacular legs quivered a little in the firelight.

"You get limits, both hard and soft. Do you know what those are?" he asked.

"Yes." She squared her shoulders. "Do I get to set any rules?"

"No."

"That's not fair."

"Life is not fair."

"What if I don't want—"

"Full consent to any activity is mandatory. That goes for whenever you're with me. I'm going to spell it out for you. Do what I say or don't. If you do, you'll always be safe and you'll be rewarded. If you don't, we'll stop."

"I don't want to stop."

Her heated rush of words bathed him with a sense of accomplishment. *First hurdle over, baby.*

She crossed her arms in mock defiance, but the way her lips quivered gave him a clue as to how she was really feeling—unbalanced.

"Can we lose the Chopin piano music?"

"Playlist. Derek Wright. Number sixteen." The music stopped. A muffled drumbeat replaced the piano chords.

Her eyes widened. "Beyoncé? How did you do that?"

"Accendos is fully wired and programmed to take spoken commands. Voice activation helps when one's hands are occupied."

"That would be so handy at my studio." She peered up at the redwood roof, where small recessed speakers were tucked into crevices to preserve the aesthetics.

"Samantha." Her attention strayed too easily. He needed to focus her. "You get three limits before we start."

Lucky

"No Britney Spears."

He laughed. "Fine."

"Let me dance until it's over? I mean, not turn it into sex in the first minute? And no laughing."

"That's three. Now here are the rules." He leaned forward.

Her eyes remained glued to his face. *Oh, baby, you are too good to be true.* She honestly seemed to wish to please him.

"You will dance nude. You don't stop until I say. You may not come." He smiled. "And you may not touch my cock with any part of your body until I say so."

"That's no fun."

"You have to earn that right."

Her lips parted on a large intake of breath. "It's a right?"

"Yes. Now show me how well you follow directions."

He leaned back and widened his knees so she got a full view of his favorite anatomical part—the part he was going to withhold from her until she fully understood how serious he was about his dominance.

∽

Oh, I can follow all right, Samantha gloated inwardly. His special world included sex rooms, Ferraris, and nightclubs, but she had special skills. He sat there, cocksure in every meaning of the word and clearly pleased with himself. With his physique and glorious sword, he'd surely conquered many female lands. Half of her wanted to roll her eyes. The other half wanted to drop to her knees and worship him with her mouth.

For long minutes, he stared at her through the flames separating them. Her gaze dropped. The small curls around his cock gleamed redder in the firelight.

"See something you like?"

Her gaze jerked back up to his face as if he'd pulled on a

leash. He had the nerve to let a lazy smile spread across his face, millimeter by millimeter, as if he could tell she was impressed.

"Are you sure you don't want me to touch you?" she asked. "It'd be more fun." She licked her top lip to make the point. So what if he acted annoyed by her earlier teasing, especially if such an activity resulted in an erotic spanking?

"I'm sure. You may proceed."

Okay, his funeral. One pivot and she gave him a full view of her back. She pulled her legs together and swayed her hips as she fluffed out her hair. With a quick glance over her shoulder through the flames that separated them, she checked his eyes. Darker in firelight, they remained riveted on her.

She extended one leg, wide, and folded over at the hips, stretching out the back of her legs and giving him a full view of her assets.

Unlike many of her students who tittered nervously when trying exotic dance for the first time, she'd never been shy about exhibiting her body. Confidence was a side benefit of growing up dancing. She never took for granted the impact she could make with a simple hip roll. Tonight, however, she cared deeply about ungluing this man so he'd lift that ridiculous rule about "no touching." In lap dance, *she* was supposed to be in charge.

She launched into the move she'd told her students to never, ever do unless they were prepared to have sex—fast. She ran her hand up the inside of one thigh, fanned her fingers over her crotch and then kept them moving down to the inside of the opposite leg. Flipping her hair back, she straightened and pivoted on one foot to face him.

His lips had parted. *Bingo*. She closed the distance between them, slowly stalking around the fire until she stood between his opened knees. His "no cock" rule would make

Lucky

her usual choreography tricky. Good thing improvisation was one of her strong suits.

Straddling his thigh, she ground her pelvis in circles, hovering over his muscled leg. With parted lips and hands fisted, he pinned her with his green-blue eyes. Her whole body hummed in gratification. He was holding himself back.

She ran her hands through his hair, the strands softer than any man deserved. The waves fell into a tousled pile, and rather than appearing disheveled, he only looked more handsome.

His gaze remained on her face, which both irritated and soothed her. She desired so many competing things of him in that moment. *Watch my body. Keep your eyes on my face. Move your fingers to between my legs because you can't help yourself.* That last wish was a definite no-no in lap dance, the recipient having to usually sit on their hands and simply receive whatever the dancer dished out.

"Am I getting any closer to earning the right to touch?" She dipped her head so her hair crossed over his face.

"You'll know when," he breathed.

"How?"

"You'll beg me to let you."

Oh? *We'll see.* She pulled herself upright and placed her foot between his knees, a half inch from his cock, now standing tall and proud. He didn't say anything about his balls not being touched. Then she got an idea. If he was going to withhold from her, she could do the same.

She pulled her leg back and rounded his body until she stood behind him. Her hands caressed down his chest until they rested on his abdomen. His rock-hard muscles moved slightly under her as if he breathed slowly on purpose.

She made sure to press her breasts against his upper back when she purred in his ear, "You didn't say I couldn't touch you elsewhere."

"No, I didn't. Good girl. You listened."

How did he turn everything around to his favor?

Her mouth hovered lightly over the nape of his neck, her lips barely touching his skin. Inhaling, then exhaling, she repeated the breath pattern over his neck until her cheeks were damp. All the while, her fingers explored the ridges in his arms and on his chest. When her fingers lowered, they met more hair on his lower abdomen. She was so close…

"Want something?" Smugness edged his tone.

"Yes." She should have kept him guessing, but answered honestly. His chest hair glinted in the firelight and his tight abs begged to be admired. She kneaded his shoulders and he let out a satisfied groan.

"Strong hands," he said.

"These hands have many skills."

"So do mine."

A trickle of her own juices escaped down her inner thigh with his words. *Damn him.* He was not helping her plans to undo him.

She'd have to get more aggressive. After circling to his front, she kneed his legs wider with her hands. Was that amusement flitting across his face? Still, he was beautiful. She'd burn her retinas out if she didn't tear her gaze away.

Placing both knees between his open legs, she tried hard not to touch what had been outlawed. She brought her breasts within a millimeter of his face. He inhaled deeply as if taking in her scent. She felt soft and pliable between her legs and knew she'd most definitely leave a trail of wet if she wasn't careful. *Ha!* As if she could stop this growing desire around him?

She pivoted and straddled his other thigh. She leaned over and placed her hands on the floor. When she wiggled her behind toward him, he cursed under his breath, the reaction she'd hoped for.

Lucky

After righting herself, she swung her outside leg so both now stood between his open knees.

"Are you sure you don't want me to get closer?" she asked over her shoulder.

"I'm sure. Dance for me here. Your ass is pure poetry."

She liked moving her derriere, especially since his gaze now appeared glued to her swaying hips.

Her thighs slicked. Her hands got sticky, and still she didn't stop. Only when her legs grew too quivery to stand, did she slink to the floor. It was time for her to take herself away from him for a bit, a signature exotic dance technique. She'd let a man think she'd get closer, but then do the opposite.

His breath hissed between his teeth when she dropped forward on hands and knees giving him another full view of her ass—and the obvious wetness that dewed her inner thighs. God, she wanted to straddle his cock and sate the ache growing deep inside her. Instead, she crawled away from him and stole a backward glance to make sure his stare followed. It did. His cock was at full mast, but his eyes remained unreadable.

She'd often wished she could read a man's mind. Tonight, she'd have given anything to read Derek's. The biology of his response wasn't enough. She wanted to captivate him, drive him mad with desire for her. Now that she'd had a small taste of Derek Wright, a type of man she hadn't known existed, she craved more of him and his interest.

After more hip rolls and rear grinds, she wearied of withholding herself from him. Time to try something else. The untenable rule denying her his cock needed to be lifted, and soon.

She rolled onto her back and goaded him with a full view of her female anatomy. She opened her legs into a wide V and took her time closing them. Her fingers played the inside of her thighs as she drew her ankles together. She lowered her legs to the surprisingly soft outdoor rug she lay upon. Shifting into a full-body, undulating move she termed Writhing Goddess, her desire for him scaled new heights. Her mind filled with thoughts of his hard body falling on top of her, his cock thrusting inside her, his lips and tongue forcing open her mouth.

Her fingers dipped between her own legs. Who cared if he watched? A sheen of sweat broke out on her chest. The cool October air was no match for her lust, fueled by her erotic visions.

"Feel good?" His deep laugh should have irritated her. Rather, that low rumble stroked her desire to a nearly impossible level. Her breath huffed in pants, and she managed to nod in answer—once. Words were never her strong suit. Moving her body was her language—and, Lord, how she wanted to converse with him that way.

He leaned forward, elbows on knees. "Tell me what you want."

"Want? You."

"How?"

"Inside me."

"Then crawl back to me." He leaned backward and crooked his finger.

On hands and knees, she made her way to him. His leg hairs scratched her palms as she latched her hands on his muscled thighs. Before she could dip her head to take his cock in her mouth, he had her up, turned and resting against him backwards. The second her slick skin touched his, the second his hard-on prodded her back—she melted on top of his body. She wanted as much of her skin on his as possible.

He caught the inside of her thighs with his large hands and spread-eagled her on his lap—resting each of her legs over one of his thighs. One hand clasped hers and stilled her.

Lucky

She'd been fondling her own breast and hadn't even noticed until he'd captured her fingers. His other hand dipped into her aching slit. She gasped at the contact, loving that he went straight to where she'd hoped he would. Every motion, every miniscule slide of her skin across his body ratcheted up her need.

"Please. God, please." He'd said she would beg, hadn't he?

When he nipped her earlobe, her body glided into an even greater boneless state. His probing fingers sank deeper and a low moan slipped through her lips. Her hands fell to her sides, ready to receive and take whatever he planned to do. With a hard twist, he tweaked her nipple, and her clit pulsed at the sensation. If he did that again and kept the fingers of his other hand moving, in seconds he'd make her come.

"Derek. Please." He held her fast, hand on her breast, fingers buried inside her cunt. Her head lolled backward onto his shoulder.

"Begging me?" His lips had brushed her skin as he spoke, and dear God, there was no rhyme or reason she hadn't shot off like a rocket from that light touch.

"Yes," she managed to get out.

His fingers left her. He grasped and lifted her hips. His cock slid into her in one long, slow, maddening glide.

"Then fuck me."

She rose and lowered herself. Once, twice, three times it took to seat him fully inside of her. A curl of sensation rose like a wave and radiated through her whole body. Her hips then took over. She rode him, hard, but when he inserted his thumb into her ass, her need to have his cock, deeper and dirtier, grew and spread. She wanted him everywhere—in her pussy, in her mouth, in her ass. Excruciating intense spasms rocked her, so she undulated back and forth. When she finally slumped forward, he tightened his hold on her so she wouldn't pitch off his lap.

As she came down from her climax, her nipples and insides tingled with blood returning, and she took in big gulps of air. His forehead rested against her back, his breath coming in big pants. She'd come so hard she hadn't noticed he did as well.

Later, she'd wonder if it was the club's atmosphere, the forced delay Derek imposed by his "rules," or the man himself that had wrung such an orgasm from her body. She'd conclude the reason didn't matter, because an inexplicable understanding crept into her heart as she regained her awareness. There were so many more things she wanted to do with this man—raw, dirty things where words were not necessary. And, for once, she didn't question if they had a romantic future. For once, that debate had been silenced. The present moment was all that mattered.

16

Derek leaned against the door frame of Samantha's studio and held back a snicker. Hundreds of little white and purple feathers danced airborne with Samantha's every push of the janitor's dust mop. The stubborn wisps of fluff defied capture.

"Been sacrificing chickens?" he asked.

She jumped backward and clutched the broom to her chest. "You scared the life out of me." She let out a huge breath. "Sacrifices only occur in our advanced classes."

"Here. Let me." He confiscated the broom and eased the pile of feathers to the side.

"Shouldn't you be at work? I mean, I'm glad to see you."

"Not until this afternoon. I came by to check on you. See if last night scared you off."

"Now that I know you can sweep, why would I let you go?"

"You can thank hours of detention at boarding school for my sweeping skills." He propped the mop, the wide cloth bottom now fuzzy with feathery bits, against the wall. "You shouldn't be here alone, you know. This neighborhood is—"

"What, Mr. Boarding School?" A half smile accompanied her crossed arms.

"Not equal to your value. Just ask your Lyra Ladies who want a million hoops." He dinged the metal hoop hanging to the side. "How are you really?"

She picked up two pairs of elbow-length silk gloves from the floor and twisted them nervously in her hand. "I'm good."

"About last night." He pulled her into him. "We probably should have talked about things more."

"Talking is overrated."

"In my world, talking is crucial."

"Then, I've decided."

"What?"

"That I loved learning more about that side of you. That's why you're here, right?" She threw the gloves in the corner.

Smart woman. Her answers soothed a raw part inside him.

Talking didn't seem to fit last night after he'd gotten the lap dance of a lifetime. Rather, he'd cleaned them up, made small talk on the drive home, kissed her at her door, and told her he'd call in the morning like a gentleman always did, despite their intentions. He'd leaned against the hood of his car until he saw her light go off in her bedroom window. He had decided to let her process, and he needed time as well. He drove around for hours, not wanting to go home.

After he finally hauled himself to bed for a few hours of restless sleep, he woke with an overwhelming desire to see her. Somewhere in the early morning he'd moved from fighting his attraction to her to embracing it.

So he'd placed a call to Jonathan that morning, hoping his fiancée, Christiana, would be willing to talk with Samantha. Derek had seen firsthand how the nature of Jonathan's sweet sub calmed the nerves of everyone around her. Plus, women liked to talk … all that sharing crap he never understood.

He could only hope Christiana would give him a ringing

Lucky

endorsement. Nothing ventured, nothing gained. What little he knew of the young woman, he liked. She'd slipped into Jonathan's and his world with relative ease. She also didn't seem hell-bent on getting pregnant anytime soon, unlike Jonathan, whose eyes took on that dreamy cast whenever a future family was mentioned. He decided she'd be perfect as a submissive mentor. My, my, how quickly he assumed they were going somewhere, as if Samantha would slip so easily into the kind of life he enjoyed.

Never assume, he reminded himself.

"Your final plans are ready." He picked up the tube he'd brought and slapped it against his palm as he lazed in the doorway.

"Already? No, wait. You give them a lot of business." Even her smirks shot inside him like a dose of happiness.

"You have no idea."

"Good timing. Cindy and I were supposed to go over some new choreography, but she must have gotten hung up."

"Shall we?" He held out his hand.

She hesitated. "I don't want to sound ungrateful, but aren't we moving a little fast?"

He scrubbed his chin. He'd seen the trepidation in her eyes a thousand times before, in others' faces. People new to construction were always afraid to commit.

He pulled a cane chair from its place next to the wall and set it in the middle of the studio floor. "Sit."

"Is it my turn for a lap dance?" She put her butt on the chair.

"I'm better at tango. Now close your eyes."

She took a deep breath, and her lashes fell to her cheeks.

"I want you to imagine your ideal studio. What are you picturing?"

"Shiny floors. Lights. Lots of mirrors."

"Good. Picture students dancing."

She smiled. "We're going to have to sweep the floor again."

"You handle a broom well."

"You handle a lot of things well."

He leaned down to her ear. "Getting ideas, are we?"

"You have the best ideas." She opened her eyes and … damn, that smile was officially his Achilles' heel.

"Eyes closed, ballerina. Now, number of students?"

"Ten."

"All adult females, I trust."

"No, a mix."

"Damn, I wanted to be the only man."

She giggled. "Okay, for today you can be the only man."

"With nine women. I like your imagination."

"Typical."

"What are you teaching them?"

"How to move. Just … move." She swayed a little in her chair. "We're dancing through a series of silks hanging from the ceiling." She cocked her head. "My grandmother is showing off fan moves in the other room. The room we don't have yet."

"You will."

She pointed to the corner. "Cindy's in the dedicated pole room. She's loud." She giggled. "We have a receptionist. God, I'd kill for someone to handle the books, too. There are students in the waiting area, happy. It's Christmas." She let out a delighted squeal. "So we're lit by little fairy lights in green, red, and white. There's a Christmas tree in the corner."

Samantha opened her eyes and gave him one of those hypnotizing smiles that made him more open to suggestion than he'd been with anyone his whole life.

"How'd I do?" Her smile faded. "Are you all right?"

He hadn't expected the whole Christmas fantasy. He hated that holiday. Damn, his eyes had moistened.

Lucky

"I'm picturing something else." She squinched her eyes shut and straightened in her chair. "Everyone left. You're still here. You want to demonstrate something you didn't have a chance to show me that first night we were together. About the silks. You said—"

"I'd wrap your luscious legs in all that fabric."

Her warm eyes opened. "Yes. Will you?"

So much for wondering what was next. They could discuss the plans for her expansion later—much later.

∼

"Samantha, dim the lights."

She wasted no time clicking off the fluorescents in the ceiling. The tiny white fairy lights she'd hung for ambience for her sexier classes remained on and bathed him in an eerily beautiful glow.

"When does your next class start?"

"An hour."

"Hmm. We'll make it work. Go to the silks. The red ones."

They were her longest pair, the ends pooled in a crimson puddle before a mirrored corner and connected by a big hook from the turreted ceiling. She placed herself between the two hanging ends and grasped them to steady herself. Had she just asked him to tie her up, in her studio, when anyone could walk in at any time?

He grasped the fabric above her fist and yanked on them, hard, as if checking their hold.

"They won't come down."

"I always check rigging." His fingers slipped underneath her tee shirt and a rush of cool air hit her skin as he tugged down her yoga pants, taking her panties with them.

"Do I get to set any rules for—"

"No." While soft, his tone did not invite negotiation.

She yanked her feet out of the bunched-up pants and kicked them to the side. "It's my studio."

"It's my dance. Anticipation is half the game. Wondering what will happen next. When the next touch will come. How it will come."

"This is a game?"

"Everything's a game. Now we need to address a few things. Answer your questions. I know you have them."

"About bondage and stuff? I'm kind of embarrassed to ask. It'd be easier if you were a woman right now."

"I anticipated that. I have someone for you to talk with. Christiana Snow."

"Seriously? Christiana? I'd have never guessed." One of her students was into BDSM. Who knew? Christiana dropped into her classes only occasionally. Perhaps she'd missed some signs along the way.

"Don't let that innocent face fool you. Come to think of it, maybe you should ask me instead. I don't want you to get any new ideas without me."

"No, Christiana is a good suggestion. I will, if she's willing." She could use someone to talk to who wasn't Derek. Now that she'd entered this relationship with him, if one could call it that, she'd go wherever he wanted to take her. She needed to know more about his lifestyle.

He cradled her cheek in one hand. "Until then, will you trust me?"

"Yes."

"Good. We'll go slow." He grasped the cane chair she'd been sitting in earlier and placed it under the tent of the silks. After grabbing a handful of the red fabric, he motioned to the chair. "Sit. Knees apart, ankles hooked on the chair legs."

The intensity of his eyes drove out any lingering thoughts about his intentions. Derek's turn to Dominant energized

Lucky

her libido like no man had ever done. The unmistakable, dark edge in his voice, the way his eyes cleared and spine straightened, flipped a switch inside her.

The chair creaked as she lowered herself to the seat. Her position put her at eye level with his chest, yet it was his cock straining against the fabric of his pants that caught her interest. The memory of him driving deep inside her—and her raw thoughts about where else she wanted that thick cock— broke free. She made a show of widening her legs, feeling every inch of the hard wood under her thighs. She circled one chair leg with one ankle. Then, the other.

He went to work.

While wrapping silk around each leg, he'd glance up occasionally to peer into her face. A second wrap with the fabric made her twitch. Watching his hands work—quickly and with confidence—drove more desire to places she rarely thought of while at work.

Oh, hell, her desire for him hadn't abated one ounce after last night's lap dance.

After he'd dropped her off, giving her a kiss at the door that numbed her lips, she'd made it to bed on quivery legs. She'd barely gotten her clothes off and crawled into bed before she touched herself. She'd never have fallen asleep otherwise. Hell, she got off twice, each orgasm called up by merely picturing his face and imagining his hands and his cock doing wicked things to her body. Even this morning she'd also woken with her hand between her legs.

Lordy, she turned into a nymphomaniac around this guy —only without the pathology.

"You'll tell me if this burns."

He pulled the last wrap of fabric taut. She gulped when the chair screeched a little as he pulled it across the floor with the force of his wrap. Oh, she'd burn all right, and not just from the silks.

"Samantha?" He grasped the curved back of the chair and held up two elbow-length gloves he must have scooped up from where she'd tossed them. "How do you feel about blindfolds?"

"The blue ones would look better on me."

"Eager to try new things, I see."

"With you, I am." She grasped her lip between her teeth.

He stepped backward. "I watched a Dominant in a club in Philadelphia go over limits with his submissive once. She listed five. No blood play, animals, sharing her, suspension, or breath play. That was it, she'd said." He focused his eyes on her face. "He then backhanded her across the face. Once her shock wore off, he asked her if she'd developed any new ones in the last minute. Like face slapping."

Samantha sucked in a sharp breath. "Now you're scaring me."

"I meant to." He put his hands on the back of the chair and leaned in so she could feel his breath. "I will never hit you. I don't hit women. But I must know what your limits are—all of them." He straightened. "This is between us. We're going to go about this a little differently, starting with a 'yes' list. What are you hoping I'll do? Then, I'll surprise you with other things along the same vein."

Oh, the things she wanted him to do. She squirmed, as much as she could bound to her creaky chair.

"Spanking?" he asked.

"Yes."

"Bondage. How does it feel now?"

"Good."

"Blindfolds?" He held up the two gloves and tied them together.

"Okay."

"Gagging?" He held up a third glove.

A pang between her thighs answered that one, so she only

Lucky

nodded. She'd never view her burlesque class the same way. In stripping, the dancer inched the glove off, finger by finger, prolonging the baring of skin, teasing the onlooker with the possibilities. Now she'd only think about the way Derek fondled the satin between his capable fingers taunting her with how he might use them. *To bind me. Gag me.* She'd imagine how the material stuffed in her mouth might mute the sharpest of her cries. Or how, if it was tied across her eyes, all her senses would heighten at his touch, his *maneuvering*.

"Good start." He circled the chair, pulling a wrist behind her. He tied one end of a glove around her wrist. "Give me your other hand." After she obeyed, her two wrists slapped against one another in a rough tug.

Oddly, he didn't blindfold her but held a glove up in front of her mouth. "Open. You're going to hold it between your teeth. If you drop the glove, I'll stop everything."

He walked across the room and propped two elbows behind him on the ballet barre. A minute and then another passed as he studied her. *Oh, please do something to me.* While he was being kind, part of her wanted him to be harder, a little harsher, a little more demanding.

"Whash oo doik?" Speaking while holding a glove between her teeth wasn't easy, but no way would she drop her makeshift gag.

"Patience. I'm admiring."

After five more minutes ticked by, she grew antsy. The chair seat cut into her thighs and her legs ached from their spread-eagle position. She flexed her butt cheeks to get a little more circulation going. Stillness posed an obstacle for her. She spent her days moving.

"You don't like to be still."

"Uh-uh."

"Then five more minutes."

Her eyesight flicked to the clock over the doorway. In thirty minutes, students would arrive. She sucked in a long breath through her nose. He never took his eyes off her.

"Feel it. Feel the tightness of the silk binding your calves to the chair and the air cooling your hot cunt. Feel the fabric of the glove that mutes your voice. Your position in the chair presents your breasts but you cannot move your arms to protect them. Feel it all."

With mere words, he'd done what she wanted. It was harsh, hard, and kept her under control. She bit down on the glove to keep a whimper at bay as her clit pulsed.

His eyes roamed her face, but never traveled anywhere else. She tuned into him, matched his breathing, followed his eyes, and sank into the restriction of the silks binding her legs open to expose her pussy in wanton invitation. Her arousal trickled down the inside of her leg and all her awareness dove to that singular, wicked spot.

She managed to widen her legs a tad more. She wanted him to see his effect on her, her acceptance of her situation and his uncompromising demands.

After what seemed like five hours, his gaze darted to the juncture of her legs and he smiled.

The moment was gone in a flash but she felt in her bones the intimacy that crossed between them—the demand and acceptance, the giver and receiver, the submissive and Dominant. She'd never considered herself someone comfortable in a passive role. Right now, for Derek, she'd be *anything* he required.

"You're beautiful." The sound of his voice cracked the silence. She almost didn't catch his words, she was so tuned in to the connection between them.

He pushed off the barre. His strides ate up the hardwood floor as he made his way toward her. "I'm not usually into that whole 'stay still' direction like some Doms. I like watching you let go." He unbuckled his belt and moved closer. "But I enjoyed those last five minutes."

When he stood inches away from her, he removed the glove from between her lips.

"Do you want to know why?"

"You like to see me bound?"

"More than that. I enjoy observing how *you* like being bound. How needy you grow, how much your body aches to touch and be touched. The needing to move but being held in place. I like when you're loud, when you thrash underneath me."

Her mouth watered at the sound of his zipper being lowered.

"I like when you surrender to whatever your body wants." What she wanted? A shift in attitude changed her thinking during the silence they had shared. Nothing interested her more than understanding how to please him.

He grasped her chin, and she sucked in a long breath. "What is turning you on right now? This?" He pulled out his cock. The erect organ thrust forward toward her from the opening in his trousers. "Or the fact I could do anything to you—while you are tied and helpless?"

She nodded into his gentle cradling of her chin. *Yes, the answer is always yes.*

He chortled lightly. He stroked up and down his length while keeping his hand on her chin. She tried to push into his hand so she could watch his movements more directly.

"Eyes on me, ballerina."

She obeyed. Even when he hooked his arms under her knees and lifted her as she gasped at his sudden machismo move, she kept her gaze on his face. The chair dangled beneath them, as the silks loosened their hold a bit. He yanked at the fabric until the chair clanged to the floor and tipped over. The silks hung loosely around her legs, now more an annoyance than a true binding.

He leaned her against the mirrored wall. "I should have left you longer, waiting, panting, but people are going to walk through that door soon, and I have private plans for this body."

"There's time." She hooked her legs around his waist.

One hand lifted the hem of her T-shirt to expose her bra. He pulled out a breast and latched his mouth on a nipple. The fat bulb of his cockhead teased her opening—for one lingering second.

Then he thrust into her. Her back smacked the glass behind her.

The niggling feeling she should be worried about cracking her mirrors surfaced. The thought was batted away with his pummeling. As he fucked her skin grew slick and she slid over the smooth panes. Only when a second orgasm came on the heels of the first did she broke her silence. She bit into his neck, damp with perspiration. God, she was so full—of him. Her world became his expensive cologne filling her nose, the taste of his skin on her tongue, and his cock taking up every inch inside her. She knew only his body and her body and the tight pull of parachute silk heating her thighs.

The silks would forever remind her of this moment and this dark, delicious, dirty feeling. This man knew things, had been places, had lived a life so far removed from her own, she grew desperate to catch up. Last night's visit to Accendos was her introduction. Now Derek's hands, mouth and other glorious parts of his anatomy promised her something even more—a true entrée into his exotic world. In the future, whatever Derek wanted from her, whatever he asked, she'd do it—just to be taken along wherever he wanted to go.

17

Derek pushed through the revolving door of the Oak Room fifteen minutes late to meet his mother. As he stepped up the marble steps into the main dining hall, he saw her sitting alone in a booth. She lifted her gaze to him. Her seething anger shot clear across the room.

"Derek Damon," she said, placing a kiss on his cheek. "I was beginning to think you were standing me up again."

No doubt she'd only been concerned about what the other diners thought. Sitting alone in a public place was akin to announcing to the world, *unwanted*. Lord knows, Betsy Carlton Wright Stanfield Pierce Barlow couldn't possibly be undesired.

"I apologize, Mother. Traffic." He hadn't expected an impromptu tussle with Samantha and silks, though he greatly appreciated their spontaneous play. When he'd left Samantha, he felt relaxed, triumphant, and more than a little obsessed with his dark-haired ballerina. Two steps inside the Oak's dining room at the receiving end of his mother's laser glare, the effects faded.

Derek snapped his napkin in place as he sat, waving off

the waiter whose deferential hovering already annoyed him. *Poor guy.* He'd likely been the recipient of his mother's angst at having to sit at a table by herself for a quarter of an hour.

She lifted her wine. "Another five minutes and Senator Moore was going to have to rescue me." She squinted her eyes at the elderly gentleman whose gaze raked over his mother as if assessing her as a potential new mistress.

"He's married, mother."

She sighed. "Why are you so angry? I wasn't the one who was late." She took a sip of her wine.

"Not angry," he said, even though a cloud of unfounded irritation filled him at having to be here. After he left a quivering and sated Samantha, the last place he wanted to be was in a DC restaurant known as a place to see and be seen by the Washington elite. Since meeting Samantha, he'd found better uses for his time.

"I suppose I should be glad you met me at all, given the brush-off I got in your office the other day." She took a sip of her wine.

Only his mother could drop in uninvited and unannounced and then play the indignant card.

"What really tore you from New York? It can't be because you're that worried about my brother."

"I wanted to see my eldest son, that's all. Since Bret has basically cut me off—"

"He hasn't cut you off, Mother. He doesn't want to be lambasted for his choice in women."

Her manicured fingers fiddled with the stem of her wineglass. "About women ... that little dancer I met the other night. How serious are you?"

"Why do you ask?"

"The way she looked at you. Full of adoration. Besides, I'm your mother. We always ask. Interesting how a girl like that could still be single."

Lucky

"Meaning?"

"She's pretty, and I recognize a woman seeking a husband, Derek." How odd she hadn't used his full, formal name.

"You see every woman like that."

She cocked her head. "Not true, though your ex-girlfriend, Margot, certainly was like that. Thank God you got rid of her," she said under her breath. "Besides, I'm very good at ferreting out the users. Remember I was married to your father. He, too, was good at seeing fake adoration, just not turning it away."

"Have you ordered?"

"Not yet. What was the dancer's name? Samantha?"

"You love crab cakes, right?" He lifted his menu. If there was a God—and he was sure there wasn't—she'd turn her attention to the food options.

"You're serious about her. Why? Why now? Honestly. I'd like to know." She almost sounded sincere.

"She has her head on straight." God knows why he answered his mother's probing question. He was a grown man, after all. "Do you want to start with a salad, perhaps?"

"Have you told her? I mean, when she brings up children and family…"

A sharp knife of anger sliced at his last shred of patience, essentially severing himself from any more small-talk manners.

"I'll never have children and you know why. I didn't have the best role models."

Her eyes flew wide.

Fuck, he thought as honest-to-God tears filled her eyes. Who knew he could cross that line? He was just so fucking sick of her subtle reminders of how he'd failed to protect his deceased little brother. He knew he'd suck at fatherhood. Did she have to remind him at every turn?

155

Jesus, he was a bastard. *A fucking bastard*. She was just curious, right?

"I didn't mean that."

"I'll have the crab," she said quickly.

"And I'll have the steak tartare." Raw meat fit his lack of grace right now—like Henry VIII.

She dabbed at her eye with her napkin. "I'm glad you found someone."

He arched an eyebrow. He'd never heard her happy about him getting involved with anyone—not that she met many of the women he'd seen.

"More wine, Mother?" He occupied himself lifting the cold bottle from its ice bucket.

"I'll have the oysters, too," she said.

"Good choice. The Oak selects only the finest from the Chesapeake Bay."

"Perhaps, someday, we'll go to Annapolis. You father once took me to Boatyard Bar and Grill."

"Oh?"

"Yes, he loved it there."

If she brought up his father, he'd speared her heart clear through to the other side. Jesus, ten minutes in and they were already having the annual chat, timed right around his late brother's birthday.

He'd order apology flowers as soon as he got back to the car. *Roses. No, orchids*. They apologized better. Flowers remained their signal to forgive and forget. The template leading up to such actions was well established. She'd arrive for a visit, unannounced. They'd fight. He'd send a garden of blooms a day later. The pattern of wash, rinse, repeat with the family drama had grown into an annual tradition.

Hell, he should send Samantha both roses *and* orchids— an advance apology for the no-kid rule she'd learn was unbreakable thanks to his own family falling apart. From the day his brother died, years ago, he'd constructed his life and future to avoid the reoccurrence of such a nightmare.

In uncanny timing, Samantha's name flashed on his cell phone screen.

"Excuse me, Mother." He was glad for the break. It would also give her time to check her tear-smudged makeup.

He rose from the table and threw his napkin over his empty plate.

"Samantha?"

"Derek." Samantha's pained and breathless voice raised fear in every part of his body.

"What's wrong?"

"It's Cindy."

∽

Derek drove straight to the police station. He'd directed his driver to take his mother back to her hotel with promises he'd show up later. He knew he wouldn't. The little white lies they told one another were part of their relationship, an arsenal of niceties and pleasantries they'd amassed to keep the peace.

When Derek arrived at the Florida Avenue station, he intercepted Samantha just as she exited a cab in front of the building.

"Cindy Carter. Mugging victim. We're picking her up," he barked at the desk clerk.

He didn't see so much as feel and hear Cindy launch herself at Samantha.

"It was Joanne. It *had* to be Joanne, that beotch," she said through gritted teeth. "Take me to her studio. *Right now.*"

Why wasn't she weeping?

"Well?" Cindy's eyes held so much fire behind that

bruised eye and cut on her lip that he almost felt sorry for anyone in her sights.

He never could predict a woman's behavior. Their emotions were whirling dervishes when calm. When pissed? The tornado became a force that could wipe out solar systems.

"Ladies. We'll talk outside."

"Good, because I can't say what I want with so many cops around," Cindy said. "It'll be considered pre-meditated murder."

"They've heard worse." He would know. Ten years ago, he and Alexander had met in a police station not unlike the one where they stood. Alexander had come to bail out a colleague and walked out with two men—the friend he'd bailed out, and Derek. To this day, Derek didn't know what caused Alexander to take a chance on the spoiled kid whose drunken, drug-induced aggression toward a cop in a restaurant alley had landed him in jail. But he had, and Derek was still grateful.

Only when they were on the road did he take a deep breath.

"I'm taking you to my office. We'll sort things out there." He had no idea where Cindy lived, and she probably shouldn't be alone until she calmed down.

"We should take her home, Derek."

"No. To DC Pole, James." She pointed from his tiny backseat out to the street.

"We're not doing either. They have your wallet, right? Your address?"

"Yeah. Damn, I loved that wallet. And, no, I don't care that I swore."

"The Kate Spade?" Samantha asked with a look of horror.

"And look." She raised her sleeve, a long tear slashed

Lucky

through the word *dance*. "I'm sorry I borrowed your studio jacket. It got ripped."

"Don't worry about that."

He turned onto Florida Avenue. "Cindy. Start from the beginning. Tell me what happened." He glanced at her in his rearview mirror.

She pointed to her eye. "This? Compliments of Joanne's boyfriend. I recognized him. Sam, remember when Janet competed for Miss Pole Whatever two years ago? That big guy with all the tattoos who hung out by the stage? He refused to leave even after two bodyguards tried to haul him off for getting too close?"

"Tattoos." Samantha turned in her seat. "Snakes up the arm? I saw him. That guy in Frost's alley had snake tattoos. The two guys couldn't be the same, could they?"

"Who knows? He came out of nowhere from behind. I got an eyeful of that cheap ink. I mean, if you're going to get a tattoo, show some effing originality. He also said he was from Joanne's studio."

"He said that?" Derek asked.

"In so many words. 'Careful there, girlie, you wouldn't want to get hurt before your next performance.' If I'd only been in front of him, I could have ensured *he'd* have trouble performing. I'd never wanted to kick a guy in the nuts so badly."

Derek's own balls tightened at Cindy's words. He'd seen this woman climb twenty feet up swaths of fabric on the mere strength of her biceps. One kick in the wrong direction...

"Let me get this straight. This Joanne person owns a rival dance studio."

"Rival my ass." Cindy pointed at her eye once more. "An enemy."

Samantha sighed. "Rival is putting it strongly. I mean, her

studio is three times as big as Aerobesque. I'm small potatoes. Why bother with me? I knew she was pissed. All those phone calls."

"Calls? You save any messages?"

"No, I couldn't stand the thought of keeping that poison. She was mad that I opened my own studio sort of close to hers. She called me on my grand opening nine months ago and left a ten-minute rant that should have melted the phone lines. 'Bitch. You'll never make it. How dare you open within fifty miles of me.'" Samantha delivered the words with amazing calm. "But she wouldn't go this far, Derek."

"Oh, yes, she would." Cindy seemed hell-bent on staying angry. "Dance studios are competitive. There's this unspoken rule: You do not open up a new place fifty miles from where you once danced."

"I took two of her classes, years ago. I wasn't a regular student."

"You don't need to defend yourself. In my line of business territory issues are common," Derek said. Only it didn't make sense for a rival dance studio to send muscle after Samantha's small outfit. No, this scenario could be driven by a different, and worse, reason. "This may have nothing to do with you, Samantha." A rival nightclub could be after him for all they knew.

His brain clicked through their options. Going to Frost, or even his downtown office, would be a mistake. Too public. His apartment was still under massive renovation, and exposing Cindy to Alexander's home wasn't wise. They needed some place for the short term. He had only one choice: Samantha's house. They'd require basic security, but whatever. He didn't believe in coincidences, and two muggings in less than a week made him suspicious.

Samantha's hand flew up to the doorjamb to steady

herself as he darted to the left lane to take New York Avenue. "Where are we going?"

"Your house. It's safer. We have video footage of the guys who harassed Samantha in the alley. Not very clear, but I'll have them sent to my phone so you both can review it. If the guy looks the same as the one who mugged you, Cindy, we'll have a better time identifying him and getting them picked up."

Samantha peered up at him. "Part of me hopes he's not the same person. Is that terrible?"

"No, you don't like conflict. But if violence has entered the picture, it'll be handled."

"You sure you're not Mafia?" Cindy asked.

I'm sorry, Samantha mouthed with a smile. He wasn't. Cindy's direct approach was refreshing. No dancing around issues, only flat-out, pointed questions.

"Not Mafia, Cindy. Just a club owner who knows a lot of professionals who, for one reason or another, are good at security."

"Yeah, I suppose this town is full of them," Samantha said quietly.

Samantha spent the entire drive up F Street, Constitution Avenue, and Connecticut Avenue trying to convince Cindy to stay for a few days until they'd nailed the idiots who'd taken things too far. She flatly refused, throwing more expletives at this Joanne person despite her moratorium on swearing. Only when Chaz's blurry video footage arrived on his phone as he pulled into Samantha's driveway did she give in to the idea. She agreed the man seen in Frost's alley could be the same guy.

Derek should have insisted they involve the police regardless of Samantha's original reticence in calling them the night of her attack. Now, she had no choice. She'd have to accept his protection.

The old landscaping of tall boxwoods and oak trees around Samantha's house made security difficult. Several large branches hovered close to her bedroom window. Mark would have declared her house a security nightmare, giving him an excuse to play hero, his favorite role next to that of Master to his wife, Isabella.

"Ladies, go inside. I'll be there in a minute." He grasped Samantha's arm before she stepped out. "Don't say anything to your grandmother until I'm with you."

"I wouldn't know what to say anyway."

Trouble was, he didn't know what to say either. Soothing angry women wasn't his forte.

After watching Samantha and Cindy disappear inside, he called a police sergeant he knew. Then he dialed Mark, followed by Alexander. DC cops were good, but overworked and underpaid. He needed a private detective, stat.

18

From the kitchen window, Samantha kept one eye on Derek in the driveway barking into his phone, and the other eye on her grandmother's moving hands, growing more frenzied with every half answer Samantha gave her.

Her grandmother had gasped and pushed Cindy's hair off her forehead to reveal a purpling bruise. *Beast,* she had signed. *And not the good kind.*

The mudroom door finally opened and Derek stepped inside.

Samantha signed to her grandmother. *This is Derek Damon Wright.*

The club owner? From the other night?

She nodded and turned to Derek. "Why three names?"

His shocked face was nothing new. "She reads lips, but also speaks," Samantha explained. "It's a myth that deaf people can't talk." Her grandmother's words weren't crisply articulated, but they were understandable.

"Yes, I talk. When there's something worth saying … or asking."

Derek bowed slightly. "Mrs. Rose."

"Wine? Or whiskey?" she vocalized. She signed an amendment to Sam. *Or champagne? He has that look about him.*

"Nothing for me, Mrs. Rose," he said.

Her hands flurried once more.

Samantha interpreted. "She says you can call her Carina."

"Beautiful name." He lifted her fingers and kissed the back of her hand.

She waved him away and again her hands moved with her usual fluid language.

"She said you'd be better off directing that stuff to the younger ladies."

After retrieving some ice and wrapping it in a blue and white kitchen towel, Carina held it to Cindy's forehead.

Cindy's eyes shone with grateful emotion as she took the ice packet. Leave it to her grandmother to quell Cindy's anger.

Samantha pulled out a bottle of white from the back of the refrigerator and glanced at the label. Was it any good? She shouldn't be concerned about the quality of her bargain-basement wine with everything going on, but Derek was probably used to the best of the best.

He gently took the bottle from her. "Allow me. Corkscrew?"

She must have looked flummoxed because he walked to one of the three drawers in the ancient kitchen. "Here, perhaps?" He pointed to the cutlery drawer.

She nodded. She needed to sit. She felt a little light-headed. The surreal quality of the last few hours crystallized into reality. Hours ago, she was having kinky sex in her studio. Cindy had been mugged and Joanne might be involved. These things happened in movies, not in the real world.

Her grandmother reached over and patted her hand. *Does he understand ASL?*

She shook her head. At least she didn't think so.

Who is he to you?

Another good question. *I'm not sure yet.*

Her grandmother hummed disapproval. She lifted her chin. "This happened at his club?" she asked aloud.

"No. Outside the dance studio," Cindy answered. "But I'm fine. Just ticked off."

"You didn't answer my first question about your name." Her grandmother eyed Derek with suspicion.

"My mother and father disagreed, so I got both names." His eyes did that twinkly thing that made most women swoon. Her grandmother wasn't most women. She'd had her share of charmers in her day, until her grandfather came along. She sat unmoved.

"You love your mother and father?"

"I try. My father's dead."

"Loving parents is important."

"It is."

What was this strange conversation between Derek and her grandmother? At least Derek understood, not flinching once during her grandmother's cross-examination.

He grasped her grandmother's arm when she stood. She waved him away. Turning to the cabinets, she pulled out three wineglasses. She placed them on the counter and sat back down as if waiting.

Derek smiled, rose, and filled three glasses, full. He then brought one to Cindy, her grandmother, and her. She waved off the wine, not in the mood to add to the fog floating in her mind. He corked the bottle and put it back in the refrigerator without having any himself.

As if reading her concern, he said, "I need to keep a clear head." Then he turned to her grandmother. "Mrs. Rose, I'd like your permission to send someone over to watch your home and Samantha's studio until we apprehend the people who did this."

Her grandmother sent her a questioning look. Her hands accused. *You didn't tell me everything.*

"Samantha, I believe it's only fair you tell your grandmother our suspicions," he said.

"You know sign language?"

"I know grandparents. She will want to know why I'm sleeping on your couch." He smiled. "I presume you have a sofa somewhere?"

She was right about Derek. He honestly cared about her. Why else would he deign to staying on their lumpy old couch?

For the first time in a while, she let herself feel hope that perhaps she wasn't a complete idiot regarding men.

⁓

Derek had never had a reason to learn ASL. Tonight he wished he had. Samantha's grandmother eyed him as if she'd had run-ins with men like him before.

The older woman was quite attractive. Her blond hair, obviously dyed, was styled in a Marilyn Monroe bob and framed sharp hazel eyes. She wore makeup. She was the type of woman widowers followed around in grocery stores asking about the ripeness of melons, but who were hoping to be brought home for dinner.

Her hands danced in the air. Samantha turned to him, flushing a little. "She says you don't need to be careful around her. She can tell what you're saying."

"Is that what she really said?" He barely moved his lips.

"No." Her grandmother stamped her foot. "I said, don't

mouth your words so carefully. I've got eyes. I know what I see."

"I can assure you, Mrs. Rose, an attack on your daughter will never happen again."

"Things like that always happen at clubs. So, you playing with my granddaughter?"

Samantha grasped her grandmother's arm.

"Samantha is afraid I'm being rude."

"When it comes to protecting Samantha, there isn't any such thing. I'll make you a deal. You let me sleep on your couch, and the two girls will share Samantha's room. Your granddaughter and the people in her life are important to me." If whoever did this was after him, he wouldn't endanger the girls' lives over some jealous club owner who wanted to send a message.

"They have Cindy's wallet, which means they have her address. They already know the studio address." He turned to her. "You had business cards?"

She nodded.

"It would be easy enough to find this house, too." He held up his hand before Sam could ask. "It's Washington. You can find out anything if you dig deep enough." And he planned to dig deep. He turned back to Samantha's apprehensive grandmother now eyeing him with contempt. He wished he could say he was surprised.

Time to pull out the big guns. "I could have this house surrounded by a SWAT team in less than an hour, if needed. I'm not bragging, nor do I mean to alarm you. I say that so you understand the lengths I'd go to. In this instance, however, some things are better done myself. It would take an army of men to get through me before they'd reach your granddaughter."

She waved toward Derek and signed.

"She said you have potential," Samantha said.

A soft knock on the kitchen door made Cindy jump. Her usual steel-and-nails bravado had vanished. Who the hell would come knocking at this house at this hour? Derek opened the door to Alexander standing under Samantha's tiny pent roof holding two bags from La Trattorio.

"You tracing my phone now?" he asked.

"I trace everyone I care about. Especially when they call me with news like you had. Carlos from Trattorio says hello." He lifted the bags.

From the small hallway, Alexander peered around Derek. His eyes softened and crinkled with his smile. "Hello, Carina." He inclined his head in an act of rare—hell, unprecedented—acquiescence. His hands made a motion. Was Derek the only one who didn't know ASL?

Samantha's grandmother's blue eyes had widened. One side of her mouth lifted, but then she turned away without responding.

"Still angry, I see." Alexander brought the food bags, fragrant with oregano and garlic, into the kitchen. "In days gone by, there was a dance club I used to go to on Capitol Hill," he said as he set them on the kitchen table. "Young gentlemen like me stood in lines that formed hours in advance and wound around the block to see Carina Rose." He waved away the flurry of her hands. "Oh, yes, they did."

Alexander gave her an amused smile. "You haven't aged a day. I take that back. You look better now."

A puff of air left her lips. She walked to him and they gave each other cheek kisses. She held onto his arms. "I'll think about forgiving you, but only because you brought the eggplant Parmesan from Carlos."

"A gentleman never forgets." Alexander released her and drew out a steaming carton. "Samantha, I don't know your favorite, but I hope you'll find something to your liking."

Lucky

"Thank you, Mr. Rockingham. It's so nice of you to do this."

"Call me Alexander." He waved off her accolades. "It's the least I can do. Plus, when I discovered where Derek was, I recognized the address."

Carina touched his arm, requesting Alexander to turn. She signed to him with an insistence that spoke of a shared history. Curiosity nagged at his insides. Coincidences in Washington were nonexistent.

After their exchange, Alexander turned to Cindy with a gentle smile. "Cindy, I apologize on behalf of all mankind. What happened to you is not uncommon, but it's inexcusable. Do you like *formaggio fritto*?"

"My favorite." Cindy, uncharacteristically mute to this point, turned to Derek. "Where the hell do they grow you guys? And where can I put in my order?"

Samantha pulled extra chairs from the living room to the Formica kitchen table while her grandmother busied herself setting out plates and honest-to-God real silver cutlery. Within minutes, only the clink of forks and knives against mismatched 1970s Fiesta Ware plates filled the space.

Chaz called halfway through dinner to say the security footage was too grainy to get an identity on the men who'd attacked Samantha. After directing Chaz to upgrade the cameras—stat—he opted not to tell the girls that identifying the attackers wasn't possible. After a while Alexander excused himself and ducked outside to make a few calls.

Derek kept his hand on Samantha's knee throughout dinner. She picked at her food and her eyelids dropped further down with each small bite. She didn't appear at all curious about this dubious coincidence of Alexander and Carina knowing one another. Every person had a unique threshold around absorbing first-time events. Once that line had been crossed, their brain couldn't process anything new anymore. Samantha had been introduced to a lot in the last few days—attacks on herself and her friend, acceleration of her expansion plans, and Accendos.

Then, there was the mere introduction of him into her life.

He knew who he was. The intensity he lived and breathed kept him going. Not everyone responded the same way, and clearly Samantha had reached her limit on new life events.

Despite waving off the alcohol earlier, Derek took a sip of the red wine that Carina took from a small wine rack on the counter, brushing off dust. Alexander had that effect on people. They pulled out bottles saved for years.

A long string of melted cheese stretched between Cindy's teeth and two fingers. She moaned. "Yes, oh, God, yes."

"Derek." Alexander stepped back into the kitchen. "You're going to get a call within the hour from a PI, Stan Toccato, best in the business."

His eyes shot to Carina, who stood with her back turned at the kitchen sink and said, "Thank you, Alexander." The private detective better get to the bottom of this mess—and fast.

Samantha rose. "Cindy, let me go upstairs with you. Guest bedroom." She stared at Derek as if sending a message, which he hoped was "come with us."

"Yeah, I'm worn out." Cindy's eyes were also drooping.

His chair scraped loudly, and as if she could hear the noise, Carina turned from the sink to stare at him. "For you, I'll make up the couch. As you said, you will stay here."

He bowed his head in answer. Something told him she knew he'd have slept in his car if she'd turned him away. Samantha and Cindy headed to the staircase. He'd started to follow when Carina's voice stopped him.

"The men will help with dishes."

Her grandmother turned to the sink once more.

Alexander took his place next to her, and Derek watched helplessly as the women climbed the stairs without him. Any other day he'd have loved to see Alexander's expensive shirt-sleeves rolled up as he loaded dirty dishes into a dishwasher. Tonight, he cursed his own manners, which insisted he obey the matriarch of the house.

19

Derek hoped the guest bedroom was far, far away from Samantha's room. He'd been with the woman seven hours ago, but the absence might as well have been seven months. The amount of female flesh he'd seen in his years was obscene, but Samantha's effect had wiped away his earlier intimacies like an ocean wave over fresh footprints in the sand.

He glanced at a smiling Carina and Alexander. They'd slipped into reminiscing—or so he thought. The hand flurries grew more animated, laughter pealing from both of them. Carina was visibly more relaxed. Alexander's presence often had that effect, as if nothing bad could happen to anyone while he was in the room.

Carina retrieved a scotch bottle from a cupboard, and Alexander took the moment with her back turned to say, "Derek, Carina and I will be a while. We have a lot of years to catch up on." His eyes darted to the stairway.

"Alexander, someday you'll have to tell me how you know each other."

"Let's just say Carina was instrumental in helping me find my people here in Washington."

His people? He'd never heard Alexander talk so colloquially. Asking him anything, however, was a conversation for another time.

"You'll reassure her I'm not going to bring ruination to her granddaughter's honor? She's bound to know where I've gone." He dipped his chin at Carina, now putting ice cubes into a tumbler.

"Don't worry. Carina is special."

He hoped so, because Derek slipped up the stairs with nothing G-rated in mind while praying, dear God, that Samantha's bedroom and the guest room wouldn't be a Jack-and-Jill set up. He should have paid more attention to the house layout a few days ago. His cock tightened at the memory.

At the top of the stairs, the dark, quiet hallway reminded him of every horror film he'd ever seen. With every step, floorboards complained. Samantha's door cracked open.

"What took you so long?"

She never ceased to amaze him. He stepped inside.

"Where's Cindy?"

Samantha peeling off her top killed any more words in his mouth. Her bare breasts pressed against him. "Down the hall. Asleep. Adrenaline crash." She unbuttoned her jeans. "Do that thing to me that you did at the club and this morning."

"Which one?"

"All of them."

She was holding more tension than an overloaded pressure cooker. Time to let off some steam.

He grasped the side of her neck and pulled her in close. "Later. Right now, you're going to let me take care of you."

Her smile was seriously going to be the death of him.

"Clothes off. Get on the bed. Hands on the headboard. Legs spread."

She positioned herself, spread-eagled, in the center of her comforter. When her hands curled into the brass scrolls, his over-eager cock pressed against his zipper. He was going to do so many things to this woman.

"We killed the boas the other night," she breathed. "I'm out of chocolate, too."

"Won't need them." Jerking off his tie, he gazed down at her. If she kept licking her top lip, he might explode. He deliberately slowed down. He released the top button of his collar and rolled up his shirtsleeves. With each motion, he grew more fixated on her quivering lips. Later, he told his cock, you will have those lips *later*.

He smoothed hair off her forehead. "Can you be quiet?"

"Probably not." She rubbed her legs against the bed as if trying to soothe an ache.

His shirt was off in less than five seconds.

"Open your mouth."

Her lips parted and he stuffed part of his shirt into her mouth. "Keep that there."

"Buff ish Amaneee."

He laughed. "Yes, it's Armani. Only the finest gags for you, ballerina. Now don't release the headboard."

After settling between her open legs, he took a moment to inspect her beauty—and silently thank his good fortune. He nipped her labia and she gave a muffled yelp. Good thing he'd gagged her, otherwise everyone in the house would have caught that high-pitched gasp—at least those who were not hearing impaired. He continued, knowing her taste, her undulations, her satisfied moans were worth the risk of waking up the neighborhood.

His cock lay trapped under him and complained bitterly about being left out of the action.

Lucky

She adjusted her hips as if seeking to place his mouth. He knew where she aimed. Even though they both needed the release and soon, his dominance kicked in. Her clit was now officially off-limits. It was time for another lesson in submission.

He grasped her hips. "You can move, but stop forcing this, or I'll make you wait 'til morning to come."

"Shoo udun."

"Oh, yes, I would. Test me." He was having fun for the first time since … *tying her up in her studio*, his cock responded.

Between her quivering legs, he licked and sucked every part of her luscious treasure, careful to avoid the one area she'd hoped he'd land on eventually.

Lick.

Suck.

Taste.

His gaze darted up as he trailed his tongue up one side and down the other of her pussy. She panted behind his shirt, now stained a darker blue from her saliva.

Her heels kicked against the bed in frustration, rattling the headboard. He needed to buy some of that parachute silk and keep it in his trunk for semi-emergencies like the one before him. She wouldn't stay still, and he honestly didn't care. Like many Dominants who barked at their subs to not move, he enjoyed seeing her squirm under his mouth's handling. She would be magnificent bucking and lurching while suspended.

For long minutes he taunted her opening, his tongue fucking her. Her head lolled from side to side and her fists grew white from gripping the metal headboard.

When she finally panted in desperation, he flicked her clit with the tip of his tongue. She jerked and let out a plaintiff moan.

"Would you like me to do that again?"

Her head nodded vigorously.

He ran his tongue over her spot once more and then again, until he couldn't stop himself. He went at her like a famished man. She came so hard, he felt the need to yank the shirt from her mouth so she could breathe. He then grasped her under ass and lifted her so he had greater access to bring her to orgasm a second time with his mouth. Her wails softened to whimpers as she bit down on the shirt as if trying to be quiet.

When she finally finished shuddering, her eyelids rested at half-mast. They then flew open when he rammed inside her with no warning. He released in less than two thrusts and didn't care if his body was responding like a teenager's. Hell, it had ever since meeting this delicious woman underneath him. Her lazy gaze told him everything that mattered. She wanted him, and for that fire pooling in her eyes, he'd risk resembling a besotted kid.

As they caught their breath, the telltale thump of the mudroom door told him Alexander had finally left. He'd have to leave her soon—at least to the living room couch. He was nothing if not respectful.

He started to rise, but her arms clamped down on his back. "Don't leave."

"But your grandmother." The clank of dishes was unmistakable through the crack under her bedroom door.

"I'm twenty-eight. It's not like she thinks I'm a virgin." She lifted her head. "Besides, she can't hear us." She dampened his leg with her crotch.

Normally a woman clinging to him to cuddle after sex was akin to a trip to the gallows. This time, feeling her arms reaching for him pulled at a heartstring he didn't know he possessed. A strange, uncomfortable feeling, as if a fishing line was pulling him in, tugged at his chest. Still, he felt inexplicably strange sleeping upstairs with her grandmother downstairs, knowing what the older woman expected of him.

"It's important to me that your grandmother trust me."

"She will. I do."

He pressed a kiss into her temple. "That pleases me, and as much as it pains me to leave you, I'm going to have to see you in the morning, ballerina."

He reluctantly pulled himself from the warm bed and dressed. As he stepped down the creaking stairs to take his rightful place on the couch, he made a mental note. No matter what state his apartment was in, next time they were going to his place even if he had to lay her down on paint tarps.

20

Samantha took a deep breath. *Just ask her.* "Um, Christiana, do you have a minute?" Cindy and her grandmother had gone out to get coffee, and she had to take advantage of the rare time alone in the studio. Plus, Christiana only came to class when she was in town, which made this opportunity even more crucial.

"Sure, what's up?"

"I was wondering if I could talk to you ... about something." She glanced over at the girls who still milled about the alcove, gathering their things. "Privately?"

Christiana nodded knowingly.

After the final student shuffled down the stairs to leave, Christiana turned to her. "You want to talk about Derek."

"I guess you know."

"Jonathan told me you two were seeing each other and you might want to talk. Good choice in Derek, by the way."

They settled on the large gymnastic mat that still lay under the lyra. "Have you known Derek long?" Samantha asked.

Lucky

"Not until Jonathan and I were engaged. I didn't meet any of his friends until we were able to go public."

"Go public?"

"He was in Congress. He couldn't be seen squiring around a nineteen-year-old."

"That didn't bother you?" She'd have hated being hidden away like a common mistress.

"At the time, yes. But I understand it now. He was protecting me."

"Protecting you." Samantha squared her shoulders toward Christiana. "So, if I asked you…" *Do you get ordered around? Spanked? Tied up with feather boas in your bedroom with your grandmother asleep down the hall while chocolate melts on your breasts? You know, the usual questions …*

"About the dominance and submission," Christiana filled in.

Her face must have registered every bit of shock she felt. The younger woman touched her hand as if she'd just told her cat had died. "It's okay. I don't talk about this stuff beyond our circle. But something tells me you're on the inside already."

"Derek took me somewhere."

"Accendos?"

"You know that place?"

"Intimately. Derek is into you if he took you there."

"So you and Jonathan?"

"Yes."

"Wow."

Christiana laughed. "That's generally what you should expect. Jonathan, Derek, Mark, Carson, all of them are unusual men. They specialize in 'wow'. You can confirm that with London."

"London *Drake*?" How many other Londons could there

be outside of one of her most advanced students in lyra? "That means…"

"Her bruises don't all come from this hoop." Christiana reached up and tapped the metal circle so it spun. "Oh, and don't worry. She loves them."

"Do you like it? What if I don't like it?"

"Good questions. So." She straightened her spine. "Answers from me. Yes, I love it, but Jonathan is my only experience. As for their demands, the rewards are usually worth it. You and Derek have talked about this, right? I mean he hasn't—"

"Oh, no, he's been great." Her body hummed at the thought of all he'd done. "It's just so…"

"Overwhelming? Deviant? Fabulous?" Her mouth lifted into a half smile.

"No, more like too good to be true."

She hadn't realized until she vocalized it how remarkable, albeit confusing, Derek had proven to be. The things he did to her? He'd flat-lined her doubts and fears about men *and* turned her sex life upside down in less than two weeks. She would never settle for ordinary missionary style after what that man had done to her.

"It's the oddest thing," she said. "It's like I had no idea my body could respond that way. And, time … it stands still when I'm with him."

"Isn't that the best?"

"It makes no sense, though. He could have anyone. Someone who's already into that stuff."

"Not to make you jealous, but he likely already has."

"Which proves my point."

"Ya know, with all these mirrors around, you might want to glance into one occasionally. I mean, look at you."

"You're sweet, but—"

"But nothing. Every student you have basically wants to

be you." She paused. "I'm going to spell it out. You're sex on legs."

Samantha nearly choked on her own laughter.

"Look, I know what you mean. For a long time I thought Jonathan could *not* be into me." She shrugged. "But I found out he needs me as much as I need him—probably more. That's the best part. This D/s stuff, no matter what you see on the Internet—don't go there, by the way—doesn't work unless it works for both of you. Jonathan once said to me that exploring what worked was half the fun. As for being with someone in the lifestyle, it's like anywhere. Except it's doubly hard finding someone you're attracted to *and* into the kink."

"I could see that." Though she still couldn't believe the angelic-looking Christiana had just used the word *kink* with a straight face.

"Be sure to talk a lot with Derek before trying anything new. So … do you? Love it, I mean?"

"I think so. But I can't spend the rest of my life just having great sex."

"Why not?" Christiana blinked at her so innocently, she knew they weren't exactly on the same page.

"But don't you want a family someday?"

"Oh, God, don't get me started. Jonathan would be driving me to the hospital right now to give birth if it was up to him. But kids? Probably. Someday. Jonathan's genes need to be passed on." Her eyes got dreamy. Their age difference was suddenly clear.

"But how?"

"Do I need to draw you a diagram of how it works?" She laughed.

"I'm serious. You can't have both worlds. How is that possible?"

"Have you seen what Derek's life is like?" She arched her eyebrow. "I think he pretty much specializes in 'possible.'"

Sam let her eyesight blur at the thought of his world full of clubs, private drivers, and expensive business suits—and surprises, of which he seemed to have an endless supply. Now that she knew more about his sexual proclivities, she realized how little she *really* knew. Where did his desires come from? When was his first kiss? She didn't even know how he took his coffee or if he drank coffee at all. As tempting as living off pure pleasure sounded, decadence had its limits.

At the echoes of Cindy trudging up the stairs Christiana stood, clearly understanding their conversation had to end.

"Call me anytime. We subs needs to stick together," she whispered.

The word "sub" hit her like a Mack truck. Was she a submissive? What if she wasn't and Derek found out? Would he dump her? That's when the second mental truck hit her. Despite the gap in their expectations that rivaled the Grand Canyon, she didn't want to lose this man. There would be time later to delve into his coffee preferences.

21

"They look like the same guy." Derek tossed the pictures onto Alexander's desk and turned to Stan Toccato, who'd proven his unparalleled PI reputation. With little information, some grainy security camera footage, and a past rap sheet dug up by the investigator, he'd delivered on who had attacked Samantha. Cindy's mugger remained elusive.

"Maybe." Stan leaned back in the chair and casually lifted his ankle to rest on his knee. "The alley assault on that dancer—"

"Samantha."

"Yeah, sure. Samantha. Well, that guy"—Stan tapped the top picture—"coulda just been trying to impress his girl."

"Joanne Bradstreet."

"The dance studio owner, yeah. He's an ex-boyfriend of hers."

"An ex?"

"Perhaps he was seeking to regain her favors," Alexander said.

"A dozen roses would have been easier."

Stan grimaced, likely his version of a smile. "But here's

what I think. They're pros. Too pro to be guys who got their nut sacks in a twist over some woman, no matter what they said to, uh, Samantha." He scrubbed his chin. "The thing is, Mr. Wright, all of this could have nothing to do with you. I've seen work like this before. But given the trouble they went to, the fact that they returned to your club, and the timing…" He glanced up at Alexander, whose gaze had turned glacial.

"You mean the Wynters." A muscle in Alexander's jaw twitched.

"Who are they?" Derek didn't like the way Alexander said the name.

"A family that doesn't see eye to eye with me."

"It's not like threatening Samantha or me does anything to you." Derek knew Alexander's power irked some, but to take on the man through him made no sense.

"On the contrary, threatening my family is the only way to get to me."

Alexander had never used the word "family" with him before. The sudden, mawkish turn made his skin prickle. He wanted action, not more layers of emotional confusion added to the pile grown from his attachment to Samantha. He'd moved from fascination to obsession with her, judging by the way his heart lurched at the thought of anyone hurting his little dancer.

"Gentlemen, this woman is…"

"Important to you." Alexander looked up at him.

Important didn't come close to what he felt about her. He'd figure out why and how later. In the meantime, getting her out of any real or perceived danger was all that mattered.

"So they dropped the DC Pole name just to distract from their true motivation?"

Stan merely shrugged at Derek's question.

Alexander leaned forward. "If anything here is more than a random act by men trying to flex their muscles and look tough for their ex-girlfriend, Stan will find it." With those last words, Stan ghosted from the room. Derek's brain seemed to go with him. An incoherent tangle of thoughts seized his mind.

"Security is in place at Samantha's?"

"Thanks to Mark. The man knows more security firms in Washington than the Secret Service."

Alexander smiled at the name of their fellow Tribunal member and friend, Mark Santos. "You can take the black ops job away from a man, but never his ability to do the job."

Mark had proven that many times—case in point, last year's run-in with a Baltimore wanna-be gangster named Weyland who'd threatened Mark's woman. He now understood how Mark felt—a strange helplessness surrounding the unknown.

Derek had promised Samantha's grandmother someone would watch over the studio—though he didn't need the urging—and when he reluctantly dropped her off there he noted the black sedan parked across the street. Now with this evidence, he'd make damn sure all three women were covered 24/7.

"They're on their way, Alexander, though Mark might be a little late." Clarisse, Alexander's assistant, peeked into the doorway and disappeared as quickly as Stan had.

Great, a Tribunal meeting. Just what he didn't need. Normally, the Tribunal stayed focused on ensuring proper BDSM behavior at Alexander's club. The Council had expanded its responsibilities in the last few years to include offering more formal support whenever one of their own needed help—whether that help was requested or not.

"Alexander, I'm not seeking a group therapy session."

"We're not offering it. But Carson's legal mind would be helpful on how to approach that dance studio to at least end the harassment."

"Afraid I'm going to take matters into my own hands?"

Alexander smiled. "I recognize that look in your eyes."

He knew why Alexander would think such a thing. They'd never broached, in any depth, the subject of his past impulsive move that brought them together ten years ago.

"Samantha being attacked in the alley … this still could be about me no matter what Stan said. Other club owners have done worse."

"You would know."

"Unfortunately, yes." He rested his elbows on his knees and studied his shoes. "I'm keeping eyes on Samantha's house. On Carina, too."

"Of course."

"How do you know her grandmother?" That coincidence gnawed at him more than Alexander's mention of his enemies. Had he said 'Wynter'? The name was familiar, though he'd never heard it from Alexander's lips before.

Alexander's chair creaked as he leaned back. "I met Carina Rose in San Francisco. A long time ago."

"Big change. From the Golden Gate to Memorial Bridge. How did she end up in Washington?"

"Same way I did. Dreams that didn't pan out. She'd heard of a new club opening on Wisconsin. In the late seventies, Georgetown was turning over. Our friendship didn't last long and we lost touch. She had the wrong idea about us." Alexander leaned back. "She once thought we might have been more."

"Oh." He'd seen many women become hung up on Alexander only to be rebuffed, gently.

Alexander's sexual preferences were never discussed. The Tribunal's Grand Arbiter didn't suffer gossip, and his closely guarded privacy was honored. He seemed more interested in others than himself. When he did reveal a tidbit, people hovered over it like squirrels over an acorn in January.

Lucky

Yet the question that burned in the minds of most of Alexander's friends arose: was Alexander lonely? *Heavy is the head that wears the crown*, it was said, and Alexander likely had a crown room. Was Alexander aware of the nickname he'd earned—The King? Oh, hell, he probably knew. Derek hoped the man found himself where he wanted to be.

Man, he'd grown soft. Must be all the estrogen he'd been exposed to lately.

"They can stay in your room here," the man said.

My room. He stayed at Accendos so much he automatically thought of it as *home* in his mind and heart. It's where he'd been staying while his apartment underwent its third renovation. Nothing in his penthouse seemed to fit, so he kept starting over, much to the glee of his favorite renovation shop and interior designer.

"I don't know if I ever told you how I appreciate having a place to go." He didn't know how to say what he'd wanted to say for ten years. "And, well, for dragging my ass back here … that day." That day they'd never talked about. He didn't know why he was bringing it up now, except his mother's visit coupled with Samantha's troubles had reacquainted him with the fragility of life. "Anyway. Thanks," he finished.

"You're welcome."

Alexander didn't move a muscle as long minutes passed. Oh, man, he did not know how to do this serious shit.

"You know, you never asked me what landed me in the police station."

"On the day we met? I was certain you'd tell me when you were ready."

"I'm surprised you didn't have me investigated."

"I learned enough. But when a man purposely comes close to drug overdose, there are some things the best PI can't uncover."

"Why me?" He looked up. "You save everyone, but…"

Words didn't exist to fully express his sheer bewilderment at Alexander saving him that day. Jesus, he'd been reduced to having the puerile fatherly talk with a man who had better things to do.

"Not everyone, Derek. I haven't saved everyone."

Derek sighed. "I was engaged to a woman I thought I got pregnant." A slice of pain lanced his heart. That old adage about ripping off the bandage all at once being less painful was utter and complete bullshit. His stomach roiled—whether at the words or the fact he'd withheld them for so long, he didn't know.

"Not yours?" Alexander's unfazed tone was honestly, truly the greatest gift he'd ever received.

"Not pregnant at all. She no longer had an incentive when I told her I wouldn't touch my trust fund. So, end of story. Funny thing was, I still wanted Margot. Hell, I moved to Washington for her." He shrugged. "She's married to an environmental law attorney. Moved to California. Two kids. Vacation home in Santa Barbara. She's better off without me."

Alexander frowned. "You're still here."

"Time flies."

"And then there was your youngest brother."

A loud buzzing replaced the growing fog in his brain. Normally, he only thought about Ethan once a year, on his uncelebrated birthday. Now, twice in one week, he'd been bitch slapped by his history. That damn kids' class at Samantha's—where he'd nearly been trampled to death—had burst the long-standing dam around his past and allowed it to leak into his conscious mind.

"Derek."

He raised his eyes to Alexander, whose image wavered a bit as unwelcomed moisture pooled in Derek's eyes.

"Yes, I know about him. Losing someone so young…"

Derek lurched from his chair. "Let's go get this over with." His legs carried him halfway down the hall until he found his ass on a prissy tufted settee under an oil painting.

Alexander's shoes appeared in his vision as he studied the carpeting.

"Take a minute, Derek. We'll be waiting for you in the Council room."

Trouble was, time didn't do shit for history, and nothing brought the past to the forefront more than trying to forget it—like how a toddler had drowned on his watch.

22

After ten minutes and one hundred deep breaths, Derek lifted his pansy butt off his perch and headed to the Tribunal room. The door clanged shut, the echo of the latch bouncing off the marble floor. The sound had always been comforting to Derek, as he knew he could say, do, or be anything within these walls.

Sarah strode over to him to give him a peck on the cheek. "I trust all worked out last week?"

Images of Samantha—ropes of feathers encircling her wrists, her shocked face when he'd shown up at her studio, red silks wrapping around her perfect legs—rose vividly in his mind. His heartbeat calmed.

"I smoothed it over. You looked like your tango was having its usual effect."

"My partner was adequate." She took the seat he offered her.

He nodded at the other attending Council members—Jonathan, Mark, Carson Drake, and Ryan Knightbridge—as they also took their places around the large circular table. Alexander's bodyguard, Tony, likely the only man Alexander turned his back to willingly, assumed his usual position behind his boss.

"The Grand Arbiter of the Tribunal network and Chairman of the Washington Tribunal Council calls this meeting to order. Third pledge Derek Damon Wright has the floor. He has some news."

Christ, he didn't know where to start. "It's nothing good," he said.

Ryan flashed his Boy Scout smile. "Do we ever meet to discuss anything good?"

"Not recently."

"We talked about my wedding last time," Jonathan said.

"Tick tock, my friend." Carson swirled ice in his drink.

"Don't remind me." Jonathan and Christiana had been engaged for more than two years. Now that her college graduation was imminent, he'd never seen a man itching so badly to get to an altar.

"She'll marry you," Alexander said. With those three words, the lines around Jonathan's eyes softened.

The assurance was another famous Alexander move. He made you believe things.

"Derek?"

All eyes were on him. Had he zoned out that badly?

He cleared his throat and leaned back in his chair. "I've been seeing someone."

Seven pairs of eyes, even Tony who rarely made direct eye contact due to his Secret Service training, bored into him. Was this so unusual? He was always with women. At least he had been until recently. He'd been taking time off. Then Samantha's luscious legs and smile that would undo any man—or woman if she swung that way—entered his club. God, his brain had switched to the damn Hallmark Channel.

"She's…" He trailed off. What *was* she?

"Special." Jonathan fixed his unnerving green eyes on him as if he and Alexander had been studying the same Oprah moves.

"Her name is Samantha Rose. Owner of Aerobesque Studios."

"The woman who danced at your club opening." Sarah leaned forward—usually enough for everyone to give her the floor. The Femme Domme had a powerful presence. "Samantha is a talented dancer, especially with tango."

"And that silks demonstration at your club was something." Mark's lips inched up into his version of a smile.

"So that's why you're still here. I thought you'd be in the Caribbean by now," Ryan said.

Yes, that's exactly where he should be.

"Bad timing, that's all," Derek said. "And I need your help."

"We launching an investigation?" Mark asked with unmasked amusement. "You had me set up security at her house for a reason. She wants a membership to Accendos?"

Now Mark was just messing with him. He oddly appreciated his friend's humor. Sharing personal details about himself wasn't his favorite pastime.

"And put her in front of you jackals? No."

Alexander's voice cut in. "She and her studio have been threatened."

As usual, spines straightened at Alexander's tone.

"I know it's not like me to ask for this Council's help with a woman I'm seeing." Asking Mark for help was one thing, but the Council came with a formality he wasn't comfortable with. He'd never had to reveal this much about his feelings to its members before.

"That's what we're here for." Carson would know. When his now-wife London was in trouble, the Council stepped in and exiled the man threatening her. Why would he think it'd be any different for him? Still, somehow, he hated to ask.

Lucky

"She was attacked in my back alley the night of her performance. One of her instructors was recently mugged. A rival dance studio owner has been making threatening calls. A woman named Joanne Bradstreet—"

"Someone attacked her at your club? That takes some guts," Ryan said. "Did he not know who you are?"

A puff of air blew through Derek's lips. "Clearly they don't know how far I'd go."

"What any of us would do for our women."

"Or our men," Sarah interjected.

Ours. Was Samantha his? He hadn't had anyone in ... well, had he ever, really?

"You have phone messages?" Mark asked.

"Erased. But I've instructed her to keep any future ones."

"Dancers threatening one another? What do they do? Beat each other with toe shoes?" Ryan was trying to lighten the mood.

"Never underestimate someone's threat to a career." Carson's face had turned to granite. As a leading attorney in DC, he'd seen his share of blackmail.

A muscle in Alexander's jaw twitched. Derek recognized the man's frustration with all this speculative talk.

He turned to Carson. "How dangerous is it to approach the rival's studio?"

The man nailed Ryan with that intimidating attorney stare he'd perfected. Hell, he'd probably invented the look. "Not recommended unless you have evidence. Even then you'd want to go to the police. Showing up and asking them why they're harassing Samantha could be deemed as harassment itself."

"Worried about those toe shoes?"

Okay, now Ryan's humor was getting annoying. Was *he* ever this irritating?

"I have another idea, and I've already set some things in

motion." Derek spent fifteen minutes explaining his plans. If Joanne Bradstreet felt threatened now, she would now see exactly how competitive he could get. His business motto was simple. When a rival tries to thwart your business, step up the success of your venture. Samantha's studio was about to become more prosperous than Joanne's. He expected an escalation in threats, which would then be captured so he could finally move in and press charges.

Not a single Tribunal member balked or, worse, laughed at him. Mark agreed to keep security in place on Samantha, Cindy, and Carina. Jonathan nodded knowingly over Derek's borderline pleas that Christiana keep lines of communication open to his budding submissive. Carson agreed to look for legal backing to file harassment charges. Ryan and Sarah offered to put the word out on the street that Aerobesque Studios was *the* place to enjoy a new, up-and-coming fitness craze.

God, he loved these people.

As for Alexander? He didn't need to promise anything. The man had done enough for him already. It was time for Derek to prove Alexander's trust in him all those years ago was well founded.

As they shuffled out of the room twenty minutes later, Jonathan hung back. "Christiana tells me she and Samantha had a talk."

"Should I be worried?" As if Jonathan would ever tell him anything Christiana said. He took secrecy as seriously as Alexander did.

"I'm sure she'll fill you in. Women like to share experiences. I doubt you could have kept them apart." Jonathan stopped. "But take some advice from me. Get Samantha out of town. Take her someplace where she can relax, and where you can focus her."

"That work with Christiana?"

Lucky

"It's the only thing that did."

Get her out of town. That idea had merit, and he knew exactly where to take her.

Jonathan slapped him on the back and pulled out his ringing phone. "Speaking of my lovely sub." He winked and headed down the hall.

Derek pulled out his own phone. Samantha answered immediately.

"Ballerina, is your passport in order?"

~

Derek's voice seemed lighter, happier, than earlier.

"I was just going to call you," she said. "Yes, I have a passport. Why?"

"It's a surprise. We leave tomorrow."

"What? Leave? Tomorrow?" Was he crazy?

Both her grandmother and Cindy threw questioning glances at her, and she put her hand over the receiver. "Derek wants to take me away. I can't. We've got the kids' recital coming up and it's just us."

"Samantha, you still there?"

"Hi, yes, um, my kids' lyra class has a recital in a few weeks and they're all freaked out."

"They're seven."

"Which means they don't want to disappoint anyone. Hey, can you come to the recital? It's the weekend before Thanksgiving. They liked you."

In the silent beat between them, she prayed. *Please say yes. Please say yes.*

"We'll see. Get Cindy to take over for you. Do you have anyone else that can fill in while we're gone?"

"Yes, but I can't go." Gabriella was a part-time instructor

who always sought more teaching hours, but his timing for a trip sucked.

Cindy yelled toward the phone. "We'll be fine. Take her somewhere. But if you say Australia, I'm coming, too. What?" she asked Sam, all innocence. "Lots of men there, Sam."

Derek's low chuckle rang in her ear. "Tell Cindy, next time she can come with us."

"You're taking me to Australia?"

"No. But tell you what, we'll leave midday tomorrow instead of morning to give you more time."

That was his version of more time?

Cindy nodded her head vigorously. "Whatever he's offering, *do it*."

"Samantha, deep breath." Derek's voice soothed her insides. "Just think. What would it take for you to leave tomorrow? Then do that."

Just *do that?* Was he kidding? "But—"

"Take it one step at a time, and pack for warm weather."

Cindy threw up her arms with a look that plainly said *she'd* go with him if Samantha didn't.

"Okay." She should at least consider his offer, right?

"Good. I'll see you after your last class tonight."

The line went dead, and despite going away being the most ludicrous, most irresponsible move she could make, a little thrill stirred her imagination. She was going to go somewhere with Derek ... tomorrow! Tonight he'd pick her up, like he had every night this week. Maybe he'd finally take her home with him. She'd yet to see his apartment. Damn, she needed to pack. But first, the studio needed to be taken care of.

"Cindy—

"I can watch over things. I'll call Gabriella to fill in, but someone else has to break it to the Lyra Ladies. They're gonna do that whiny thing."

Lucky

"I hope I'm not making a mistake."

"Hell no! Oh, sorry, Mrs. Rose."

Her grandmother waved her hand away, then she signed to Samantha. *You go. Then you'll know.*

She didn't respond. She didn't want to get into her relationship with Derek with her grandmother, especially at a time when she essentially had twenty-four hours to rearrange her entire life.

Cindy abruptly stood. "Hey, we better get going. I hear a dance mom downstairs."

Her grandmother tapped her on the arm before she could turn away, too.

What did he say about the recital?

Sam signed her conversation with Derek, leaving out the recital pieces. Her grandmother arched an eyebrow.

She signed. *He said no to the recital, didn't he?*

He's busy.

Her grandmother frowned. *Remember what I told you, don't pay attention to what they say. Only what they do.*

Samantha had a feeling her grandmother wasn't just talking about Derek, but also men from her past.

Fine, she'd take her grandmother's advice. She ran a list in her head. Derek had stayed with her the last two nights. He'd uncorked an endless well of lust inside her. He'd grown possessive and protective—no, downright covetous—of her and her time. He'd also arranged for security, two of whom were stationed outside right now. They pretended to blend into the landscape outside. *Ha!* Two guys the size of Mount Everest didn't blend.

Honestly, she liked the additional protection. She hadn't felt unsafe before, but now she felt a curious sense of freedom she hadn't known she'd lacked. She didn't hold her jacket closed in case she had to dart out in a rehearsal costume to walk one of her students to her car, or hold her studio keys in her hand, sharp edge out, like a weapon. Things she hadn't realized she'd done as naturally as breathing.

Her grandmother said to watch what he did. She liked his actions so far. So what if he didn't come to a kids' recital?

Two of her young students rushed into the room, their energy lighting up the space.

"Miss Rose!" Amber Lynn squeezed her legs. "Can I try the ribbons today? Pleeeeeease?"

"We'll try. And I have other news, too."

With an excited squeal, the little girl peeled off her jacket and dumped it on the floor at her feet before tearing through the curtain to the dance space. Watching her, Samantha's elation dimmed a tad. It mattered to her if he came to see her girls. It actually meant everything.

She sighed. One step at a time, like Derek had said.

23

Samantha ran her hand over the armrest of the cream-colored couch.

"I can't believe you have a sofa on an airplane." They had buckled into seats for take-off, but she now freely roamed a cabin as large as the living room in her house. A table with four chairs, a desk, and a seating area with two swivel chairs facing the couch she now admired took up most of the space.

The floor underneath her tilted slightly and she gasped. "Whoa."

"Mild turbulence." Derek pulled her down to sitting. "Nothing to be concerned about."

A flight attendant dressed casually in a khaki skirt, crisp white shirt and matching white beret brought a tray of drinks to where she sat.

"This is a mocktail that Derek thought you might like."

Derek let go of her hand so she could take the frosted glass topped with two tiny yellow and pink umbrellas. "No alcohol," he explained.

A quick sip and the coconut and pineapple instantly

transported her far, far away from Washington and its bleak fall skies. A low purr of contentment rumbled in her throat.

"You like it." He smiled. "Your drink is clue number two as to where we're going."

Derek had said he'd provide five clues about their destination. She rather liked his game.

She turned in her seat to face him. "Okay. Pack my bathing suit was one. Piña colada is two. Let me guess. Key West?"

"Aim farther."

Her heart jumped with a thrilling idea. "You can't be serious. The Caribbean?"

"One of my resorts."

She gasped. "I didn't bring resort-y clothes." Damn, she should have packed her little black dress; but black in the Caribbean? She'd roast. Her old tee-shirts and shorts just would not cut it, either.

He laughed openly. "You and clothes. Karen?" He signaled to the flight attendant, who scooted a large rolling suitcase to them.

"Everything you need is right here." She threw her a kind smile.

"They should fit, if my hand memory is correct. Your body is hard to forget."

Heat flooded her body from head to toe. Karen was listening!

With a neutral expression the flight attendant returned to the front of the plane as if nothing had transpired. Had Karen seen this little scene before? Samantha tamped down the thought she might be female number one hundred who'd been handed a suitcase of resort clothes at thirty thousand feet.

"Come." Derek rose, took the suitcase, and walked past several more large leather seats to a door at the back. A large

Lucky

W had been etched into the fabric covering of the door panel.

At his gesture, she stepped inside a bedroom. Bolted-down lamps topped night-stand countertops on either side of a king-sized bed. Amber-colored, ruched curtains waterfalled down windows on either side of the room. Three steps in, her knees met the satin gold and crimson comforter. He threw the bag onto the bed and then situated himself leaning against the tufted headboard, legs crossed at the ankles. "Try something on for me."

She closed the door behind her. "Any requests?" she teased.

"Surprise me."

"You don't like surprises."

"I'm making an exception if it involves you taking off your clothes."

She unzipped the bag and a small thrill ran through her at the rainbow of colored fabrics wrapped in tissue paper. She lifted each folded square, the paper crinkling with a promise that these clothes wouldn't be like anything she'd ever owned. She was vaguely aware that she might have squealed a little when her fingers touched the expensive material of a long, floating, vivid green chiffon dress, a faint pattern of tropical flowers dancing across the bias. Releasing another square of tissue paper, she found a pale yellow sundress with a Marilyn Monroe-esque halter top. A large-brimmed sunhat lay upside down, ostensibly not to crush it. Six bikinis in varying hues lay folded inside the crown. More unwrapping revealed a pair of impractical but oh-so-cool cropped linen pants, a more formal ivory silk dress, lingerie, and so many tops she wondered if they were staying for a month.

"I prefer you nude," he said. "But in our restaurants, you'll have to wear clothes. Health codes."

She gasped. "We're going to a nudist colony?"

"Not exactly."

He was joking, right? "Only if you have SPF 100. If I burn in certain places, it will put a damper on how I'm going to thank you for this." She lifted the green dress, not willing to wait another second to feel that delightful fabric on her skin.

She relished the feel of the diaphanous cloth that slipped over her body in an airy tease. She instantly felt more resorty. She twirled—as much as she could in the space—and the asymmetrical hemline lifted.

"Shoes should be on the bottom," he said.

Indeed, the suitcase revealed more outfit goodness, including two pairs of strappy sandals, a pair of sturdy walking shoes and two rather ornate flip-flops.

She raised the black pair studded with tiny matching crystals. "Cindy would kill for these."

"Then I'll send her a pair for filling in for you while we're gone."

"Thank you. She's helping me get my little girls ready for their recital. Hey, you're coming, right? Amber wants to know when you're bringing the pink ice cream." She pulled off the dress, wanting to try the bikinis next.

"I like those pink nipples. Bring them closer." His gaze raked over her bare torso. Her panties—the only thing she had on—dampened.

"You have a one-track mind." She climbed up onto the bed and over his legs. "But I like the way you think." She reached for his zipper, but he grasped her wrists.

"Samantha. Permission."

"You don't want…?"

"I do want. But from this moment forward, we're going to do things a little differently." The blue in his eyes turned a ferocious gray. "Ask me."

"Please sir, may I have some more?" she asked in her best Dickensian cockney accent.

Lucky

She moved to sit up but his grasp behind her neck stopped her rise. "Yes, ballerina. You may have some more. In fact, in coming days we're going to explore a whole lot more." His words were slow, as if he meted them out for emphasis. His face held no smugness or humor.

"Lean back on your heels."

He released his hold and she settled her butt on her ankles. Her nipples pebbled in the cool air conditioning, but the rest of her warmed under his regard. The short distance between them was uncomfortable. When had she gotten so used to constant contact with him, some part of her body pressed against his, even if just fingertips?

He reached over to the small nightstand next to the bed and opened a drawer. He lifted a small robin's egg blue box wrapped in a white ribbon.

Tiffany. God, let her not have said that out loud.

"To complete your outfit." He handed the box to her.

She untied the bow on the grosgrain ribbon. In the case was a set of diamond drop earrings.

"Oh, my." She'd never had real diamonds before. "They're beautiful."

"Put them on."

She unhooked her plain gold hoops and glided the silver wire through her ear. The diamond's weight instantly made her feel more sophisticated and expensive—if someone could feel that way.

His eyes smiled at her. "You make those look good. In fact, maybe that's all you should wear this week."

"I know you're kidding."

"I'm not. Let me look at you." He put his hands behind his head. "Samantha, in a minute I'm going to ask you to take off my belt."

Oh, yes, please.

"First, though, I might just enjoy that smile you're giving me."

She felt her cheeks lift even higher as he smiled in return. "Whatever you'd like, sir."

His body shifted as if settling into his lean against the headboard more. "The sir is a good start."

"To what?"

"To your journey to my side of the world." He sat forward and took her hand. "Starting right now, you no longer have to concern yourself with anything that's happening in DC. You only have to be here. Right now, in the moment."

"I'll try. I'm not good at slowing down."

"I gather that. But this week, I'm going to open up your world, show you places you may not have known existed. Slowing down is part of that. Willing to try?"

"I'm pretty sure you could get me to try anything."

"That's good." His low chuckle made her skin prickle. She loved hearing him happy. She also wanted him to do things to her—things he'd alluded to with half promises.

"Even tying me up." She might as well lob it out there for the hundredth time.

"Hmmm. Eager."

She studied her fingers, now twisting as if that would keep her from asking what she wanted to ask. "Ever since I talked with Christiana…"

He lifted her gaze with one fingertip under her chin. "Go on."

"I've been thinking back. Right from the start, I knew she was different. London Drake, too. They remind me of those women I saw at Accendos. Confident. Gratified. So sure about themselves and their life. I'm not being very articulate."

"You are." He laid his hand over her nervous fingers, stilling them.

Lucky

"It's like they've been loved all the way through to the other side."

He cocked his head. "Interesting way to put it."

"It's something my grandmother used to say to me. *I love you all the way through.*"

He didn't say anything, just nodded once. "You want that."

"Doesn't everyone?"

"Perhaps. What you see in Christiana and London is deep trust. They trust the men in their lives will take care of all their needs. So, I have a question for you. Do you trust me?"

"Yes."

He leaned back. "Then take off my belt."

The sudden turn in their conversation gave her a jolt. Take off his belt? What did giving him a blow job—his obvious ploy—have to do with anything?

"Trust me." One side of his face lifted into a smile. He settled his hands behind his head. Her gaze settled on his trim waist that she knew tapered into a perfect Adonis belt. Her fingers reached the flesh-warmed metal of his belt buckle. Oh, she wanted to be that lucky buckle.

Once his trousers were unfastened, instinct told her to wait before proceeding.

His eyes blazed. "Keep going."

With eager fingers, she slipped his cock free. She cradled his hardness in her hand and discovered his erection anew. Deep, fleshy red skin stretched taut over his length. How something could be both hard and soft was a wonder. Her eyes remained on him for longer than she'd ever stared at any man's anatomy. Before Derek, she'd never considered this part of a man beautiful. She could see beauty now.

The smooth crown of his head begged for attention. As she ran a fingertip around the circumference, a long exhale from him gratified her. Her touch affected him. He hardened more in her hand.

She'd given blowjobs in the past, usually an act to revive a man's sexual interest after too much alcohol or when she didn't feel like having sex but was afraid to appear frigid. Now, her wants in the past meant nothing. No, she hadn't truly *wanted* before Derek.

She drew closer. His musky scent made her mouth water, and an urge to take him between her lips overcame her senses. When her tongue finally made contact with his bulging crown, moisture from the small slit slid over her lips. She sucked him fully inside, lifting her lashes to watch its hopeful effect.

"Christ." His back bowed slightly.

She pushed and pulled his length over her lips, slowly. She sucked. She ran her tongue on the underside, tasting every ridge and vein.

His hands grasped the sides of her face and stilled her movements. "Remember, Iceland. Hold both hands up if you can't speak it when you need to."

His statement registered just as he slammed his hips upward sending his cock deep. Her traitorous gag reflex seized her throat.

"Just breathe." He stroked her hair. Twin tears escaped her eyes and ran down her cheeks. Still, he didn't pull out.

"Trust me," he growled.

There were those familiar words—not spoken like a question, but not a direction either. She understood. He was giving her the choice to either understand he wouldn't hurt her, or believe he might.

He eased out so she could get some air. Just as her lungs filled, he pushed back in even further as if testing her choke response. She willed her throat to relax even though his grip on her head increased.

His cock flattened her tongue and she let him go farther than she'd ever let a man go. As he breached that boundary,

Lucky

the muscles in her pussy contracted and rippled to her clit. She grasped his hips and moaned against his invasion. Vibrations ran over her lips when the sound escaped her throat.

"Oh, baby. Your mouth is so fucking hot." His words made *her* hot. She couldn't speak with her mouth so full of his cock. She could only *take* whatever he gave.

Something in her mind flipped over at that realization. She was taking, too. She received him as her choice. She could shut down this activity at any point. A flood of power surged over the fact she held his most vulnerable part engaged in an act so intimate that in some parts of the world it remained illegal. Yet there she was, freely enjoying him and enjoying her effect on him.

He moved out for her to breathe again. He didn't push in immediately, as if testing her resolve.

"I'm going to fuck your mouth, ballerina."

She flicked the crown of his cock with her tongue, and he got the message. *Go ahead.*

His hips thrust upwards in understanding what she wanted. She wanted him to use her—all of her.

Years ago, before she'd been so concerned about marriage and family, she'd had secret fantasies like this, of being stripped down to her skin and taken, of being *made* to do things. Somewhere along the way, she'd shelved those desires. Why?

"Coming. Soon. Fuck, I'm going to come." A warm, salty flow of liquid spurted down her throat. Drops of fluid leaked down her chin, following gravity. She didn't care. She greedily sucked on him, milking every last drop.

His hold on her head loosened, and his cock slipped free of her clasping mouth. She felt the loss and didn't like it.

"Are you okay?" he asked.

Her lips felt bruised, her throat raw, her cheeks sticky

with his fluid, but she was more than okay. She felt used, but potent.

So this is what Christiana, London, and all those women she'd seen during her quick trek through the Library at Accendos felt. To be the object of such focused attention was addicting.

She licked her lips and climbed his body. He grasped the back of her neck and pulled her in for a kiss. His tongue thrust where his cock had stretched her so brutally, rudely exploring every part of her mouth as if he owned it. He did.

Something else inside her loosened and gave into the inevitable. She would be helpless in Derek's wake. This man not only made her crave things she'd only imagined before but sated those cravings. His attention didn't feel dangerous, either. Instead, for the first time in eons, she trusted a man—*this* man. He was decent, wild, and something straight from a dream. She vowed right then and there that she'd learn more about Derek during this trip, because she was *all in.*

24

When the buzzer went off on the nightstand, Samantha startled in his arms. She'd drifted easily into sleep after Derek had ferociously fucked her mouth. Who could blame a man? After she'd leaned over him, eyeing his cock as if she wanted to devour him, he'd let his animal instincts take over. He'd laid claim to that rosebud mouth, stretching her lips brutally and ramming himself home repeatedly. She didn't look worse for the wear, a good sign for the week's plans.

Karen's voice drifted into the room via speaker after he hit the button. "Sir, we're about to land. May I suggest getting back to your seat?"

"You may."

Samantha lifted her dreamy eyes to his.

"Good morning," he said.

She answered by snuggling her face into his neck with a little mewl of contentment. His cock twitched alive at the sound. *Huh*. This cuddle thing wasn't so bad.

After they tidied themselves and he chose the yellow sundress for her to put on next, they emerged from the cabin. Karen smiled at them, and Samantha flushed from head to toe. Ah, well, Karen's discretion was locked in. By the looks of her bored expression, she knew exactly what had just gone on despite the fact she hadn't seen him with anyone in over a year.

They silently settled into their seats and buckled seatbelts. Sleep still lingered in Samantha's eyes as she peered out the small oval window to her right. Her peaceful face strengthened his understanding. She'd fit into this lifestyle well. Already he felt better about his decision to take Samantha away from Washington and the myriad of obligations that town held for them both.

This coming week could be pivotal. For her, she'd see what life could be like outside the one she'd likely designed as a little girl while she played house with her dolls. For him, he'd be able to focus and assess her ability to slip into a world that could hold so much. A woman hadn't kept his interest this long in years.

The jet landed as smoothly as it could given a severe crosswind over the runway. With any luck, the tropical storm predicted for next week would skirt St. Thomas and the usual sunshine and clear blue skies would greet them every morning. He didn't want to return to DC too soon.

He'd told Barton & Sons construction if they got Samantha's studio done while they were gone—and no chintzing on quality—he'd pay double their bid. He couldn't wait to show off his surprise—a brand-new studio in her building of choice.

Buying the commercial building where she wanted to expand and move wasn't hard. Due to the state of the building, the current owner's suspicion of Derek's generous offer was well warranted. Older commercial real estate wasn't easy to move in DC. Still, the man wisely agreed to sell on the spot. Derek chuckled to himself. What was the fun of having money if you couldn't make problems disappear?

Lucky

Despite his earlier decision to stay out of her expansion plans, he couldn't wait until she saw the three dance rooms with floor-to-ceiling mirrors and, thanks to opening up the ceiling tiles, all the best rigging to hang any apparatus in any room. The expansion included a full dressing room with five makeup stations and a wall of lockers, a storage closet for all those feathery things, a private office with a new state-of-the-art computer, printer, and scanner, and a small kitchenette. Also being installed was a significant security system to include indoor and outdoor cameras. She could operate rent-free for a while. Hell, forever, if he had his way. He didn't need rent. He needed her happy.

When he'd called Cindy to share his plans, she erupted into those squeals women were so fond of making. He'd had to tell her in case new signs indicating the building's change of management went up. He never underestimated women's observation skills, especially when it came to their territory. Cindy swore she wouldn't tell and began babbling about a special open house. He let her go on, amused by her enthusiasm. He looked forward to a similar reaction from Samantha. A major stress point in her life would be eliminated for good.

The jet door popped open and warm, tropical air scented by jet fuel mixed with salty sea wind gushed in. He'd never grow tired of that sultry hit whenever he visited, which wasn't nearly often enough. Perhaps he and Samantha would make quarterly visits, something he swore he'd do but hadn't in recent years.

The engine's roar from outside filled the cabin. Once the stairs were wheeled into place, Derek held Samantha's arm as they descended to their waiting Jeep.

"Karen," he called up. "Thanks. Just send our luggage on."

"She knows where to send it?" Samantha asked as she settled into the passenger seat.

"She knows everything." He shrugged off his jacket, rolled

up his shirtsleeves, and jumped into the front seat. Before starting up the engine, he glanced over at her and was pleased to see her eyes reflecting excitement. "Ready?"

She stretched in her seat, sending her arms into the sunshine. "More than ready."

The drive to the Regal Crown took less than thirty minutes. Samantha kept rising from her seat, peering over the cliff's edge they drove along as if they'd pitch over any minute. After the tenth time he told her to sit back and enjoy the view, she finally returned her fine ass to the seat and relaxed.

A rush of attendants met them when they pulled up. His brother, Bret, jogged down the steps and threw them his famous blinding smile. He helped Samantha from the Jeep. "Samantha Rose, so we finally meet. I finally get why my brother wanted to stay in Washington." He kissed her hand.

"All right, Casanova. Where's Ava?" Derek pounded his back in a brotherly hug.

"Finally!" Ava swept down the stairs, her dark hair curls bouncing with each step. "You're here! You're here!"

"Wow, Ava, the islands look good on you." Derek returned her embrace.

She mock punched him. "Flatterer."

"Meet my favorite dancer, Samantha."

Ava directed an equally dazzling smile at her. "Hi. I'm Ava. Derek's sister-in-love."

"Hi, Sam."

Bret drew Ava closer to him. "Man, Derek, you've got Frank and Carly all excited." He turned to Samantha. "They're the lead concierge team. They love to serve beautiful women."

"Let them know they're off the hook. We only need access to the Rig Hut and our room."

Bret glanced at him sideways. "You got it, big brother."

Lucky

Ava hooked Sam's arm and led her up the wide steps. "If you need anything, and I mean anything, call me. Just pick up any phone and tell the operator 'Samantha calling for Ava.' They'll connect you to my private cell right away."

"Thank you. Do you have a spa? I could use a pedicure. I wasn't prepared for this weather."

"Consider it done. The champagne and rose pedicure is the best, and…" Ava's voice disappeared as the women grew out of earshot.

Derek held back with Bret as the women entered the main hall. He got a glimpse of Samantha's appreciative glance at the large glass mermaid sculptures gracing the center of the large lobby fountain.

"So, Samantha." Bret eyed Derek up and down.

"Yeah."

"Man, you could use some sun. That lily-white skin'll blind our guests."

"All work and no play."

"The Rig Hut will cure that."

Derek hoped so. Introducing Samantha to rope bondage had to be carefully handled. Being tied up by cheap, easily-torn boas and silks were one thing. Being suspended mid-air by unbreakable ropes was an entirely different matter.

Bret threw him one of his signature grins. Perhaps that's why Samantha's smile had hit him with such force. Bret was the only person he trusted outside of himself, so meeting someone with an equally guileless smile calmed his nerves.

"So, Samantha's into—"

"Still exploring."

"One wrap at a time, big brother."

He had that right.

25

Samantha paused in the entranceway of their suite. And she thought *Frost* was over the top. Derek's footfalls echoed on the marble flooring as he made his way through the wide foyer and jogged down two steps into a large living room that could seat thirty people.

Before following him further inside, she stopped at the large, colorful painting that hung in the hall. A winged woman lay on her back with a dog standing on top of her.

"It's an Orestes Gaulhiac original. Cuban artist. You like?" Derek beamed over at her.

"Sure."

He frowned at her response. Guess her real feelings showed on her face. She liked all forms of art, but this one perplexed her. Rich people and their odd art always had.

She continued further into the room, taking in the ivory, taupe, and teal decor. A long marble rectangle dominated the center of the room, a long row of flames dancing through its center. A bank of floor-to-ceiling windows looking over the turquoise ocean below caught her eye. She had to get closer.

"The water is so blue."

Lucky

Derek's hands descended on to her shoulders. "Nothing like the Potomac."

"I'll say." The dirty gray river that ran through DC looked cold and muddy year round to the point that she didn't register the Potomac as water at all—more like liquid steel.

"I have an idea." He turned her to face him. "Let's go for a swim."

"They don't have sharks here, do they?"

"I'm pretty sure the ocean has everything and the wildlife go wherever they want. But rest assured, nobody gets to bite you but me."

A slight pang hit between her thighs, but when a trickle of sweat trailed down her back from the humidity, the idea of a swim trumped any other desire.

After Derek selected the black and white bikini as his choice for her afternoon wear, he disappeared into the bathroom only to emerge wearing a pair of surfer jams in a red and white flower pattern. She'd have laughed if he didn't look like a surfing god in them. Did this man ever model? He could pull off any look, any item of clothing, depicting instant cool.

"Samantha?" Derek lifted her chin, which had drifted south as he grew nearer. "See something you like?"

The sizeable bulge behind the tie-string closure of his suit drew her eyes like a tractor beam. He'd turned her on so quickly and thoroughly on the plane yet she hadn't orgasmed. At the time, she'd relished in a strange power over not having one. Odd, she supposed. Serving him had been enough. But now?

"Those swim trunks seem happy to see me. I mean ... " When she cupped his cock, a tangible, growing hardness met her palm.

"You're in the room. Of course I'm getting hard." A shock of reddish blond hair fell over his forehead as he stared down at her hand, which curiously had grown a mind of its own. She slipped her fingers inside the waistband and down, down, down until she met the soft hair dusting his balls. *Yes, so beautiful.*

"So you're eager to be tied and bound?" he asked.

Her gaze shot up. "With you, I am."

This man called up desires in her she hadn't names for—like bondage. Such a thing hadn't been in her choreography, ever. Now she couldn't stop thinking about it. Was that part of his ploy? Dangle a carrot and see if she'd lean in for a bite?

One side of his mouth lifted in an amused yet skeptical half smile. "That's good, but consent goes both ways."

"You don't want—"

"I want more than you can possibly imagine. Get on the bed. Assume the position." His voice, rough and edgy, brooked no room for disobedience.

As she crawled to the center of the king-sized bed, she felt a pull on her back and fabric fell toward her elbows. He'd untied her bikini top. Such a boy.

"Hand it to me." Slipping off the top, she handed him the two small triangles of fabric. "Present your hands."

It took him less than ten seconds to bind her wrists with her top, have her flat on her back, legs spread wide, with arms overhead. By the time he was finished, she was in a state of wet longing, as she always grew under this man's unorthodox handling. Oh, who was she to call something unconventional, especially when that *something* had her panting in seconds?

He hooked her bikini bottom and forcibly jerked them down and off. "God, I like seeing you bound."

"At your mercy?" *Yes, please.* She tugged on her wrists and the pressure ratcheted up her lust. How did he so thoroughly bind her with essentially eight inches of stretchy material?

Lucky

"How does it feel?" His eyes glanced up at her captured wrists.

"Different. Good. Add it to my 'yes' list."

He chuckled over how quickly she'd answered. Heat flashed across her chest and a slight pulsing grew low in her belly at the flash in his gorgeous eyes.

After clicking on a ceiling fan overhead, he climbed down her body and split open her legs. The motion was so lasciviously possessive, she moved from a state of desire to a female in raging heat. The dark thick lust between her legs made her quiver. She wanted to rub her nipples against his chest, wrap her legs around him, be filled everywhere by him. *God, please fuck me.*

His mouth descended on her pussy and garbled cries bubbled up from her throat from the immediate intensity. No warm-up, his lips and tongue worked her savagely. Without warning her orgasm arose like a tsunami and submerged her in pleasure.

Before her insides could stop contracting, he thrust inside her with brutal, welcomed force. God, she was so full of him. Pillows dropped off the bed, sheets bunched and the headboard racked against her hands as she steadied herself. His hot mouth clamped down on hers and inhaled groans she was incapable of stopping. Once more he laid claim over her body, and she willingly allowed it.

Their skin grew slick and the room filled with their panting and the click-click of the fan rotating overhead. The slight breeze produced from the blades whispered over her skin in sharp contrast to his large hands gripping her ass tightly, as if he needed the leverage to push himself deeper inside. *Yes, go deeper.* Her heels dug into the small of his back. If she could inhale Derek, she would. She'd never been so physically close to another human being before, and it still wasn't close enough.

He didn't come for a long time. She, on the other hand, didn't hold back. At some point he released her mouth and stared down at her, a look of pure adoration etched across his face.

"Welcome to the Caribbean," he said. "I'm glad you came."

She burst out laughing at his double entendre and the spark of happiness in his eyes.

She reached up and cradled his face with her hands. "You should pass on these eyes. They keep changing color. Sometimes they're blue. Then, green. Sometimes gray. It was one of the first things I noticed when I met you."

"And here I thought you were after my performance space."

"Oh, I want that, too."

"You want it all, huh?" He lifted himself off her and released her wrists.

"If it involves you, yes."

Hesitation crossed his eyes but vanished as quickly as it appeared. "You have a fantastic smile, Samantha Rose." He cradled her wrists as if checking them.

"It's not my best feature."

"I'll be the judge of that." He eased off the bed and held out his hand. "Come. Shower, then pool, then your toe massage—"

"Pedicure."

"And then dinner." He flashed her a brilliant smile as he pulled her to standing. "This resort has many more offerings you have yet to sample. I plan on acquainting you with extreme pleasure this week, ballerina."

Extreme pleasure. Perhaps that could be enough.

~

The fading afternoon's sunshine slanted over her body as she drifted weightlessly on her back, bobbing in water as warm as a freshly drawn bath. A slow current floated her through the maze of man-made tributaries that comprised *Regal's* pool.

Derek coasted alongside her, his hand gripping hers possessively.

"Why are you giggling?" he asked.

"Otter families do that, ya know. They hold hands while drifting in the water. Guess they want to stick together."

"Hmm." His low grumble held contentment. The man had come twice that afternoon, which was half of what he'd given her. She'd never considered herself multi-orgasmic. Of course, her old self didn't have a man whose sex drive proved relentless and whose talent for arousing her was matchless.

"You have a lot of energy." She corrected herself, not meaning to sound so dismissive. "I mean, you don't seem tired after we messed around so much."

He laughed heartily. "Messed around?"

She splashed him, embarrassed she hadn't come up with something more original.

"You have no idea how much messing I plan to do with you, my prima ballerina." He pulled her into an embrace, righting them so their toes touched the bottom. The current still continued to pull their bodies forward. The sunshine vanished and they found themselves inside a cave-like structure. The current stilled. He pulled her to two stools, submerged underwater in front of a long bar cut into the rock. As if on cue, a man stepped through a hidden door in the gray surface.

"Mr. Wright, what can I get you and your beautiful friend?"

"Samantha?"

"Grapefruit juice. What? It's low-calorie. I'd rather eat."

"I'll have the same, Fred, only add a shot of tequila." He smiled at her. "It's one of life's pleasures."

"You're good at pleasure."

"I'll let you try some if you're a good girl."

"What if I'm a bad girl? You remember what happened the last time we were together in a pool," she whispered into his ear.

The crack of a can caught her attention. Fred smiled at her as he poured golden liquid into a tall glass full of ice. He set it in front of her.

"Next time I'll squeeze some fresh for you." He winked.

Derek's muscled forearms surrounded her waist and pulled her onto his lap.

"That's all, Fred. Thank you." He frowned.

The bartender disappeared through the hidden door.

"You don't like him."

"I do. I don't like the way he ogled you."

"He was just being nice."

"I recognize not-so-nice thoughts."

"Is that what you're having, now that I'm in your lap?"

"Here." He lifted his drink to her lips. "Tell me if you like this."

She took a sip and wrinkled her nose at the acidic tang.

"You don't like it."

"It's, um… " No, she didn't like it, but she did like the idea of warming to something he enjoyed. Perhaps the more she sampled, the better it would taste. When he reached for the glass, she held fast.

"Greedy, are we?" he asked with a lazy smirk.

"For whatever you're having." She downed another full swallow, proud of herself for not wincing.

He watched her as she continued to sip. "Samantha, you don't have to like what I do. You need to be forthcoming with me or we won't get anywhere."

Lucky

Where are we going? Had she said that out loud? Thank God, no, she hadn't. It would sound like the typical annoying ploy to ferret out the direction of the relationship. The tequila must be going straight to her brain. She did feel a little woozy all of a sudden.

She was in the Caribbean on the lap of a hot Viking, her legs still tired from the multiple orgasms of a mere hour ago. Not the time to launch an interrogation—despite the dozen questions sitting on the tip of her tongue.

What was your childhood like? Who's your best friend? How did you meet Alexander? How did you get into bondage? Have you ever brought anyone else here?

Yeah, she would definitely *not* ask that last one. She wasn't stupid.

Who was your last girlfriend and was your break-up horrible? Why are you so certain about not having a family of our own?

She shook off the questions, telling her brain to shut up. Tequila was officially on her make-me-crazy list. The grotto's pool water lapped lightly against the cave-like walls, making the silence that stretched between them more pronounced.

"What else do you like besides tequila?" *There.* She'd settle for an easy question.

"You." His hand gripped her knee.

"What do you like about the Caribbean?"

"Seeing you in a bikini."

"I thought you preferred me naked."

"Only when we're alone. But if you'd like to go to the nude side—"

"Do you like owning resorts?"

"Full of questions today, aren't we?"

You have no idea.

"Okay." He set his empty glass down and turned to her. "The Caribbean. What's not to love? Great food, warm people, sunshine. This is one of my favorite places on earth."

The relief from learning *anything* about this man was more than ridiculous, but she'd still take whatever scrap of information she could.

"It is peaceful ... and quiet," she said.

"It's adults only."

"You seem to be so certain about that ... no children, I mean."

Was she crazy or did that make him flinch?

"Yes, I'm certain." He swirled the ice in his empty glass and turned to her. His gaze pinned her with his intense eyes. "Because, Samantha Rose..." He eased her off his lap and stood, pulling her with him. "When it's adults only, I can do this." He twisted her and repositioned her on his lap facing outward. The ocean view rose in the grotto's open mouth. Waves curled and climbed the sand.

"And you can have this view"—his breath whispered over her damp skin—"while I do this." His fingers slipped down toward her crotch and did their own curling—around her clit.

Oh, God, his fingers should be registered as a weapon, because they obliterated any of those stupid, negative thoughts and questions from her mind.

"You are such a tease, Derek Wright." Her words were no more than a breath.

Ripples formed all around them in the water as she undulated slightly against his hand.

"Feel good?"

Not even close to good, she thought. *Off the charts.* Despite being sore from their earlier sex, she *almost* came.

He abruptly stopped his machinations when Fred stepped back through the hidden door in the fake rock.

He eased her off his lap. "Must be time for your pedicure, ballerina."

"Is it three thirty already? I hope they have food."

He pushed wet hair off her forehead. "They will. I told them to stock chocolate just for you. Then we'll go to an early dinner in time to catch the sunset."

"My hero." She pecked him on the cheek.

Yes, he was heroic. She shelved any lingering discontent about Derek being so private and not sharing much about himself. He'd open up to her later. Besides, she had an idea for a surprise at dinner. Something she was sure he'd love.

26

Derek pulled out a chair and Samantha nestled into the soft cushion. Her stomach gave an unladylike growl.

"Hungry?" Derek's eyes did that twinkly thing she loved.

"How can you tell?" She was starved. After some afternoon swim time and a minuscule late lunch consisting of chocolate and fruit during her and Ava's decadent pedicures, she could eat a cow for dinner.

She gazed at the water. "It's beautiful here."

The sun had begun to set behind the tinted glass of their private dining alcove—one of several that made up *Liaisons*, the most unique restaurant she'd ever seen. Derek had told her the design was his brother's brainchild. The pride in his voice over Bret's achievement was unmistakable. She could see why.

Liaisons sat at the end of a pier jutting so far out into the ocean they had to take a golf cart to reach the end. Heaven forbid women had to walk the seven hundred feet in high-heeled sandals over sun-bleached planking. The trip was worth the extra effort. Each alcove promised a spectacular view of the orange sun slipping into the ocean and dolphin fins cutting the turquoise water.

"You and your brother certainly like making a statement." She hoped her tone came across as she meant—appreciative and not admonishing.

Pride once again flicked across Derek's face as he circled to his chair.

"You have other brothers and sisters? I hadn't asked."

"It's just Bret and me."

"What about your father?"

"Dead. Got a string of stepfathers, but I don't see them." Derek snapped his napkin in place and leaned back. "How adventurous do you feel? Do you like sushi?"

"Never had it."

The curtains rustled and a man in formal wear smiled down on them. "Ah, Mr. Wright, Miss Rose, I understand your palate demands sushi tonight. Excellent choice, as the boat docked today with some extra special selections."

"Aldo, have the chef put together whatever is freshest. Samantha has never had sushi."

The waiter gasped.

"Would you have sushi for the first time in DC?" she asked the incredulous-looking Aldo.

"You have shown remarkable restraint, mademoiselle. After tonight, you'll demand only the best." He disappeared behind the curtain.

"You're spoiling me." She fiddled with her diamond drop earring.

"More like acquainting you with a lifestyle you should grow accustomed to."

Derek lifted a bottle of wine from a sweating ice bucket. "I hope you don't mind. This Sancerre is one of our finest white wines."

"I'll have some." She cocked her head toward his disbelieving stare. "I do drink sometimes. Only not when I'm performing, and unless you're going to demand another impromptu dance…"

"Oh, you're going to dance." He poured her a small glass. "Just not the way you're used to."

"Like I said, such a tease."

"Says the woman who likely invented it. That dress should be illegal. I should order you to take off your panties. Right here."

"I'm not wearing any." *Surprise.*

His gaze lifted from the bottle he held.

She'd walked the length of the hallway from their suite, through the lobby and the restaurant sure a breeze would catch her short hemline at any minute and reveal her bare ass. It hadn't, but the uncertainty had been killing her—until now. The look on his face was worth the risk.

"Good. I'm taking you some place tomorrow."

"Any clues?" She tamped down the urge to bounce in her seat.

"It's something you asked for." He lifted his chin. "Now, show me."

Her lips parted. Before she could protest, he leaned back in his chair and said, "Go on."

She flipped up her skirt to show one bare hip.

"More, Samantha."

She glanced at the curtain, her ears straining for an approaching Aldo. Hearing nothing, she stood and lifted the front of her skirt to bare her sex to him.

His eyes narrowed approvingly as one finger ran over his lips. "I might have you for dessert. Back up, ballerina. I'll tell you when you can lower your skirt."

She stood before him for more minutes, her pussy clenching as he ran his gaze over every inch of what she presented. She bit back the teasing retort that sat on her tongue. Instead, she let herself feel the full weight of his admiration.

His eyes darted up to her face. "Thank you, Samantha. You may sit."

After she took her seat, he slipped a long turquoise box with a white ribbon in front of her. More Tiffany?

She lifted her gaze and found Derek smiling at her. "Having you walk around with just earrings wasn't fair."

Inside the box lay a sparkling, diamond tennis bracelet.

"Derek, I..." She, what? She'd never met anyone so generous.

"You aren't going to say you couldn't possibly."

"Oh, no. Thank you. It's so much."

Maybe diamonds were de rigueur for him, but she now officially owned more real jewelry than she'd touched in her life. Even her grandmother's jewels were paste. *In case I lose them while dancing*, she'd always said. Samantha knew the truth. Dancers weren't exactly rolling in cash.

"Samantha?" He frowned.

She was being rude. She lifted the bracelet and presented her wrist to him. "It's amazing. Put it on me?"

After the bracelet was secured, she took a moment to watch the yellow-orange light from the setting sun sparkle over the jewels. His gift was spectacular.

"I think you do like it."

She gazed into eyes that held an unsettling hesitancy.

"I do." She jumped out of her chair, circled the small table and threw her arms around him. *"You* are amazing."

He honest-to-God blushed a little.

The curtain blew backward announcing Aldo's return. She instinctively drew her skirt down as she returned to her seat. Aldo set a tray between them, swirls of sauces making intricate patterns around bits of fresh fish and curlicues of ginger and cucumber.

"Thank you, Aldo." With chopsticks, Derek placed two pieces on her plate. "Start with the mahi-mahi. It's mild."

She was finally going to see what all the fuss was about sushi.

After several attempts she managed to lift the lump between two chopsticks and get it to her mouth. The cold flesh hit her tongue. The taste reminded her of stale river water. On second thought, more like exactly what it was. *Raw fish*. A quick gulp of wine forced the fish down her throat. She took another sip. And another, until all the taste was gone.

Derek placed another piece on her plate. "Tuna. It was likely swimming hours ago."

She lifted her chopsticks. A vision of scales and fins hit her mind the second she bit down on the dark pink fish. She was going to retch. More sips of wine did little to rinse the ocean from her mouth.

"Now the octopus." He placed a white and pink spiny looking piece of rubber on her plate.

She knew she couldn't do it, but he was watching her. She lifted the rubbery piece. Her stomach roiled as she placed it in her mouth. Tears stung her eyes, and an involuntary gag reflex spit the octopus out. It landed left of her plate onto the tablecloth.

"I'm sorry." She pressed her napkin to her lips and then reached for more wine.

"No. Don't apologize, but you do owe me something."

She looked up at him, a little frightened at his vehement tone. "What?"

"You need to tell me you don't like sushi."

"I hate it."

"I could tell from the first bite, you weren't a fan." He leaned back and appraised her. "Why did you eat the second piece?"

Lucky

"I didn't want to disappoint you."

"The truth never disappoints me. You also don't like tequila or that painting hanging in my suite."

She slowly shook her head. "Sorry."

"Don't be."

Aldo slipped through the curtain once more and placed a small plate of pasta in cream sauce in front of her.

"I ordered this for you," Derek said.

"Thank you." At least she recognized this dish. "You expected I wouldn't like sushi?"

"I had no idea what you'd think. That's the point. Tonight, and every night, you will tell me exactly what you're thinking. This isn't about whether *I* like it or not. It's what works for both of us."

She felt a sliver of hope that she hadn't scared him off with the whole children conversation. Perhaps he wouldn't mind questions after all. She just hadn't found the right timing.

She lifted a small forkful of pasta and bit into it. Juicy spices exploded in her mouth. "I like this."

He chuckled.

In silence, she finished every last bite of her dish and sipped on her wine. With more in her stomach, she was in no danger of getting drunk, a state she didn't entertain ever. She still felt woozy. It had to be the way he watched her with those ever-shifting eyes. As he lifted bites of sushi to his mouth, he studied her as if concerned she'd like what he offered, despite what he said.

Aldo swished through the curtain one more time. He laid a small plate in the middle of the table and disappeared without a word. A thick caramel sauce draped a small chocolate soufflé surrounded by a puddle of white cream. *Oh, yes.*

"Come here." Derek's voice ripped her gaze away from

the decadent dessert. He scooted his chair back and patted his lap. He wanted her to sit on him? Well, they were alone.

She rose and situated herself on his lap. He swung her so she sat fully on both of his muscled thighs, her feet dangling over the edge. One sandal slid off and hit the floor with a *plunk*. His fingers slipped under her hemline and possessively cradled her bare hip.

He lifted a spoon, scooped up a generous portion of the chocolate soufflé, and held it in the air. "For every truthful answer, you get a bite." He lifted it to her lips.

Heaven burst in her mouth. He set the spoon down.

"Truth equals chocolate?" she asked. Finally, they were going to talk?

"Now you're getting it. Tell me, what else is dancing in that pretty head of yours? Something's been on your mind today."

Earlier she'd almost initiated the whole "Where are we going?" conversation. Now, on his lap, feeling his muscles under her bare ass, she had something completely different on her mind.

"During our pedicures earlier, Ava said something." *Just say it already.* "She called you and Bret 'special guys with special tastes,' and said I should come to her for anything. It was the third time she'd said something like that, so I could tell she expected I'd need her. I flat-out asked: *You mean for bruises?*"

"And?" His face was unreadable. He scooped up more chocolate and brought it to her mouth.

After swallowing, she licked her lip. "She said, quote, *Or rope burns*, unquote."

"If you get burned, I'm doing it wrong."

"Is that the surprise?" She hadn't meant to sound so breathless. Only ever since he mentioned tying her up and then binding her in silks in her studio, and then today with her bikini top, the vision of what else he could do hadn't ever fully left her head. This activity was clearly part of his life. One trip to Accendos showed her he was serious about his extra-curricular activities, too.

"What would you say if it was?"

"Good." The word burst forth on the heel of his question, not an ounce of space between them. Yes, she'd wanted to know more about Derek, but after her talk with Ava, something new occurred to her. The best way to get to know the man was to meet him in his world.

Derek wasn't anything like the man she pictured for herself. He was better, albeit a man set in his ways. Maybe she could change his mind someday about children. Hell, George Clooney had, and he'd been the poster child for the "no marriage-no children" movement. Yet even if he didn't, she wanted to be with him, all of him, which included pleasures she hadn't known existed. What was the harm in fully exploring what he offered? She didn't like being left out of any part of his life.

His spoon offered more of the chocolate soufflé, which she took. "Aren't you going to have any?"

"No. This is for you. Everything about this week is going to be about you, about finding your 'yes' list."

"So, you'll…"

"Tomorrow, ballerina. I promise." He didn't need to expound. She understood.

He lifted another spoonful of the warm dessert to her mouth, and she gratefully accepted his offering.

27

"Man, am I glad you called!" Little-girl voices screamed in the background. Saying Cindy sounded harassed was an understatement.

God, she missed her little girls.

"How are my Lyra Ladies?" Samantha leaned against the balcony railing and lifted her face to the sunlight.

"Let's just say when the cat's away the little girl demons come out to play. They listen to you. Me? Not so much. Gabriella is handling them with her mom voice. Creeps me out. Anyhoo, want to tell me why the FBI wants you? Two hot guys in men-in-black suits dropped by flashing wallets of badges or whatever they call them. Derek really is in the Mafia, isn't he?"

Sam would have laughed, cried, and gasped all at once at the rush of Cindy's words if she could have figured out which emotion to feel first. She glanced through the glass doors, taking in Derek's broad shoulders as he faced away from her.

"FBI? What do they want?" She sucked in a sharp breath as her last conversation with Craig arose. "Oh, wait. They probably want to ask me questions for Craig's security clearance stuff. He mentioned it the night we danced at Frost."

"Shit—sorry—I missed the chance to tell them he has a teeny tiny pecker and would totally fit in with Capitol Hill. Next time remind me of these things! I could have soooo made Craig go away."

Samantha laughed. A pang of missing Cindy *and* her Lyra Ladies hit her in the chest.

"They left a card." A rustling came through the phone. "Here it is. Want their number?"

Like she'd call from the Caribbean? "I'll deal with it when I get home."

"Yeah, you're too busy getting laid."

"Getting tan." *And* getting lucky.

"When you get back I might have something to tell you, too." She lowered her voice. "Chaz has been coming by every day. You sure we're not in trouble?"

"No, he must be coming to see you." Or, Derek was being overprotective as usual and wanted to keep an eye on things through his security guy. She'd have to ask him.

"Yeah, right. He is kinda hot, though. Maybe I'll invite him up for some cha-cha. Oh, wait … Amber, no! Listen, the natives are getting restless. Everything's fine, despite the FBI visit. Go get laid. Don't get pregnant. Not at least until you find three more instructors for the influx of requests we've had. The phone's been ringing off the hook. So expect to be busy when you get back. You *are* coming back, right?"

"Promise. In a few days. I trust you. And thanks, Cindy. I really, really—"

"I know, I know. You can't live without me. Just make sure to lock in Derek's interest. He's our good-luck charm."

After ending her call, she took a moment to gaze over the turquoise water from her balcony perch. Despite the fact she'd gotten a visit from the FBI and Chaz was probably directed by Derek to stop by, she did feel lucky. Being warm, rested, and, as Cindy pointed out, well serviced, had amazingly catapulted her into a sense of good fortune.

∼

Derek had always enjoyed living alone. Being drawn into constant conversation, having to work around someone else at the coffee pot and knocking over their stuff in the bathroom had never held any appeal for him. Now his ears strained to hear Samantha if she left the room. Seeing her through the glass oddly comforted him. He was getting used to having a woman around.

Samantha pushed open the balcony door with a soft slide and one of her killer smiles.

"Did you send Chaz to check on Cindy while we're gone?"

"No, why?"

"Oh, my God, that means he *likes* her." She danced from one leg to the other. "He's been dropping by every day since we left. Don't get mad." She held up her hand. "This is a good thing. Cindy's also had bad luck with men. I mean, not that I am now. What I mean is—"

"Slow down," he said. "I'm not mad. Why would I be?"

"That whole never mixing business with pleasure thing, which by the way you've totally broken with me."

Yes, he had.

"I am so happy for her." Samantha's eyes got that dreamy quality that usually had him heading for the hills.

"He hasn't proposed yet."

She crossed her arms but smiled. "Not what I said. It's just nice to have the attention."

"Hmm. Ready to go? Downward dog awaits." He had his

Lucky

own attentive plans for Samantha today, starting with a good limbering yoga session.

"So you really do yoga?"

"For years. Come. Maude is waiting for us. We'll do a session and then"—he scooped her up into his arms—"it's off to your surprise."

~

An hour and twenty-five sun salutations later, any conversation about budding relationships back home were long forgotten. Samantha lazily sat back in her seat on Derek's latest favorite toy, his fifty-foot Aeroboat. The speedboat cut through the water at half its capability, about thirty knots, and he longed to let her loose once out of the safe speed zone.

"Samantha, want to drive?" He had to shout in the wind.

"You seem to be doing fine." Her face was up toward and sun, blissed out from their yoga session.

"Okay, then." He eased the throttle forward and the boat's bow pitched upward as he hit top speed. He heard a delighted squeal from Samantha's direction. Her hair streamed behind her in the wind, her eyes on fire from their increased speed.

"Can you go faster?"

He laughed. This woman barrel-rolled to the floor from twenty-five feet high. "Slow" wasn't in her repertoire.

"I see land." She pointed toward the small island that rose from the water in the distance.

"That's Bret's." He pointed to a second island to the left. "We're going to mine."

"Of course we are." She tried to stand only to land back in the seat once more as the boat bounced over the small waves.

As they neared the island, he slowed and headed to the

short dock to his private island. Given what he planned to do to Samantha today, prudence dictated a guaranteed privacy.

"Is there anything you can't do?" Samantha finally stood. He pulled her between his legs.

"I'm a terrible cook."

"Me, too."

"Good thing I own restaurants then."

"You do?"

He spun the wheel by the heel of his hand. "Six. Take off your bikini top."

"Aren't you getting sick of me being naked?"

"Is that a trick question?"

She untied the top, drew it through her cover-up dress, and hung it over his neck. After slipping the boat alongside the long dock, he tossed her bikini top down into the cabin.

"Hey, I'm going to need that later. There might be people here, ya know."

"Anyone who is here will also be nude, and they will be preoccupied, ballerina. As you will be soon."

While he knew the only people on the island were emergency staff, she needn't know that. Let her think she was being watched, which would add to him having the upper hand.

28

Samantha stood on the dock, clearly in awe of the seemingly untouched white sand beach framed by swaying trees, large rocks, and flowers in a dozen hues of red, yellow, and orange. Its beauty had always had a similar effect on him. It's why he bought the place.

One hundred feet from where they stood, a shadowed, three-walled pavilion rose between several large coconut palm trees. As they walked the short path, yellow Ginger Thomas flowers and red hibiscus blooms swayed lightly in the tropical breeze.

At the small structure's opening, wide louvered panels hung like barn doors between rich brown teak columns. Derek slid them open and beckoned her up the two wide steps. The gentle lapping of the calm afternoon ocean, about fifty feet away, followed them inside.

He breathed in the ocean spray mixed with the scent of caoba wood. *The best scent in the world*. One click of a switch and small red lights glowed from corners and rafters to cast a warm and ominous light. The room was empty.

Face upturned, Samantha examined the high timber frame ceiling and blinked at the ropes and levers hanging from rafters.

"What is this place?"

"Someplace I've wanted to bring you since I first saw you spinning above my stage."

She stepped deeper inside. "Why did you wait?"

"You weren't ready."

"Or maybe you weren't." The lilt at the end of her voice did little to soften her cheekiness.

He chucked her chin. "You have no idea how ready I am now. Strip. Everything off."

Her gaze darted to the beach.

"Don't worry about being nude. It's a clothing optional island."

With a smile, she slipped off her cover-up and kicked her bikini to the side. She was so eager, so willing to please him, like most submissives he'd played with, but her authenticity was unparalleled.

"So this is why we did yoga first. To warm me up."

"Smart as well as beautiful. I needed to know if you had any mobility problems."

"You could have asked."

"I'll be asking many things of you today. Watching you in various poses tells me more than simple words. Go light the candles." He indicated a long table at the end of the room that held a dozen pillar candles in various sizes.

She eyed them and returned her gaze to him. "How romantic." She walked over and did what he asked.

Oh, if she only knew what was coming.

With the flick of another switch, a screen rose revealing mirrors strategically placed on three walls. Samantha didn't say anything about them as she lit the candles with a lighter wand.

He strode to hidden storage areas to his left. One push and a drawer clicked open. He chose six bundles of hemp rope, each with embroidered ends in varying colors. Bret had teased him for the dramatic flourishes. Today, he was glad he'd had the foresight that someday he'd bring a woman here who deserved such adornments.

At the last second, he also drew out two bundles of green and gold ropes. Her legs would look fantastic in a karada, perhaps with double coin knots, the two colors contrasting against her tanned skin.

He dropped the bundles in a pile at his feet in the center of the room and positioned himself under the largest suspension ring.

Samantha's head bowed toward her task, elegant muscles moving in her back as she lit each candle. Watching her move was akin to church. He hadn't a religious bone in his body but if anyone could make him believe in a divine being, it would be Samantha.

Not one inch of rope had touched her skin and already he'd begun to second guess his delay in sharing the pleasures of being bound and suspended. Yet he also knew why he'd waited. From the first moment he'd laid eyes on her body stretched out on a hoop, he'd been captivated. Once he wrapped a single limb, he'd want more and more until he was truly, soundly addicted.

Too late for that. He was already a goner.

"Samantha, come here."

She spun upon hearing him release one hemp bundle in a snap. When her gaze ran down the long rope trail, she licked her bottom lip seductively.

As she sashayed toward him, he looped the unfurled rope once, twice, three times and then hung it around his neck. His cock responded to the light abrasion of the material in his hands—or perhaps it was the way her hips rolled with each step.

With tentative fingers she reached out to touch the rope.

"Turn around."

She jerked her hand back and turned to face away from him. The skin on her arms had risen in gooseflesh despite the tropical air. He picked up another bundle from the floor, his eyes trained on her reflection in the mirror ten feet away. He ran the skein up one arm, over her shoulder to under her chin. He lifted her head with the rope in his hand so she'd be forced to see herself in the mirror. Her eyes locked on his.

"Remember, Iceland," he said.

She laughed. "It's hard to think of an ice-filled continent here."

"Remember it anyway, ballerina. It's important you know how to get out of anything you don't like."

"With you, I don't want to get out of anything." Her face morphed into a thoughtful stare.

He rubbed the rope lightly under her chin. "But know you can. You're going to be honest with me, right?"

She nodded. "Yes."

Alexander and Club Accendos had drilled BDSM protocol into him so thoroughly he naturally gravitated to ensuring spoken consent at every major step. Gaining permission from his past submissives was satisfying. Gaining Samantha's trust, however, filled him with an incomparable pride. She made him want to slow down and take her through experiences deliberately and perfectly, so neither of them would forget the moment.

He picked up another bundle of rope and teased her skin with its rough surface. Up one arm, across her back. and down the other arm.

"Samantha, today, I want you to look like you do when you dance."

Lucky

"How's that?"

"Like you're flying." He roughly rubbed the rope over her nipples, now pebbled and hard.

She gasped. "Everything you do makes me fly."

"We'll see."

He kicked open her legs so he could treat her inner thighs the same way, getting her skin ready to receive. She sucked in a breath when he got close to her crotch.

Her eyes closed and she let her head fall back. That's when he truly began.

"Kneel for me, baby."

∽

Samantha lowered herself to sit on her calves. Her chest expanded as he pulled her arms behind her in a boxed position. With so many mirrors, she could watch him from several angles. She swayed as he roughly wrapped rope around her chest.

He was so fast, looping and snapping the ends of the rope even though he held her close. His chest thumped against her shoulder, and his obvious excitement both invigorated and scared her.

More wraps of rope went around her torso and eventually pinned her arms to her middle back. Oh, God, she was being held in place. She flinched and shuddered as sharp scratches reddened her skin. She wore so much rope she'd grown shackled.

He formed a beautiful knot at her sternum, and as she took in the intricate pattern, her lungs demanded she take a larger breath in response. Constriction stopped her short. The compression only made her want to inhale deeper. *Don't panic.* She willed herself to steady her breathing as she did before a performance.

"Rise up on your knees." More rope encased her hips and thighs. Oddly, being fully nude felt less naked than wearing the rope harnesses he now formed.

His capable hands didn't show an ounce of hesitation as he crouched behind her, looping, tying, drawing more rope up, over and through her bindings. His consummate skill obvious, he moved swiftly, assuredly, and with growing force. His breath grew more ragged, and arousal tented his thin linen pants. She understood his reactions as her own ramped up. Blood roared in her ears … and everywhere else.

She stopped watching him and tuned into the scratch of the jute, the yanks, the pulls. She'd worked with silks for years, had them wrapped around every limb, hung suspended with no fear, but nothing compared to the bite and restriction she now felt. Exposed, helpless, but oddly cradled by her bounds, a quiet exhilaration from receiving his focused attention built.

He lifted her to standing so quickly, her head rushed with blood. Holding her close, he looped more rope through a large ring overhead. One yank and the tension from the rope overhead took over. She felt she could spin like a top under the secure point.

He smiled down on her, his blazing blue-green eyes making her swoon a little. The rope kept her from falling completely backward. She wasn't too steady on her feet but amazingly she wasn't going to fall, either. *What a strange sensation.*

"Let it go," he said. He put his hands underneath her knees and she let herself lean backward. Her feet lifted from the ground and her body settled into a semi-seated position.

Oh! He'd yanked her right foot backward. After connecting her ankle to the ropes along her back, she placed her other foot back to the ground in a defensive response.

Like a ballerina in an attitude position, she spun with one toe as if in a pirouette.

A single drop of perspiration ran from her throat to between her breasts, provoking a trail of nerve endings. A ripple through her pussy made her whole body ache for a release. If he could run a rope through her slit, she could turn on pointe and rub against it, bring a little relief.

Another strong tug and her other leg lurched upward, both feet now off the ground. Suspended in mid-air, cradled in natural jute rope, she twisted in a pose as if she'd frozen in a ballet leap, facing up to the ceiling. Reality sank in hard. She couldn't move, couldn't touch the ground. Now a little claustrophobic, she made a Herculean attempt to drive out any rising fear that now competed with her heightened arousal.

"Samantha, how does that feel?"

"Good. Strange. Flying." Three words that didn't quite track with her unclear feelings, but nothing else came. Tendrils of heat licked at her skin where the rope bit into her, like invisible teeth holding her in place.

She stared at the large suspension ring as the ropes creaked in time with her sways. She lifted her head to face Derek. He held a long length of green rope.

"This is going to look amazing on you." Deep satisfaction filled his face.

With quick hands, he created a diamond rope pattern up one leg. She watched, fascinated, as he did the same to the other. The slither of the rope as he slid it through small knots produced a cascade of sensation up her legs and spine, while soothing ocean sounds roared in the background. Her ass clenched and her hips moved up and down as if begging for more rope placed *there*.

She peered down at the beautiful pattern on one leg. She pointed her foot and the ropes hugged her tighter. Her vision swam a little, and the room took on a surreal quality, her reflection in the mirror oddly mesmerizing.

Her head hung down, and he turned her so she faced the opening to the water, now upside down in her pose. Red-orange sunlight bounced off waves in the near distance. The setting sun glowed large and wavered in her sights. How much time had passed?

Derek's broad chest filled her vision as he stepped backward as if examining his work. In turn she examined him, from the tanned muscles peeking through his open shirt to the trail of red-gold hair that disappeared into his loose-fitting pants. If only her mouth could reach the drawstring on them, loosen them, so they dropped to the floor revealing the cock she suddenly was desperate to suck into her mouth. With her head now thrown back, she could do it.

He drew closer and his palm touched her cheek. "You're beautiful."

"No, you are." She swallowed back the rising want in her throat. Her jaw ached from desire to suck him inside, her pussy now begging so hard she couldn't stop clenching her thighs so her hips rose.

He circled around her, split her knees wider and pushed himself between them. A small groan escaped her throat as rope bit into her skin more from the shift in position. The scrape of his linen pants against her inner thighs heightened the sensation of her bindings. The feeling also raised up an even greater carnal need.

His clever, strong, magical fingers that she wanted everywhere slipped in between knots and length of rope as if checking their tightness.

He pulled her tightly to him and ground his cock into her crotch. *Oh, yes, please.*

"Now you're mine," he growled.

She raised her gaze and caught his eyes. She'd likely been

his for some time, but while she'd have done anything he asked before, now, hypnotized by his handling, the rope bindings, the tropical air, his ocean-green eyes, he owned her.

Jesus, what would it take for him to fuck her?

29

Derek held on to her foot as he leaned over to retrieve a candle from the table. Her eyes had taken on that faraway quality, alerting him she'd grown rope spacey. Her hips also taunted him, moving and seeking his cock. He needed to bring her back a little, keep her on the edge.

With the candle held high to ensure the first hit of wax wouldn't burn too badly, he dropped white wax on to her foot. She jerked in her bounds, and her beautiful mouth shaped a sharp inhale. He dripped more down her calf until the rope stopped the long rivulets. He'd ruined the ropes—and couldn't care less. Her head rose and her eyes locked on what he was doing. Not smiling, not grimacing, her face showed pure, dreamy fascination.

Her head jerked backward, her hair swishing with her movements, as he dripped more wax.

Soon both legs, her stomach and chest wore the wax, not too much given she wasn't oiled, but enough to keep her edgy, awake, *with him.*

Her whispers brought him back. *More. Tighter.* Experience told him what she truly craved. She wanted more wrapping, more rope—*his* rope. She didn't smile. She didn't need to. She gave him something infinitely greater. Pure need shone from her face.

Cupping her cheek, he bent near her ear. "I have more for you."

He blew out the candle and picked up one last bundle of rope. After snapping it loose, he looped two lengths. He positioned himself between her knees, getting a full view of her weeping cunt. She liked being bound—more than liked it.

With one piece on either side of her swollen clit, he sawed lightly with enough pressure to be uncomfortable but pleasurable. She moaned loudly. No building, no nightclub, nothing he could put into the world could compare to how she responded to him. Was that his ego talking? Fuck, he'd take it.

Next time, he'd rig her in a position so he could take her mouth while he played with her. He didn't want to stifle her cries, rather capture every sound he caused. He'd inhale her orgasm, owning her response fully.

He ran the rope, now wet with her juices, up and down. She jerked, tossed her head. She climaxed quickly, and God love her, she didn't try to hold back her cry.

Bringing her here was right. Today was about the two of them, the ocean lapping feet away, yards of rope weighted in his hands, and her noises.

His mind flashed forward to nights and days of moving her into different positions. An endless list of bindings, suspensions and patterns that would mark her flesh lay before them. He'd secure her to pillars, trees—hell, anything that didn't move, just so he could see her mouth drop into an O, have her face twist in orgasm like it did now.

She'd been up long enough. As much as he could have powered through with a more seasoned rope bunny, it was time to free her. One rope at a time, he released her from her bindings. One leg down and another, righting her so she leaned against his chest. She rested her head on him, bits of cold wax loosening from her legs and belly and falling to their feet.

Once the ropes were yanked free of the suspension hook, her whole weight fell into his hold. He lowered her to the floor as he loosened her leg bindings. As beautiful as the green ropes were, she'd had enough. Skeins of rope spidered in all directions around them.

She curled into him, shaking a little from the circulation in her body returning to normal. He ran his hands down her arms, her back. His cock, as hard as it'd ever been, pressed painfully against her hip. He brought her small hand to him until she cradled the head of his shaft. She swiveled her gaze up to him and gave him a spellbinding smile.

"We're not done yet, ballerina." Fuck, his cock had answered for him.

~

Samantha melted under his eyes. *Such beautiful eyes.* They blazed with hard-core desire.

Pillows were suddenly nestled around her, seemingly from out of nowhere. She was grateful for the padding.

He jackknifed her legs apart and hilted himself in her. A moan of satisfaction echoed, and only when her mouth latched onto his shoulder, muffling the sound, did she realize it came from her own throat.

His chest hairs tickled the indentations in her sensitized skin as he held on to her, his hips rising and crashing down on her with another thrust.

She'd have grasped his hips with her legs if she had the strength. Instead, she was left to receive him, take all of him. Candle flickers, wicks gasping in the humid air, and the

Lucky

steady hush of waves faded into the background as Derek's heavy breathing and male growls called to her as if beckoning her to focus on him, only him.

Her orgasm came quickly, faster than she thought possible and with little build-up. His own release followed shortly after, and still he didn't stop, never fully softening.

He grasped her knees and lifted them. Gaining purchase on the back of her thighs, he thrust them upward until her ankles rested on his shoulders. God, he was still hard, taking her just as hard. She was nearly bent in half when his mouth latched onto hers. His teeth nibbled on her lips; his tongue searched her mouth.

Grinding her pelvis against him escalated yet another orgasm. Before she could crest, he lowered her legs and flipped her to her stomach. Pillows slid out from under her. With his uncanny swiftness, he yanked her hips backward. He seated himself in her once more and pounded against her ass. The lack of direct stimulation slowed her orgasm but didn't remove the possibility—not one little bit.

Her earlier fog cleared and she saw herself on all fours in the mirror, Derek on his knees behind her. His face was taut, the muscles in his forearms straining as he gripped her hips savagely, like a true Viking. In her mind a fantasy flashed of being found by him on one of his pillaging voyages, captured, bound in ropes while he fucked her mercilessly because he could. She'd never been this hot, felt so used, so taken by a man.

She focused on his face intently as he bent his head back and roared as another climax took him over. His tight growls were all it took for her to pitch into another orgasm herself.

∽

She turned her face up to Derek, his hand lazily drawing

circles on her arm. For the last hour they'd lain on the mass of pillows watching the sun disappear into the water through the large doors.

"What time is it?" she asked.

"Does it matter?"

"No, actually." Samantha stared at the indented pattern along her leg. She still wore a rope dress. He'd fashioned it for her when she asked if he could show her more of his mad skills. She wondered if she could she sleep in it.

"How did you get into rope bondage?"

"Prison," he bit out. "Also known as boarding school." A spear of panic lanced her heart. Samantha didn't need to hear his life story to know something bad had happened. No one released bitter words so quickly without a hidden reason behind that hostility.

He nestled his head back and resumed his stare at the ceiling. "I was on the wrestling team. One night one of my teammates and I snuck into the gym. We were going through some holds for a match later in the week. We weren't supposed to be there. So when the superintendent caught us, let's just say she had an interesting way of disciplining us. She tied us up together and left us overnight to be found the next morning."

"Seriously?"

"Yes. We spent the whole night talking about doing it to her. How we'd bend her over. Strap her to that intimidating executive chair she barely got out of. Got a hard-on so bad I thought Chaz would never talk to me again."

"Chaz, as in *Chaz*?"

"Yes, and if you tell him I told you any of this I'll have to come up with a creative punishment."

"Are you kidding? This is the most I've learned about you in one sitting. I'm not about to jinx it." She laughed lightly. "So then what?"

Lucky

"Chaz and I made a deal. When we got out of that mess the next morning, thanks to the wrestling coach, we'd made a pact to learn rope work. So we did. Used to leave various knots on her desk as a threat. Something tells me she took it as a compliment."

"So she knew about rope bondage?"

"Since then, I've learned anyone who can tie a decent TK knot and double columns like she had knew what she was doing. And it wasn't from learning to sail."

"You never found out, um, what she was into?"

"Jealous?" He peered down at her. He didn't wait for her reply, which would have been a resounding *hell yes*. She didn't like the idea that Derek had experienced so much without her. True, he was older, richer, and more well-traveled. She still didn't like it.

"She intimidated the shit out of me. I wouldn't have asked her a thing. Then I graduated, went to college and found great riggers in New York to work with."

"And Chaz?"

"Not his thing."

"What is his thing? I'm asking for a friend." She smiled down at him as she sat up. Whoa, head rush.

"Not my story to tell, ballerina. Have more water." He handed her a small bottle, which she gratefully drained. Who knew being bound made you so thirsty? *And cold*. She snuggled closer to him.

"I'll get Cindy to spill. She's certainly asked a lot about you." *Oops.* "I shouldn't have said that."

"I know how much you women like to talk."

"How do you find out anything if you don't?"

"Observation goes a long way. Like how when I do this," he murmured, trailing a fingertip down her side, "you wiggle."

"I do not *wiggle*."

He took the empty bottle from her grasp and flopped her to her back on the cushions. "I know how to make you move." His lips descended on hers. After plundering her mouth for a long minute, he broke the kiss.

"Hungry?"

"Starving."

As he led her to the boat, his arm gripped hers as if she'd pitch over any minute. She had to admit, she felt spacey. As they bounced back across the bay under starlight, she sprang between feeling both out of her body and deep in her bones all at once—the epitome of contentment even in the shadow of the discovery of bitterness in Derek's past.

Sunk into her happiness, she felt the little patterned indents in her skin with her finger, trailing it along her leg, and let her gaze rise to the stars.

30

The next morning they lazed in bed, another first for Derek. While his nighttime schedule ensured he rarely rose before noon, when he did wake, he shot out of bed.

After a long shower with Samantha, which involved exploring her body and all the ways he could make her respond, they finally made their way into the living room.

She immediately lifted her cell phone. "I should check in with my grandmother." Her face fell at what she saw. "Oh my God."

"What?"

"My grandmother texted me ... from San Francisco. She's with *Alexander*. It's the Burlesque Hall of Fame event. I wonder if she's dancing. Man, I should be there to see her!"

"Do you want to go?"

She turned to him. "Are you serious?"

"Why not?"

"But I can't interrupt them. 'Cause ya know—"

"She's not his flavor, if you know what I mean. I'm sure Carina knows."

"Huh. Still, I shouldn't show up. She hates it when I hover."

She scrolled through her screen. "What time is it there? Too early to call. Here she says she'll be back in two days, in time to plan for Thanksgiving. Hey, you should come to dinner." Her eyes shot up to his.

Ah, another holiday he usually avoided as if it were the plague, Armageddon, *and* a meteor strike. Probably because, in his family, it was all those things and more.

"I'm usually here with Bret."

"Oh, good. At least you're with your brother."

"You're into holidays, huh?"

"Isn't everyone?" She lowered her phone and circled her arms around his waist. "Come to my house. My grandmother makes great stuffing."

"I have some stuffing I'd like to do."

"You're incorrigible." She giggled loudly when he lifted her up in his arms.

"Now I'm going to have to prove that."

"Can I check in with Cindy first? It's just…"

"You want her to spill." He laughed. Women truly were from a different planet. He took the opportunity to phone Jills. While Samantha took her call out on the balcony, he moved back to the bedroom. Jills reported all was well with Frost and that his penthouse renovations were complete. *Thank fuck.* Now he could take Samantha there. He couldn't imagine returning to her house and inadequate bed space. In recent weeks he'd learned how she loved to be moved around a king-sized bed, and he'd fallen in love with all those little noises she made as he fucked her. Who cared if her grandmother was deaf. He'd missed the privacy his sound-proof apartment offered.

After hanging up with Jills, he dialed Mark. One last check-in was required.

"Yo." Mark's voice boomed into his cell phone. "You tan yet?"

"Everywhere. Hey, how's the studio?"

Mark had promised he'd stop by Aerobesque's new space while Derek was gone and assess the workmen's progress during Derek's absence.

"Checked in last night. They were finishing up the painting. Should be done by tomorrow morning. Expect an embarrassing amount of genuflecting from Samantha."

"Looks good?"

"Home run. I can go by later."

"No, thanks. I'm sure it's all fine. We'll be home tomorrow."

"No problem."

"What's the word on Samantha's attackers?"

"Stan's still working on it. Still think it might be that rival dance studio."

"Doesn't compute."

"Alexander isn't worried. Hey, you may not know this, but he took the grandmother to San Fran."

"Samantha told me. I have no idea what that's about."

"Probably figures he could help smooth things over. Ya know, you marry the whole family."

"Who said anything about getting married?" He'd been waiting for this from Mark, now married to a woman he'd loved from afar for ten years. Derek might soon be the only single man left standing amongst his friends.

"It's not a death sentence, Derek."

"Says you. Listen, I gotta go."

From the other room he could hear Samantha's rising voice. Something was wrong.

∽

"I told you not to freak out. Amber Lynn will be fine. It's just a broken wrist." Cindy was too calm for the news she'd delivered.

"How, though?"

"She let go of the lyra and fell. Hell, it's a good lesson to hold on."

"Cindy! Oh, God, I should be there."

"No, we're fine. Her mother freaked, but hey, I didn't drop any F bombs." Her voice grew hushed. "Chaz drove us all to the emergency room. He came by as we were leaving to go."

"But—"

"Amber is *fine*, Sam. I bought some sparkly unicorn stickers for the girls to adorn her signature, shocking-pink cast. Colored casts are all the rage now. Man, I was born in the wrong era."

She should have bought the sparkly unicorn stickers. Not Cindy. "Get colored pens."

"Already done. Silver to match the tiara her mother bought her. Oh, hi, babe. Be there in a sec."

Babe?

"Look, Sam, Chaz just arrived. Go back to your hot Viking and likely even hotter sex. When you get back you can tell me all about it." Her tone grew hushed. "I might have something to share, too." The line went dead.

"What's wrong?" Derek was on the balcony. He rushed over to her and pulled her into his chest. "Your grandmother okay?"

"It's Amber Lynn."

∼

Derek was acutely aware of how his heart overreacted and stilled. Why? He'd met the little girl once, for Christ's sake.

Lucky

"She broke her wrist."

Overblown relief preceded his long exhale.

Her voice cracked. "Derek, I should be there."

"Oh, baby," he said, drawing her into his arms. "She has a mother."

"You don't understand. It's my studio, and she's my responsibility and I—"

"Hey." He cradled the sides of her face. "It's sweet how you care about your students."

"She's my—"

"She's not *yours*."

She visibly stiffened under his hands. She stepped backward, her face escaping his hold. It was only when she turned and went inside, a mask of shock covering her beautiful face, that it occurred to him his choice of words held a certain insensitivity.

She reached the center of the living area and spun on her heel to face him. "Why do you hate children so much?"

"I don't hate them."

"You told me to be honest with you. So level. Why are you so against them? What aren't you telling me?"

"Look, I'll order up some lunch."

"No, tell me why."

He took a deep breath, trying to ignore the thread of anger he was feeling. "I told you. I spent all my formative years in a military boarding school. That's perfect training for a close family, don't you think?"

"They were mean to you? You're angry at your own mother?"

The psychoanalyst shit annoyed him. "No."

"Then why?"

"Sit down, Samantha."

"I'll stand."

"Sit."

257

She lowered herself to the couch. He sat next to her. Another fucking Band-Aid—this one the size of Texas—was about to be ripped off. Samantha was a dog with a bone when it came to finding out things. If he had any chance with this woman at all, she'd have to find out about his past eventually.

He rested his elbows on his knees and studied the carpeting.

He couldn't do it. The words wouldn't come. Instead, he reached over and pulled her into his lap. "Things happened in my past. Let it lie. We go home tomorrow. We should make the most of our last day here."

"Someday you'll tell me?"

He sighed. "Yes."

She bit her lip but didn't ask him anything else.

"Let's go down to the beach. We'll get a cabana and pull the drapes closed. The sound of the waves will mask your cries." He slipped his hand between her thighs.

He was all too aware she wasn't smiling. Oddly, that concerned him the most.

He took her down to the beach anyway and spent the afternoon trying to get her to forget all about home and the little girl's broken wrist. The ocean didn't come close to concealing her excited moans. He didn't care if the whole world heard what he was doing to his woman. He just needed to keep her occupied and away from questions about his past.

31

The only good thing about landing back in Washington, DC was that he had yet another surprise for Samantha: her new studio. The skies were gray and overcast when they descended the stairs to the tarmac and his waiting car. His driver, Rich, waiting patiently, threw Derek a set of keys.

"Thanks, man."

"No problem, sir."

"Samantha?" Derek held out his hand to help her into the front seat. Ever since yesterday's argument, he'd tried to keep his voice light. She seemed to be walking on eggshells around him.

Still, they'd enjoyed their last dinner on the terrace of his suite. He'd made love to her as dessert. All through packing this morning, saying good-bye to Bret and Ava, and the flight, she'd not raised a single word about kids or what he wasn't telling her. He was grateful for that silence.

The children conversation was bound to come up. It always did if a female was involved. He hadn't expected the direct approach, however. When he felt the time was right, he owed it to her to be direct back and tell her why he landed in boarding school in the first place.

"One last surprise, ballerina." He pulled through the gate of Dulles Airport's general aviation terminal.

"I can't take any more!" Her familiar teasing was a welcome balm to the tension he'd held in since yesterday. So what if he spoiled her? A full life could be had without all the trapping of family complications. Hadn't he proven that?

Despite her obvious pull to the suburban dream, he wanted to stay with this woman—at least for the time being. A girlfriend, perhaps? He could handle that. Nothing too permanent to encroach on what they each needed to do. She had goals. He had goals—some, anyway. He'd met most of his life's objectives already. Now he was going to help Samantha reach hers.

When they pulled up to the building housing her new studio, she glanced over at him. "You did something, didn't you?"

"Perhaps." At the entrance, he punched in the key code on the door.

"A security system!"

"That's the first surprise." Damn, the code that Mark texted last night didn't take. He tried the door, and it swung open easily. Someone must still be finishing up. "Wait," he said. He pulled out the men's tie he'd worn on the trip over and secured it over her eyes. She squealed when he hoisted her up into his arms and took to the stairs.

At the top, his shoes crackled on something.

"What did you do?" she asked. Her excitement was devastating against what he saw.

"We'll come back later."

"No, Derek, what—" she pulled off the tie and gasped.

He set her down, gingerly. "Careful."

"What happened?"

He had no idea. Cracked mirrors threw broken reflections at them. The custom-ordered teak desk lay upside down. Broken cane chairs lay in shambles around the room. Slashed and ripped silks hung from the ceiling. A lyra lay on its side with dents hammered into its surface. Dance poles lay strewn like tinker toy sticks. But it was the feathers, everywhere, as if dozens of fans and boas had been plucked like dead chickens, that roiled his gut. *Violence incarnate.*

She stepped into the space. "Who would have done this?"

A cold rage clouded his mind. "Someone must have broken in. I had … " He had done what? *Not a thing.* He had delivered *nothing.*

"You had it renovated. Oh, Derek, I can see it. It was beautiful."

He could see the pristine finished product in his mind's eye, too. Underneath the rubble would have been a space as beautiful as Samantha's dancing. That vision made the destruction hurt even more.

A hardwood sprung floor capped by base-to-ceiling mirrors. Brand new silks in red, blue, deep purple, and white swaying in the air conditioning. Hoops of varying sizes to accommodate the little girls to the women hanging from the ceiling. Dance poles lines up like soldiers in a rack. Colored theater lights that would have shone down on the dancers.

Now? *Trash.*

He stepped into the space, somewhat spellbound by the destruction. Frustration pounded against his chest. He'd delivered on Samantha's dream, and someone had the audacity to crush his plans.

He should call the police. He pulled out his phone, turned and came face to face with large red letters sprayed onto the cracked mirror on the far wall, long red drips like blood running toward the floor.

Next time it will be her face.

Forget the police. He needed Mark.

~

Derek held Samantha's arm in a death grip as he hustled her down the stairs. Anger shimmered off his skin. She understood his surprise was ruined, but her heart felt it would burst with love for this man.

"Derek, stop."

He continued to hold her arm too hard and rush them down the stairs, his phone in his hand. "We need to leave. Now."

"Ow."

He relaxed his violent hold on her arm. "Sorry. We're going to my place. I'll tell Alexander to keep an eye on your grandmother. Perhaps not come home as scheduled."

"But—"

"But nothing." He pushed her toward the door leading to the outside.

"Stop." She locked her legs so he couldn't move her easily. "Derek Damon Wright, you are an amazing man. I can see your vision. You did such a wonderful thing."

"No. I hired people. A lot of good it did."

"But you imagined it." He stepped backward as if burned by the sight of tears in her eyes.

"We need to go." He peered down the hallway, suspicion emanating from every pore.

She let herself be led outside and into his car. His strained voice cursed into the phone. His anger made her uncomfortable, but his pain frightened her more. His reaction to some smashed mirrors and decimated feather boas made no sense.

"Derek?" She touched his arm and he flinched. He was unreachable. She sat back in her seat and waited for an answer to come about what she should do or say. She was in uncharted territory, an emotional country for which she was wholly unprepared to navigate.

She still knew nothing about this man—at all.

Except I'm in love with him.

32

Samantha stood in the doorway and absorbed Derek's large bathroom. Sunshine streaming in from a picture window on one side mixed with enough theatre lighting to put Carnegie Hall to shame. Her gaze ran over gleaming quartz counters and the blue-and-gray tiled shower that could fit an army. How much space did one person need? Apparently, if that person was Derek, a lot.

Three master-sized bedrooms, five bathrooms, and a living room larger than the footprint of the first floor of her grandmother's house comprised his penthouse. Oh, and naturally he owned the building. She'd discovered that when she looked up his address on the laptop sitting on the granite kitchen counter. What else was she going to do after he'd slipped out this morning?

Derek's note said he was going to "check on things." She hoped he hadn't gone back to the wreckage of her new studio, though he probably had. She didn't know much about handling men, except for one thing: sometimes you just had to let them do whatever they felt they needed to do.

With no classes to teach until later that evening, she

sought out scraps of information online about a man she was in love with, but who remained a mystery. They hadn't had sex last night, which gave her an odd, distanced feeling. A strange reason, she presumed, for trolling the web. Finding pictures of him with other women didn't help.

She checked her phone. He still hadn't answered her two texts. She knew when a man was backing down. Lord knew, she'd been there before.

She rose. Taking a shower would feel good. She hadn't had one since the Caribbean, twenty-four hours ago. Had she really been in a five-star resort only yesterday? She'd been happy, sated, and so sure she and Derek had a future, though unspoken. *And then there was his refusal to talk about family.*

Her bare feet padded across the bathroom's mosaic tile floor. She stopped to trace one of the large swirls of ocean blue that formed a soothing pattern with her big toe, now sporting red polish.

A loud buzzer echoed throughout the apartment, and she jumped at the intrusion.

Abandoning her shower plans, she hit the intercom button at the front door. "Uh, hello?"

"Miss Rose, a Mr. Rockingham is here to see you," a man's voice said.

Alexander? Her grandmother might be with him, too. She would know what to do about her predicament—what to do next.

"Send them up!" She threw open the door, her leg dancing in anticipation. She had on yoga pants and a sweatshirt, not the best of receiving clothes. Her grandmother would notice, but she didn't have time to change.

What felt maddeningly like ten minutes later, the private elevator doors across the small alcove opened and a gray-suited Alexander stepped through, alone. He held two white plastic bags, Italian food scenting the hallway. Her stomach growled.

"If that's from Trattorio, I'll love you forever."

He gave her a kiss on each cheek. "I suspected Derek wouldn't have food. Your grandmother says hello."

"She didn't come with you?"

"No." After that non-answer, he ducked inside.

"I should text her."

His hand descended on hers, lowering her phone. Jesus, he had large mitts. "She thought you and I should talk."

Talk?

"She sent along her génoise cake, which I understand is your favorite."

"She made it? How long have you been back?"

"A day." He lifted a carton from the bag and set it on the table.

"Thanks for taking her to the burlesque convention. I'm sorry I missed it."

"She got to see a lot of old friends. Besides, my absence gave *my* friends time to talk about my surprise birthday party."

She gasped. "You know?" Derek had mentioned the party to her when they'd been floating in the pool. Her heart flipped stupidly at the memory of how happy she'd been just a day ago, so sure he was *into* her.

"Secrets are hard to keep from me. Tell you what. My knowing about it will be our little secret. Now, let's eat."

Samantha rummaged in Derek's cabinets for plates. Alexander expertly dished out mushroom ravioli and they settled on two stools in front of the granite island—an outlandish centerpiece in his gourmet kitchen.

Alexander cocked his head at her sudden laughter.

"Look at this kitchen. Derek doesn't cook." Her last word

Lucky

broke a little. She wasn't going to do that goofy laughing-crying thing that women did in the movies, was she?

Alexander laid his fork down and turned in his stool. "Samantha."

The way he said her name stopped the bizarre thoughts in her head. Tranquility settled in her belly. A rush of everything that was good in her life drowned her earlier fear. She was in Derek's apartment. He hadn't kicked her out. Alexander was here. Her grandmother was home.

"How do you do that?" she asked.

"What?"

"Calm everyone. At my house, I saw you do that with my grandmother, and also Derek."

He gave her a small smile. "Thank you. That's one of the best compliments I've ever received. Do you like your food?"

Another changing of the subject? These guys were good, but she'd had enough of that technique. "I do like it. Thank you. I guess that means you're not going to tell me. Wait. I'm sorry. That's rude. It's just I'm so…"

"Worried about Derek."

"Yes, and you are, too."

"You're quite perceptive, Samantha."

"It comes from living with someone who's deaf. I read facial expressions. But Derek—"

"Is upset about your studio. Yes, I heard about that unfortunate occurrence."

"He's so angry. My grandmother doesn't know what happened, does she?"

"No, and she's not in danger, Samantha. I made certain of that."

"How do you know each other?"

"I met Carina in San Francisco. I lost someone important to me a long time ago, and she gave me the perfect advice to help me through the grieving process. *Live the life that would make him proud*, she told me."

"That sounds like her. She likes giving advice."

"There's another person who could use some guidance." He paused. "Derek. Despite what most people believe about him, he hasn't had it easy. How much has he told you about his past? His upbringing?"

"Not much. I know he went to boarding school quite young. He was in cotillion. He can dance. I met his mother—"

"You did? Forgive me. Continue."

"I also know he's generous. I mean, what he did for me was more than anyone ever has." She twisted her napkin in her lap.

"Derek likes to bestow gifts. It's how he shows love. When they don't go well, he believes he'd failed … and he grows distant."

Alexander's eyes showered kindness on her. She suspected he spoke those last few words for her.

"He worries too much. Money doesn't bring happiness. Except my grandmother said the fastest way to make a rich person unhappy is to take it away."

"Money doesn't interest Derek. Making people happy does. Did he tell you he took over his father's failing companies at age twenty-four?"

"No." But then, why would he? He kept so many things from her.

"He turned them around and saved his mother from a penniless future, a fate worse than death for her. He then refused his own trust fund. He felt he didn't deserve it. He wanted to be his own man. Make amends."

"Amends? For what?"

"I'm afraid I've said too much."

"No, please. Tell me more." Her voice sounded over-eager

Lucky

even to herself. "One minute he's lavishing me with trips and diamonds, and then the next he pulls back. And why his aversion to family? Do you know anything about that?"

Alexander's lips tightened. Yes, there most definitely was a story there.

"Samantha, these are conversations that you both need to have. You are right to keep prodding him to open up, gently, of course. I believe you may be the only person in the world who could."

"It hasn't worked so far."

"Keep trying." His hand descended on hers, stopping her from flipping her fork over and over on the granite.

"Remember this. We all eat lies when our hearts are hungry." He let go of her hand. "Another Carina Rose saying."

"I'm familiar with that one," she said with a laugh, only to choke the levity back as a lightning crack hit her brain and her memory opened up. Another saying she'd shared with Derek—but who obviously hadn't really heard—bobbed to the top.

Alexander threw her a curious look.

"There's something else my grandmother says. 'People aren't whole until they're loved all the way to the other side.' I suspect it might apply here."

"Like I said, you are quite perceptive, Samantha."

If she was, why hadn't she recognized that state in her own life? Many men had only wanted her for her entertainment value, leading her to make terrible choices in her past. Perhaps it was easier to see your own troubles in others. That would explain why Derek felt the need to fix everything for everyone around him, but not see his own need.

He was raised with so much money—another internet discovery—yet she found no signs that his life had been happy. No childhood memories and no pictures of him having fun beyond the endless snapshots of him with gorgeous women at club openings. Had he ever felt loved for himself?

"I came by to tell you something else," Alexander said. "Derek will want to tell you this, but I don't withhold information from people if I think it can help. The men who destroyed your studio and who attacked you in the alley are the same. Fingerprints were left and they matched with police records. My people have confirmed it. If they *are* linked to that rival dance studio, things will get bad for a bit."

"I can't believe Joanne would have anything to do with it." She shook her head, not fully grasping how anyone could do such a thing over dance, the most beautiful art form in the world. "Derek thinks it has something to do with him."

"Men often lose sight that not everything is about them. I'm leaving it up to Derek to press charges since both attacks occurred on his properties. I believe that's what he's doing now."

"I should go to him." She leapt from her seat.

"Sit down, Samantha."

At his commanding voice, she lowered herself to her seat once more.

"Let him do this for you." He lifted his fork. "And let's finish our lunch, shall we? I expect you to have some raspberry génoise. Afterward, I'll take you to see your grandmother." As she picked up her fork, she wondered if anyone had the guts to disagree with Alexander.

33

Derek leaned against his car in front of the DC police station, flipping a jump drive between the forefinger and thumb of one hand. With the other, he tossed his cigarette butt into the street. Smoking hadn't been his thing for years. He knew it would kill you. But he was in a mood. He'd have laughed at himself for feeling so dark over slashed silks and dented lyra hoops, but his perspective about such things had left long ago.

After a sleepless night, he'd lifted himself from his brand-new bed and abandoned a still-slumbering Samantha. At least he'd had the presence of mind to leave her a note.

Alexander had sent a text to both him and Mark last night with the names of Samantha's alley attackers and confirmed his suspicions that they'd also trashed her new dance studio. Some men were so witless. Security cameras were everywhere in DC After handing over the drive with the evidence earlier this morning, Alexander suggested Derek call his attorney and let him handle getting the additional proof to the police. Derek had wanted to drive over to the likely dilapidated Southeast row house where Samantha's two attackers lived and acquaint them with his wrath, but he wasn't an idiot. Instead, he drove to the police station himself, his version of a compromise.

Now, staring at the front door, he wondered if he'd regret not taking matters into his own hands. A car door slamming behind him interrupted his debate.

Great, a babysitter.

Derek pushed himself off his car and widened his stance.

"Just here to make sure you really walk in." Mark jerked his chin toward the building.

"Think I'm afraid?"

"I think you're debating whether or not to drive to Southeast."

Alexander likely called Mark to ensure he, Derek, didn't get into trouble. Derek couldn't seem to shake his reputation of being one step from another brainless mistake.

"Not a fan of police stations."

"Who is? But don't be rash. You've got Samantha now."

"Just because you're pussy-whipped doesn't mean I am." He regretted the words immediately. Mark didn't deserve his anger. If he'd been Mark, he'd have punched him for even suggesting the man was taken in by a woman. Mark's mastering of Isabella was famous at Accendos. Derek, on the other hand, had what? A handful of topping scenes with Samantha under his belt?

"Giving you a pass on that one, brother, because I know how uncomfortable it makes you." Mark leaned against the car next to him.

"What's 'it'?"

"Being in love."

Did he hear Mark Santos, the ex–special ops guy, say the word *love*?

Not that he'd ever been comfortable with that four-letter

word himself. Anyway, he wasn't in love. He was something far worse. He was obsessed, which meant he was also out of control. It was the only reason for his over-the-top anger at a minor construction job going south. Far worse things had happened.

"So you going in or what?"

He huffed, turned away from Mark, and strode to the entrance. He'd turn the evidence over and forget all about this conversation.

He cared about Samantha. He wanted to keep seeing her, but a little perspective on where they were going was necessary for everyone around them, including himself.

~

Samantha pulled in to her assigned parking spot, averting her eyes from the building that held the smashed dreams of her new studio. Derek had texted that the guys who trashed it were being "taken care of" and that she shouldn't worry. He'd also assured her that her new studio would be renovated over the next two weeks.

She couldn't give a rip about the studio space.

Surely, the distance she felt from Derek last night was merely a minor monkey wrench, nothing to be concerned about. Only a spoiled girl would launch into a dramatic tirade. She'd just returned from a week-long Caribbean excursion where Derek had lavished her with attention and expensive gifts. That niggling feeling that something was off would go away.

Her grandmother had kept her preoccupied all afternoon with stories from her trip. The organizers had wanted Carina Rose, the East Coast Burlesque champion many times over, to take the stage, a last-minute addition to their "Legends" presentation. She'd declined, simply stating she knew when it was time to put up the high heels. She'd also remarked favorably on Samantha's tan, though expressed concern that she didn't look as happy as one would expect after a Caribbean vacation. Samantha didn't fill her in on the recent bump in the road.

She mentally pulled up her big-girl panties and drove straight to her old studio. Cindy needed a night off, so she'd handle all three classes tonight. Until then, paperwork would keep her busy. She'd address Derek later.

Just as she was about to step in, a strong hand grasped her arm. She wheeled around and came face to face with the last person she'd expected to see. Cold fury emanated from his eyes.

"Craig? What are you doing here?"

"Came by to see what the hell you said."

"I don't know what you're talking about."

He gripped her arm more tightly, which only reminded her of how Derek had done the same only yesterday. "I was fired. What did you tell the FBI?"

She wrested free. "I didn't tell them anything. I wasn't even here. I was in the Caribbean. With my new boyfriend. Derek Wright." She lifted her arm. "See? Tan."

"Boyfriend, huh? Wright, as in the club owner? I doubt that." He nearly spat the words.

"What do you mean?

"Are you kidding? Derek Damon Wright is not known for sticking around. I mean, I know what you want, Sam. The house, the minivan, the kids. He's not it."

"And you were?"

"Don't be gullible. Pinning your hopes on someone like that is—"

"I have to go, Craig."

She spun on her heel and jogged up the steps. Pinning her hopes? When did she ever do *that*?

Lucky

When she got to her desk, she pulled out her iPhone and dialed Derek. She prayed he'd take her call, even if he left her texts unanswered.

"Samantha?"

"Hi." God, her voice sounded relieved even to her. "Just wanted to hear your voice." No need to worry him more by bringing up Craig's visit.

"I'm with some people." The formality of his voice stung.

"Oh, okay. We can talk tonight."

"I thought you might want to spend time with your grandmother. I have a lot to catch up on. Work."

"Derek, is something wrong?" Because something most definitely *was* wrong.

"Right now I'm not good company."

"Trying to scare me away?" she teased.

"I'll see you later, Samantha."

He didn't take the bait. He also didn't call her ballerina.

The Derek on the other end of the phone wasn't the Derek she'd fallen for. The guy she loved didn't back down. This guy was avoidance and hesitation and … He was the guy who'd met her Lyra Ladies. The guy who was afraid, who'd backed away inch by inch with a smile. The guy who refused to be pinned down instead of focused on pinning *her* down. She recognized his hesitancy, having experienced it oh-so-many times from other men.

She wasn't having any of it, damn it.

After hanging up, she ran through her night. She had to teach three classes. Then she'd be free. Derek likely wouldn't be home until midnight anyway.

Think, Sam.

Craig's visit was well timed. It reminded her where she'd come from, and where she was never returning. In the last month, her life had split in two. There was Before Derek and

After Derek. She was not going back to Before. Or worse, be stuck in the In Between.

She took a deep breath. She knew how to fix this situation. She was going to have to go for it— all the way, one hundred percent, no backing down, the full monty.

I can do this.

34

Derek pulled into the underground garage at Accendos. He was vaguely aware he parked, took the stairs up to the first floor, and found his way to the back in the gardens. He took a chair on the terrace and stared out at the fountain.

"I thought you'd be with Samantha." Alexander's voice boomed behind him.

"Nope."

Alexander scraped a second chair over.

"Care to tell me what happened?"

Jesus, here it comes. The fatherly advice. How many times had he willingly sat here and listened?

"Just need a little space. We spent seven days together."

The man leaned back in his chair and assessed him as if he wanted to say something.

"I see."

Did he? Derek needed time to cool off, reorder his emotions, and regain control. What was the big deal?

"Derek, I should have said something the day I bailed you out of that police station."

"Don't get caught again?"

"No. I should have told you, you aren't special."

Wow, that was some cold shit. "Never said I was."

"Yes, you do. By the way you live. As if you're above it all. None of us is above love."

"Not interested. And, besides, you're single."

"Right now, yes. By choice. But you're not choosing anything. You're letting your past do the choosing."

"Man, this place has turned into a therapy center." He almost stood, but something in Alexander's eyes made him stop. Jesus, the man could freeze Medusa. His friend's serious face unnerved him to the core. Alexander wanted him to hear what he was saying. Trouble was, he didn't want to hear it.

"Derek, you aren't special," he repeated in the harshest tone he'd ever heard from a normally patient Alexander.

"What the hell, Alexander?"

"You're unique, and that's the good news. Have a life that is your own. Stop trying to have the opposite of your parents. You're privileged to be alive on this planet. Not everyone gets that chance."

"So why did you try to rescue me, Alexander? Since I'm not special and all."

"You remind me of someone who also had an unsupportive family." He stood and rose to his full height, which normally didn't intimidate him. Alexander had seen him at his worst—mouthing off at DC cops in his dirty European suit and high on whatever he'd gotten his hands on earlier that day.

Alexander placed his large hand on his shoulder. "More than that, Derek. You deserve better."

He knew he should go. But Alexander kept talking.

"Every day I feel the loss of a certain person. You ask how I knew to save you that day. I recognized something in you."

"You've been binge watching Dr. Phil?"

Lucky

He smiled lightly but didn't stop. *Please stop talking.*

"You reminded me of someone I once knew. He also had a good heart, and it was abused badly."

"I'm fine, Alexander."

"Fine isn't great, Derek." He slapped him on the shoulder. "Go for exceptional. It's time."

Alexander headed back to the house. It was time for him to go, too. He rose and headed back to the garage. Fuck, not even Accendos was safe anymore. Maybe he'd stop by Frost where no one sought anything beyond a good time.

~

Samantha cleared her throat and spoke into the intercom at Accendos' entrance a second time. "Samantha Rose? Um, Derek asked me to come here. I'm to wait for him inside."

By some miracle, the gates opened, but only after three cameras trained down on her had swiveled around, giving her and her car a thorough once-over. She'd been thoroughly, virtually frisked.

When she pulled up to the entrance, she hadn't expected Alexander to be at the top landing of the stone steps. A valet took her keys, which gave her a nanosecond longer to think about how she was going to explain herself.

"You're not here to meet Derek, are you?"

She bit her lip and faced a stern-looking Alexander.

"I am. He just doesn't know it yet."

A jovial laugh erupted from his amused face. "You remind me so much of Carina. She rarely took 'no' as an answer, too."

She climbed the steps to greet him. "I could use your help. I'm in love with Derek."

"I know. Come inside."

She stepped inside the vestibule with him, where the two

guards who stood before the gabled archway ignored her just as the two previous sentinels had.

"I know I should have called. It's late, too. But I thought…"

"Let's talk in my office, shall we?"

"I was hoping the Library."

He stopped short. "I'm sorry, Samantha. Protocol says I can't take you there."

"Protocol." She measured the word in her mouth.

"Yes. Only Derek can accompany you to a playroom, given the nature of your relationship. It's also quite full tonight." He peered down at her. "Would you like to see his room? While you wait there, I can call him for you. He was just here, actually."

"He was?" She thought he was at work. *Damn*. Now she was doubly glad she came because her instincts were right. He was backing off. Why? Because of what happened at her new studio space?

The Library was important tonight, however. During her trek through that room with Derek, she'd seen an apparatus that called up enough curiosity in her and seemed hard-core enough that she required its use tonight. She needed Derek to see her *on* it as an offering of herself to him. She needed him to see her in *his* world.

Alexander didn't wait for her, however.

She traversed the long hallway, taking two steps for every one of Alexander's long strides. A man in black leather chaps was cuffed flat against the wall. Alexander walked by him, not acknowledging his presence.

At the end of the hall, he turned into another wide foyer. A nude woman whose male companion held a leash attached to her collar lightly stepped past her. Alexander didn't flinch.

Well, she wouldn't either. This was Derek's world, and she'd come here of her own volition.

A wide staircase led to a second floor. This place was like Tara. At the top of the stairs, Alexander led her to the right and stopped at a door with an ornate carving of a white raven at eye level.

"Why don't you go inside. It shouldn't be more than thirty minutes before Derek gets here."

"You think he'll come?"

"Most definitely."

"I have one more favor to ask." She reached into her bag and pulled out a bundle of rope she'd swiped from the Rigging Hut on St. Thomas. She'd stuffed it in her bag when Derek wasn't looking and smuggled it home. She wasn't a thief, but she'd wanted a souvenir. She'd hoped to please him by learning how to create a rope dress and one night when he stripped her, he'd find her surprise. No time for that. She had work to do tonight.

"I don't know how to do it—create a rope dress. YouTube was *no* help."

Alexander's chuckle quelled her embarrassment in asking the elegant man to do this for her.

"It's been a few years. But I think we can figure it out. After you." He pushed open the door to Derek's room.

35

Derek sat at the bar at Frost, alone, the crowd fairly light for a Sunday evening. He was grateful for the emptiness. He took a swig of his second tequila. He should check in with Jills, see how things had been going. Working would feel good after being gone for weeks playing tour guide to one dancer who now threatened to encroach on his formerly-free life.

He scrubbed his face, which was growing a little numb from the alcohol's effects. If only the liquor could obliterate the stitch of discomfort from Alexander's little chat.

The problem was the man was right. He had been playing it safe. Then a woman with dancer legs and a killer smile walked into his club. His plans to seduce her with pleasure worked. He just hadn't expected their relationship to keep going beyond that.

"Relationship," he huffed into his glass. He rarely thought the word, let alone spoke it. He was supposed to be the one seducing her, and instead she'd gotten her hooks into him. Her *you're amazing* echoed in his mind.

Lucky

"Said the spider to the fly." He was losing it, talking to himself like a homeless person on Fourteenth Street.

He stood and stretched. When he turned, three sets of eyes met him. Jonathan, Carson, and Mark.

"Gentlemen, buy you a drink?" He lifted his arm at Greg, at the far end of the bar.

"No thanks." Mark leaned against the bar. "We're here to talk."

Great. One look at their faces and he could tell they'd been drinking from Alexander's Fountain of Confrontation. Why else would they be here?

"What, no formal tribunal meeting?" Derek stood too. At least they wouldn't look down on him.

"This is more important. Heard about the studio. Talked with Alexander. We know what's going on around Samantha."

"You don't know anything."

"Shut up and listen, because, one, I know you know better and two, I've seen you worse. I also recognize that look in your eyes."

"Oh, yeah, what's that?"

"Pure avoidance." Carson stepped forward. "Here's the deal. You're a fool not to go for her." The man always had cut to the chase.

"Jesus, what is it with everyone today? Like a fucking Oprah show."

Mark smirked. "You stopped me from putting my car into a concrete wall over Isabella. Now I'm returning the favor."

"Oh, yeah? You don't understand. I got a little wake-up call, that's all. Long-term, I'm not cut out for what Samantha wants. Kids. Picket fence. They're *my* concrete wall."

Carson sighed heavily. "You think any of us were ready for the disruption a woman brings? London was hell-bent on marrying her career, not me. And Jonathan? With a nineteen-year-old?" His eyes darted to the man who stood behind Derek. "No offense, man."

"None taken." Jonathan regarded Derek with piercing green eyes as serious as he'd ever seen. "I'm going to cut to the chase, and it's a bitch. So I'm only going to say this once. Picture Samantha pregnant with another man's child."

Carson and Mark visibly winced at his words. Hell, so did he. He had to re-straighten his spine after Jonathan's words sunk hooks into his heart.

"Just what I thought," Jonathan said. "That's what it did to me."

"We done here now?" Mark pushed himself off the bar, and the three men left.

Hell yes, he was done. So much for tequila's numbing effects. The men's words had done their job, piercing through the alcohol fog and letting loose the jealous beast he hadn't known lived inside him.

∼

Derek strode back into Accendos, not acknowledging a single person he passed. Manners be damned.

After Jonathan, Carson, and Mark had left Frost, his phone buzzed with a message from Alexander, alerting him that Samantha was waiting for him in his room at Accendos. A cold, possessive panic set in. He knew who else was at Accendos—half a dozen men who'd line up for a chance to try their hand at mastering her.

Taking the steps two at a time, he stormed down the hallway and slammed open the door to his room. He met empty space. She wasn't in the bathroom. Hell, not even under the bed. Given her love of games, he didn't believe she was above hiding.

Alexander had explicitly said she was in his room. Nothing but the ticking of a small wall clock filled the void.

Where could she be?

She wouldn't.

Oh, yes, she would.

He dashed into the hallway and back down the stairs, not even bothering to shut his door. The Library was at the other end of the house, and never before had he experienced the length of Alexander's place as much as he did in that moment. It took far, far too long to get through the gabled arches and large oak door that hid many pleasures and many dangers for someone like Samantha.

He had no idea what was going on with him and the little ballerina, but he'd be damned if he'd let anyone home in on her and bring more confusion to their mess.

Why the hell had Alexander allowed her to roam Accendos unescorted? But knowing Samantha, she snuck out of his room without telling anyone, no small feat at this club.

His worst fear was realized as soon as he stepped through the wide door held open by Tony. The man peered down at him and arched an eyebrow. "She's been waiting for you."

At the far end of the large room, Samantha knelt before Alexander, eyes downcast, nude, and wearing a rope dress. The material looked curiously like the special gold rope he'd used on her in the Rigging Hut. Ironically, a large spider web suspension unit stood behind her.

Alexander's amused eyes darted to Derek.

Derek prowled to Samantha. "What are you doing here? Who put that on you?"

"Alexander." Her eyes remained downcast.

The thought that another man's hands had touched her, even Alexander's, lit his skin on fire.

"However," Alexander said, "it seems Samantha didn't

acquaint me with all her plans. She was to wait in your room. When I was alerted by the staff, she'd stormed—"

"I didn't *storm*." She lifted her gaze.

"Quiet." Derek's bark caused her to return her gaze to the floor. "*Master* Alexander was speaking." She wanted to play? She would abide by some rules.

"Yes, sir." She settled her hands back to her thighs. A curious calm from her movement descended over him. Also, more than a little suspicion arose that she might be manipulating him by play-acting submissive. Her defiant face, chin up despite her downcast eyes, proved his thought. She knew exactly the impact she was having.

"As I was saying, when the staff told me she was here, I decided to wait with her until you could get here." Was that respect flickering in his eyes? Over what she'd done? Samantha was way out of her depth at Accendos.

In his periphery, he noted several flogging scenes unfolding. A man to the left lay strapped to a spanking bench, and couples milled about, no doubt wondering where *this* little scenario would lead. Alexander wasn't one for much public play. His presence alone would cause a stir. Add the new potential submissive kneeling at his feet, and the Dominants unengaged in play were hovering like wolves in the shadows.

"Alexander, thank you. I'll take it from here."

Alexander dipped his chin, cast a small smile down at Samantha, and stepped backward but didn't leave.

Derek took a long moment to study her kneeling form, tanned skin against the gold rope. *Rope that should have been tied by me.*

"Stand."

As soon as she was upright, he forcefully grasped her chin and her eyes widened.

"You don't ever come here without me, Samantha. Remember what I said about manipulation."

"I'm not trying to manipulate you. I wanted—"

"I know what you want." His eyes glanced over to the spider web's steel chains.

36

Samantha's breath hissed between her teeth. So what. Though harsh, his grip on her chin didn't deter her one bit.

"Why are you here?" he growled.

"You came here without me." Screw him if she laid her jealous hand on the table. When she heard he'd come to Accendos instead of coming to her when something clearly bothered him, splinters of pain had lodged in her heart. For a second she hated him for what he'd done. Then her logic had kicked in, and for once, she understood that a man's retreat said something about him, not her. She'd seen enough in his eyes to know he loved her.

He released her chin. The loss of his touch was unbearable, even if he was annoyed with her. Well, she was irritated, too. Couldn't he see all she wished was to be with him in whatever way he needed? He'd said he was in charge of pacing, how things would be done and when, but she wouldn't let him back away. She had to act.

"Derek—"

"Sir."

Her hands reached for his chest and he stepped back. He

couldn't have hurt her more than if he'd backhanded her face.

"I-I'm here for you."

"Here for me," he repeated. "You offer yourself to me? Show me how well you can serve me? Submit to me?"

She let her arms fall to her sides. "Of course."

His eyes roamed over her rope dress. "If you truly were my submissive, you'd have known a punishment was in order for this stunt. And, afterward? Your ass would be so bruised, your throat raw from me fucking your mouth, you'd never again show up here and put all of these people around you in danger."

"Danger?"

"Anyone allowed in this room has been vetted," he continued. "You have not. It's unfair to put yourself on display, Master-less as if available, and have them believe you know more than you do. It's dishonest." Each word landed like a punch.

His words made sense. When someone inexperienced showed up at her studio bragging about their previous dance experience or thought the fact they "worked out" meant they could be an instant aerial artist, they endangered not only their own life but also the people around them.

She lowered her gaze. "I understand."

"Do you? A true submissive shows loyalty through obedience, not abandoning all good sense. If you get hurt, then it's my job to pick up the pieces. It's my job to make sure you *don't get hurt in the first place.*"

Shame that she'd disappointed him dampened her bravado. She *had* been reckless and desperate, but he'd pushed her away, began the retreat dance she'd experienced from men too many times before. *Not this time.*

Derek had opened up her world and shown her the pleasures from being spanked, bound, and *delayed.* She'd orgasmed to near blackout. He couldn't abandon her now, act as if they hadn't done everything they'd done. She wouldn't let him.

She shelved the rising sentimentality that threatened to veer her off course. She turned to face the spider web and leaned into the chains. "Then vet me." She turned her face so he could see her eyes. He had to believe her. "And then punish me."

Derek let out a puff of air. Who cared if he remained incredulous at her actions and words?

Turning her face to the wall behind the web, she cast her eyes downward and curled her fingers tighter around the metal links.

"I'm sorry, sir," she said quietly. "I promise never to endanger you or anyone here." *But I'm not leaving.* The cold steel bit into her palms, but he'd have to rip her arms off her body for her to let go. She'd stay in place until she collapsed.

The webbing lurched as he placed his hands alongside hers, his large hands grasping chunks of the steel chains. His chest pressed against her until the ropes scratched at her skin. She nearly cried out in joy at the contact with his body.

"No, you won't." He began to pry her fingers loose.

She didn't know where the renewed courage came from, but fear was a powerful motivator. "If you take me off this, try to make me go home, I swear I'll find someone else who—"

A hard slap against her ass pitched her whole body deeper into the webbing, the tight chains grinding into her skin. Pain and pleasure reverberated straight through to her clit, now throbbing in instant anticipation. His action had been swift, as if instinctual. He'd reacted exactly as if he were her Master.

The other people and ambient music playing through the room receded into white noise as the sting faded to a faint

Lucky

prickle. She homed in on Derek's presence behind her, willing him to press his crotch against her backside, growl in her ear, and demand her obedience. Only then would she have his full respect, and God, like a junkie who shook with desperate need, she had to have it. To earn that, he had to *be* who he said he was, fully, and she had to take it. If he didn't, the chance of him walking away would no longer be merely a possibility. Their separation would be reality—and permanent.

Derek fisted her hair. "Don't test me, ballerina."

Test him? Wasn't that what he'd been doing to her? Binding her with silks in her studio and taking her to the rigging hut in St. Thomas were not enough—not for him, not for her. They'd had fun but she was left with nothing more than postcards in a scrapbook of experiences. She needed his commitment, and she'd earn it by showing him *hers.* They belonged together, here and everywhere else. She knew in her gut they were inevitable.

She ground her ass backward against his hardening cock.

"Derek. Sir, please."

He released her hair, pushed off the web and her body swayed a little from the web's sudden shift in balance. She squeezed the chains and clung to the frame as if the web were a life raft in a hurricane.

"Alexander, thank you for your oversight." He'd adopted his formal voice. "Will you be our witness?"

She'd forgotten Alexander stood nearby, and her head craned back to see the tall man step forward. She wasn't sure why Derek tacitly agreed to move forward, except perhaps he needed this scene as much as she did.

She swallowed as Alexander's large body blocked a red light that had been shining down on the spider web. The dark shadow cut into her courage, but not enough to back off. She was going forward if it meant she died at the end of tonight.

"Samantha Rose, you are about to enter a scene with Derek Wright. Do you consent, fully and willingly with no reservations?"

"Yes." The ragged whisper slipped through her tight throat. She could only hope they both caught the word.

"Derek, you may proceed." Alexander disappeared from her peripheral view.

Derek's breath puffed along her cheek as he leaned forward. "You got a pass on that one. Given your indiscretion, he has every right to throw you out. But I'm glad he didn't." He captured a damp curl alongside her face and twisted it around his finger. "Since you're such a brave little ballerina, I'm going to show you exactly how things are done here."

"Whatever you wish, sir."

As he let the hair slide through his finger, her hair teased the side of her neck. "Then let go and face me."

She did as he demanded—*because* he demanded.

As she turned, his eyes had cleared to that hard blue she'd grown to love. He pushed her back against the spider web, the rough rope and steel chains both now nearly rubbing her raw. She clasped the chains to keep her feet from sliding out from under her.

"Your limits." His authoritative tone relieved her doubts and the fire in his eyes pierced her anxiety like a pressure valve release. He'd flung aside that polite mask worn for the outside world. She witnessed the real Derek Wright. He was harder, sure of himself, and coiled so tightly veins pulsed in his neck.

"Samantha." The way he said her name, deep and direct, sent a spiral of heat through her body. She blinked. *Limits.* She had to think beyond the heady anticipation that she was getting exactly what she'd asked for. She had to tell him *something*, even though right now she'd let this man do whatever he wanted. No, what he *required*.

The conversation she and Derek had in her studio when he first bound her in silks rushed to the forefront of her brain. She opened her mouth and spoke. "No blood, no lasting marks, no face-slapping, no letting anyone else touch me."

Her heartbeat ratcheted up with each verbalized boundary, and instead of clarifying her situation, a new chaos whirled in her brain. This was part of the dynamic, right? Unbalancing her by asking her to think what was possible was part of the game.

When she couldn't come up with any other limits, she closed her lips … and waited.

He had listened intently and his breath had grown more even, as if he'd relaxed in the face of her list.

"Agreed," he said.

~

Derek yanked at the knots on her dress, freeing her. He couldn't stand the sight of the ropes on her body.

She didn't protest but peered at him with frightened eyes. *Good*. She should be scared witless of the monster that lived inside him.

Despite himself, Derek appreciated Samantha's ballsy move to sneak into the Library. Finding her kneeling, waiting for him, in front of the web, in a place he could so easily bind her, both unnerved and titillated him.

Now that she was freed, the rope pooled at her feet, the diamond indentations on her skin taunted him.

"Pick up the rope," he demanded.

She lowered herself to the floor, settled on her knees, and

lifted one long piece to him. Jesus, she presented the abandoned dress like an offering. He nearly came in his pants as he glared down on the crown of her head, her hands holding up the gold rope.

He took in long breaths. Behind him, the Library buzzed with activity. Floggers slapped against flesh, and murmurs and groans floated in the air from the crowd playing, some just feet away. The din goaded him as much as the siren kneeling before him who'd traipsed into the room—unannounced, unvetted, unprepared.

Fuck, anger returned. "You stole this."

"Borrowed. *Sir*."

A dark chuckle came from someplace deep inside him, despite the bubbling irritation still very much part of his emotional landscape.

"Stand."

She didn't hesitate. In seconds, he faced her toward the spider web. "Feet up on the first rung."

Binding her to the unit took some time, but when he completed the task, both arms and legs spread to the four corners of the frame. The night he met her flooded his mind. The fantasy of putting her in a four-point bind on her lyra rose up as if he was having the vision for the first time again. She did that for him. She made him feel things anew. Like a siren, this woman fucked him up six ways from Sunday, calling up emotions he'd carefully boxed and put away years ago. Now it was her turn to feel something wholly new—the real man he'd spent ten years putting back together piece by piece after Alexander's just-in-time intervention.

Carrie materialized and held out a hair band to him. He managed to maintain his composure at the submissive assistant's sudden appearance, and took the elastic from her hand.

After securing Samantha's hair, he stepped backward to

Lucky

admire his work, the gold rope securing her in several places. He pressed his foot on the pedal that maneuvered the back-and-forth motion of the unit and lowered her to a forty-five-degree angle.

"Very nice," a male voice said behind him.

She'd re-curled her hands over the links. Afraid he'd invite someone to their party? *Not likely.* The man's intrusion was not only unwelcome but also rude. Derek's only response was to glare at the man, who replied with a casual shrug of his shoulders before stepping away. *Men around the block, as usual.*

Derek ran fingertips over her tight ass, slowly, in a silent treatise to the perfection he'd admired the first night he'd met her. His anger paused for a second, but returned when she shuddered under his hand. If he had any sense, he wouldn't be doing this scene—one orchestrated and demanded by a willful maybe-submissive he'd grown dangerously obsessed with. But damn, he hadn't played publicly in over a year. He had enough ego to know they'd draw a crowd, and she was fresh submissive meat.

"I'm going to start with my hand and then work up from there. Remember Iceland."

37

A whirring sound had sent the spider web to rest at a sharp angle, her face pressed in between two of the metal chains. The links cut into her thighs, her arms, and her belly, which only ignited her libido. Her thighs dampened as he ran slow circles with his palm on her backside.

First, a light, attention-grabbing slap. Perhaps he was testing her to see if she was serious. She curled her fingers into the steel. The next smack wasn't unexpected, but the strength he'd used to deliver the harsh blow was. She cried out a little, but hung on. As if she could have gone anywhere … neither her body nor her resolve could have her be anywhere else.

The next set of spanks came harder and faster and with a skill apparent by the way he knew exactly where to cause the greatest sting. He still hadn't used all his strength, and without needing him to vocalize his intention, she knew what was coming. His arms had held her. She knew what his muscles could deliver.

He alternated with hard and soft, and she shifted on the webbing, which only kindled new sore spots. Welts had to be forming. He rubbed firm circles on her bruised ass, stopping briefly to squeeze. He knew exactly how hard and where to put pressure to cause the most pain. She swallowed back any whimpers that dared to escape and dove deep into that buzzing that began in her belly and traveled up her torso.

After long minutes of him applying pressure and then backing off, her body cried out for him to stop—but also to squeeze harder. Like testing a sore tooth with her tongue, she grew desperate for him to slap her again and ignite those sore spots.

Now that he took her seriously, she relaxed—sort of—into her bonds. If he'd held back, it would have been worse.

A series of new blows made her legs dance in their bindings. More pain from the steel webbing and the rope woke up new parts of her body, and still he didn't stop smacking the fleshiest part of her ass.

But it was a fast whipping noise followed by a red-hot stripe of pain that caused her to cry out. She couldn't have kept her lips closed if Derek himself had muzzled her. The sting rippled up her backside to her nipples. Her hips would not stay still; if only she could move over an inch she could rub herself against the smaller chains that crisscrossed in the middle.

She turned her face to rest against one of the metal chains. Voyeurs had gathered but they were distant ghosts who stood in the shadows. A deep breath helped her manage the pain that kept her from sinking deep into the sensation, kept her just on this edge of awareness.

"Want it harder?"

Had he asked her a question? Her ears buzzed with her blood rushing. *Fuck*. His next blow *hurt*. The bottoms of her feet aching from standing on the thin metal links, her skin rubbed raw from ropes, and sharp points along her chest from leaning into unyielding metal—all these sensations competed for attention.

Powerful claps against her flesh signaled he wasn't asking her anything. He teased her. She'd begun to feel warm, loose, and a little sluggish—except for her pussy, which ached for his attention. She liked the floaty feeling that danced around the stinging throbs coming from all parts of her body.

"Samantha. Your master asked you a question."

"More," she gritted out.

His hand circled her waist and his fingers circled her clit. The ripples in her pussy and ass morphed into a deep pulse. If only she could push forward and capture his finger…

"Bad little ballerina." When his finger pressed inside, a long moan traveled up her throat. "Jesus, so wet and just waiting to be fucked. Is that what you want?"

Without thought, the truth fell from her lips. "I want what you need."

His hand left her. A long swipe as light as a whisper trailed down her arm. She turned her head. He held a long black feather, which he lazily ran up and down her forearm. She jerked her hand against the rope binding her to the frame—but only when he ran the feather from her face down her neck and down her spine did her nerve endings erupt into a maddening cruel itch, layered on top of the maze of agony that trolled up and down her body. After a dozen passes along her back, he moved to her legs. This pain was unbearable. Not a sadist, he'd said. He'd lied. He was.

She cried out as he trailed the long feather up the inside of one thigh, over her ache and down the inside of the other leg. Her jaw clenched down so hard she could barely draw in breath.

Anger returned with a vengeance. She was bound and secured, ready and waiting for him, and he teased her with a fucking *feather*. She shuddered again, igniting new sore points along the front of her body. It did little to squelch the fire-y itch on her back and legs that slowly drove her insane.

"Derek, p-please." She hung in her bindings, gasping but needing something that skirted the edges of her understanding.

"Say Iceland," he growled in her ear. He trailed the feather through her aching, wet slit.

"No." Why couldn't he just take her, use her, let it all out *on her*. Why this tease, why drive her insane? *Fuck*. If he trailed that feather along her leg again, she'd scream.

The suspension unit rose again so she was upright. Bloodflow cascaded down her legs raising up new pinpricks of sensation.

He slapped her ass hard once more and the sting eased at least some of the itch. For long minutes he worked her over until she felt warm tears paint her cheeks. She'd given up trying to keep herself in place. When she finally gave in to the rope's hold, she realized she hadn't needed to hang on at all. Until Derek freed her, her body was glued to this unit, open and available to whatever he wanted to do. The irony of that understanding nearly made her laugh.

He moved his hand around her waist to rub her clit in steady circles until she strained against her bindings so hard the pleasure and pain mixed until neither one was recognizable.

"Oh, God." She ground herself against his erection, now pressed into the small of her back. He flexed against her as if fucking her, but not. If he had penetrated her, she'd release in seconds. Instead, he kept her on the edge.

Once more, he left her and the loss of his body made her cry out. Another hot tear ran down her cheek.

He circled the suspension and stood before her. Even though her skin was on fire, her pussy ached and her thighs grew wetter from his penetrating stare.

"Samantha." His growl matched the intensity in his eyes. "You want more, don't you?" he asked.

She sank further into her bindings. "Yes, more. You."

"Be careful what you wish for."

After he circled around to her back once more, her ass and thighs took more blows from him lashing at her with something hard yet flexible. A leather strap? The wash of heat made her crave more despite hurting like a bitch. One last smack, harder than any before, exploded up her backside to her throat.

The only words left came out, stilted and raw. "I love you."

∽

Samantha couldn't have slapped him any harder than with those three words, and a crushing panic built in his chest. He dropped the leather strap he'd used to punish her ass, though he wanted to strike her repeatedly as if he could drive out any lingering feeling she might have for him.

She kept presenting her ass and letting out those yelps of pain that called up the deep, carnal parts of himself he'd kept under wraps for so long. He didn't know shit about love, and now this beautiful woman pushed him toward it like no female had before. By doing what? Giving him what he'd wanted since the first moment he'd met her? By offering herself and her flesh so willingly?

Despite Alexander lording over her in the Library, he knew the truth. He'd always known the truth. While Alexander watched, Samantha had knelt in a rope dress waiting for *him*.

He squeezed his eyes shut to clear his vision. When he opened them he drank in her face, slack and pale with pleasure and pain and that stubborn resolve that landed her here

Lucky

to begin with. Fuck him, she was beyond her limits … way, way beyond.

He touched her back and she shuddered as if he'd struck her anew. "Easy, girl."

"Derek. I love you … love…"

"Ballerina. Breathe. I'm taking you down."

"No!" She rattled the steel chains.

He'd gone too far.

"I *love* you." She gritted out the words, not hearing him. She was so lost in subspace she'd never hear him like this.

"Stop," he said.

"Make me." She shot out the words, hard.

While he fisted her hair so she'd be forced to look at him, he gave her ass another slap. Her flesh wobbled under his hand and, damn her, she met the pain as he recognized the hardening lust in her eyes.

"Iceland," he gritted out.

"W-what? I'm not done."

"We're more than done."

Alexander appeared to his right in seconds. He'd been there the whole time. Disgrace ate at his insides. Only his experience kept him from throwing his rope to the floor and heading to the door.

"Carrie." That was Alexander's only word.

The submissive assistant placed her hand on Derek's arm. "I've got her."

"Back off." He reached for his rope coiled around Samantha's limbs. No one else would touch it. After ensuring her legs were free, he moved to her arms. Coiling his arm around her waist, he eased her off the unit and caught her in his arms. Her hot tears stained his neck, and breath ran through her lips in short pants. She was more than done.

Thankfully, neither Carrie nor Alexander followed him as he exited the Library and carried Samantha down the hall toward his room. After laying her on the bed, he slowly undid her hair, careful not to pull on the strands too harshly. Her hand clutched at his arm, even as he rubbed a special ointment of Arnica and lavender into her bruises.

"Derek." Her soft voice sounded unsure. "I love you." Those words again.

"You don't know me."

"I do. You're my ... mine ... my gentleman. Master." Her eyes had colored with that milky quality, just like a submissive, floating and unbalanced beyond their right mind. "With beautiful eyes."

"You're beautiful." He meant his words. Everything about this woman deserved more than him.

His hand found its way to her face. "Sleep, ballerina. I'll be here when you wake."

He sank to the small club chair in the corner of the room, more to distance her from his rage about nearly losing control tonight than any real need to sit. She stared at him until she couldn't. As she drifted to sleep, he grew more awake. He wasn't going to sleep—maybe never again.

But, Jesus, he was tired. He leaned back in his chair and tried to drink in the peace that emanated from her.

Jonathan's words still rang in his ears. *Picture her pregnant with another man's child.* He didn't want a child, yet the ridiculous thought of her round and full rose in his mind like a harvest moon. Fuck, he'd spanked and flogged that woman to the point of no return and now jealousy arose? Samantha deserved more than him, despite what his friends thought.

Every smile she'd given him held secret messages of what she needed—a normal life of Sunday morning pancakes and men who played with their children in the park. It didn't matter how many studios he built her. Studios wouldn't be enough. There wasn't enough rope or parachute silk to stop her longings, despite her audacity to storm her way into his world.

Hell, he could concede his world. He could marry her and give her children. They might sneak away for a week a year, get a handful of scenes in, secret their desires away for fear the kids could find out.

That's not the reason and you know it.

Even if he weren't into kink, he'd soon grow so resentful he'd fuck them up somehow. Not in a big way, but he'd begin with small things that wouldn't seem so bad at first. His transgressions would pile up, destroying her inch by inch, until they were both crushed by disappointment. They'd become two unhappy people coexisting until they were shells of their former selves.

He was going to have to crush her with the truth about himself.

Tomorrow.

38

Derek stretched his neck, stiff from nodding off upright. After spending hours watching Samantha curl around his pillow, her face a mask of pure peace, he finally stood and moved to the one window of his Accendos bedroom. He watched the dark sky change to gray, as he had so many nights from this very place. The steel gray lightened to pale yellow and then blazed orange with the rising sun. As cliché as it sounded, something about the breaking dawn did provide him a jolt of well-being, as if perhaps today would be different. Now with Samantha sleeping in his bed behind him, her lips parted in long, soft breaths, her very presence reminded him he was the same.

"I'm not doing this," he said to the Washington skyline.

"Do what?"

Samantha's soft hazel eyes blinked up at him. Jesus, even battered from their scene, hair askew from a deep sleep, he could have fallen on her and ravished her body.

He eased himself down to sit next to her on the bed. She sat up in response. "Are you okay?"

Lucky

He huffed out a small laugh. Once more, she was worrying about him. "How are you?"

"In love."

He sighed and gazed at the dark gray carpeting. "Don't be."

Her small hand landed on his arm, and he shuddered from her caring gesture.

"Today you'll stay in bed. Master's orders." Even his voice betrayed him as it cracked on the honorific she'd bestowed upon him last night.

She slowly sunk under the sheets and smiled. "You'll stay with me? You won't leave?"

"I have no intention of leaving you." He couldn't have left this beautiful creature if he tried, and he had no idea what to do with that truth.

"Good. I'm never leaving you, either."

"You will." He turned to face her. "You asked why I'm not having children. I had another brother. He died right before his second birthday. Drowned. My mother was … distraught. That's how I ended up in boarding school."

"Oh, Derek. I-I'm sorry." Her hand once more descended on his arm, and goddamn him, this time he flinched.

"It was my fault. You need to know that."

"It couldn't have been. You were a child."

A completely inappropriate smile played on his lips. God, she was so trusting. Beautiful—stunning, actually—but she was, oh, so naive.

"It was my fault all right."

His mind did what it always did when he'd allow it to wander. He sifted through every detail of that day. The way the rope on the swing felt in his hand. The high-pitched yell from Bret around the side of the barn. The feathery sways of Ethan's blond hair in the water as he floated face down. His

305

mother's howls. The sharp-pointed thought that his life would never, ever be the same.

He had to stand again.

"I was supposed to be watching him. It was my one job when my parents were off somewhere. Our nanny—"

"You had a nanny?"

He stopped his insane pacing. "Of course. She was off that day and I was left in charge. We were at our country house. Bret went off to explore this old barn on the place. I thought Ethan was with him. He wasn't. He was playing in the creek. He must have fallen in." Derek lifted his eyes and hoped she didn't want any more details. "That's where he died. Drowned."

"It wasn't your fault," she repeated.

"Samantha. Stop it."

"No. I love you anyway. All the way through to the other side." She was a terrible submissive. She sat up, kicked off the sheets and slid her arms around his waist, fully nude, her hair smelling of springtime and sleep. Her nipples grazed his chest. As his arms encircled her, his hands meet indentations on her back. A hardened lust rose up like a beast. It shot clear through his head, spearing any logic.

So what. Let her finally have all of him—including his rage.

"Get on the bed and spread your legs wide."

∼

Samantha didn't need to hear that story to know something bad had happened. No one bit out sharp words as quickly as he had in recent days without a reason behind the hostility. His past tortured him. His pain bled into the room every time the subject of family was raised. Did no one ever tell him his brother's death wasn't his fault?

Lucky

He thinks he's unlovable. What a load of bull. Last night she'd floated on a dream, slept hard and now, sore and aching from receiving his pain, her world had never been so clear.

Derek was *everything*—generous, beautiful, noble, and *hers*.

The thought his own family let him steep in this pain for so long raised a fury so harsh she had to shelve it for fear of veering off course. Then she remembered he didn't let much out. Did they even know?

Before she could puzzle out what she could say, what she could do, his sharp, steel-blue eyes bored clear through her thinking as they had last night. They colored to that shade that indicated he was on a mission.

She crawled to the center of the mattress.

Derek ripped his shirt off, buttons bouncing across the carpet. Shoes and jeans were next, abandoned and kicked to the side.

"This is who you want?"

"Yes."

Her pussy ached and her thighs instantly grew wet from his penetrating stare. Even if he'd burn her to cinders and ash, she'd take it. If all he could do was use her body, she'd accept his wrath just so long as he didn't run—didn't abandon her.

He climbed onto the bed, his eyes pinning her to the mattress as if she'd been strapped down.

His growl matched the intensity in his eyes. She hadn't the faintest interest in withholding her body from him or punishing him for taking out his anger on her. She'd meet him wherever he was willing to go, even if that place held so much pain she'd have to take it for the both of them.

His cock was inside her so fast she cried out. He didn't stop to check on her, instead battered her insides with long thrusts. So much fluid had gathered, he slid inside her to the hilt with no difficulty.

She wrapped her legs around him wanting him closer, deeper. She let her head fall backward and lifted her chin to give him access to her throat, baring more skin for his hungry mouth to devour. His lips punished her neck, his hands roughly manipulating her, positioning her where he wanted her—spread wide and taking him fully.

"I love you. I love you. I love you," she whispered into his hair. She wouldn't let him avoid what she knew in her heart. He loved her, too. So she'd say it as many times as needed for him to accept the truth.

Sounds of flesh slapping together filled the room, the bed shaking underneath them as he pounded her body for long minutes. The pure silk bedcover under her back rubbed her skin until it was on fire, and she still wanted more. She'd always want more from Derek.

As he came, he barked a choked curse into her neck, her skin wet from his mouth working her over, or perhaps from faint tears. She didn't care so long as some of his pain was released.

Their bodies clung together until their skin cooled. He didn't let go of her as he slowly lifted his weight off her. He cupped her face with one palm and turned her gaze to him. Miserable, beautiful blue-green eyes shone down on her, definitely wet.

"I'm sorry," she said. "I shouldn't have pushed you. I should have waited until you were ready, but maybe you were seeking the right place to put your pain. I can be your safe place."

No woman could have loved more in that instant than she loved this man. If she had to stalk him to the ends of the earth to be with him, to take care of him, she was going to do it.

Lucky

"You're going to regret this, you know."
She felt her brows furrow in question.
"Making me love you," he continued.
"No, I won't. Not ever."

39

Hours of paperwork and still the stack of work on Derek's desk didn't seem to diminish. It was going to be a long night. Especially since he longed to see Samantha. She also had classes to teach until nine. He didn't care how much work was left on his desk. He was picking her up at 9:01.

He caught his reflection in the glass. Nighttime had fallen heavily over Washington. He stood at the window and watched traffic slowly crawl up Pennsylvania Avenue. His eyes honed back in on his reflection. He didn't look any different.

Last night's reveal of his past to Samantha had a curious effect. He now understood the Catholic Church's sacrament of confession. He did feel a little lighter, though not entirely saved.

Yet his friends were right. He had been a fool trying to contain his emotions around her. Being loved and being in love still felt like he had on the wrong suit, as if it belonged to another man. He supposed one had to break in a new emotion like you did new shoes. His body certainly was getting used to the idea, his cock complaining loudly about being separated from her all day.

Part of him wanted to take her back to Accendos, bind her to the Library's spider web suspension and see how long she could take the steel chains biting into her skin. Perhaps another time. He hadn't fully forgiven her for going without him. He'd withhold that desire of hers a little longer, and cool off more. Besides, they had plenty of rigging spots to explore in his penthouse.

His phone buzzed.

"Nick."

Derek's attorney never called with good news.

"Mr. Wright. The two gentlemen you pressed charges against? Got word they've made bail."

"How?"

"We're trying to find out. In the meantime, I thought you'd want to know."

"Thanks, Nick. Keep monitoring."

He killed the call. This town was fucked up. Damning evidence should have set bail so high no two-bit criminals, nor their friends, could make it.

His text to Mark was direct and to the point.

Security back on, Mark. Guys made bail.

In case the thugs got any bad ideas to pick up where they'd left off, he wanted to make sure Samantha and her crew were covered. Moving on them would be the stupidest thing anyone could do, but he never overestimated the intellectual capacity of criminals.

He pulled on his suit jacket. He'd head over to Samantha's early. With any luck, it was an adult-only night and no Lyra Ladies.

His footfalls echoed in the still parking lot. A quick double-click on his key fob and the lights of his Ferrari flashed on. He reached for the door handle. Without warning, he was pushed forward. His head exploded in pain as his skull cracked against the hood of his car. Strong hands twisted his arm behind his back. His legs were knocked out from under him, and blacktop slammed into his jaw.

Dazed, he felt himself being lifted by his jacket lapels. Instinct from years of basic fight training brought his hands up between him and the brawny, tattooed arms that grasped the material of his suit. He leaned back away from his attacker. Derek rocketed a right uppercut to the man's jaw, breaking the son of a bitch's hold. A head-butt to the attacker's face splattered blood into Derek's eye. A wounded roar sounded from the animal, undoubtedly due to the unmistakable crunch of the bastard's nose against his forehead.

He hadn't fought in years, yet the memory flooded back to his muscles. A second aggressor punched him in the side. Derek rounded on the man and let loose with a right hook followed by a left uppercut.

Shouts echoed in the distance. Others were approaching. Security guards, no doubt. He didn't care. Fury and adrenaline had taken over his very soul.

He pinned the man against the chassis of the car and unleashed his rage in a flying series of hits to the man's body. It felt good to let loose, remembering a time when polish and poise didn't matter, when a man could take matters into his own hands. He released all the heartbreak and pain, everything he'd held inside for far, far too long.

∽

Derek cracked open one eye and fire seared his retina. A football stadium's worth of lights shone down on him.

"I didn't take you for a fighter." Alexander Rockingham's voice thundered through the too-white space. With supreme effort, Derek turned his head. Alexander sat in a chair too small for his large frame.

Oh, yeah, he'd been in a fight.

"Clearly I'm not a good one."

The events in the parking lot came back to him with unusual clarity. He was surprised he was alive, as one guy had at least fifty pounds on him, the other maybe seventy.

"Samantha." Her name came out in stuttered syllables.

"She's fine. She's with your mother. She's one tough cookie."

"You have no idea. My mother's made of steel." Derek tried to sit up, but his muscles protested. "Go rescue her, will you?"

"I was talking about Sam's strength."

"Samantha."

"She prefers Sam. At least that's what she told your mother." Alexander had the gall to smile.

"Good girl. So how are the other guys?"

"Back in jail. Not going to make bail this time. I've taken care of it. Cindy's mugger, apparently, was a brother of one of the guys who attacked you. He confessed to putting him up to it. So the mugger's going down, too."

"Oh my God!"

Derek winced as his mother's voice nearly broke the sound barrier. A jarring of his bed made him wince harder. "Oh, my poor boy." Her cool hand touched his forehead, the metal of her rings even colder.

"I'm fine, Mother. Samantha—"

"I'm right here." The sight of her bathed him in relief. He hadn't realized how high his shoulders had risen until he lowered them.

Samantha circled the bed to stand on the other side. "How are you feeling?"

He flinched when her fingers pressed into his bruised and swollen hand.

"Oh, I'm sorry."

He latched onto her hand. Contact with her skin was the best medicine.

"Are you in pain? Do you need me to get the nurse? Where is that woman?"

"Mother, please. I'm fine." He kept his eyes on Samantha, who wore concern across her forehead.

"Truly?" She drew in a stuttered breath.

Alexander stood. "Mrs. Wright—"

"Barlow. It's Mrs. Barlow now."

"Mrs. Barlow, I was wondering if you'd accompany me to the nurse's station. The police have a few questions."

"Police?" She threw her hand to her chest in mock horror.

"I'll go." Samantha's concern cooled. She slipped her hand free from Derek's clasp. "It was me they were after anyway."

His mother threw her a visual pitchfork.

"Mother," he said sharply to her.

"No, Derek. It's okay." Samantha smiled at him and, Jesus how did she do that? Her smile was a counter measure against anything, even visual bombs. "I won't be long. Alexander, if you don't mind going with me?"

"With pleasure."

Alexander extended his arm, which Samantha took with another dazzling smile.

His mother scooted the chair Alexander had vacated closer. She pulled out a handkerchief from her bag. Instead of dabbing her eyes in mock sadness, she pressed it against his forehead. "Five stitches. Not too bad. Your hair will cover—"

"I don't care about my forehead, Mother."

"I do. I care about every inch of you." His mother's voice

Lucky

sounded strange—not at all like herself. Then again, it could have been the painkillers they gave him.

He lifted his hand and examined the IV piercing the back of his hand, where his skin was marred with small red cuts. "Oh, you know me. I bounce back."

"Yes. You and your brother are strong men." She focused on her hands. "I've always admired that about you both."

He didn't know what to say to this stranger inhabiting his mother's body, so he leaned his head back and stared at the ceiling.

"You love her."

That was not what he expected to hear.

"Yes."

"She has a sunny smile. Warm." What do you know? His mother nailed the perfect word for Samantha Rose. She was the sun. No wonder so many people gravitated to her, circled her, wanted to be in her orbit, himself included. Still, he hadn't a clue how to reconcile the whole children thing. *Fuck him.*

She patted his hand. "It's good you found someone."

"Oh, really?" He started to count the ceiling tiles but they kept shifting. His eyesight was so wobbly. It had to be the drugs.

"I know what you think of me. The truth is, you and your brothers are the only things that ever mattered to me. Ever. When Ethan died..."

His head careened around, his neck wrenched. He must have flinched because she said, "Do you need the nurse?"

"No. Please, let's not do this."

"Samantha said something. She's right that maybe you need to hear it again." *Here she goes.*

"It wasn't your fault. It wasn't. I was supposed to be there. I was the adult, Derek."

He craned his neck so he could look at the window and

315

not her face. He'd never thought about it that way. What did you know? His mother had a sliver of responsibility in her after all. Still…

The snap of her purse went off like gunfire. "I know I'm the last person you want to see right now."

"You're not the last person." That sounded so much better in his head. It didn't matter that she'd been a terrible mother —hell, no mother at all. She didn't deserve the amount of hostility he lobbed at her. "I mean…"

"I know. I love you, Derek." She stood, gave him a shaky smile, and walked out.

"I love you, too, Mom." That was the problem, wasn't it? He did.

He loved her and Samantha, and he hadn't a clue what to do with that information.

40

Samantha eased Cindy away from a shaking Joanne Bradstreet.

"Cindy, why don't you go—"

"No. Fucking. Way." Cindy's eyes bore holes in Joanne, who responded to the hostility with a visible swallow.

"I came here to apologize. I got a call from the police station. My ex—"

"The asshole."

"Yes. That's him." Joanne straightened, obviously tired of being berated by a viciously angry Cindy.

"Ladies. Students." Samantha cocked her head toward the curtain where four of her teenage students had to have heard this whole exchange. They were too silent in there, even though they were supposed to be helping her set up for the kids' recital and invasion of parents in three hours.

"I'm not going to stay long," Joanne said. "Like I said. I came to apologize for any trouble Curtis and his idiot brothers caused."

"You mean the mugging, the attack on Sam and destruction of property owned by a member of the Mafia. See? No swearing, Sam."

"*Cindy.* He's not Mafia. Go help them get ready." Samantha pointed at the curtain. Cindy sashayed by Joanne and threw back the curtain in a flourish. Four girls straightened from their crouch and backed into the room. They'd been listening.

"Go on," Sam said to a clearly nervous Joanne. If she'd been a part of the last week's violent acts, she sure was hiding her cooperation well. Of course, many dancers were also great actresses.

"My ex-husband wasn't a good man. It's why I left him. And his brothers? They're worse. I'm sorry they went after you. I mean, I told him I needed something for myself. If I was successful, then, well, maybe I'd consider seeing him again. *Maybe.* He took that as an action plan."

"I can tell."

"Curtis always was a little delusional. The court-appointed psychiatrist said he has socio-pathic tendencies, and he doesn't see the world right. I didn't know his brothers had been in prison, and they and Curtis had been coming around. They must have heard me leaving a message for you or something."

"Yeah, we got your messages."

She sighed. "Sorry about that, too. It's been hard. Stress doesn't bring out the best in me. I shouldn't have taken it out on you."

"No, you shouldn't have."

Joanne bit her lip and turned to leave.

Sympathy and anger fought with each other in Sam's brain. She chose to just let it go. There weren't any more words to say.

Before heading down the stairs, Joanne turned back once more. "Oh, the East Coast Aerial Extravaganza moved up their deadline. Saw it on the website this morning. You shouldn't miss it."

"Thanks."

The last thing on her mind was entering a dance competition. She appreciated Joanne's gesture, however. It meant something.

"Joanne. Truce?"

The woman nodded. "Truce. One last thing. I heard about you and Derek Damon Wright. Be careful, okay?"

Why was everyone warning her away from Derek? He was a good man. Clearly, Joanne was no one to judge. She had terrible taste in men, even worse than Samantha had. Well, her taste had improved.

She and Derek were now a couple. She'd practically moved into his penthouse with him last week as he recuperated from his fight. The bruises on his face faded, like the memory of what it was like to live without him. She couldn't imagine them *not* being together. The world would just have to catch up to that fact.

As for now? She had a kids' recital happening in three hours and a transfer to her repaired new studio later in the week. Derek planned on supervising the move. As for her Lyra Ladies recital? He didn't have to come if he didn't want to. She was done pushing him. She now understood why kids scared him. If he showed up, fine. If he didn't, fine.

I think.

~

Derek stood outside Samantha's new studio, watching parents and children climb the rickety stairs to Samantha's old studio. Where would she fit them all? Her new studio would be ready in a few days, but she staunchly refused to delay her recital. She cited how Washington parents had trouble enough with scheduling; throwing a new date at them less than two weeks out wouldn't work. She was right.

He leaned against his sedan. Rich sat patiently in the driver's seat, likely wondering when he'd push off and go inside.

Perhaps he'd take one more trip to her new building next door to see if the 24/7 security he'd hired was in place. *What a weak stalling tactic.* A few parents milled outside, mostly men. The fathers seemed as uncomfortable as he was, delaying their entrance. He recognized Fitness Mom talking to a tall man. Amber Lynn clung to his leg. A strange sensation cut through his chest at the sight of her arm engulfed in a too-large, horrendously bright pink cast adorned with scribbles and decals. He couldn't tear his eyes away from it.

"Mr. Wright! Mr. Wright!" Amber ran over to him. "Look what I did." She lifted her cast. "You have to sign it. Daddy, Daddy, this is Miss Rose's boyfriend." *What a pair of lungs.*

The man walked over to him. Derek shook his hand. "You have quite a talented daughter."

"When she holds on." Her mother had sidled up to him. "Mr. Wright, good to see you. Come on, Amber Lynn, we don't want to be late."

Before the little girl could be dragged away, she turned to him. "You'll sign it, right? I saved you a special sticker, too."

Her large, innocent eyes focused up at him adoringly. Oh, what the hell.

"Sure I will. See you inside."

She smiled and bounced back to her mother's outstretched hand.

He turned to his driver. "Rich, we need to go somewhere."

∽

Samantha's grandmother sat on the couch, eight-year-old

Lucky

Jessica banded to her side. She formed the young girl's hands into a fist.

"A," Jessica repeated.

Her grandmother smiled down on her. "Very good."

Samantha loved those little girls. For the last few months, her Lyra Ladies had been trying to learn ASL, which touched her heart even more.

Amber Lynn careened into the room. "Miss Rose, Miss Rose, where are the stickers? I saved one for him."

"They're in the third drawer, Amber. Who?"

Amber didn't reply but took off like a shot toward the new teak desk Derek had sent over a few days ago. While he'd been recovering from his injuries, he hadn't slowed down one bit. From his penthouse, he'd ordered furniture not only for her new place, but her old one, too. That wasn't all. She fingered the sparkly Tiffany necklace he'd draped over her neck two days ago. The man had a serious shopping addiction.

Amber Lynn returned waving a paper that held stickers, though most of them had already found their way to her cast. She'd made a major point of choosing which stickers her fellow students and the adults got to pick for adorning her broken arm. Forget Broadway. Samantha had a feeling Amber was on her way to becoming a CEO.

"Sam, you about ready?" Cindy stood in the entrance to the studio space. "It's five minutes past."

She peered inside. On one end, thirty or so parents on folding chairs chatted with each other. Six of her Lyra Ladies, clad in pink tights and sequin bodysuits, nervously tittered behind a screen she'd set up in the far corner as their dressing area. The little fairy lights hung from the ceiling made the lyra hoop gleam in the center of the room over a gymnastic mat. Everything was perfect, except for one thing. Derek was nowhere to be found. In her heart she was so sure he'd show, despite her earlier self-talk about it not mattering.

She needed to get a grip. He meant what he said. Children were not his thing, not in any shape or form. Despite her acceptance of Derek and all his former pain around his brother's death, a tiny corner of her heart held out hope that she might be able to shift his perspective. She'd done what countless women before her had done: believed he would change for her. But when it came to children, he couldn't—or wouldn't.

Did it matter?

The truth rang inside her like it usually did—loudly and with force.

Of course it did. She'd blame it on the fact she was surrounded by little girls, except she knew the truth. Her inner critic really had the *worst* timing.

Cindy dimmed the lights. The show was going to start whether she or Derek were ready. In that moment, the old adage of "the show must go on" never felt more oppressive.

∼

Derek pulled open the door to Samantha's studio, a familiar song wafting down the staircase. *Don't Deserve You* by Plumb. He climbed the stairs carefully, not wanting the creaking steps to interrupt the dancing.

As soon as he reached the top, he surveyed the scene through the open curtains to his left. A little girl in a blue sequined leotard sat in the hoop, spinning faster than he recognized as safe. Samantha crouched near the gymnastic mat underneath the tiny dancer as if she'd lurch to catch her if she fell.

The low lighting illuminated Samantha's face like an angel. She regarded the little girl with such awe, such

Lucky

palpable gratification, he felt his eyes go soft. He glanced at the parents, who wore similar looks.

"Sir." Rich's voice behind him caught him off guard. "Allow me. I'll handle it." The man took the two bags Derek held from him.

Derek eased inside the room and leaned against the door frame, a little mesmerized by the small dancer. She tumbled backward, landed on her feet and bowed to an appreciative, clapping audience. Another little girl, this time in white, stepped onto the mat and grasped the hoop, replacing the girl in blue.

They traded places, back and forth, each taking a turn at spinning, dropping, stretching, and showing off flexibility any adult would kill for. Their movements were smooth and confident, faces betraying not an ounce of fear. He grew spellbound by the power they didn't know they possessed. He knew more than most that a lack of fear was the most potent force on earth. Not strength, not even intelligence could compete with the magical, *worry-free* ignorance of youth. Had he ever been that innocent?

On a long musical note, the little girl's lithe body leaned backward, impossibly arched. When she slipped backward, her feet caught on the outside of the hoop, leaving her in an upside-down suspension. He nearly gasped aloud. A few parents weren't so silent; they quickly erupted into applause.

Her little hands reached toward the floor, her hands flourishing. He recognized the move from Samantha's performance at Frost.

She taught them that.

The recital lasted forty-five minutes. When the show was over, the girls hugged each other, like little adults, and bounced around the room with no loss of energy from their performance. The adults wore fatigue along with their conservative Washington outfits, their faces a mixture of concern and delight. Rolling his shoulders, Derek loosened some of his own tension amassed from watching the little bodies bend and twist in impossible positions—whose miscalculation, he knew, could too easily result in a shocking pink cast adorned with stickers and colored writing.

Small arms grasped his legs, breaking his admiration. He peered down at Amber Lynn, who gaped up at him with excited eyes. "Hi!"

"Hi."

She let go of him and shoved a half-empty page of stickers up toward his chest. "You're this one." With a silver pen, she pointed to a small horse. "I saved it for you."

He lifted the paper closer to his face. The sticker of a small white horse with a knight on its back came into focus in the dim lighting. If Amber Lynn knew the truth about him, she wouldn't have reserved this sticker. He glanced down at her.

"This one, huh?"

She nodded, vigorously. "It's you."

He didn't know how or why someone so pure could equate him with a knight in shining armor. Eh, little girl romanticism, he thought. Who was he to argue? He lifted it from the backing and placed the sticker on her cast, which she held up like a queen presenting her hand to be kissed.

"Now, sign." She said the words with such conviction she could give his managers a run for their money.

He took the pen and initialed under the knight sticker.

Amber Lynn appraised his work and nodded up at him as if she'd approved.

"You came." Samantha's voice rolled over him.

He straightened. "You invited me and ... I promised." *Speaking of which.* He turned to go retrieve his gifts for the girls when he found Rich standing behind him.

Lucky

"Sir." He lifted the two bags. "I stored them in their mini fridge. Not ideal but they didn't melt too much."

Derek took the two bags and turned to Samantha who held Amber Lynn in a close embrace. "Pink ice cream."

Amber Lynn squealed. "Jessica! Ice cream!" she yelled to another little girl off to the side. "You're the best!" She latched on to Derek's legs again and gave him a squeeze that shot up his whole body.

What do you know? He actually felt like that dime store knight sticker. The Queen of England couldn't have bestowed a greater title.

Amber Lynn ran to where Rich had set up a mini ice cream dishing station on Samantha's new desk. Yep, those little girls were going to rule the world someday, judging by the way they immediately ordered Rich to make the scoops *really, really big*.

Samantha's eyes welled with tears. "Thank you."

One of the Washington mothers grasped her arm, seeking her attention. Congratulating parents, beaming over their children's achievements, swamped her. She radiated joy. So, this was her greatest accomplishment—seeing others do well. He was awestruck.

She was better than him, he realized. Only happy when other people were, Samantha Rose was an exceptional human being. No man on this earth was luckier than him.

The kids swarmed her next. They all wanted her praise, her encouragement. He understood their need. Basking in Samantha's approval was like being adopted into the rarest club of all—the club of unconditional love.

Jesus. He was now on the inside of that club.

He had always seen women as something to put into the cracks of his life—like flowers bursting through flaws in the sidewalk. They weren't part of his real life. Opening properties, amassing a fortune and a fortress, making sure no one could get inside—that was his reality. What an asshole thing to believe.

Samantha Rose threatened to push out what used to be the main parts of his life and take over. Why wasn't he panicked? Rather, a sense of privilege overcame him.

Alexander was right. It was time to go for exceptional.

While Samantha said good-bye to her students and their parents, he managed to pull Cindy to the side.

"Cindy, how would you like to be my cohort in crime?"

"You're speaking my language. Does it involve trashing Joanne's studio? 'Cause I have a crowbar and a big hammer."

"No, something better. Much better."

Derek knew one thing about himself. Once he made a decision, he didn't turn back—until a new, better option came along. One had. It was time for him to pay his membership dues to Samantha's club.

41

"You sure you don't mind, Derek? Cindy seems kind of freaked out about something. She wants me to come over and have a sleep-over. I swear to God, if Chaz did something..."

"I'm sure she wants to dish about him."

"Did you just say *dish*?"

"Cindy's rubbing off on me. I can part from that gorgeous body for one night. You can make it up to me."

"I'll have to go straight to the studio in the morning. Cindy booked me three privates starting at nine and my grandmother also wants me to come by for a late lunch afterward. I don't know why everyone suddenly wants to see me."

"I know why." Man, did he ever know why. He'd arranged her suddenly packed schedule. Occupying her wasn't a hard sell. Everyone wanted to be with Samantha. "They love you."

"Hey, why don't you come to our house for lunch tomorrow?" The "our" stung a little, a subtle reminder she'd only half moved in with him. A few drawers holding her clothes did not constitute a full move. Not after tomorrow, however. He was going to seal that deal.

"Another time," he said. "I have a meeting."

"On a Saturday afternoon?"

"Club owner, remember? Spend some time with Carina. I'm sure she misses you and wants you to herself. I'll have Rich pick you up at four thirty and bring you back here."

"I have a car, you know."

"So I've heard." That reminded him. She needed a new car. Stat. He added it to his internal shopping list. She'd look great in the new Jag F-type—red, of course.

"Ballerina, see you late afternoon. Text me when you leave in case I have to rescue you from the side of the road."

"I love you."

"Same here."

After hanging up, he turned back to his texting app. Everything was in motion. He even asked Jills to come by and help in case he panicked at the last minute. She was responsible for him meeting Samantha in the first place. That woman deserved a raise.

∼

After she and Rich got stuck behind an accident on H Street, Samantha finally made it to Derek's thirty minutes late. Funny, he didn't answer her texts. Maybe his meeting went long. She wasn't going to panic, like before. They'd gotten over a major hurdle. She'd take the win.

Still, good thing she now had a key to his place. She wanted nothing more than a good long soak in Derek's enormous bathtub. She was tired, sore from showing the helicopter move on the pole this morning a hundred times, and full. Her grandmother insisted she have two slices of her lemon génoise cake, her second favorite to the raspberry.

Samantha pushed the code into the console and waited for the elevator to appear. Everything appeared on half-

Lucky

time today. When the elevator doors opened to his apartment—or sky mansion, she liked to call it—silence met her ears. The door *snicked* behind her, echoing off the cold marble floor of his penthouse. Hmm, perhaps she wasn't the only one late getting home. *Home.* What a funny thought. She could never live here fully. The place was ridiculous—flat and perfect and sterile. Marble floors were cold.

Man, she was cranky. Good thing Derek wasn't here. She headed to the bathroom. Before turning into the master suite, she was stopped in her tracks at the entrance to the small office next to the master bedroom by a fresh paint smell and Derek on the floor washed in a blue light.

Oh, no, was he hurt? She ducked through the doorway and found him ... asleep. A paint roller was off to the side looking like it'd cemented in bright turquoise paint. She turned slowly.

The freshly painted walls were a deep Caribbean blue, the trim left white making the walls appear framed. Off-white tarps splattered with various colors were tucked close to the baseboard, more piled to the side as if hastily pulled back.

Her eyes locked on the far corner of the room. It couldn't be. What she saw was inconceivable.

In the corner, a brightly colored, slowly revolving, fish mobile hung over a baby crib. Plastic still lined the spindles on either side. She stepped closer. *Oh. My. God.* It was the DaVinci Kalani four-in-one convertible crib. Surpassing all safety standards, this one had a four-mattress height adjustment and a toddler rail for easy conversion. Made of New Zealand pine sourced from sustainable forests, it was the Mercedes of all cribs. She'd chipped in money to help buy that same one for two of her older students having babies.

Babies.

She blinked again.

A sudden deep breath made her twist around. Derek still slept, but had adjusted his arm so it lay over his head.

She sunk to her knees and leaned against the crib, feeling the solid wood against her back. For long minutes she studied him. Blue paint splatters covered his arm. White and blue paint etched the cuticles of one hand.

Her hand touched something. A screwdriver.

He'd done this—himself?

She took in more. Half a dozen Babies R Us shopping bags occupied the space where a desk had once stood. A stuffed yellow elephant peeked out of the top of one sack. Her eyesight wavered as tears pooled in her eyes. Any minute she'd wake up. Any second, this would all be a mistake, right?

She crawled toward him. She lay beside him, tucking her head into his shoulder. He didn't stir, his breath heavy through gorgeous, parted lips. Dark circles under his eyes made her think he'd been up all night. She took a long look at his profile.

That first night they'd met, she was struck by his good looks, his manners, his larger-than-life, unwavering confidence. He'd lifted her knee, bandaged it, fed her, made her feel better. He made her feel lucky and special. Her eyes pricked at the thought he'd lived thirty-four years with no one telling him he was *magnificent* at caring for someone. She only had to look at the half-painted Caribbean blue walls to know this man had an exceptional heart.

Feeling his chest rise and fall under her cheek, she also recognized Derek wasn't impervious. He'd been wrestling demons inside himself nearly his whole life, and in this room, perhaps, he'd battled them and won. Yet she felt somehow that *she* had won.

"What?" His sleepy voice broke through her overwhelming emotions.

Gah, she'd said her words out loud and woken him up.

Lucky

His arm descended on hers as he sucked in a long breath. She'd been gripping him tightly across his chest this whole time, like she wanted to hang on and never let go. He eased himself up, taking her with him.

"Samantha. I must have fallen asleep."

"It's perfect. You're perfect."

He rubbed his eyes. "There goes my surprise. I was going to blindfold you and everything. Hey, are you crying?"

"A little. What happened? How? When?" She swept her arm through the air.

He stood, taking her with him. "Got the urge to paint. Looks good on you." He lifted a strand of her hair with a drop of turquoise. He swiped a thumb under her eye, then shrugged. "This is what I know how to do."

"Paint?"

"Build things." He scrubbed his chin. "You like it? I mean I can change the color—"

"No, it's beautiful. I'm just … "

"Surprised?"

She nodded.

He smiled down at her, pleased, and took both of her hands in his. "You make me want things, Samantha. Things I didn't think … Well, I won't know how to do this, you know. This … kid thing."

"No one does. Not really."

"You will. You'll know exactly what to do. You're great at improvising."

"You're doing pretty well with me."

"Family is new to me. You'll have to show me." He dipped his chin. He was embarrassed?

"That means your commitment will be stronger."

One side of his mouth quirked up. "Not sure it could be any stronger where you're concerned."

He uncurled her hand. She hadn't realized how hard she'd

been gripping the key to his penthouse the whole time. An indentation had formed on her palm.

"My key. You weren't coming to return it?"

She snatched her hand back. "Not on your life, baby daddy."

A grave pallor washed over his face. "You don't ever have to worry about anything. I won't ever let anything happen to you or our…"

"I know. But I do have one question." Full monty, right? She sunk to her knees, dropped the key, and gripped his calves. "Will you marry me?"

His face cracked into another smile. "Admit it. You just want my gene pool."

"I do. I want my sons to be just like you. But I want more than that. I want all of you. So, say yes?"

"Since you asked." He lifted her to standing. "You better believe I'm going to marry you, Samantha Rose."

He led her over to the crib and picked up a small turquoise box that lay on the mattress, also still encased in plastic.

"The last piece of Tiffany. For today anyway."

The white ribbon floated to the ground. Inside was a small black velvet box.

He sunk to his knees. "Don't get used to me being in this position." He took the box from her and cracked it open. The sun couldn't have competed with the giant rock sitting atop a platinum setting.

"Yes," he said. "I will marry you."

Her lips stretched into a wide grin. "Good. I'll marry you, too. Though we're going to need to address your shopping habit."

He rose and slipped the ring on her finger, which immediately fell to the side from its weight.

"I love you, Samantha."

Lucky

She took in his beautiful eyes, now a clear green.

"You know what that means, don't you?" he asked. "We're going to have to go to Accendos, the Library. Kids and mad rope skills don't mix."

"Fine by me. But for now, Derek Damon Wright," she said, grasping his T-shirt, "want to make a deposit of your genes?"

He laughed, and then his lips silenced her. His body, on the other hand, spent over an hour telling her everything she needed to know. She'd chosen well. *Very well.*

Epilogue

"No, give him to Derek." Samantha leaned back in the hospital bed.

The nurse in the ridiculous pink top with the chicks and ducks splashed across the front turned away from Samantha and handed him the tiny bundle swaddled in a blue blanket as he fought down incipient panic. Good thing he was sitting.

As soon as the nurse placed the fragile being in his arms, heat seeped through the thin blue blanket. He stared down with disbelief. "I cannot believe I was ever this tiny."

"He didn't feel small a few hours ago."

"How are you? Do you need anything? I can—"

"Derek. I'm fine." Samantha cradled her head with her arm and stretched. The grimace that ran across her face vanished as soon as it appeared. "More than fine."

He had no idea how women gave birth more than once. After witnessing Samantha deliver their son, he understood why fathers called their wives their better half.

The nurse gave them both a smile and eased out of the room. He leaned into the tall back of the upholstered rocker he'd pushed beside Samantha's bed, keeping one eye on her and one on his son as he rocked back and forth.

"I think he likes it." The baby squirmed a little and his upper lip curled in pleasure—he thought. What did he know?

"See? I knew you'd know how to do this." Samantha tucked a piece of blanket between his arm and the baby. She stared at their son. *Their son*. Wow, they'd made a human—a living, breathing creature.

His tiny mouth opened in a grimace.

"What's wrong?"

Samantha looked amazingly calm that their son just experienced ... something.

"He yawned."

"Oh, huh."

"You know, this"—she lifted the Tiffany rattle he'd gifted her—"will be totally lost on him."

"Only the best for my son."

"Oh, just look at him." His mother's coo entered the room like a cannon. The baby flinched from the sudden voice. She leaned over Derek's shoulder. "He's got your eyes, Derek. Hmm, and your father's chin." She straightened. "Your grandmother and I are off to meet your parents, Samantha."

"Thank you for going to get them."

"I couldn't let Derek just send a car. Too impersonal."

"Don't be surprised if they're a little jittery. This will have been their first trip in a private jet."

"But not their last." Derek lifted the baby so they could see each other face to face. "I think he has Samantha's chin, Mother."

"Well, he's going to get your stellar education," his mother continued. "I have the best news. I got him on the waiting list at Fort Henry Military School. It wasn't easy but—"

"Take him off the list. He will never see the inside of a boarding school. We're considering homeschooling."

His mother sighed heavily. "I don't suppose we could talk about this?"

"We just did. Mother, thank you for picking up Samantha's parents. You better hurry."

"And that's my cue. You should unbundle him, Derek. Let him feel your skin. It helps in the bonding process."

He had no idea who this woman was, standing before him in her Chanel suit giving advice about connecting with a baby. Wonders never ceased.

He watched her leave the room. Finally! For the first time

in over twenty-four hours, he, Samantha and his son could be alone. Nurses, doctors, and her grandmother had hovered efficiently and with irritating calm during the whole birthing thing. He, on the other hand, had been reduced to engaging every deep breathing exercise he could remember. At least his mother stayed in the waiting room. Thank God he'd had the foresight to book a private hospital room months in advance of the baby's arrival.

The baby popped an arm free of the blanket. "Doesn't look too coordinated yet." His forearm was like silken cream, and more than a little red.

"Derek, open your shirt, put his face up to your neck."

He cradled his son so he could rest against him. A soft gurgling sound bubbled against his skin. He could spend hours like this—the little heat missile against his chest making alien grunting noises. A ferocious protectiveness rocketed through his whole body, and he had to be careful not to crush the little guy closer to him.

Samantha rested her hand against his leg and he nearly came undone at the contact.

"About his name," he said, more to distract himself from dissolving into a puddle of girly tears. "You sure? It's not cheesy?"

Samantha laughed. "Not cheesy at all. It's a beautiful tribute."

"Okay then." He brought the baby down to the crook of his arm so he could look him in the eyes. "Alexander Ethan Wright. Yes, the name fits."

He looked up at the woman he was going to spend the rest of his life making happy, and his vision clouded. Damn, guess he was just going to be emotional about the whole thing. Her smile coursed through his veins like he was mainlining heaven.

His son squirmed a bit, as if wanting his full attention. "He's pretty strong for being a few hours old."

"Like father, like son."

Oh, yeah, those emotions coursing through his limbs were on a rampage. He cleared his throat and handed her little Alexander. He leaned against her body, as much as he dared knowing what she'd just gone through. He needed the contact, however. He might never be able to be away from either of them ever again.

"I love you, Samantha." The words tumbled out as naturally as a breath. "I love both of you."

"We know." She grasped his fingers.

He lifted her hand and laid a kiss on her knuckles. "No, I want you to know that I *love* you … all the way through to the other side."

And then he wasn't the only one who spilled tears.

~ The End ~

Don't miss the next Elite Doms book, **Fearless**.
For a sneak peek, turn the page!

FEARLESS

Chapter One

The soft-close doors on her fire-engine red Maserati GranTurismo made a soft thunk. The elegant machine gave a quiet chirp when she hit the key fob. With a grimace, Sarah shifted on her new Valentino Rockstud patent-leather pumps and limped to the garage elevator for Club Accendos. While the heels were to-die-for gorgeous, an hour ago she'd lost all feeling but pain in her feet. She'd been on them since eight that morning with three client dress fittings, including one Senator's wife who could not make up her mind—as if choosing a blue tulle A-line over a black crepe shift was akin to national security. Ah, well, beauty had its price, and in the end, all that mattered was that her patrons were happy. With any luck, she'd make it to her private bedroom unnoticed despite what had to be a large crowd in the club. The garage was full. Thank god for her reserved parking space. She needed a lavender-scented bath and eight hours of blissful, uninterrupted sleep.

Fearless

The elevator doors slid open, and she came face to face with the owner of Club Accendos, Alexander Rockingham.

"Sarah, just who I was looking for." He stepped back to allow her to pass.

"Hello, Alexander, aren't you on your way out?" Ignoring the complaint from her throbbing feet, she rose on tip-toes and gave him a peck on the cheek.

"I saw you come in on the security camera. Have a minute for a walk in the garden? Everything's in bloom, and it won't take long." He jutted out his elbow in invitation.

"Of course." She slipped her arm through his. For her friend of fifteen years, she had all the minutes in the world to give. To hell with her aching feet.

"By the way, nice car. What made you decide on a Maserati?"

"It's beautiful? It purrs?" she offered with an unapologetic laugh. "Indulgent, I know. What can I say? I have a weakness for pretty things. Besides, if I have to be stuck in DC traffic as often as I am, I might as well do it in style."

"Nothing more than you deserve. You're working too hard, aren't you?" Alexander's handsome face formed a concerned frown.

She shrugged lightly and patted the arm that held hers. "It's spring. It's what I do, though I thought Mrs. Darden would never make up her mind this morning. When she finally did, she chose the first of the fifteen dresses she tried on."

"That brings me to good news. Your charity fashion show last week broke a new record. The battered women's shelter will be able to add 300 beds with the $200,000 raised."

"*We* raised," she reminded him. "I'm thrilled. I can't thank you enough for getting Senator Markson there. Perhaps I can get her to come to my next one. I've decided four events a year isn't enough. We should do more."

Fearless

"Ambitious."

"It's the least I can do. I spend my days fitting the wealthy and elite of D.C. in Gucci and Prada, while the Washington Shelter for Women and Children does meaningful work. They give people their lives back." While as a personal stylist and wardrobe consultant, she had the ability to enjoy luxury and glamour, she would never lose touch with what was really important in this world—freedom to live your life without fear. "So, was that what you wanted to talk to me about?"

"No, I have a request. Let's talk where it's more ... private." As they strolled leisurely down the hallway, he nodded at the security team standing before the massive oak doors leading into the Club's main play space, The Library.

An arousing series of slaps followed by a man's long wail filtered through the closed doors. She grinned. "My, we're starting early today."

Alexander chuckled. "You know what they say about spring. It brings all the boys and girls out to play."

She made a small murmur of agreement as they strode by. How easily she could dart upstairs to her private room and slip into a dress, perhaps the red one with the lacing up the back which coupled nicely with her new Chanel black suede boots. Having a man crawl to her, lower the zipper with his teeth ... *mmmm. Perhaps another time.* She'd made other plans for her rare weekend off. Plans were important. Having the discipline to stick to them was more important, and one of her rules was only Alexander could interrupt them.

They entered the long breezeway, blessedly empty, that led to the back of the house. Her breath stilled at the view through the glass French doors that opened to the stone terrace. Alexander's extensive, walled grounds were a sight to behold in any season, but as if overnight, every flowering tree, shrub, and flower bed, had burst into a color—whites,

Fearless

reds, blues, violets, yellows, and oranges, against a backdrop of every shade of green. The color warmed her soul. She'd outfitted too many people today in drab navy blue and black.

"Washington DC springs are spectacular, aren't they?" Alexander cracked open the doors, and the scents of rich earth and roses drifted over her.

"Nothing like them. So what's this other news? Clearly it must be bad if you're trying to distract me with your enchanted gardens."

He winked at her. "Plan foiled. We have two new candidates for membership."

"Ah, I see. No one else can do it? I had hoped to take off a few days." She often vetted new members for Alexander and determined if they were a good fit for their Accendos family before they presented the application to the seven members of the club's Tribunal Council. This weekend, however? She needed some much-delayed "me" time—and sleep. Insomnia couldn't last forever, though this recent bout was testing that limit.

"I'm sure they can, but a request has been made for you, specifically. Let's walk."

"Oh? Don't tell me. A famous politician? Military general?"

"Not exactly."

Now she was intrigued. It never ceased to amaze her that Alexander had kept Club Accendos secret for so long. Ninety-nine percent of the town had no clue his mansion on Q street in Georgetown was the private play space of the kinky elite—members of the U.S. Congress, military heads, and other bastions of Washington DC power.

They stepped down the three wide steps to pause at the Greek God of erotic yearning. Pothos looked down upon them from his center stage placement in the oval. As she often did, she sent up a silent prayer of thanks to him for whatever force was responsible for connecting her to Alexander, the man she called mentor, brother and sometimes, in her heart, father. An overwhelming sense of gratitude for her well-ordered and privileged life arose—as it often did when she stood in his gardens.

She eased off her heels, hooking them over her index finger. Normally she'd never take them off, as they were important to her overall presentation, but, as usual, Accendos' permissive atmosphere urged her to take a moment of pleasure. The sunlight had warmed the stones, and her toes stretched in delicious freedom.

"You said these potential members asked for me?" With eyes closed, she lifted her face and let the sunshine pour over her. *Heaven.*

"Yes, Derek met them in Copenhagen. Apparently one of them was quite complimentary of you. That's why Derek felt he could invite Steffan to check us out."

Her eyes snapped open. "Excuse me, did you say Steffan?"

"Steffan Vidar. He impressed Derek. Watched him handle three female submissives at once, and now that he's moving to DC—"

"Wait. He's moving to DC? To here?"

"You know this man?"

Know him. Familiar regret followed by a budding panic swelled up inside. "I met him in London. Club 501. It was a while ago." She lifted her foot and put a heel back on, then the other.

"I sense you don't agree with Derek's assessment of him?"

"Oh, no, it's not that …" She stepped around the fountain. How could she talk to Alexander about Steffan? He couldn't be moving to DC. He said he'd never leave Sweden, never leave "those who depended on him." His exact words that morning she'd left him—after a night that *never* should have happened.

Fearless

"Do I need to know something about this gentleman, Sarah? He seemed rather eager to see you. A little too eager in my estimation. He was quite ... adamant."

"You talked to him." She stopped in front of him, having made a full circle of Pothos.

"Of course. No one steps foot in this place without speaking with me." He smiled as if trying to put her at ease. "Derek seems to believe he is quite seasoned. Did something happen with him? Is he safe? You look rather shocked."

His questions speared her heart. She knew what Alexander asked. Did he adhere to all the rules of safe, sane and consensual BDSM play? Yes, he did. But was he safe? Not for her. In an instant, the two years it had taken to erase every memory of his ice blue eyes, that shock of blond hair that fell across his forehead, were gone. His face crystallized in her mind as if she'd seen him last night—in the flickering red light of that basement club.

She'd been in town for London Fashion Week, and, on impulse, she'd skipped an official event. She found herself teetering down stone steps into an old wine cellar the owners had converted into a secret space. She'd seen Steffan immediately. Or he'd seen her. As she roamed by the scenes unfolding around her, his cobalt eyes had tracked her. It took less than ten minutes for him to introduce himself and invite her to co-top a red-haired woman in his care. Funny the details you remember and the ones you don't when emotions run high, like the way his lips had curved against her ear as he pressed her into that other woman they'd sent so deep into subspace—together. Steffan's eyes had shaded to violet when he stood directly under the red light that had shone down on them. She vividly pictured the desire in them when she'd said "yes" to his later proposal. A shaft of pleasure moved through her body at the memory of how they'd celebrated their meeting later that night in his suite at the

Dorchester Hotel. Neither had topped or bottomed for the other. They'd indulged in pure, unimaginably delicious, raw, *foolish* vanilla sex.

They'd argued the next morning. He'd wanted more time with her, wanted to *get to know her*. Those were his words, right? When he'd pushed for her to stay, that cemented her decision to leave. She'd slipped out when he'd stepped out to the balcony to take a phone call. She'd left a cordial note, thanking him and did *not* leave her phone number. On the flight over the Atlantic, she'd assured herself that she could—she would—better manage herself in the future. She'd let herself go with him, broken a deal she'd made with herself decades ago. Many years before that she'd once hurt a man, deeply, but she'd recovered and made a wise, responsible, lifetime decision—all romantic liaisons would be relegated to a dungeon where protocol and rules kept everyone safe. Anything else led to dangerous consequences. She couldn't afford to be one of those women who just followed her heart and acted rashly around men. By the time she'd gotten through passport control in the States, she had thoroughly let Steffan go. She couldn't—wouldn't—have Steffan fall in love with her or her fall for him. Instead, she tucked her time with him away like a treasured souvenir from a trip to some far-off land that one places in a box under the bed. She knew it was there. She had no need to pull it out.

"Sarah?"

Her eyes snapped open, not realizing she'd disappeared so deep into memories they'd drifted closed.

"Are you sure you're all right? You know you can tell me anything."

Her chest squeezed tight at the kindness in his eyes. She had worried him, and she made a point of never worrying anyone about anything. "I'm fine." She added a slight laugh to her voice.

Fearless

Alexander didn't look convinced, but she couldn't have him believe—what? Two years and she still couldn't quite nail down her feelings about what had happened, as if feelings mattered in this scenario. Steffan had *impacted* her to the point she'd let her long-held policy about men and how she got involved with them slip. In the heated darkness, she and Steffan had said things they didn't mean. They were both Dominants, for God's sake. Even if she didn't have an iron-clad rule in place around relationships, how would they ever get over *that*? A headache began like a low drumbeat behind her forehead.

"He would go through the usual vetting process," Alexander said cautiously.

"Of course, and background checks. Interviews. Tribunal Council deliberation." The mechanics kicked in quickly. She hadn't even had to think about those words. "Carson would be a good person to—"

"No, by you. It was one of Steffan's requests. He wanted you to be the one to assess his suitability and his partner's. He has a man with him."

"A man?" He was gay? A sliver of illogical hurt bubbled up that she could have been an experiment. No, Steffan's voracious sexual appetite that night with her would belie that probability. Perhaps he was bisexual, which wasn't anything new in their world. See? Already things were ... messy.

"Wait until you meet Laurent. I believe you'll be intrigued. But, Sarah, if you'd rather not—"

"No, I will." Her mind had shuffled rapid-fire through decision points. Declining his request based on personal feelings would show a weakness of character that she would not allow herself. Rather, she'd alter the *significance* of his memory by recasting their roles in present time. This could be an opportunity to stuff that past experience in the bin of failed experiments. Things one did just to see what would happen. She'd be a professional with him like she was with all new potential members. He would *not* take away her control from her again.

"Good," Alexander said. "If we get started today, his thirty-day probationary status will be in place by the time the plane leaves for St. Thomas. Steffan and Laurent can join my birthday party."

"Today?" A strangled laugh died in her throat. "Wait. You want them to attend your party? You have over one hundred people on the waiting list."

"Yes and yes." Alexander smiled down at her. "They're here. In The Library."

Good-bye, relaxing weekend.

∽

Fearless can be found at most online retailers
or visit Elizabeth's web site at www.ElizabethSaFleur.com

ABOUT THE AUTHOR

Elizabeth SaFleur writes romance that dares to "go there" from 28 wildlife-filled acres, dances in her spare time and is a certifiable tea snob. Find out more about Elizabeth on her web site at www.ElizabethSaFleur, like her Facebook page or join her private Facebook group, Elizabeth's Playroom. Follow her on Twitter (@ElizaLoveStory) and Instagram (@ElizabethLoveStory), too!

Also by Elizabeth SaFleur
Elite
Holiday Ties
Untouchable
Perfect
Riptide
Lucky
Fearless
Invincible

The White House Gets A Spanking
Spanking the Senator

Shakedown
Tough Luck
Tough Break
Tough Love

Printed in Great
Britain
by Amazon